# THE STONE CIRCLE

by

Karen Cracknell

Grosvenor House
Publishing Limited

This book is published by
Grosvenor House Publishing Ltd
28-30 High Street, Guildford, Surrey, GU1 3EL.
www.grosvenorhousepublishing.co.uk

A CIP record for this book
is available from the British Library

ISBN 978-1-908447-53-1

I dedicate this book to my late mother Eileen and
my brother Ian.
Through it all, I always loved you.

Take care of your Thoughts because they become Words.
Take care of your Words because they will become Actions.
Take care of your Actions because they will become Habits.
Take care of your Habits because they will form your Character.
Take care of your Character because it will form your Destiny,
and your Destiny will be your Life.

There is no religion higher than the Truth.

Dalai Lama

# When the end became the beginning

October 1980

I could not see.

I looked around me, but there was only darkness.

Nothing.

Looking down, I tried to pick out my feet but the blackness was impenetrable. Fear swept through me, where was I?

Then I realised.

This was the unlit room of my Soul. The blackness came from within. Swiftly it all came back to me.

Why I was here.

Suddenly the pain came flooding back, the wretchedness never seemed to leave. I was in a cave of my own despair. The tears flowed like rivers down my cheeks, but they never helped, they never took the self loathing away.

I cried out in anguish, must I continue to live like this...... surely I had suffered enough?

But pain knows no boundaries or time, seeping into all dimensions of life. Only now it had become too much.

Why not end it here and now?

Nothing could be any worse than living like this.

I began to cry again, I wanted to leave this place but I didn't know how or if I could even find the courage to do so. But still, my mind automatically flipped through the options.

Then I remembered, a neighbour had hung himself from the banisters, maybe that would be quick and not too painful.

The darkness took me again.

Was absolute.

Pressing in on me from all sides. I had to leave and leave soon. Before I merged into its vacuum, because then, I'd be nothing at all and that was a far more terrifying thought than this.

Suddenly a voice spoke out of the darkness.

"You are here for a reason." It said.

Jolted out of my misery I looked about me, but no one was there, I was still alone. Had I imagined the voice? And where had it come from? But there was nothing more.

I sat for a while, pondering. Should I stay? But I wanted to go, to leave all the unhappiness behind, but the voice had made me hesitate.

Finally I made a decision. Not yet, I would not end it now. Later.

With enormous effort, I willed the darkness away. Reaching out, I felt the silky fur of our golden retriever Cindy, whom I'd lain against all those hours ago. Lowering my face to bury it in the soft hair and stroking her lovely head I said.

"Thank you for loving me, when I can't even love myself." Then, feeling her soft warm tongue lovingly licking the salty tears away and I knew suddenly with an inner knowing, everything would be all right. Here I had something to hang on to, as tenuous at it might seem, something that would stop me spinning away into the darkness again. I scrunched a ball of fur into my fist cherishing its softness in my hand before raising my head to look at her. Her soft brown eyes shone back at me with so much love and understanding I wanted to cry again. She knew my pain when no one else did. She loved me unconditionally when others had turned away.

Our loving family dog had comforted me in my darkest hour and for that I would always be grateful. For in that moment, I believed she saved my life and had given me a reason to live.

With just her love.

I leant down to kiss her noble head and then like holy water washing over me I suddenly saw the light. I would live, even though I did not want to and during this existence I would search for answers and find the Truth.

To make sense of everything that had happened.

I would try to find ways to heal my wounded and damaged Soul and in doing so I would strive to learn to find a meaning to my life.

And if I was lucky enough to do so, I would share these answers with others.

For I knew what it was to feel immeasurable pain like so many of my fellow humans, and if my quest could make some small difference to them and help save them from their own torments, then I knew all my pain and suffering had been worth it.

June 2011

"You are here for a reason," the voice said.

I believe that reason to be this book.
This is my humble gift for humanity.
Go heal your life, like I have.

God bless you all.

KC

If you don't wish to read the story turn to the back of the book to begin the healing.

# Chapter 1

# Trekking

We'd been trekking for more than four hours. I wondered not for the first time my amazing good fortune to have found myself here. It was my last foray, the last time I would have the freedom to do exactly as I pleased. Everything had gone according to plan, like clockwork and I was determined to enjoy this last adventure on my travels into the Thai jungle.

I had loved every minute of my gap year, even after six months of arduous travelling. The contrasts in culture, the polarity in wealth and poverty, had made this trip new and exciting in every country I'd travelled. Hawaii, New Zealand, Australia and now finally Thailand. The other boundless possible lives I could live in these places, in once unimagined places, had opened my eyes to the real world. A world full of colour and diversity in the ever changing landscape of infinite human lives. An unending education in the trials and tribulations of other people's experiences.

I was due to fly home once I had completed this final adventure and the thought of returning to the reality of my life and what this entailed brought with it a fresh stab of sadness. Home was definitely not where the heart lay.

Not in my case at least.

It was one of the very reasons I'd made my escape and visited countries on the opposite side of the world.

The trekking expedition had been booked through the hostel I'd made my base while staying in Chang Mai. Since I had exhausted all the other sights around the area I felt the trekking experience to an amazing waterfall, riding on elephants and staying in the stilted jungle huts of the Karen tribe, a native village in the jungle, would be a fitting ending to my six months gap year before returning home to England.

Here, the undulating landscape was as strenuous as I'd imagined, for once making me glad of my physical fitness. Some of the others in the group were finding the terrain challenging, making conversation stilted and the pace slow. The ever constant changing scenery and the feeling of adventure lightened my step in anticipation. The falls had been one of the highlights of this trek and I was as eager to experience them as everyone else. The much talked of local beauty spot was on the itinerary of virtually every backpacker I had spoken to and I hoped the long hot walk was going to be worth it.

Our group consisted of a mere five others, plus the mandatory two guides. In any normal month there'd be more than double the number on the trek, but with local festivals in full flow, many people had opted to visit these instead. Not that I minded. Far from it. The lack of numbers gave me some measure of solitude, a good excuse to be on my own. One of the reasons I'd come to this remote part of Thailand had been to get away from the hustle and bustle of the cities and people who inhabited them. Bangkok and Chang Mai had been particularly frenetic with their hot dusty polluted atmospheres and the throng of motorbike driven tuk tuk taxis crowding the roads. In the beginning I'd found it thrilling, riding in the open aired cabs and feeling part of the chaotic urban landscape only a hands breath away. Until your lungs choked with the stench of pollution and your clothes and hair became covered in a film of grimy dirt.

Such a contrast to my home town, the quiet, well ordered and wealthy Harpenden. Here the Thai people were poor but seemingly happy despite their ramshackle living arrangements and lack of money. Perhaps their cheerfulness could be attributed to living in tight family groups. I'd always thought home was not a place or country, but was where the people you loved resided.

Only a couple of weeks ago I'd visited Bangkok. Another world entirely to this, with its markets of fake designer goods and seedy night life. The hordes of blubbery men in the company of young Thai girls had wrought a deep loathing at what had been created out of the innocence of others. I knew then I could never be a part of anything which caused such degradation to these young girls.

This city had branded itself as the sex capital of the world and from what I saw in those few days, it had certainly lived up to its name. A honey pot of fantasy and gratification for those who couldn't get it at home and for those who wanted it anyway. Overflowing with titillation and pornography on a gargantuan scale. Nothing about this place held any interest for me and I couldn't wait to get away from the testosterone thronging sex clubs and false touristy fodder. I wanted something more and exciting, something real, and unbeknown to me, this trek was about to tick all the boxes.

Not that life at home couldn't be called uneventful or unpredictable but I'd had enough of that kind of volatile existence. Travelling had given me a means to escape and leave my troubles safely back in England. Being out of my natural environment had enabled me to shed some of my shortcomings. Here, I could reinvent myself, be anybody or anything and to some extent I was happy.

After finishing my A levels I'd booked my gap year backpacking trip when life at home had suddenly become too much, too crowded and claustrophobic. I wanted to see something of the world, expand my horizons as I knew I might not get another chance once I got a job. Others at school were not as adventurous as me, only planning to start the autumn term at Uni once they got their results. I couldn't see the rush, knowing there was the rest of my life to be weighed down with responsibility and mortgages. I wanted freedom, to spread my wings and spend sometime exploring new horizons.

Over the last few years, I'd saved all my birthday and Christmas money and combined with my holiday job salary and it had been enough to bring me here. The tidy sum of money accruing secretly under my bed had become enough to pay for the multiple plane ticket rides and support me for a good six months if I wasn't extravagant with it of course.

Booking the trip had been easy. The travel agents, Trailfinders in Kensington, London attracted a certain type of well travelled young employee, who had seemingly. extensively travelled the length and breadth of the world for themselves. They made excellent suggestions on how to plan my trip, countries to travel too and which places to visit. Besides wanting to see New Zealand and Australia, I had no idea where to go on my homeward leg of the tour. So they'd suggested Asia.

I had plumped for Thailand, its appeal had been its for its cheapness and a well worn track for backpackers. I was travelling on my own after all, I didn't want to face anything too challenging. I'd had enough of that sort of thing at home. Besides, money would go further here, allowing me to continue my travels for much longer than I'd first imagined on my budget.

People at school thought I was foolish to spend the money on an extended holiday instead of saving it to pay for Uni. I just put their acid criticism down to jealousy, not liking it when someone stepped out of the norm and making them feel their own mediocrity.

Travelling I knew, would put my own insular existence and home life into perspective. Growing up in a middle class commuter town called Harpenden some twenty miles north of London had made it easy to feel like a big fish in a small sea and to live blinkered from to the real trials of the world. Cocooned and swaddled in money, people here had little understanding of the hardship of others or the dangers outside this safe and sheltered town. With their parochial attitudes and a healthy undercurrent of gossiping, they had taught me the value of silence and goodness knew, there was plenty to keep the gossipers busy for months on the subject of my family.

School life had been much easier to handle due largely to the privileged catchment area. All three Harpenden State schools churned out Oxbridge candidates like no other. Highly qualified teachers flocked to work within the area. Success breeding success levered my own comprehensive into the heady heights of a national top ten school.

Along with the academia, most girls I knew had begun to explore the unchartered territory of the opposite sex. Snogging and groping at parties, some persuaded to go all the way. Boys had never featured particularly in my life. Perhaps it was just me, but they acted far to immaturely and down right annoyingly for me to take much notice.

Yet, despite my lack of interest I seemed to attract far more than my fair share of attention. Remarkable all the more because my appearance had never paid homage to the fashion of the day by any stretch of the imagination. My untamable straight hair style was as far removed from the curtain straight hair adhered to by my peer group. Nor did I wear the orange coloured foundation or thick layers of mascara so desired by many other girls my age. Perhaps most surprisingly for a girl, was that, horror of horror, I loved sport. Some would say I did it just to be able to proudly walk out of school lessons early and watch the teacher's irritation and the resentment from my class mates. Yet I actually enjoyed pitting the strength of my body against others in an arena where I knew I could be somebody for once and win. Surprisingly the number of girls who competed in after school sport activities dwindled to virtually nothing. Girls my age seemed to think moving in anything faster than a walk was uncool. Nonetheless, I was good at running, a fact which helped me through some difficult times in my life, when everything else conspired to make me feel totally and utterly crap.

Perhaps my hormones hadn't kicked in yet like the other girls, or maybe there were still too many other things crowding my life, but boys seemed like an alien race. Their conversational topics as incomprehensible as talking to a garage door. Not that anyone would be attracted to me anyway. Not with my untidy appearance and indifferent air. I wasn't foolish enough to pretend otherwise.

Growing up a full head taller than the girls and boys in school had made life difficult for me. Being 5ft 9, my towering height brought unwanted attention, singling me out. Teachers always noticed me misbehaving or talking well before other more worthy candidates. Combined with the ill fitting school uniform and lofty height, these attributes conspired to present opportunities too good to miss for the bullies always on the look out for a suitable victim.

Yet, during the infrequent visits of my relatives we visited who oohed and ah'd over my long legs and curly hair, telling me how lucky I was, the compliments embarrassed me to the core, invariably sending me to the safety and quiet of my bedroom for the duration of their visit. For how could they know how I considered these afflictions caused me so much trouble at school. How the other girls would deride these unusual characteristics with hurtful names until I believed I was nothing short of being a freak.

Admittedly my legs had been useful in getting me out of trouble at times. Running away from all those irritating boys and aggravating brother in my younger years. Now they only served to make my gym skirt look ludicrously short and the nylon knee length socks toddler size. Never quite long enough to cover the full length of my calves due to my mother's habit of absentmindedly putting them through a few too many cycles on hot wash. My school uniform as a whole was something left to be desired. The black stretched acrylic jumper held no shape whatsoever and the low hanging bat wing arms could flap impressively against my sides on a particularly windy day. The old straight grey skirt was not designed to contend with my father's pointy racing seat on top of the bike I used to ride to school, messing with the seam at the back and causing the stitching to fray and break and in need of continual darning and mending.

I'd thought my neglected and shabby appearance would thankfully allow me to merge into the background and to be nothing special, camouflaged from the rest of the other marauding Roundwood Park School pupils. But it never ceased to surprise me how many times I was proven wrong.

My last year in sixth form and 'A' level exams couldn't have come soon enough. School had served its purpose. It had provided me with a means of escape. I had no worries about failing my exams. I knew I was reasonably good at my studies and they were always a welcome break from my real life. Class had been somewhere I could lose myself and engage fully with a subject that did as it said on the front of the book. Solving a maths equation or working on my still life pictures in Art absorbing me in subjects other than myself and time passed more easily.

Although I had some friends at school, I would not say they were particularly close. I preferred it that way, for mastering the art of crafting superficial relationships did not necessitate forming bonds too strong. Letting people in and trusting them was always a recipe for disaster.

*People always let you down in the end, they just couldn't help it.*

Besides, I preferred my own company and actively sought it. For in solitude how could anyone hurt you? Shutting people out meant no pain, no criticism, no remorse, no mood swings, no guilt or anyone else's expectations to live up to.

*It was where I'd become most comfortable.*

From far away, someone was talking to me, abruptly bringing me back to the present.

"Alice, take a look over here!" Naomi called from up ahead.

Naomi was one of the girls I had met from the backpackers hostel, who like me was taking a gap year break before starting University the following year. We'd got talking one evening in the little backpacker's hostel 'Changs' tucked away down a small, narrow unremarkable alleyway at the back end of town. Finding these hostels had not been as hard as I'd first imagined namely because of the backpacker's bible 'The Lonely Planet Guide', the one indispensable item to take on a trip like this. I'd hardly seen anyone using anything else. With its in depth, accurate dissections on what to do and where to go, directions and ratings for local hotels. Even write ups for top end expensive hotels (if you were feeling flush) were honest, to the point and something I'd come to depend on. Knowing what to expect when travelling on your own was a bonus I'd never thought I'd have and over the last six months or so the guide had never let me down.

"Alice!" came Naomi's insistent voice again.

I quickly scampered over the uneven path to catch her up. Following her gaze down the now visible ravine I saw that it stretched far beyond where my gaze could follow. The sound of the river below filtered up to us, rhythmic and soothing in its continuum of melody, neither too loud nor too soft. Plants and trees from the jungle drifted out from the sides. Draping leaves and branches wafted in the gentle breeze, and ferns glistened and shuddered in the dappled sunlight.

"Take a look at that!" Naomi said awestruck.

Naomi and I had hit it off on that first night. She owned the most amazing green eyes I'd ever seen. The colour of dark emeralds, almond shaped with long lashes to die for and holding a permanent twinkle. She was from 'up north' near Manchester. Her Bolton accent contrasted vastly with mine, finding my pronunciation a constant source of amusement in what she considered to be my 'posh' southern accent. Like me, she was travelling on her own, occasionally hooking up with other backpackers for companionship, to trade stories and indulge for a short time in the comforting presence of others. Although not tall, probably only 5ft 3, she made up for it with almost permanent chatter or giggling. I knew she'd be a sought after gap year companion and never short of company, whereas I always had to work hard to form friends. I found the knack of keeping the conversation flowing always such an effort. The need to sound interested, to laugh or interject in the right places were always a constant reminder of how awkward I felt in company, but Naomi hadn't seemed to notice.

Pulling quickly away from the substantial drop I replied. "Nice." Trying not to sound shaky.

"How far down do you think it goes?" she said bending over even further.

"No! Don't lean over like that, that really freaks me out!"

"You're kidding me, right? I thought you didn't mind heights cos of your bungy jump in New Zealand!!!" Naomi giggled, her nose scrunching up into little creases as she laughed.

"Yeah, but I didn't say that bungy jumping didn't scare the life out of me! Please Naomi, come away from the edge."

Bungy jumping really had terrified me. During my month tour round New Zealand I'd visited Queenstown in the South Island, with the sole intent of becoming a member of the "A.J. Hacket" bungy jump club. Jumping off the famous Kawarau bridge, fifteen storeys high, the original home of bungy jumping, had seemed a great idea at the time and in the backpackers world the only thing worth doing in Queenstown. There'd been an unstated rivalry amongst us to do it, respect for those who where brave enough, and a great deal of ribbing for those who were too chicken.

We continued to walk along the narrow, winding path. The waterfall couldn't be far now due to the roar of water building steadily as we approached. Dropping below the ridge heading downwards, the path became more hazardous, it was strewn with small boulders fallen from above and just wide enough for one person. It would be all to easy to topple over the edge and disappear forever, I thought with concern. No one would find you out here.

We came to a stone staircase hewn from the rock face, narrowly descending from view. Uneven in their spacing and depth the steps were difficult to navigate, but having long legs does have some advantages.

Naomi's chatter gradually drained away under the growing noise, not such a bad thing after long hours of listening to it, I thought to myself. Although I enjoyed her company, quietness was really what I craved.

Finally we reached the ravine floor, the sound of crashing water became tremendous. The air around us seemed to reverberate with its tempo and the atmosphere took on a damp and clammy feel despite the heat. As the path took us round a last turn, the terrain opened into a surprisingly large expanse of rocks and water. Lush emerald trees fringed the foaming white waterfall, creating a perfect frame for the enormous wall of water ahead. The unrelenting surge of water crashed heavily over its lip into the pool below, bubbling and seething under the cascades entry. The heavy pounding of falling water felt tangible even from this distance away. Plumes of light misty spray rolled away from the waterfall, settling on our hot sunburnt skin and surrounding vegetation.

With an unspoken protocol the two guides led us forward towards the waters edge, gesturing towards the pool and where the river surged away.

The first guide shouted in halting English.

"Werrry, dang-er-ous, no swim," he said pointing to the pool.

Naomi and I spluttered as we tried to conceal our giggles. Bing's broken English never failed to make us laugh, made worse by the fact that we tried to hide it.

I looked towards where the water swirled away beneath the deceptive calm of the pool's surface. A shiver ran down my spine. I'd heard several people had been swept to their deaths in this very river and I didn't doubt Bing's warning.

Pushing the thought away I walked towards Bing with my camera.

"Hey Bing. Could you take a picture of me and Naomi please?" I said, still fighting to keep a straight face when he nodded seriously.

Handing my camera over, I returned to my place beside Naomi with the waterfall directly behind us.

"Ready? Okay, wun, two, free," he said. Only serving to set us off again, no need to force a smile this time!

I set about taking pictures of the ferns, the pool, the waterfall and my companions. Over the last six months I had compiled thousands of photographs on several memory cards before downloading them onto CD and posting them back home. I wanted a record of everything. This was a trip of a lifetime after all, I doubted I'd ever be doing anything like this again. Luckily my compact camera was easy to use. I didn't have to think about shutter speed or aperture, just turn the dial to the correct icon, point and shoot. No need to engage any brain cells!

I explored the terrain to gain a variety of view points for my camera. It was so beautiful here, so out of the way and remote and apart from our group, there were no other people.

Naomi came to rejoin me.

"This is amazing!" I shouted. "I never imagined it would be like this."

"Too right. It's supposed to be the largest waterfall in south east Asia," she yelled back. The noise was such, that we gave up trying to talk any further.

Flicking the dial onto 'landscape' to catch some last shots of the waterfall and river, I glimpsed something that looked suspiciously like a wild elephant way down river at the water's edge. Quickly walking forward to gain a better vantage point and making sure my camera was properly prepped, I wasn't watching my footing as carefully as I should have been. I was in a hurry, we'd be leaving soon and wild elephants didn't hang around to have their picture taken.

It all happened so suddenly, as if in slow motion. One moment I was striding purposefully towards the water's edge, the second, my toe snagged on a jutting rock sending me flying. Nothing to grab, only empty air rushed through my fingers and with the same sickening feeling I remembered when bungy jumping, I knew I was past the point of no return. Nothing could prevent it now.

My face hit the surface first, the shock of cold water on hot skin paralyzed me momentarily before an explosion of fear and terror tore through me. I had to get out quickly before being syphoned away into the full force of the river. Already I could feel the fierce pull of water beneath tugging at my legs. I kicked them hard in reflex, trying to propel myself back towards the ledge from which I'd fallen, but the current was too strong. I was being sucked away from the relative calm of the pool towards the full force of the river, where others had been sucked to their deaths.

Utter panic tore through me as I frantically clawed at the water. Surely someone had seen me fall in? But the current had me now, pulling me away from safety, away from my trekking companions who'd gathered by the poolside to watch in horror as I was being whisked helplessly away. Bing shouting in words I could not hear, Naomi's expression told me everything. There was no hope of getting to safety, panic stricken, I realised it was too late for that, I'd been taken too far.

Nothing could save me now.

Still, I frantically fought the water and with each spluttering gasp for air, I was being taken further away from the waterfall. Away from everyone and everything I had ever known, when everything went black.

# Chapter 2

# Waking up

Something buzzed and fluttered in my ear, stirring me from my dreams. My mind unhurriedly whirred, slowly becoming aware that something was wrong, not quite right. I was not in my bed at home that was for sure, the lumpiness beneath me was far from being that of my comfortable soft mattress. Red light filtered through my closed eye lids, the heat on my skin burned hotly. Faint sounds of water sifted into my brain, making me strain to make sense of the unfamiliar sounds and sensations that rolled in haphazardly, as if from far away. A sudden recognition jolted me awake, unprepared for the assault of the sharp jagged sensations which stabbed painfully through me. My eye lids fluttered open, trying to focus, brightness too blinding, nothing, colours swam, shapes merged, everything was hazy, blurred and it hurt like hell.

Closing my eyes quickly from the blinding dazzling light, my awareness shifted to my head, throbbing as if to a drum beat rhythm. Tentatively I tried to move, first my fingers, then my arms and legs. Everything felt heavy and stiff as if being held under water. Even the smallest of movement felt cumbersome and ineffectual. I tried to surface, struggled to recollect my other life before this, but the tiredness dragged at me, overwhelming and all consuming. Through the haze the throbbing pain slowly helped me to focus, piercing slowly the cloak of numbness, ushering my consciousness towards fully understanding the meaning of the unrelenting pounding that seemed to emanate from every inch of my body. Slowly I lifted my hand to face, wanting to feel the source of the torment. As my hand scraped through my hair, it became snagged and tangled within the matted strands, caught with twigs and leaves. The effort was too much, my hand flopped back down uselessly to my side. Exhaustion overwhelmed again, allowing me finally to slide back into nothingness and under the beckoning cover of painless sleep.

I awoke again, my mouth and lips felt dry and swollen, my tongue like a piece of driftwood and much too big for my mouth. The lower part of my body rocked comfortingly and gently but was cold, so cold. I heard the distant roar of a river and realized suddenly my body lay half submerged in its shallows. Raising my head a fraction and hardly able to open my crusty eye lids, I located the sounds once so confusing. Nearby rocks and small trees swam into vision, the sparkle of tumbling water in the distance, but there was nothing close enough to shade me from the hot sun scorching my skin. I was strewn at an angle on a small shingle beach, resting in the shallows on a quiet curve of the river. Tentatively, I tried to shift my weight, until I realized I could feel nothing below my waist. The numbness must be caused by the cold water, or was what I hoped. My mind would not entertain anything more serious.

Time stretched onwards, I felt my strength ebbing away like the water around me. I must be dying, I thought suddenly, I could not survive this. I allowed my mind to drift, to help ease the torturous pain and sharp barbed agony which came with each and every breath. The light had become hazier, softer as I gave myself up to the sensations I could no longer fight. Peace enveloped me, warming and soothing until I felt as if I was floating. Somehow separate from my body but yet still connected. Maybe I was already dead I thought impassively. That would be all right, there'd been nothing to live for anyway.

Then somehow, along the meandering and uneven path which led away from consciousness, I managed to find oblivion. A place so peaceful and painless I never wanted to leave it ever again.

I had not idea how much time had passed when I found myself waking reluctantly, gentle hands were lifting my head, a bowl was being held to my mouth, water touched my dry and chapped lips. Suddenly I became aware the inside of my mouth felt like the Sahara desert, only drier, grittier and much more parched. Moving my lips to receive the water my tongue stuck to the roof of my mouth causing me to choke. The water was all I could focus on now, all that I desperately wanted. Yet it had all but dribbled down my chin and escaped my desperate attempt to swallow. At least it had loosened my swollen and sandy tongue.

Again the bowl was held to my mouth and this time the water slid down my throat, soothing, sating my need, as sweet as honey and never tasting so good. The effort to swallow had taken every ounce of strength. Exhaustedly, I lay back, hardly registering that someone had found me, for now I hardly cared. I only wanted to sleep forever, like before, and never have to feel anything ever again.

When I next opened my eyes it was twilight. Moving my head gingerly I looked around me, taking in my surroundings. I lay on an animal hide which had been spread underneath my supine body with wads of soft ferns piled beneath. I'd been placed under a large curtain tree, so named because of the large number of vines that hung thickly to the ground from its branches. Beside me and within the shelter of the vines, I could make out other items. A number of other hides and a large leather pouch close to me which I guessed contained water.

*What was I doing here?*

And more importantly who had brought me? For there was no sign of anyone close by. Something stirred in my mind, images of water swept to my attention. Lots of it, that much I remembered. The image of my river nightmare suddenly faltered back to me. The amazing waterfall I had trekked to see before slipping on the mossy rocks covered by misty spray. My fight for survival after falling into the water. How I'd never noticed the uneven surface over which I'd walked so carelessly, the jutting rock tripping me and sending me head first into the water. How the boiling waters of the river pulled me this way and that, spinning me round like a wooden top as if in a giant plug hole, bashing me against the huge boulders which sat so silently stoic against the careering current. The only clue to their presence, were the huge mounds of water racing over their surface, and where they rose high above the tumbling water, white waves beat rhythmically against the rocks impeded from joining the surge and current of the rest of the river. The rapids had spun and tossed me, heedless my to my plight, from one rock to another, knocking the very air out from my lungs I laboured so hard to pull in. Water stole into my nose while the undercurrent repeatedly dunked me beneath the surface of the water. The deafening roar muting, as I was pulled into a silent, bubbling, disorientating underwater world. I remembered the battering I'd sustained within the cavernous waters of the river, until finally, after how long I knew not, the water had carried me with benevolent mercy into a quiet curve of the river. Leaving me strewn haphazardly upon a shingle beach just above the tide line. Small waves had lapped continually at my legs like a million tiny dog tongues washing and cleaning and giving thoughtful loving reassurance I was safe at last. I'd hardly noticed the sheer sides of the gorge towering magnificently above me as the sun had risen high in the perfect turquoise sky. Beating down on me, warming, then burning my broken and senseless body. Here, nature both ferociously cruel and yet achingly beautiful, showcased perfectly within the spectacular gorge. The power and full force of natures powerful elements having nearly conspired to take my life, had inexplicably deemed seemly to allow me to live.

*But how had I come to be here?*

Glancing around, I searched for my small hiking pack containing my passport, plane tickets, toothbrush and mobile phone and a few other items I'd needed for the trek. My large backpack containing all my other belongings had been left in the hostel in Chang Mia. It really hadn't been necessary to bring all my stuff with me when the trek was only five days long.

*It didn't look like it had made it.*

Sighing deeply, my predicament began to dawn on me, and then a pulse of fear crept through me. I was in the middle the wilderness, with no phone, no way of contacting the outside world, having been found by one or several people, as yet, I did not know. What if they were drug smugglers or feral natives? A shiver of fear ran down my spine. I had no way to protect myself, who knew what they would want with me? They'd know I was far from home and with little hope of escaping. They could keep me here forever and no one would ever know. My mind raced to the horrors that could lay before me. My predicament looked bleak, I had really got myself into deep trouble this time. So far from home and out of my natural environment. It was hard for me to make a plan like I'd do at home, but this was not a normal situation. The jungle and all it contained was a whole new ball game, and one I had little idea how to navigate.

I cursed under my breath. Feeling my heart hammer and the bile to rise in my chest. I should calm down. I was still alone and nothing had happened yet. There was no sign or movement of anyone close by. My mind rapidly flipped through the facts. I was lost in the jungle, probably miles from anywhere, no rucksack meaning no phone, no passport, no way of contacting anyone to my whereabouts. I'd been found by one or several people, there was no way of telling. If there had been others surely one would have stayed behind to look after me? I shifted my weight, suddenly becoming painfully aware that all was not as it should be as far as my body was concerned. Looking down at myself and trying not to become alarmed I saw a large palm leaf wrapped around one leg just above my ankle and held neatly in place with thin twine. My other leg was covered in deep purple bruises, little of my true colour was evident anymore. Suddenly I noted with concern my shorts had disappeared and all that remained to cover my modesty were my Marks and Spencers knickers. Once pearly white and now reduced to a dirty brown shade.

*That did not bode well, not good at all.*

My fear careered away again out of control as I trawled through all possible reasons I no longer wore my shorts. Holding onto the fact the extent to my injuries were obviously pretty bad. It would have to be a sadist who'd want 'that' from me as well. Trying to calm my nerves I glanced over the rest of my body. My skin appeared to be clean enough although the dying light diffused the ability to see with any great detail. Certainly, someone had spent a little time cleaning and patching me up. At least I still had my T shirt, even if it was dirty and ripped. My clothes or what was left of them were torn and filthy, large holes intersected the Marilyn Monroe printed T-shirt. Perhaps it had saved me from the worst of scraps. Lastly, inspecting my arms and torso I noticed they'd remained relatively unscathed but the injuries to my palms gave evidence of another scenario. Although not bandaged I could see clean, ragged skin hanging in places from the deep scratches and my fingernails were torn and broken.

I searched to recall any other details but nothing came to mind. Only the vague memory of gentle hands holding my body.

Inspection over, I lay back down to mull over my predicament, trawling through the facts. Before heading out for the trek I hadn't felt it necessary in leaving information of my home address or next of kin. The trek was only meant to be five days long. What could happen in such a short time? I knew it had been foolish but I wasn't the only one, for Naomi hadn't bothered either. With growing unease I realised there'd be nothing to trace me to my whereabouts. I'd left no passport or any documentation in my backpack back in the hostel. All important papers I kept with me and my small backpack was now probably half way to the Indian Ocean by now. I sighed, no one would ever know where or how I'd disappeared or even that I was lucky to be alive. The trek guides certainly wouldn't know who to contact concerning my disappearance. Even if they notified the authorities, everyone knew that these treks where frowned upon by the Thai government. Taking tourists to stay within remote mountain villagers, poor by anyones standards and having to supplement their meager incomes by growing opium and cannabis, was at the best of times risky. With the high number of drug lords operating in the area, transactions could quickly become volatile and sometimes fatal for those who got in the way. The government's disapproval stemmed from wanting to avoid the embarrassment of foreign blood on their hands or the reasons why in the face of the international clamp down on the drugs trade. Just further north of our trekking route a tourist had recently been shot dead while boating on the ungoverned Koki River, thinly separating Laos, Burma and Thailand and famously known as the golden triangle, it was an easy transfer point for drugs.

No, nobody would know where or which country I was in because over the course of the last six months I'd contacted home perhaps only half a dozen times and only by way of the internet. Certainly not to speak to anyone directly since the whole point of this trip was to get away and forget about anything home related. I didn't want to hear my mother talking about her depression or how the world conspired against her. Maybe it was selfish or self preservation, I did not know, but I'd wanted this trip to help me shed, lizard like, the layers of myself I had come to dislike. For over the course of the last few years I'd forgotten to pay attention to the seeds of change, this unfamiliar person I'd now become. Now I was paying the price of my forced independence, my foolishness and unheeding determined attitude to do things my own way. The single minded approach to find some semblance of normality, balance and inner peace over the whirring chaos that had been my life up to now, had now landed me in this place.

Crap.

The darkness had deepened and now only the stars were lit up, shining so clearly and brightly like precious jewels held in a velvety backdrop. Unlike back home where the dirty orange city street lamp glow leaked into the inky night. Spoiling the beauty of the stars and hanging smog like over the sleeping towns and cities.

The heat from the day had cooled considerably. Up here in the hills the nighttime temperatures could drop very low and I already missed my warm downy sleeping bag lost to the river. Instead I'd been provided with a scratchy thin blanket, hardly enough to keep me warm against the chilly damp air, but it was all I had.

I grew tired of waiting. It must be very late, for now I could hardly keep my eyes open. I gave up waiting to see who had brought me here, who I needed to fear. The anxiety and fears could wait until morning, for ultimately it would not make any difference.

The warmth of morning sunshine woke me from my fitful sleep and the drone of early insect activity brought me to my senses. Mosquitoes where the bane of my life and I always had to be vigilant for any furtively landing on my skin. Constantly getting bitten had made me a popular companion at home. People knew it was prudent to sit next to me when relaxing outside on a summers evening. For some strange reason, I seemed to attract the stealthy blood suckers more than others. Maybe it was the scent of my skin, but I acted as favorable decoy for everyone else, much to their amusement. Here the mosquitoes were vicious little buggers. My pale skin was festooned with hundreds of angry, red lumps, giving me little peace day or night.

Suddenly, me stomach groaned in recognition of the aroma of food cooking not very far away. I was ravenous. Sitting up slowly, careful not to move too quickly, I found the source of my torment. Over a low fire, a spit had been constructed with some sort of dead animal skewered over the smoky flames. My breath suddenly caught in my chest, for beside the fire crouched a man. His elbows resting casually on his knees, his gaze thankfully only concentrated on the cooking animal. My heart leapt and I felt myself stiffen. Fear gnawed at me, this had been the moment I'd been dreading. Coming face to face with the unknown rescuers. Not knowing what they would want with me or who they were. For all I knew they could be the dangerous drug lords that the trek guides had warned us about and I knew they would not take kindly to a white European girl lost in their territory. My instinct told me to stay perfectly still, I didn't want to attract any attention. Not until I had time to access the situation or to see if there were any others.

Yes, the camp was definitely empty apart from the man.

*That was good.*

I looked closer at my rescuer searching for clues to his origin. He was obviously strong by the look of the well toned body. The honey brown skin accentuated the contours and outline of his muscles beneath where the colour fell into shadow. The skin was smooth and virtually hairless. Drawing sharp contrast to the long cascading black hair draping casually over his bare shoulders and back. Some of his hair was braided, woven with many colourful beads. He wore brown fabric trousers snuggly hugging his hips but no shirt. A diagonal leather strap hung from shoulder to waist interspersed with small pockets, one holding a sheathed hunting knife. I noticed a leather pouch held by a thin leather string hanging from his neck and a colourful woven beaded bracelet tied to his left wrist.

*Crap, he was looking at me.*

Feeling the weight of my stare he'd turned to look at me, examining my alert gaze with interest. I found myself momentarily shrink backwards to have been caught so blatantly staring, but despite my recoil I couldn't help but gape at his handsome face. The square jaw and prominent cheekbones served as a perfect foil to the soft expression in his eyes and concern that now creased his brow.

*Not what I was expecting at all.*

Don't be taken in by his handsomeness, keep up your guard, I chided myself, good looks were a facade, they only drew you in.

His nose was straight but not large, his lips full without being too big, everything was in proportion and just right. He rose to his feet in one fluid motion, unexpectedly taller than I'd first imagined. He must be more than six feet tall I thought, not at all like the small stature of the fine boned local Thai men.

Even from this distance I couldn't help but notice the muscles rippling under the shift of his posture, drawing my eyes to sweep once again over his body. He was not what I would have called overly built up. Not like the puffed up body builders I'd seen down the gym. His body had the appearance of a martial arts expert. The muscles worked not to look good but sharpened for necessity of function and purpose. Strangely, he didn't look like a Thai at all. His features belied anything Asian as was his height. Maybe there was a mutant tribe who lived in these parts.

*Crap, now he was coming towards me.*

He approached me slowly, not shifting his gaze from where I lay but abruptly stopped when he saw me shrink backwards. My movement had been involuntary. A product of all my dire imaginings. I just couldn't help it.

I relaxed a fraction when he returned to the fire and began slicing chunks of meat from the carcass now presumably cooked. I was grateful for his sensitivity, this was all too new and scary. Next time he approached I promised myself I would be more prepared. I saw him pour water into another bowl then made his way back towards me cautiously. Encouraged to continue when I neither flinched or cringed as he neared.

The aroma of hot barbecued food had travelled straight to my stomach making it groan in anticipation. The overwhelming hunger helped me to overcome my fear when the native next approached. I couldn't think of anything else.

He crouched slowly and sat down beside me, no sudden moves, careful not to frighten me and laid two bowls at my side. Tentatively he stretched out a hand to feel my brow. His touch was light and cool, despite the growing heat of the day, his palm was not as rough as I supposed it would be for someone who lived by their hands.

Seemingly satisfied, he motioned for me to eat and drink. I needed no further encouragement. I was hungrier than I'd ever thought possible as I reached for the bowl. The food tasted amazing, better than any barbecue I'd had back home, but flavour was not my main concern. My frustration lay in the fact the meat took too long to chew, I couldn't satisfy my ravenous hunger fast enough.

Finally taking my last mouthful and washing it down with a slurp of water I turned my attention back to the native. He'd returned to the fire and was just finishing the last scraps in his bowl, not glancing in my direction nor taking any notice of me at all. He got up to distinguishing the fire, wiping down his hunting tools and putting away the wooden bowls. Moving about the camp with a quiet proficiency. His seemingly lack of interest calmed my nervousness as I assessed his demeanor. He didn't seem dangerous or aggressive but he was a native, who knew how they behaved? His life style would be as alien to me as mine would be to him, our worlds poles apart. I had no idea of any native customs or native etiquette. They didn't teach any of that kind of thing at school. I wondered if they hated foreigners wandering into their territories. Especially those who fell into raging rivers and blighted the countryside with their presence.

How had he found me I wondered? Many questions burned inside my head but I assumed I had little way of finding out. He probably didn't speak any English I decided, and why would he? We where deep in the Thai jungle, miles from any English speaking places or anything remotely civilized, I couldn't expect him to understand me, anymore than I would understand him.

More importantly, where was I and how was I going to get out of here? The area we'd been trekking had been very close to one of Thailand's National Parks. I knew roughly the area in which I must be. Considered uninhabitable due to the inhospitable terrain. The mountains too steep to grow crops (or opium) or to graze any cattle. With no roads or infrastructure and miles from anywhere, I'd thought this area would be unpopulated.

*How wrong I'd been proven to be.*

So I was deep in the Thai wilderness, isolated from anything or anyone other than my native rescuer, safety a distant concept. At least my initial fears had been allayed for now. It appeared I'd been rescued by just this one native for I hadn't seen any indication of any others.

Yet.

The man at least seemed genuinely concerned about me. I'd seen it in the way he'd looked at me, assessing my progress. Then an uncomfortable thought came to me. I was going to have to depend on him for *everything*. My gammy leg meant I would be unable to do much for myself. The thought struck a cord of consternation. I wasn't used to relying on other people. Self sufficiency had been my mantra.

The native returned to my side causing my heart to hammer in consternation. I hadn't noticed until he came to sit down next to me the woody scent that pleasantly emanated from his skin. I'd been expecting him to be smelly, weren't natives supposed to have permanent body odor, and dirty finger nails? Surely they didn't have the same Western cleaning compulsion to wash twice a day? It wasn't like they had soap and showers to nip into morning and night or aftershave to slap on to disguise their 'BO.'

The movement of his hair as it slid over his shoulders suddenly captivated my attention. It was so glossy and straight, but still, his closeness was unnerving.

"Full now?"

My astonishment at his words rendered me momentarily speechless.

"Yes.....thank-you." Came my stilted reply. I didn't seem to have gained full control of my speech yet, or for that matter my emotions.

He shifted his attention to the vine leaf encircling my leg, motioning towards it for permission to touch it. I nodded, I was curious and anxious to see the damage which lay beneath the foliage bandage.

He gently untied the twine, pulling back the palm leaf slowly as if aware this could be painful. A warning for what was to come. Revealing beneath a layer of something soft and mossy, the texture like cotton wool and stained a deep shade of red. Very gently he began pulling the covering away, revealing something that should only belong in a horror movie. A long gash, at least 30 cm long, horizontally traversed my shin. The skin gaped swollen and torn, blaring an angry red colour. What little flesh there was didn't look good at all and I was certain I'd caught a glimpse of bone. I reared backwards, feeling the queasiness suddenly souring my throat. I wished I hadn't eaten the food so quickly now churning sickeningly in my stomach. I no longer wanted to see what he was doing, for now the pain was stabbing right through me. The sight of raw meat and bone was enough for me to be grateful to leave the task of doctoring the wound to the native.

I tried to divert my thoughts away from the sharp excruciating pain emanating from my leg, despite the man's gentle hands. Instead I concentrated on the top of the natives head. In another world the sort of hair I would have loved to have owned. Silky, soft and hanging obediently straight. Not like the crazy, frizzy ends of my own hair.

Impossible to control, hopeless to style.

Finally the native was done, reapplying the foliage bandage and retying the twine. Looking up as he smiled, little dimples appearing in his cheeks, the white teething flashing in the sunlight. Looking more like a movie star on location than he had any right to be.

"Okay?"

I nodded trying to hide the pained expression I'd been wearing only seconds earlier.

"Rest." He commanded softly before moving away again, leaving me stunned and confused.

*Who was this man?*

I mused over the last half hour, it didn't look like we would be having any deep or meaningful conversations with the single monologue language he'd been using. That was okay, I could live with that. I presumed he was ignoring me to make me feel safe.

It was working. Already I could feel my fear lessening by small degrees. In the short time I'd been awake he had done nothing to frighten me despite my scanty attire. Perhaps my predicament was not as bad as I'd first feared.

I was curious to know more about him. Who was he and where he had come from, and how had he found me? I was alive because of him, I was in no doubt about that. I could never have survived in this deserted jungle, not with my horrendous leg wound.

One thing was for certain, my life was still in his hands and I wasn't sure whether to still feel frightened or intrigued by my native, handsome rescuer.

One thing was for certain, I was going to enjoy watching him while I recovered.

Besides, there wasn't anything else to do.

# Chapter 3

# Life at Home

The sun shone high in the sky when I next woke. I guessed it to be close to midday, for the trees and shrubs cast hardly any shadow at all.

Was this a new day or the continuation of the same one? I had slept so much lately I hardly knew how many days had passed since I'd fallen in the river. Time appeared to have little meaning here in the jungle. Everyday was the same as the next.

The trees stretched high above me, the trunks were spindly in comparison to the wide canopy spreading away from their tops. The sunlight only reached the jungle floor in dappled patches and I was thankful to the shade for keeping the air cooler.

The colours were vivid. Rich shades and contrasts of colour shimmered in the sunlight, dancing off the leaves. How had I not noticed before? As I glanced around me I observed how the emerald green vegetation fluttered in the light breeze, variations of browns and beige, golden tones and the grey of the rocks and earthy mulch of the jungle floor. Around me, I noted the abundance of unrelenting bug activity. This place must be the creepy crawly capital of the world I thought, for the soil was in constant turmoil as ants and beetles twice the size of anything I'd ever seen at home trawled through the soil and leaf mulch. My body frequently acted as a favourable decoy as countless creatures tickled my skin, aimlessly wandered over its undulating landscape.

The native had gone. Again. He seemed to spend most of my waking hours away from the camp. I couldn't blame him, I wasn't much company (in my present state). He was probably ticking off the days until he could return me to civilization. Being alone had never bothered me before, but strangely I had come to find comfort in watching him move about the camp, even if he did mostly ignore me. I was getting used to that, it was usually how I treated others anyway. Yet, the strangeness of my whereabouts, the unfamiliar animal noises, aromas and vegetation made me feel vulnerable. Being out of my usual environment my only tenuous link to humanity lay in the quiet, golden brown native.

Despite the shade the heat prickled beads of sweat over my skin. It was March, the beginning of the hot season. Temperatures could get into the mid thirties but combined with the humidity it could feel much hotter.

I lay back on my makeshift bed allowing my mind to drift, caught up with the lazy movement of the canopy high above me, hypnotically stilling and soothing my thoughts. Reminded me of when I'd lay under the dappled shade of the oak tree at the bottom of the garden back home, returning my thoughts to the real reasons why I had left, to my other life, the one full of sadness and pain.

In the last eight or so years of my life, home had become unbearable. In the latter years of my childhood, growing up with a progressively alcoholic mother had been a painful process and I'd learned early on that hurt and angry abuse was never far away. How could they be when my mother violently reared between being sober to drunk, from lucid to anger, self pity and depression? Being battered between her mood swings and drunkenness had left me wrung out emotionally.

In the beginning, her the drinking had begun as a method by which she'd relax. My young and naive mind had thought it to be only a simple matter of will power and self control for her to stop. Now I knew better. An alcoholic does not want to stop or to have any help. Not if the festering wound which drives them to forget is still in need of healing. Nor if the world appears to be a dark and dangerous place in which to live.

My mother had become lost in this world, and then lost to her drinking, leaving my brother Harry and me bereft of any adult guidance. There'd been no point of focus from which to orientate ourselves because now the anchor was already adrift. My mother, a single parent, was the ship of this family but now she had no idea where she was going or how to steer us along the dark and stormy seas of life.

Over the course of my childhood, my mother sank ever deeper into her alcohol abuse. Becoming ever more self involved, the needs of Harry and myself had inevitably slipped into the backseat. We were just appendages to her turmoil. Another strain to stress over, another reason to sink herself into the drink.

Left in limbo.

To survive the ever prevalent angry onslaughts, and vicious tongue, I'd shut myself away within the internal, safe confines of my being, for therein lay safety. To remain unnoticed lest it invoked the rain of verbal abuse, until the criticisms and twisted accusations coated with a heavy dusting of venom had left their scars.

Now it was as if there was a blankness or emptiness inside me. Any semblance of real emotions had been forced away. I'd learned that feelings were dangerous things that could provoke a tirade, or push people away. Gone were the hugs, the words of encouragement and the displays of affection on which I'd once depended. Now, in turn I struggled to know how to feel the naturalness of showing any form of feelings. I'd become stiff and awkward, making it difficult for me to connect to people in any real way. Keeping friends had always been a struggle, as if people sensed the void inside me, this hollow person I'd now become.

Over the years the toll of my seeming lack of compassion was how everyone had judged me. The indifferent exterior, the reverse to what lay inside. I understood other peoples pain in a way I could never show, felt it as keenly as if it were my own, yet, my clumsy ham fisted attempts to sympathise with others were pushed away, preventing any further attempts to show concern.

In our teens my brother and I gradually found life on the outside. We were largely left to run wild anyway, mother being usually too drunk or asleep when we eventually crept in at night to notice the lateness of the hour. I found it a form of escape, to be able to leave the oppressiveness of what was our home life for as long as possible. The atmosphere stank from the stale cigarette smoke of thirty a day, and the sickly sweet smell of empty whisky glasses littered all over the house. Palpable depression hung thickly in the air like smog. Sapping the very substance from even the most cheerful of person who entered.

I stayed away as much as I could, but if on my late return my mother was awake and still drinking, oblivious to the hour, she would slurringly begin to recount excerpts from the day (from where she had left off at supper time) spurring me to extricate myself as soon as I could to save myself from the one way conversation that would have sent any insomniac to sleep. It was as if she possessed a form of Alzheimer's, repeating these stories over and over again without any need on my part to comment at all. The stories were always along the same themes. Never deviating away from how hard she worked, how unappreciated she was, or how so and so had been an absolute bitch at work. It all just sounded like a normal day at school to me.

I thought of one incident when I was 14. I had been out late at the pub with my regular older friends. When on my return I was greeted by my mother's thunderous face and I knew I was in trouble.

As soon as I entered the house she hurled the words." Where the bloody hell have you been?" she said, spitting the words at me with such force the spittle landed on my face. Whether a symptom of the booze or from sobriety I could not yet tell. But I saw she was hardly holding it together, best not to say much. It was often like this. A seemingly small incident suddenly becoming a disaster of world magnitude. The day's stresses and strains finding an outlet, namely that of taking them out on Harry and me, the two closest and easiest targets.

This outburst surprised me and for a moment I couldn't speak. She'd never asked me of my whereabouts before, she'd never been that interested, always being too wrapped up in her own troubles to notice.

"Out with Jess," I replied in a monotone, I was always careful with my replies. Any tone of voice she didn't like would be sure too incense her even more. I could not yet work out where this was leading but decided to conceal the fact I'd been at the pub. I was sure it wouldn't go down too well with me being under age and all. Not that I looked it, with my height and build people often told me I passed easily for eighteen.

"Do you know what the hell the time is?" She shouted. "I've just had Jessica's mother on the phone wondering why you weren't back yet. I didn't have the faintest idea where you were."

That was not unusual I thought, but it wasn't as late as my usual return to the house. It was only 1am. The swearing did not surprise me either. Her use of foul language when she was drunk had escalated with every passing year.

"What's the problem mum?" I asked, but I already knew. When Jessica's mum had phoned, it had made her feel guilty because she'd had absolutely no idea of my whereabouts or what time I'd be back. It had made her look stupid and a bad mother and now she was taking it out on me. She was trying to make herself feel better, trying to lay the blame firmly at my feet, even though it was partly her lax parenting controls that allowed me to roam so freely unchecked.

To a certain extent I did feel a pang of guilt. In any normal family I would have been grounded long ago for my nocturnal habits, my late night soirees. For someone as young as myself to be out so late doing whatever I liked was totally inappropriate, I knew that, but this was no normal family and having an alcoholic mother made it all too easy to flout the rules and live my life the way I wanted. Besides, my mother didn't have control over her own life let alone the ability to govern mine or my brother's.

"Mum, we went back to a friend's for coffee, that's why I'm a bit late," I said, still not mentioning the pub.

"Shut the bloody hell up, I haven't finished speaking," she slurred but didn't continue because a glassiness had begun to form over her eyes and confusion was replacing the fury. The drinking numbed her memory, in the morning she probably wouldn't even remember what this argument was about. Besides, I knew better than to take her mood head on in her current state, she would be particularly difficult if she recalled an argument. It wasn't worth the hassle.

The glazed faraway look was reinstating itself, the drunkenness and the lateness of the hour were taking their toll.

"Okay I'm sorry I'm back late, I didn't think you'd mind, we were only round the corner," fudging the last bit, I only wanted her to stop feeling bad and not blame herself. In the long run that would be worse for everyone. Her face softened. She saw a way out, of not losing face or appearing the bad, uninterested mother that Jessica's mother had made her feel. I knew the crisis was over.

"See you in the morning mum," I said before she could object, not waiting for an answer as I darted up the stairs to my bedroom.

As my mother's influence diminished with each passing year Harry and I began a quest to find some semblance of normal life, moving us imperceptibly away from our mother's nemesis. I learned to fill the gaps in my life with art and my love of animals, spending my weekends and summer holidays volunteering to help muck out and tack up at the local riding stables. The reward for my toil would be a free, bare back, half hour ride back to the horses nighttime grazing, a route which would take us through the woods strewn with logs to jump and fields over which to gallop. I'd found some measure of solace in animals, who loved you no matter what. They did not judge you for your failings, criticize your mistakes or dislike you for what you were not. I found their company and love more satisfying and rewarding than any humans in two small but significant facts. They never hurt you or took their love away. Cindy our golden retriever and the horses at the stables filled my life with feeling needed, a valued part of their lives, poles apart from where I felt my home life to be. This aspect of my life remained unfed, unwatered and undernourished.

Sometimes I would become depressed that this was the sum total of my life. Relying on animals to make me to feel loved when all other sources had dried up. Having a mother who had internalised herself and shut herself away from the world meant she hardly noticed much of what was going on around her, and that included Harry and me.

I only knew I didn't want to be like my mother. Wallowing in self pity, blaming the world for her misfortune and drowning her sorrows in drink. Life, I knew with conviction, had to hold more than just that.

*I only had to find it.*

I suddenly came back to myself, my daydream over, finding myself still gazing up at the swaying canopy above me, noting how the sun had passed from it's zenith to one side and had begun lengthening the shadows once more.

The native eventually returned towards the end of the day, carrying a backpack that suspiciously looked like mine, bearing the same dark blue colour and the familiar name 'The North Face.' He looked up and smiled that smile again. Did he know how disarming he could be? I didn't want to be taken in or relax in his company, but it was difficult not to be affected by his looks and easy manner. I wondered how old he was. He appeared to be not much older than myself, but I knew darker skin aged considerably slower than white.

He walked over to me, abruptly crouching down and began fiddling with the fastenings on the rucksack. His appealing woody scent now mingled with another I could not place, making me only too uncomfortably aware of his closeness again.

"Okay?" he asked, assessing me with an interested glance.

I nodded.

"Is this your rucksack?"

He handed it over to me allowing me to take a closer look. His little speech had surprised me. He'd said more words in one sentence than he'd said altogether since he'd found me. I glanced at his face, noticing the impossibly long eye lashes and the warm brown eyes looking at me intently, waiting for my answer. No sign of malice or leering even though I was decidedly underdressed. Must be my hair and my untidy appearance I thought, they would put anyone off.

"Yes, that looks like mine, where did you find it?" I wondered if he would understand all the words, even though I had said them slowly.

"Down river, near where I found you," he replied.

Obviously no problem understanding I thought. His voice was slightly husky, warm and had with melodic undertones and a hint of an American accent. This didn't surprise me, often when visiting foreign countries the English spoken by the foreigners sounded American. I guessed because of the numerous American teachers in schools here in Thailand or perhaps from the influence of American films and music. I decided it was an appealing voice, one that would catch your attention in a crowd and was easy to listen to.

Taking the bag I turned it over in my hands studying it carefully. It had not suffered nearly as badly as myself. Just a few rips in the sturdy fabric. Some of the clip fasteners were missing and it still contained some of my belongings. Its presence in my hands seemed to suddenly snap a vision into my head, like a film playing over. The images unexpectedly coming to mind as I remembered those gentle hands. I wondered how long I'd been lying half dead on the rivers edge before he had found me. How long ago had it been since I'd been trekking with Naomi, Bing and the others? It already seemed a life time ago, another world.

I was brought back to the present when I felt the native's eyes still on my face, suddenly embarrassed under the intense scrutiny, knowing how awful I must look even to a native. My hair stuck out at all angels, dirty and neglected. My clothes ripped and torn or what was left of them. I looked away to avoid his scrutiny. I still had some pride, even here in the jungle.

"My name is Jaya," he said, a ghost of a smile flickering over his lips. What was the joke? Probably my hair I thought.

"Alice," I replied, looking down with embarrassment, I did not want him to see the embarrassing blush even though I was glad we were on first name terms now.

"How long have I been here?" I asked.

"A little over a week," he said. His grasp of English really was amazing.

He suddenly looked troubled. "You took a long time to wake up."

*Had I really been gone all that time? A whole week!*

My mind drifted off to my trekking party. They would have arrived back at Chang Mai by now. Perhaps they'd alerted the authorities who could be looking for me right now. They'd have to use helicopters to find me of course, there would be no other way to search the miles of jungle and the tough terrain. Hope suffused through me at these comforting thoughts and I began to feel more optimistic.

"You are a long way from home. Nobody ever comes this far into the jungle, especially not Europeans," he didn't ask me out right how I happened to be in the jungle, but I could hear the unspoken question and how did he know I was from Europe?

"I was on a hiking trek, with some others, we were at the waterfall, but I fell in," it sounded so pathetic, so feeble. I wouldn't blame him for thinking I was a complete idiot because it was exactly what I thought of myself.

He smiled kindly "It's many miles from any touristy trekking areas, you're very lucky to be alive. The river is very treacherous in this area especially since the rainy season has just finished."

*No wonder there were so many mosquitoes!*

"Your English is very ......good," I said noting the sudden watchfulness before he replied.

"I haven't always lived in the jungle," He seemed reluctant to tell me anymore as he looked away. I had the distinct impression he was being cautious in how to reply. He turned back to look at me, studying me more closely than was warranted before he rose in that causal fluid movement of his effectively concluding the conversation.

Taking a look inside my old rucksack I was relieved to find some spare clothes I'd packed for trekking. My passport, toothbrush and phone were still in there. Excitedly I flipped the phone open only to find it was completely dead and soaking wet. I probably wouldn't get a signal here anyway. Sighing, I put it back and pulled out some clean, wet clothes to lay them out flat to dry. At least I would soon be half decent.

I smiled inwardly. I had to congratulate myself, I had certainly got what I wanted. Seclusion, the desire to get away from the hurly burley of life, from people and from home. Yet Jaya, I mused, wasn't like the people I'd wanted to get away from. There was something different about him. Something comfortable and dependable, something I realised I was beginning to really like.

# Chapter 4

# Bath

Several days had passed since I had woken up and found myself in the care of Jaya. We had got into a familiar routine. Jaya would go off to find food and I would wait patiently for him to come back. That amounted to my day. There was nothing to do. The seconds ticked away like hours. Time passed achingly slowly and I was bored. I tried to occupy myself by counting ants or humming songs, but with no book to read, no phone or ipod to play with the time dragged slowly. Nothing worked long enough to take away the dullness of boredom. Moving without help was impossible. My leg was too badly injured to risk attempting to get anywhere by myself, and in an effort to occupy myself my thoughts would frequently drift back to home. At times the memories would be unwelcome, the very reason I had left home in the first place had been to escape ever thinking about them again. Yet, thoughts are hard to control, especially when there is little else to think about and mine were no exception.

When people talk about their happy school years I knew they must be lying because it wasn't like that for me. I remembered the bullies at school, the gaggle of girls who would huddle in groups in the school playground always on the look out for a suitable victim, someone to torment. Maybe I just had 'victim' plastered all over my forehead or perhaps it was my height that made me stand out, but somehow I always seemed to draw their attention. Usually it would be the names at first, hurled slyly in my direction. The old chestnut 'scaly' or 'reptile legs' by the less imaginative ones who laughed at my eczema. The flaky, sore skin had plagued me most of my life. Appearing on the backs of my knees and wrists with persistent resolution. Thankfully not manifesting anywhere near my face, but still, I had to be careful to avoid certain types of shampoo which could create a major snow storm in my hair. The summer months I dreaded when I could no longer hide the angry patches under jumpers or tights, bringing unwanted awareness to my affliction and the cutting, taunting barbed comments would begin. Now glancing down at my scabby wrists and elbows I wondered if they would get any worse without the army of creams I had to apply to them to keep them under control.

Looking back, it seemed to me, most of my school years had been spent trying to avoid drawing unwanted attention to myself. Preferring to spend my lunch times either practicing sport or scurrying to the school library on the pretence of studying or doing my homework. One particular incident from school had stuck in my mind not only because it proved to me the immaturity of boys my own age, but how sex never seemed very far from their brains.

"Hey curly," he annoying nick name was hurled across the play ground drawing me to look in reflex towards the voice. Regretting it immediately when I saw Matt grinning with amusement, enjoying his ability to irritate me.

"Going bowling tonight with the gang?" he probed. On Friday nights I sometimes joined a group to play a few games of Ten Pin bowling, the loser picking up the drinks tab. We alternated bowling with a visit to the Wicked Lady, the real ale pub with its home brew scrumpy in nearby Wheathampstead.

"No, I'm heading home tonight, you?"

Seeing he'd got my attention, he quickly sauntered over to me. The bell was about to ring for class, he'd have to be quick. Suddenly he was leering down at my chest and I realised anything he was likely to say wasn't going to be nice. Turning to move away he stopped me by grabbing my arm, pulling me round to face him.

"I bet you £1 I can make your boobs wobble without touching them," he snickered.

"Piss off," he replied angrily, pulling at my arm to get free.

"I lose!" He laughed smuttily before lunging forward to grab my breasts.

I gasped, angry and shocked. How dare he! Without thinking my foot shot out aiming at his shins as he ducked away. Unfortunately my shoe being of the clog variety and completely open at the heel, flew off with the momentum, sending it flying, not stopping until it had smacked straight into Matt's mouth.

"Ow!" he yelped as his hand flew to his mouth, coming away with two bloody front teeth nestling in his palm while his mouth and remaining teeth were covered in a thin film of pink.

Like I said boys, had always been annoying and the girls mainly bullies, but don't get me wrong, Roundwood was a really good school, it was just the pupils who sucked.

Not that I minded the lack of school friends, I had just enough to keep away the embarrassment of standing alone in the school playground. Besides, my real friends were much older and far more mature than the spotty, bratty adolescent school boys and girls I endured in the classroom. I met these friends down the pub or travelled to gigs with them up in town. We talked about politics and sport, about climate change or the state of the country and government. A good subject for the Tory led Harpenden residents. They did not mind me being underage or gawky, including me in their mature conversations and debates, and this acceptance meant far more to me than anything else. Here I was one of them, not questioned for my motives or my reasons in staying out late. They accepted me for who I was, or that was what I thought.

My thoughts flitted back to Jaya. It was ironic to think how I'd expected him to be smelly when I lay here smelling more like the armpit of Calcutta. Being completely paralyzed meant there was little I could do to rectify the situation. I couldn't move, certainly not walk. There were no crutches or wheelchairs in the jungle. I would have to be patient and try not to mind. Not something I was particularly good at. I'd never been the sort of person who allowed myself to rely on other people. My past had seen to that. Now my helplessness made me cringe every time Jaya had to do something for me, especially a native who'd I'd only met a few days ago.

Over the course of the last few days Jaya had helped me to a place where I could perform my bodily functions, then thankfully leave me in private, it was so embarrassing. The loss of dignity made me squirm with humiliation. Jaya never seemed to mind, always able be to anticipate my needs and now was no exception I noticed. He was making his way towards me through the camp. I wondered how long this exchange would last this time. For he deliberately kept our time together to a limit. Perhaps because he had seen in the beginning how much he'd frightened me and as if gentling a wild animal he had kept our exchanges brief so that I could become accustomed to him in my own time. Or maybe there was another reason for keeping a distance. Something about the way he seemed too cautious had enlivened my interest. No, I decided, his aloofness was most definitely caused by the foul stench I must be emanating. I could even smell it myself. A good enough reason as any to keep as far away from me as possible I thought, mortified.

"Bath?" he asked without any hint of repulsion at the disgusting mess before him. His eyes sweeping over my body as if really seeing it for the first time, making me cringe inside again. Its stinking, bedraggled appearance next to his clean and tidy handsomeness, made me feel all the more unkempt and dirty. I was suddenly consumed with embarrassment. He must want me to clean up, to save himself from the shameful aroma that emanated from every pore of my body. I knew the smell must carry for meters. He didn't need any other excuse to stay well away from me. The jungle had been very hot these last few days, causing me to perspire heavily. My skin carried layers upon layers of dried sweat and body odour, not to mention my hair which still contained twigs and smelly river silt within its tangled tresses.

The shameful stench's only benefit as far as I could make out was in keeping the mosquitoes away, but the flies seemed to find me more interesting.

I looked around, as if I'd suddenly spot a bathtub waiting for me to get in.

"I'll carry you to water," he announced, reading my expression correctly. Then smiling at the look of horror in my face as I realised I'd have to be held close to him in this horrible state. Before I could protest any further I was swept up into his arms as easily as a child. I knew I was no feather weight.

*Impressive. I thought.*

All the same I was now way out of my comfort zone and fidgeted in his arms. I worried about the horrible smell, how could he bear it? I tried to shift my weight to hold myself away from his chest as if this would lessen the hateful aroma, but his grip was too tight. I was pinned against his smooth, hairless torso uncomfortably aware of his woody scent, the feel of his hands on my body and the shift in his muscles as he carried me. The proximity and this almost intimate closeness made me feel intensely awkward. I had no experience of this kind of thing, of being held, or touched. It had been a very long time since anyone had been this close. Now the startling nearness and the hardness of his muscles stirred something in me. The sensations that pulsed through me confusing, contradictory.

*Normally I didn't feel anything about anyone.*

He carried me like this for quite some time along such a narrow and heavily obscured path that I would surely have missed. The motion of walking gradually lulled me into a sense of security I had not felt since I was a small child. I was happy that he walked in silence and I was just as content to listen to the growing volume of noise of the river up ahead. I presumed the lack of conversation helped him not to breath in so often.

We emerged into a clearing of flat rocks and shallow pools next to the river. He set me down gently and I gingerly straightened my legs allowing most of my weight to be taken on my relatively good leg. The dizzy feeling I attributed to not having been vertical for quite some time, it felt strange.

We stood by a pool some distance away from the main part of the river, audible in its seething, ferocious roar in the distance. The pool in contrast lay undisturbed. The trees and plants that edged its rim, caste a mirrored double effect into the water. Good I thought, finally I would be able to get a good look at myself.

Jaya was still holding me close into the side of his body making sure I wouldn't lose my balance. His presence and the way he touched me were always gentle and with respect. Over the last few days I'd largely lost my fear of him and I no longer worried about the intentions of this man. Now a growing curiosity had replaced the apprehension.

"The pool's not too deep, there is no danger as it's completely contained and only fills again when the river is in full flood. The water is still fresh and drinkable," he said confidently.

"I won't get washed away again?" I said smiling shyly. It was the first time I had tried to joke with him.

"You'll be quite safe here, just mind the fish."

"What fish." I asked worried now "Are they big?"

"Big enough to nibble!" He grinned. "It could be painful!"

"You're joking right?" I said looking worriedly into the dark water.

Before climbing in I glanced into the mirrored water to catch a reflection of myself before my entry blurred the surface. I smiled to myself. I wouldn't be winning any beauty pageants if ever, I looked more like an extra in a horror film. I could see a gash to the side of my face, long and ragged. Dark bruises on my temples and cheeks had formed here and there. As I had feared, my hair usually my defining feature stuck out at all angles making me look like a half crazed mad woman. This was the essential part of me by which people associated me. I remembered a wig party back home, an 18th birthday of a casual school friend. Nobody had recognised me at first because of the red, straight shoulder length wig so different from my usual curls and frizzy ends.

It wasn't until years later I found the answer to my hair problems, neat conditioner slapped on at regular intervals throughout the day and to avoid getting it wet at any cost. Rain of any kind spelt frizzy disaster.

I tentatively moved to the pool's edge still balancing on Jaya's arm and lowered myself into the cool, still water. Allowing it to envelop my aching and bruised body. It reached only up to my waist, the water buoying me, allowed me to stand on my good leg without too much effort.

"I will be in the next pool," Jaya announced once I was safely in the water. I saw him walk away and strip off his few clothes to reveal even more of the perfectly sculptured body before diving into the pool next to mine. His neat bottom shockingly pale before disappearing into the water.

I was amused rather than shocked, I'd grown up with a brother after all. I decided on for a more modest approach, taking off my clothes beneath the concealment of the water. Although these were the fresh clothes from my rucksack the smell from my body odor had already dirtied them.

The water although cold, was refreshing and invigorating as I washed my skin's grimy surface and dunked my head under the water several times to loosen and the remove the debris from the river. I turned my attention to the vine bandage pulling at the twine to remove it. I wanted the wound on my leg to be properly cleaned. The surface of the gash was now forming a thick scab puckering and wrinkling the skin around the edges. I really didn't need the vine bandage any more but it had stayed in place to keep the flies away and to prevent me from knocking the scab accidentally.

Chores over, I lay back in the pool and allowed the refreshing water to wash away the rest of the aches and pains, the coldness taking the heat from my skin allowing my mind to drift and be still. Baths back home were never as relaxing or revitalizing as like this. I'd always preferred to take a shower. Sitting in a bath with its scummy surface and cloying heat had always made me feel drowsy and unrefreshed afterwards.

I redressed beneath the water before getting out. Although my clothes were wet, the temperature of the air meant that they would dry soon enough and their dampness would keep me cool for a time.

I glanced up as Jaya had rejoined me, his lower half already dressed while his body and hair were still dripping from the pool. Thin rivers of water rolled down his lean body and suddenly it was hard to look away, not to watch in fascination how the water droplets clung to his golden brown skin or how they trickled in thin rivulets over the muscles, like gleaming jewels I thought distractedly.

Get a grip, I told myself, this wasn't Mills and Boon.

He'd been busy while I'd been washing. Several large fish hung from his hands. How had he caught them so quickly?

"Nice," I said. Adding hastily. "Catch," I murmured, suddenly embarrassed to have been caught gaping.

"You smell better," he laughed drawing a deep embarrassing blush to spread over my face and neck before becoming annoyed with myself for not being able to think of an appropriate clever retort.

Within a short time Jaya had built a fire and had expertly gutted the fish.

"I don't think I have thanked you yet for saving me, if you hadn't found me......." My voice trailed off and I changed the subject. It looked like he didn't want any gratitude. "What were you doing in this part of the jungle anyway? I've been lead to believe these areas of Thailand where uninhabited." I suddenly thought my question sounded stiff and too prying. I knew nothing of who he was or what he was doing in the jungle. For all I knew he could be working with the drug Lords and would not take kindly to impertinent questions.

He paused what he was doing for a second before continuing, but did not look at me when he spoke.

"I live here."

"On your own?" I asked

"There are others in the jungle but not in these parts."

Definitely cautious, but I couldn't think why.

Changing tack I asked, "how did you find me?"

He looked up this time when he spoke.

"I was walking above the gully, I saw you in the shallows of the river. I thought you were dead but I came down to check all the same." he smiled. "I have never seen a person covered in so many bruises or mosquito bites! I couldn't leave you, not while there was still breath in your body."

My mind processed this last bit of information before I asked him my next question.

"Where did you learn English?"

His eyes shifted away from mine again. The caution was there again and uncertainty played briefly across his features before they smoothed.

"Here and there," he said in a non committal manner.

I didn't press him any further but I knew for certain it wasn't the truth. Besides, the set of his strong jaw told me he wouldn't divulge any more information on the subject and I hardly knew him well enough to ask more.

"Where is your home?" he countered.

I smiled inwardly. "Good question," I replied. I'd always thought that home was somewhere you'd wanted to return to. Your haven from the frenetic life and stresses in the world. Home didn't mean any of those things to me anymore, being the very reason I'd left, but I couldn't tell Jaya that.

"England," I replied. "Not far from London." I wondered if he knew geography.

He nodded. "What is your purpose in coming here?" He looked at me searchingly. Was there more to the question than it appeared?

"I'm taking a gap year before I go to University. I wanted to see the world while I still had the chance," I said. I didn't add that I'd needed to run away, from home, even from myself. The latter two I'd managed admirably.

He seemed satisfied with my answer. Looking at me intently he spoke in a low soft voice, the wonderful resonance coupled with the intensity of his golden brown eyes caught me off guard.

"Don't worry, I'll get you home," he said with certainty. I stared back unnerved again at his closeness. Its effect. Jaya was so self assured in himself and his confidence and maturity belied his young handsome face. I knew that I believed him, that he would get me home and he would look after me until that time. Yet, staring into those golden brown eyes I suddenly felt like I didn't want to go, not just yet. For some strange reason I wanted to stay here for longer.

But whatever those reasons were, I didn't entirely know why.

# Chapter 5

# Wanting to Stay

Over the course of the last week I had become accustomed to living in the jungle with Jaya. There was nothing complicated to worry about, no bipolar alcoholic to side step, no reminder of my awkwardness. In fact there was nothing here which reminded me of home or the memories I wanted to forget.

I certainly didn't need people or company to be happy, back home or here in the Thai jungle and I had seen enough during my gap year to satisfy my wander lust for years.

My life had already changed beyond all measure and entirely because of the native called Jaya. This place was beginning to grow on me. The jungle was becoming an increasingly attractive place to stay. Not just because of my fascination with Jaya, but because I felt more comfortable and content than at any time I could remember. All the years of feeling the joker in the pack, all the awkwardness I'd felt in other peoples company had melted away in this new and different environment, a place where I didn't have to try so hard. Home had been like living on a merry-go-round, never knowing where or when you could get off, it's unpredictability creating uncertainty in every corner of my life. Here I could watch Jaya live each day with authenticity and conviction. Self contained but in a different way to me. The ease in with which he lived in this environment and the self assurance by which he undertook each task, his knowledge of the jungle and how to live in it showed me something I had not seen in a person for a long time, confidence. Confidence in what he did and confidence in who he was, engendering a trust in me as well. A trust in him. Gone was my fear of him or the marauding animals, the worry over the imagined hidden dangers in the jungle. Perhaps a product of my boredom but lately I had began to wonder why I would ever want to return to the uncertainty and chaos at home.

Yet, Jaya was steadfast in his desire to deliver me safe and sound back to Chang Mai, such was his feeling of responsibility.

Leaving me in little doubt that I only had a short time left in the jungle and I worried that I had come to rely on him in more ways than I would care to admit, by forming a connection that inevitably would have to be severed. Yet, he was all I had, no matter the dangerous ground this was leading me into.

Yes, I was beginning to toy with the idea of staying here in the jungle even when my injuries had completely healed. This outlandish idea all depended on Jaya and if I could persuade him. To second guess his response to my proposal was more than just a grey area, it was an unchartered territory. I couldn't deny that being in his company had been infinitely more enjoyable than anything I'd left behind. Over the last few weeks I'd come to feel so comfortable, so easy in his company, no awkwardness and no feelings of embarrassment anymore. His company and conversation were effortless, not that there was much of it, but that didn't matter, I'd never been much of a conversationalist either. Now the thought of returning to my former life struck a cord of consternation, I didn't want to go just yet. I was more than happy here because I was untroubled for the first time in ages. Besides, the jungle met all the criteria I'd craved for, to get away from people and be by myself. Jaya didn't count, being more like an oil painting you wanted to study all the time, always finding something new and interesting to enjoy everytime you looked.

"What if I don't want to go back?" I said suddenly. The thoughts had been playing over on my mind all morning, all week in fact. "What if I stay here with you?" I added suddenly feeling sheepish to have asked. Jaya's expression suddenly made me feel embarrassed as his eyes flickered over my face.

"Why would you not want to leave? I thought it was what you wanted?" he said studying my face, a sudden watchfulness flaring.

Searching for the right words, hardly knowing all the reasons myself I replied.

"I want to........to stay because........" I paused, suddenly finding it difficult to get the words out as they got stuck in my throat. "There's nothing for me back there."

"But your Mom and Dad will be worried about you," he said simply.

I shook my head. "No, the only company that my mother wants to keep is with Jack Daniels and her cigarettes." I added bitterly.

"Why would you want to stay here?" he said quietly, his eyes suddenly dark and unfathomable and instantly I felt foolish to have even asked. Was I giving him the wrong idea? I tried again.

"I like it here, I don't care about going home. I feel comfortable, I like.........the jungle," I sounded like a petulant child. Crap, how was I going to explain myself.

"What of the rest of your family, your father?" Jaya said.

Yes, what of the absent father? "He definitely wouldn't miss me."

Jaya looked at me as if he didn't know what to say. I pressed on. "I can't leave yet anyway, my leg won't get me very far. You said there were others in the jungle. Is there a village or tribe near by, perhaps we could go there for a while? Until I get better, if it's safe?"

Aside from visiting the waterfall I was still curious to see what a real hill tribe looked like. Being one of the very reasons I'd undertaken the trek in the first place. Jaya couldn't be living in this wilderness all on his own. Like he said, there were others in the jungle. Besides, staying with Jaya's tribe would be like living in five star accommodation in comparison to this.

Jaya's body stiffened and something changed in his face.

"You can't stay in the jungle," he said with a firm edge to his words.

"Why?" I stared at him suddenly interested in Jaya's reaction.

"That's not the best option, we should get you back to Chang Mai where you can tell them you're okay." His abruptness surprised me, he'd only spoken to me with gentle words before.

"I don't care about that," I said bitterly, sounding like a typical rebellious teenager. Blaming the parents, always their fault. Only this time it wasn't me who'd gone off the rails. I felt a blaze of anger at what my life had become, the misery I'd left behind.

I certainly didn't want to return to that now I had found some semblance of happiness.

"Alice you cannot stay here," Jaya said suddenly becoming angry, his face oddly dark, making my stomach twist strangely inside.

"Why?" I wasn't going to give up that easily.

He gave me a hard look, a muscle twitching in his jaw.

"You don't belong here and it would be dangerous." He looked away and I thought he must be referring to the drug barons. Perhaps there was a real possibility this area was unsafe, I knew little of how or where they moved about the jungle.

"Surely if it's dangerous it would be better for me to stay with your tribe. Until I can walk again and get my strength back. Wouldn't it be safer there?" I pressed, realising too late I'd touched a raw nerve, because abruptly he jumped to his feet and was striding away, disappearing from view behind the thick green foliage of the jungle, leaving me stunned and confused to have caused this unexpected reaction.

*What did this mean? What had I said to upset him?*

I had touched on a subject he was uncomfortable with. But what? Nothing came to mind. I resolved to remain quiet in future, to keep my thoughts to myself when he came back.

*If he came back.*

Because now I worried I had driven him away.

He was my only hope.

I knew I was clinging to straws. Perhaps he didn't like the thought of spending anymore time in my company than he had too. Yet, I couldn't blame him for disliking me, not many people did. The sparse amount of friendships I could make claim too had never been particularly close, apart from Georgia, my best friend and my brothers girlfriend.

Sometimes I felt like a human punch bag, taking the rap for someone else's insecurities or irritations. I knew I was an easy target, easy to blame, being a person who kept their feelings to themselves. It wasn't as though I couldn't lash out with my hands or my tongue. Yet, the years of biting back the words to save myself from the volcanic reactions at home had curbed my ability to retaliate. Holding it all in, keeping it all together had taken all my strength in an attempt to keep the peace, eventually taking its toll and leaving me sterile in my responses. The impossibility of growing up with an abusive mother and one totally out of control had left their mark. In the beginning I'd been too young and powerless to say or do anything about it and later too repressed to be able to fight back.

I had tried over the years to help her, Harry and I both had. To hide her bottles of whisky or return them to the supermarket shelves before she got to the checkout, thinking with the innocence of our young minds that this was all she needed to stop. Later we tried to confront her about her drinking, but our efforts were shot down in angry flames. She did not want to listen, she did not want her faults and failures to be flagged up and especially not by mere children.

Eventually, the only way to survive the hap hazard mood swings and unpredictable fury had been to remain quiet. To bite my tongue because whenever my brother and I tried to steer her away from the alcohol, we were only rewarded with her wrath and the full force of her parental power. A fact she wielded to her full advantage when she became irritated with us or when we questioned her reasons to drink. To challenge an adult in our mothers eyes was disrespectful and rude. We were only children after all and still under her ultimate control. A balance which would remain uneven until adulthood if ever at all. We learned early on an alcoholic never wants to give up their crutch. The very thing they come to rely upon in order to survive, even for the ones they supposedly love. For what else is there to stave off the darkness?

I only wanted my mother to come back, to return to how she was before. Not this poor replacement, this alien that now inhabited my mothers body. The mother who used to take my brother and I with all our friends to the adventure parks, swimming pool and bluebell woods had gone. Who'd once loved me for myself despite my personality defects, my shyness and crippling hypersensitivity. She'd stood beside me through the trials and tribulations of school, the fall out with friends. Shielding me with her love and compassion from even my biggest critic.

Myself.

All that was gone.

Taken away by the drinking.

I still loved her, but it had became harder with every passing year. I missed the old mum, the lovely dinners, the fabulous stews, roasts, cakes and puddings now replaced by supermarket frozen ready meals from the microwave. I missed the laughter, her dry humor, the cuddles and the loving words. Now superseded with bitter sadness and displeasure in everything around her.

As the drinking insidiously took over, I had felt a sense of failure that my brother and I were no longer enough to make her happy. No longer anything in which she could find pleasure. We became little more than an irritation, an aggravation to add to her pile of other problems rather than the children she had born and loved. We were only teenagers, making a mess, leaving shoes or clothes haphazardly around the house, not tidying our bedrooms, nor noticing the product of our disorderly lives. Yet, to our mother we had become an another burden, another strain to add to the scores of others.

We never told anyone, could never divulge what was happening, she was still our mother after all. She was our last pillar of security despite how tenuous this proved to be and if this was taken away, what would become of us afterwards? No, sharing our troubles had never been an option or even a possibility. Harry and I had both known that.

This was how life had become until we'd both found a means to running away, because living with my alcoholic mother had become like riding a runaway train, running a marathon with no end, enduring an agonizing pain that never goes away.

*In the end, leaving home had been the only way we'd known how to survive.*

It was getting late, the sun had now dipped far below the trees. Its golden light streamed through the branches causing the shadows to become long and thin. Jaya had still not returned and I was beginning to feel anxious.

*What if he didn't return?*

I couldn't imagine Jaya would leave me, not after the trouble he'd taken to help me recover. He'd cared for me in a way I had forgotten another human being could do. Even in the short time I had known Jaya I knew he was different from other people. There was an integrity, a sense of something I could depend upon, yet I was scared he wouldn't come back.

Surely there had only been a small misunderstanding? I was sure whatever I'd said could soon be put to rights.

*It had too be.*

Because I could not bear the thought of him disliking me.

I had tried not to be taken in by the winning smile, the engaging features or be attracted to the athletic physique, but it had been difficult. Perhaps this was what happened to people when they were taken out of their natural environment and their entire existence depended upon another. The barge pole distance I usually kept people at bay could no longer be applied. Not when I was almost intimately manhandled. A necessary requirement due to the sickness in my body. Jaya had come to know my needs almost as well as I did and with almost uncanny predictability.

Far ahead, from the edge of the tree line, a brisk movement suddenly caught my attention. With an exaggerated swagger Jaya emerged from the jungle. He appeared taller, more imposing than before and I shivered involuntarily when I saw the anger shimmering through him with every jagged movement. He covered the ground swiftly, tautness shouting from every fibre. His movements oddly shuddering and I wondered what had made him so angry. I glanced round, expecting to find the cause of this strange behaviour. With a sudden consternation I realised it was only me he was looking at, only me his eyes never wavered from.

*But this couldn't be for me, or could it?*

He was holding something that looked like a stick or a spear and it's presence in Jaya's hand caused a sharp recoil in my stomach and the barbed twisting fear began. This wasn't the Jaya I knew, this was someone else. He was coming for me, I was in no doubt about that and there was nothing I could do but watch as he quickly covered the distance between us. Not giving me anytime to think, to work it out, or what it all meant.

Abruptly he stopped before me. Malevolent emotions cursing over his face and shimmering over his body. The anger hardly bridled or held in check.

This was it, I thought, there was nowhere to go, no way to escape, because now being held at my throat, was the jagged tip of his spear.

# Chapter 6

## Interrogation

I felt the shaking begin and a cold weakness spreading through my body. What had turned Jaya into this inferno of fury? What had been the spark which had kindled this anger? I hardly knew how to act in the face of my unknown crime, but the spear which now rested firmly against my neck told me otherwise.

"Who are you?" He spoke quietly but the menace in his tone made me shiver. I felt a lump forming in my throat and suddenly I was rendered mute, unable to speak.

"Who sent you?" he said again more firmly this time, his voice now underlined with threat. I told myself to keep calm, this must be all a mistake. There had to be a simple explanation to all of this and would soon be resolved. I fought to keep my face impassive for fear of provoking more fury, I knew there was little I could tell him. What was there to say? Who did he think I was? I sifted through my mind, desperate to find the right words, to find anything that could help me. What did he want to know?

My lips began to move but nothing came out, like the volume control had somehow been turned down. I noticed the two angry crease lines deepening between his eyebrows, the set of his mouth pulled taut and angry, his eyes hard and glinting. A strong pulse throbbed in his neck and his nostrils flared with every pull of breath. His expression hardening in the face of my silence. It seemed my time was running out.

"I....I don't know..." I managed, croaking out the words and sounding more like a hardened smoker of sixty a day.

"Why did you come here?" he said, his voice came louder, colder as he adjusted the spear. The tip now wavering under my throat, leaving me in little doubt to his intention. Fear, fear, fear, the beat tore through me. The jagged shards cutting, the adrenaline pumping, the tension unbearable, my breathing now coming in ragged gulps. My original instincts must have been way off. The unforeseen aggression now bounced off him in huge waves hitting me deep within my core. I was falling apart. I couldn't think, the Gobi desert that had been barren to my tears erupted in full force. The drops rolling down my nose and chin. Deja vue, like the other time. I remembered how crippling panic could be.

Like a frightened rabbit caught in the headlights, I could only stare back at him, the sobs escaping haphazardly from my chest. The calm facade now broken to pieces and laying about me like confetti. The river had failed to take my life but now I was in no illusion that Jaya was about to. Such was the stab of the spear aimed at the artery of life, pulsing in pace at the exposed tilt of my neck.

I finally found the strength to stammer.

"Don't hurt me, please." As my face contorted in anguish before I buried it in my hands. I was beyond all point of self control. I had reverted back to base instincts. The tears wrought to find pity, for compassion and mercy. I swiveled away from him to hide the unrelenting river running unchecked down my cheeks. Then bowing my head into the hard plains of my knees. What did it matter if I faced him or not? I had little doubt at what lay in store. Let it be over quick I thought, wondering what was taking Jaya so long to finish it, for wasn't this what he threatened if I did not answer him? To end my life with his spear? Now he cruelly prolonged the agony as the seconds stretching away into eternity. A vision I'd soon be joining Jesus and his happy gang of angels flittered weirdly into my mind. I was detaching from reality, spinning away from myself and from the horror of this moment in an effort to save this last intact piece of myself.

I jumped as a hand lightly touched my shoulder, its fingers squeezing gently. For a moment I could not connect that this was Jaya's hand, Jaya's fingers that softly grasped my flesh. But why? Confused and dazed, I fearfully looked up. Gone was the fierce hatred and unbridled anger, gone the aggressive stance and the spear that had moments before stabbed at my throat. Standing before me was the Jaya from before. The one I'd once thought I had known.

His eyes flickered over my tear stained face, dipping lower to take in the fearful strobes of emotion still quivering over my body.

I had been stripped as bare as a newborn. The thick wadding of protection mechanisms no longer in place, leaving nothing to conceal but the coward that lay within.

Abruptly Jaya crouched in front of me, balancing on the back of his heels, levelling his eyes with mine. He reached out to gently cup my chin. A hand only moments ago which had brutally thrusted its spear at my neck, a hand threatening to kill.

"Don't move," he murmured as I quivered under his touch, recoiling in reflex as if from being burned.

"Don't move," he repeated firmly. Bewildered, I mutely stared back, the intensity of his gaze stilled something in me. Calming the velocity of my racing heart then regulating the rhythm of my breathing, before becoming lost in the sea of his golden brown eyes. Holding me captive more than any spear had been able to do.

*What did he see, what did he search for?*

He gazed deeply into my eyes until finally he dropped his hand, freeing me from its captivity. A quietness had befallen Jaya. He remained silent, thoughtful, his eyes never leaving my face. It seemed as if he was trying to reach a decision and it was difficult for him. Finally the spell was broken when he looked away.

"I want to show you something," he said, then he added, "You have nothing to fear, I won't hurt you."

Won't hurt me, nothing to fear, who was he kidding? I knew I could never trust him again.

"Can't you just explain yourself first?" I managed bravely while fighting to contain the grenade of emotion still exploding through me.

"I will, I promise, but not here."

The anger ascended first. Elbowing its way through the rusty pathways of my being.

"What the bloody hell was all that about Jaya? I thought you were going to kill me."

"Alice, keep your voice down, please."

"NO! Not until you tell me what the hell is going on."

"There isn't anytime for this, we have to move. NOW," the urgency in Jaya's voice stalled me.

"What?"

"There are men nearby in this jungle. If they find us, they will kill us."

I stared incredulously at Jaya, daylight dawning. He'd thought I'd been one of them, a spy. That I was trying to find out information about his tribe and God knows what else. I suddenly felt as if I'd been hit in my solar plexus, the dots were slowly joining. Most likely it was the drug barons nearby. What else could instill that sort of fear into someone like Jaya? He'd suddenly changed his mind about me. Maybe it was my pathetically, cowardly performance that had contributed to that?

*Undoubtedly.*

Because now, he'd swung me up on to his back before heading into the thick of the jungle.

Jaya cautiously entered a large clearing, empty except for a smoldering pile of ash and a couple of charred logs still burning at its edge. Allowing me to slip gently to the ground, he gestured towards the fire.

"There are people, bad people in these parts. They have been close to us not so long ago," he said looking at me intently, a fire flickering behind his eyes.

"When you started asking questions and wanted to stay in the jungle I thought you may be one of them." He paused. "Your reaction ...........it was too strong for me to doubt you. These people who hunt us are tough, well trained, possibly military, and you? You are like a tender fruit, soft, but with the appearance of something more substantial. It only took a gentle prod to reveal your underbelly, your true colours. For that I am sorry but it was necessary......" He trailed off, taking my hand in his in a comforting gesture.

"I saw who you are Alice," he murmured looking intently down at me, seemingly to convey something more than just words. Could he really know me, know the person inside?

*I hoped not.*

"Who are the people who are looking for you?"

"They are greedy men, money is what they worship," he said releasing my hand suddenly, allowing it to flop back to my side.

"Do you have something they want?" I asked.

"What they want is ...... I cannot tell you," he paused looking towards the tree line. "We cannot stay here, we must leave."

He pulled me onto his back once more before making a swift exit from the clearing. Whoever had made the fire could not be very far away and we both knew they could return at anytime.

He followed a faint path beside the river, taking us deeper into the mountains, stopping after a short distance beside a vine to pull off a length of its string.

"This is necessary to prevent any stray fibers from catching on the overhanging branches. We do not want to leave any evidence of our passing," he said giving me some string with which to tie my own hair.

"Have you lived like this for very long?"

"Long enough," he said.

He avoided damaging any foliage, fringing the path and walking wherever possible on rock, I presumed so not to leave any trace of a foot print.

"How dangerous are these men?"

"They would kill if it served their purpose. These people are skilled trackers, they've never managed to follow me further than the pools we bathed in earlier today." That was comforting I thought, but I wondered what he meant by further.

*Further to where?*

"They followed your trail?"

"Yeah, but never close enough to see me."

It became tiring clinging to his body as he walked swiftly and silently through the jungle. My arms ached from holding myself upright and my legs still felt stiff and sore from their wounds and bruises. Now they'd become numb with fatigue and from binding myself to his body. We had been moving for several hours before he stopped and gently set me on my feet. At first I was too stiff to stand upright, my legs felt like jelly and my muscles fibrillating with the effort. Jaya stood beside me with a hand placed around my waist to steady me. I was too tired to appreciate the gesture, for in some ways I'd already taken his attentiveness for granted.

The caress of a hand for reassurance or an arm placed prudently to support me. It had always been like this but now I shivered involuntarily. Remembering Jaya's brutality of only a few hours earlier.

"We will rest for a while." He told me and pulled the large pouch of water from his hip before offering it to me. Taking large gulps, I watched as Jaya expertly readjusted his ponytail, pulling back stands of hair that had escaped before retying the twine.

Much later he said. "We will continue until dark." I nodded, handing back the water pouch too tired to answer while I mused over his long. I decided how male it looked, the abundant glossy mane somehow gave a sense of strength and self assurance, a statement of not needing to conform. I knew Jaya was a native but still, his long flowing locks seemed to set him apart, making him different from the short cropped hairstyles of men from back home. The act of pulling his dark hair from his face had revealed a strong smooth neck. The skin such a lovely colour, the workings of the muscles and tendons as they moved were fascinating.

Get a grip. I told myself again, tearing my eyes away.

We continued again in the same fashion until the encroaching darkness obscured the path to the extent it became too treacherous to continue. I was relieved when Jaya finally put me down to make camp for the night.

Almost as soon as Jaya had lain upon the animal skins he was asleep, laying close enough for me to touch tonight if I wanted to. Previously, he'd always slept well away from me. Never too far for me to worry about prowling, marauding animals but never as close as he was now. His woody scent hung in the air, strong and earthy and bringing a sense of security with its familiarity. Helping to keep the fears and nightmares away that dogged my sleep.

"The nightmares will fade," Jaya had told me. "They're only the subconscious fears from the trauma, it is only natural you will have them for a while."

But even before I'd come into the jungle nightmares had always been my constant companions at nighttime.

Tonight, I lay unable to sleep. Instead I watched the stars brightening in the sky one by one. I could just make out the Milky

Way, Pegasus or the Bear, the constellations my father had been at pains to show me on a cloudless night before bedtime. The moon almost full, gave just enough light to make out the smoothness of Jaya's skin. A light dusting of fine hair over his arms and chest, the straight strong nose and prominent cheek bones, his silky black hair falling back into the pillow of soft ferns. Looking at Jaya sleeping, the gentle fall and rise of his chest I realised suddenly I had more feelings for him than I cared to admit, despite what had happened earlier today. This wasn't just about enjoying his company anymore, these feelings were a far more dangerous and frightening prospect. It wasn't just because of the way he looked, it was the strong but gentle person he was inside. His face and body just window dressing, just making it easier. He was beautiful and completely unaware of it, not like the boys back home. The ones who knew they were good looking. Using their looks to full advantage, to flirt, to grab attention and charm the female teachers, I thought with distaste.

I turned my face away, berating myself for being taken in by his looks. Beauty was an illusion, no better than the pretty packaging of a Christmas or birthday present. Never knowing what you would find inside, sometimes pleasing sometimes not. What was it about beauty that people admired so much? Why strive for something which was only skin deep, that would fade with time? Wasn't it more important to nurture the person inside, to strive to gain admirable human qualities and be remembered for who you were? The West had become fanatical in its striving to achieve the impossible dream, to have that flawless body, that perfect face. Whole industries revolved around this undertaking, the gyms and beauty parlors, the diet products and weight loss clubs. Maybe it was a result of living in a judgmental and critical world that propelled us to enhance the exterior rather than work on what lay inside. Because inevitably that was how people judged us.

I'd known that even from my time at school.

I'd survived the criticisms and the wreckage of my home life purely though numbing everything and everyone out, blurring the hurts. Watching the life around me with a healthy dose of cynicism. Yes, maybe I was a coward in facing my emotions, but at least this had saved me from humiliating myself and relying on others for happiness. Self reliance is a hard, but safe road to travel, and I seriously doubted, worse than that, much less cared whether I hurt people with this attitude or not. Because this was my armour, the only thing that kept me from falling apart. To open my heart would be like opening the flood gates and I never wanted to feel that amount of heartache and pain ever again.

*If I did, I knew next time I might never survive.*

# Chapter 7

# A New Vista

My mind was still too active. Sleeping looked a distant prospect for now and I felt my thoughts inevitably returning to the day's events. Too many questions, too little in the way of answers. So many things I did not understand. I wondered what it was Jaya and his tribe had in their possession the men wanted so badly? Was it valuable? What could be so precious in the middle of nowhere? Glancing at Jaya again, his face silhouetted against the moonlight, I wondered at this man. His strength of purpose, his kindness towards me. I was someone who could have endangered him yet still he'd attended to my needs.

Could anyone be truly that good? Suddenly I felt a stab of shame for being such a burden. I hated the thought of being so totally in Jaya's debt. The trouble he had gone to in looking after me when danger lurked all around us.

It had been a huge undertaking.

Despite this, he had endeavored to do the best he could in the face of these risks. Thinking back to when Jaya had found me, I realised the care he had taken in disguising our camps, leaving the area just as we had found them. Never leaving any remains or discarded food from the meals he prepared nor any evidence of the ashes from the camp fire. Deftly smothering the ashes in leaf mulch and rearranging the leaves. I had never considered the real reason why he'd been doing this, now it all made sense. It was not for the sake of leaving the jungle undisturbed, but to conceal our presence of ever being there.

Over the last few weeks our position had remained relatively the same, due mainly to my inability to move anywhere at all. Now we appeared to be going somewhere. Jaya seemed to have some goal he was heading for. Of course, we could just be moving out of the area where these men were located, yet I had a sense there was something else. Something Jaya wasn't telling me.

But what?

Later, the drone of insect activity swarming beneath the trees and the warmth from the sun pulled me gradually awake. The jungle seemed to constantly vibrate with the quiet humming of millions of insects flying untiringly in search of food or a mate. The sounds, scents and sights of the jungle no longer worried me or drew my attention to what had been once an alarming amount of bug activity. Even the mosquitoes seemed to bother me less. Jaya had told me they were attracted to the smell of soap and shampoo, and the sweet foods I had a penchant for, now just a memory of my other life, another world to this.

I found I was laying disconcertingly close to Jaya, curled up tightly next to his warm strong body. To anyone looking we would have appeared as a young couple snuggled together in a relaxed form of intimacy.

Jaya had not moved at all and was still laying on his back just as he'd been when I'd watched him last night.

*As I was watching him now.*

I seemed to spend most of my waking hours trying to find ways to observe Jaya without being noticed and lately I'd felt I was getting good at it.

"Did you sleep well?" he asked softly, jolting me in surprise before feeling a slow flush scorching my cheeks. Obviously not that good at it.

"Yes," I mumbled chagrined. Moving myself away so not to cause him any embarrassment. I couldn't imagine him wanting a bedraggled European girl getting sweet on him.

"We need to get going soon but first I want you to practice a few steps. You need to get some strength in those leg muscles," he said.

It was the first time Jaya had suggested any form of physiotherapy and I smiled to myself wondering what he had in mind. Zimmer frames were in short supply in the jungle, I couldn't imagine how I was going to manage this.

Almost immediately I was hoisted to my feet, the speed at coming vertical brought on another spell of dizziness.

"What? I have to do this now?" I said catching my breath.

"No time like the present," he said responding to my dubious expression. "Support your hands on my arms and start walking forward." I did as he instructed, tentatively resting my hands on the bulge of his biceps. They felt hard and warm under my touch.

*This wasn't going to be so bad after all!*

My progress was slow but I managed a respectable distance before my bad leg began to ache with the effort.

"That's enough for today," he said glancing down at my legs. "You did well. Take it easy while I pack everything up."

The small compliment swelled my heart, I suddenly realised that I wanted him to be pleased with me. No, even more than that, I wanted him to like me. Yet, in my present condition I was under no illusion anyone would give me a second glance, least of all Jaya.

In the past I'd never given much thought to my appearance because I'd never wanted anyone to notice me, until I'd met Jaya. I knew it was ridiculous to worry about my appearance in my poor physical condition, but being so close to Jaya's immaculate handsomeness only made me too fully aware of my own scruffy appearance.

*I was still a girl after all.*

Stupid! What did it matter? I was lucky to be alive, I should just be grateful I was here at all I thought, while twisting and smoothed a tendril round a finger. I was suddenly struck how my presence here made Jaya so vulnerable. As long as I remained with him I would be a hinderance, a regular pain in the ass. How I would give anything to be able to walk again. This inability to do anything was becoming frustrating and my recovery tediously drawn out for Jaya and me.

"I slow you down don't I?" I said suddenly, blurting out my inner most thoughts and then suddenly wishing I hadn't. Jaya stopped in mid track and turned to consider my remark.

"So you think I could leave you to your own devices in the jungle do you? How far do you think you would get?" His tone was almost stern his eyes had darkened and suddenly I felt foolish to have asked the question under the affront of his gaze. Satisfied I had taken his meaning, he continued his chores leaving me feeling stupid and chastised.

"So where are we going then?" I said under my breath in a sarcastic manner, not for a moment expecting an answer.

"Let me worry about that," came his reply, his jaw flexing. "Just get yourself better."

Yeah well, I couldn't argue with that.

We were soon silently following the trail through the jungle. I wanted to ask questions, lots of them, but my nerve failed me. After my last mistake, I didn't want to feel stupid if he wouldn't answer me.

"What's it like living here in the jungle, is it lonely?" I asked.

"The life here is simple," he replied. Strands of his long, black hair had escaped from his pony tail and tickled my face.

"Do you spend time with anyone?" My mind wandering to the gorgeous exotic native girls thronging the local villages, or a girlfriend or wife patiently waiting for his return. A silence lengthened, another question he wasn't prepared to answer causing me to cringe inside again. I felt like I was walking a tight rope when asking for information about himself.

Our conversations were generally short and I was beginning to understand that idle chatter did not have a role in the jungle. Not like back home where it made up the very essence and fabric of life amongst people at school. Jaya was economical with his remarks, speaking largely with his eyes and body language than with anything he actually said. I was learning by example too, asking only about specific topics rather than to speculate about anything out loud. I found this to be the best way to draw Jaya out and learn more about this intriguing man. I asked about the plants and wild life, the climate and it's people and at times offering small snippets about my own life back home.

*But not too much.*

I was careful to paint a bland enough existence to prevent any attention being drawn to myself. It was a method I had employed deftly to deflect people's tiresome curiosity and unwanted sympathy. Besides, I hated people knowing anything about me because then they could not judge you.

"How is your life in England?" he asked.

"Well, there are less mosquitos," I quipped. "And I had a few more clothes!" I was still wearing the one set of clothes that had survived in the backpack. They were already beginning to take on a shabby appearance, the colours had faded and small holes had appeared where I had caught them on overhanging branches. My touristy garb hadn't been designed to survive in this environment.

"The lack of clothes is *definitely* nothing to worry about," he said grinning at the suggestion in his remark. Only in me it twisted a shard of apprehension.

"What? You mean less is more?"

"Something like that!"

"Is that why you strut around half naked?"

"Yes, and I highly recommend it!"

"For your benefit or mine?"

He turned towards me with a lop sided grin. "You're in the jungle now Alice, it's the way to go."

Crap. I thought, that's the last thing I need.

The landscape had opened up the higher we had climbed. Although the gradient had not been too steep I could see the beads of sweat appearing through Jaya's pores. The walking was arduous without a doubt. I wondered how he had the strength to carry me for so long, but he never complained or made me feel that it was inconvenient to him. His generosity and good natured approach to caring for me put me uncomfortably in his debt and he never took advantage of this fact.

*Thank God.*

I had a feeling he was enjoying this task somehow. His manner had changed in the short time since he'd threatened me with the spear. Since showing me the smoldering pile of ash in the clearing I'd had the sense he was watching me more than usual. As if there was something he was trying to work out. There seemed a curiosity lurking behind his eyes that had not been there before. Perhaps he still considered me a threat, that I was here under false pretenses, but still, it made me nervous.

*Because I was the watcher of everything. Not him.*

The scrub had disappeared as we walked out onto an expanse of jutting rock when Jaya lowered me carefully to the ground. The view panned out exposing a vast and cloudless sky interrupted by only the jagged pinnacles of distant mountains. The jungle stretched as far as I could see, the mountains thickly covered by trees and vegetation. Dotted over the landscape wafts of damp mist hung in patches, collecting in hollows and above the ridges. The white vapour drawing sharp contrast with the dense emerald green of the jungle. It was breathtakingly beautiful. The huge panorama of pure, vibrant nature. The amazing power and diversity of plant life caught at something in my chest.

"You like it?" Jaya asked, looking at me intently.

I nodded.

He came to stand close behind me. I could feel the heat emanating from his body. His proximity when he *chose* to stand so near was disconcerting, and suddenly I felt my heartbeat kick up a notch. He pointed casually ahead, his arm over my shoulder.

"Over there about 800 kilometers from here is Bangkok, and that way," grasping my shoulders he swiveled me round, then pointing again in another direction." Is Chang Mai where you came from on your trek......... and over this way." He pivoted me again in a new direction. "Are the Pi Pi Islands." The warmth of his hands on my shoulders lingered even after they had dropped to his side.

"Where they had the Tsunami?" I questioned.

"Yes."

"I didn't realise this was going to turn into a guided tour!" I shyly teased. "What lies in the direction we're walking?" I asked.

"You mean the way I'm walking?" He grinned. "You haven't exactly had to work too hard have you?"

I stared at him perplexed unsure how to answer him. Jokes had never featured particularly in Jaya's vocabulary before.

"You've hardly given me much choice!" I said. "Dragging me across the wilderness. You haven't even told me where we are going!"

We had been travelling for several days since leaving the bathing pool and I realised this wasn't just about getting out of the way of the mercenaries anymore. He hesitated before replying. "I'm taking you to my home."

My interest piqued. I waited for more information.

"It's better I don't tell you," he said before looking at the ground to avoid my gaze.

I knew he had secrets and I knew there were reasons why he did not want to speak about them but suddenly I felt suspicious. Why was he now taking me to where he lived when he'd been so reticent before? What had changed his mind? Dark thoughts swirled inside my head and I felt a stab of disquiet.

I hated secrets, especially when they were at my expense.

"You're not going to tell me? Why?"

Silence.

The realisation that Jaya had no intention of divulging his plans suddenly hit me like a stone dropping in my stomach.

*That changed things, changed things a lot.*

"And I'm supposed to just trust you even though you can't tell me where your taking me?" I said coldly.

He sighed. "Do I look like the sort of person who would harm you, have I ever given you any reason to fear me?" He said patiently.

"Yes," I replied simply, thinking of the spear incident.

"Apart from that?"

"I don't really know, you don't tell me anything."

"It's for your own safety."

"I thought you were taking me back to Chang Mai."

"I will, but not yet."

"When did you decide this? I thought you were just moving us out of reach of those men."

"We are."

"Jaya, I think I deserve to know where you're taking me."

"Does it make any difference? Your out of your natural environment anyway."

"Yes, it does matter, it matters to me."

"Well, I'm afraid you don't have any choice Alice."

I stared at him in confusion.

"You can't just take me to places against my will without telling me where we're going, that's almost kidnapping!"

"If you want to get back to Chang Mai you'll have to trust me."

I digested the information for a moment. He levelling his eyes on mine with almost a challenging expression I did not like, his words triggering something in me. This was the first time he had ever forced his will over mine and for a moment I could not think.

*But what choice did I have?*

I felt a sudden twist of uncertainty, the situation had rapidly escalated away from my control, from were I was most comfortable. I wasn't sure what this new place would be, why Jaya was being so forceful. Making me.

*But that wasn't my main concern.*

I didn't usually follow other peoples rules or directives. Rules were for other people who lived normal, narrow, stiff, cardboard lives. Who'd never had to think for themselves like I'd had to. I'd learned to live by my own morals, my own set of protocols for therein lay safety in being able to steer my own course, following my own gut feelings. Rules at home had never made my life any easier, had never been consistent. The goal posts forever changing depending on how far my mother had slid down the slippery slope to oblivion.

Suddenly I felt out of my depth and unexpectedly angry. I turned and tried to hobble away to give myself time to gain control over my wayward emotions. Hadn't I wanted to stay in the jungle with Jaya? Hadn't I wanted to avoid going home? So why was this making me frightened and angry?

*I knew why.*

Because I wasn't being given a choice and when anything was forced on me against my will, when I had to do as someone else said, I panicked.

"Alice?'

I felt Jaya come to stand behind me before placing a hand on my arm.

"I'm not going with you until you tell me where we're going." I said angrily but knowing my ultimatum was useless.

I felt Jaya's hand drop from my shoulder and silence yawned between us. Eventually I felt it, the shimmer of annoyance but with the undertones something else.

"When you're ready we'll move on," he said abruptly before moving away to gather our belongings.

*Crap.*

No choice.

None whatsoever and I suddenly felt very small, so very vulnerable and I did not like it at all. Because now, I no longer felt safe. Jaya had just burst the imaginary bubble of security I'd begun to feel in his presence. When I'd believed he'd protect me from those men, when after all this time I'd begun to think he'd been different to everyone else. Somehow better.

My thoughts descended into confusion. I was my own worst enemy when it came to trust, for nothing over the years had engendered confidence in people and their supposed promises. My errant ways and my forced detachment from others had been deliberately construed because fundamentally, I didn't trust anyone.

*Because then they could hurt you.*

I could not stomach others who tried to control you, who tricked you into believing their lies, who thought nothing of bending your will to theirs. Intimidation, threats and bullying, all grew from the desire to force. To bend a person against their will, to conquer and to rob you of your freedom for their own unfathomable and twisted reasons. Terrify someone enough and you cheat them of their liberty, ruining their life forever. The echoes of those fears forever lurking beneath.

Paralysing anyone who wished to live a full and normal life.

*I knew, because it had happened to me.*

# Chapter 8

# The Caves

I had not noticed the passing of the day, the change of scenery or vegetation. My thoughts had frozen, something had shifted inside, despite the heat I felt cold. It was my usual repertoire of defence mechanisms coming to my rescue. A well travelled road in my short existence but nonetheless necessary. I had returned to my hiding place, that deep unfathomable pit where I had mostly lived over the last few years, but recently from which I had begun to tentatively emerge. Like a hermit crab from its shell. Now I had all but scurried back to its safe confines from where I could watch the world but not be seen. Where I could exist out of sight and mind and find comfort in the familiar incarceration. I hid because I never wanted anyone to know what lay inside. The fears, the hysteria had nearly bubbled to the surface and now I'd thankfully pushed them away.

*This time.*

I had to pull up my guard. It had been too close a call and I never wanted to be taken that close to the edge again. It was too dangerous. I knew it was my own fault. My hypersensitive nature meant every pressured situation threatened to pull down the well constructed brick wall. Yet, Jaya had said he'd already seen what lay beneath. Knew the confident exterior belied the coward that lay within. The one I was always running from. For no one ever wants to face their failings. Especially not one so flawed and weak, the person I virulently detested.

Sure, Jaya had forced me to come with him, but he had not imposed any other stipulations or anything else that would frighten me. I only had to follow him to God knew where. Surely that could not be so bad? I should welcome the excitement of adventure. Embrace this new and uncertain turn of events, but force of habit extinguished any flame in this diversion. Fear icing over any feelings of excitement.

We stopped abruptly at the mouth of a cave. Its dark recesses stretching away into its cavernous bowels and beyond where my eyes could follow. Was this our destination?

Jaya carried me to the far end of the narrowing cave, allowing me to slide to my feet before stooping low and disappearing from view behind a thin gap.

Leaving me perplexed. Was I meant to follow?

I had to bend down low to enter the long tunnel into which Jaya had disappeared. Shuffling along and leaving through a low exit I was unprepared for the sight that met me there. Compared to the glare of the white heat outside, I'd walked into an enormous cave. The atmosphere appeared crystal clear, as if everything had been brought into sharp focus. Ribbons of sunlight streamed through broken cracks in the cave's roof stretching loftily above us. Small groups of ferns and other vegetation hung precariously to the steep sides, and where the sunlight caught them, I could see their fronds glistening as they leant outwards in search of light. The air was cool, a welcome change from the roasting temperature outside and the air smelled damp and earthy. I noticed how the haphazard sound of water dripping into pools broke the hushed silence with echoing resonance, and somehow amplified. The cave was large, extending further than I could make out due to the shadows hiding its true potential but serving to outline more sharply the shafts of slanting sunlight slicing through the darkness.

Jaya returned to my side. The watchfulness had been replaced with an openness and childlike enthusiasm I had not seen before, making him seem almost, innocent. Until I remembered, it had not been my choice to come here.

"Hey," said Jaya looking at me closely. "Okay?'

"Fine," I replied sullenly. It would take me a while to get over being forced to come here.

If ever.

I looked about me, awed by the immense cave, drawn into its reverent atmosphere. I could stay here forever I thought. Never leave the safe confines within its walls, it reminded me of myself. Dark and gloomy with little to illuminate the interior.

"What is this place?" I said hearing my words echo through the cave, marveling at the ethereal atmosphere. A welcome change from my other thoughts.

"An anti-chamber." He replied.

"A what?"

"It is the prelude to a sacred cave further back."

"Sacred?" I scoffed. What was so sacred about this place? For God sake, it was just a cave.

"Tribes worship here." Jaya said simply, as if this explained everything.

"Why?"

"Because of the energy," Jaya studied my face thoughtfully as I assimilated this last piece of information, but pressed on. "Look over there." He pointed to the far side of the cave, the only wall in fact, illuminated in the gloom.

Abstract shapes interjected the flat plains of the wall. Varying in shapes and sizes, some were arranged in tight rows as if written in some strange language. Others bore stick like resemblance I presumed to be people. Their meaning seemed alien, undecipherable to my eyes but that did not mean anything. This was a different culture to mine after all.

I turned to find Jaya watching me with interest. Something flickered behind his eyes but was gone before I could interpret its meaning.

"What do the symbols mean?" I spoke quietly, hardly wanting to break the stillness.

"Their meanings have mostly been forgotten."

"Do you know anything about them at all?"

He looked towards the wall of symbols before replying.

"There are stories which have been handed down through each generation. I only know a little of them. It is said they speak of a time of when man still knew his great power, when humans remembered their origins, their purpose here on earth. How they passed into other dimensions. They used their knowledge to do unimaginable things, things we have forgotten. There is talk that something precious has been lost, something which is connected to the earths energies but we do not know what it is."

"Sounds like they had a warped grip on reality. *I mean really*, cross into other dimensions!" I almost laughed.

"And you know better about such things?" said Jaya tightly. I suddenly noticed a small muscle clenching in his jaw.

Yes, I probably did, I thought, for how could it be possible? It was beyond my understanding and everyone else's, surely? I'd nearly said how primitive, how barbaric to believe in such things when in the West with all it's scientific discoveries, we knew better.

Without another word he pulled me up onto his back and headed to the caves furthest point, carefully stepping over fallen rocks and debris. Stooping low we passed under another jutting rock into a larger cave, titanic in comparison to the previous one. I could see the dimensions more clearly this time because of a large almost round hole high above us, allowing a huge shaft of brilliant light to slash diagonally down to the cave floor. Thousands of tiny insects lit by the shaft aimlessly meandered, rising and falling within its illumination. I was struck how reverent this cave made me feel, almost like the hushed silence that pervaded the air in a church. The atmosphere had a quality that prickled the hair on my skin, sending goosebumps shimmering down the curve of my back. The ambience here was strange, like nothing I had ever felt before and suddenly I began to get a little nervous. What had Jaya said about this place? That there was an energy which was sacred. Well, whatever it was I didn't like it.

*Because now I could feel it.*

Creeping cobweb sensations fluttered across my face and crawled through my hair. The air once inert now took on an oddly heavy quality. Thickening with each passing moment, pressing, pushing invisibly against me. Suddenly I realized in panic there was something else in here with us, an unseen force, something powerful and very much alive.

"It is nothing," said Jaya, looking down curiously at my hand gripping his arm.

This was nothing? I had never considered anything like ghosts could be real. The stories I read and the horror films I'd watched I'd considered built upon nothing but mere fantasy. A product to entertain and thrill, invented for the adrenalin rush.

*But now?*

Somehow the sensations did not feel evil and perhaps need not strike pure terror through me. This was something else altogether, this felt ___ *good*.

Over the years, I had thought little about the hereafter, never questioned the need of others to trot obediently to church each week, to worship their God. That was their life, their beliefs, not mine. Maybe they felt something I didn't, an unseen presence only perceived by devoted worshippers. Perhaps it was only the worthy who deserved the love of God. Obviously not me, I'd made sure of that. My life had never been filled with Angels or blinding light, nor had I felt the guiding hand of fate or synchronicity. Or if it had, what an utterly crap life HE'd chosen for me. I'd had to pull myself out of the rubble by my own fingernails, my own will, because the only alternative had been unthinkable. I'd come to rely only on myself, no one else, trust my own instincts, act on my own agenda, for in what else could I have faith?

*If HE did exist, then I blamed HIM for everything.*

My life had been left in tatters after what he'd taken from me. *But now?*

Now as the love descended and wrapped its arms around me I felt the sensation of coming home, of finding that place we all searched for in our deepest, darkest moments. That feeling of utter peace, of safety and unconditional love. To be loved no matter what, to be loved for my mistakes as well as my failings.

*To be loved for who I was.*

I had forgotten this love even existed and now I never wanted it to leave. I wanted this feeling to stay forever and suddenly I knew I could not be content until I had found a way for it to do so. The years of pain and heartache were being washed away, as if my Soul was being painted with a brush of clean, healthy emotions. Feelings which had remained nocturnal in the daylight of my life, dormant in the winter of my being, were shyly edging forward to embrace this unconditional love. Until suddenly, this loving caress was taken away.

*Like it always was.*

I shuddered. A shocking memory bubbled upwards too fast for me to withhold of another time, another love that had been torn form my life. A memory of my father struck down by a fatal heart attack at the age of 45. Who had left this planet so suddenly without even enough time to say goodbye. A father whose absence had left a huge hole by his untimely departure, sucking the love and joy from my own life and from all those closest to me.

Grief is like a cloying smog holding you under its veil of darkness. As if a light had been smothered and taken from your life. Your purpose now erased. For how can anyone return to their life unscathed after a loved one is ripped from their life? How can anyone understand the abyss of emotion in the aftermath of death? No one can, until it happens to them, and the chill from that time still reached deep into my heart. The ache of loss never far from each beat of my own vibrant life, unjustly keeping me alive while failing that of my fathers. Since that awful day, the quagmire of dark emotion sat never far below the surface. The world was no longer a vanilla, quilted or cocooned, instead it was full of pain and torment.

I remembered how it had happened one morning before school when we heard something heavily falling on the floor above. Sending our mother rushing upstairs in panic before milliseconds later, hearing the distressing phone call to the doctor and then the quiet sounds of her muffled sobs that followed.

On the day of the funeral I was left at home with a neighbour while the rest of the family went to pay their respects. How utterly alone I had felt on that day, for it was unseemly for me to go to school and apart from the neighbour who was little more than a stranger, I was alone in the house.

*Alone except for my grief.*

Everyone that I loved was where I wanted to be, saying goodbye. I was not allowed, I was too young to join the adults and my brother. My mother felt it would protect me from any more distress, and for that I could never reproach her. Yet, she could never have foreseen how it led me to never truly accepting his death. Every morning when I woke, I lost him all over again and with it, the dawning realisation he was never coming back. For a long time afterwards I refused to believe he had gone. I imagined one day my father would walk through the door, take up life where he'd left it, whistling his usual tune, and resume his fatherly role once more. I often thought that I saw him riding in another car or walking down the street. The image catching in my throat until logic berated my stupidity and the old ache of grief would return.

I remembered the pain, feeling it physically in my body, the endless tears and aching like hot shards of glass in my heart and head. The power of these emotions had frightened me and in the beginning I had let myself cry. Until eventually I'd realised its futility, the tears and sobs never did any good, never took the pain away. For how could they after what we had just lost. How could anything feel better again after that?

My young mind had been unable to comprehend the man who'd been my father was never coming home. He'd never again be there to hold me in his arms or jiggle me on his knee. Nor to comfort me when I'd fallen and kiss away the tears. Never see his smiling face, never hear that deep warm laughter, never, ever again. People told me he'd gone to heaven and was never coming back, but where was this place and why couldn't I go there too?

During the first few years after we carried on as best we could, adjusting our orbits to exclude a now extinct planet that had once been our world. The gravitational pull no more, we had to learn to live a new but empty existence. The driving force behind the family absent and extinguished, casting us adrift, directionless, having nothing to stay afloat for.

And this was the reason my mother turned to alcohol for solace. Never getting over losing my father and never adjusted to the life of being a single parent.

My mother's pain I could only imagine, for when you are so deeply in your own trauma how can you have room for anyone else's? I had little idea how she carried on in those days after, the memory of that time now seems blurred and sketchy. It wasn't until much later that I recognised the bitter anguish, the loneliness and the ever prevalent pain. She never recovered from my fathers death and how could I blame her.

*I hadn't either.*

Only she had found an escape route, a method by which to anesthetize the pain. At first my brother and I thought nothing when we heard the scraping sound of a metal whisky bottle top being unscrewed, then the soft glug of spirit pouring into glass. When the bottles began to pile up for the recycling, we realized too late a new evil presence had entered and changed our young lives forever. It's ability to take control of our mother was frightening in its totality. Taking her to a place we could not follow, extinguishing any real presence of our last remaining parent.

Later the unexpressed stress and grief, induced a paralyzing lethargy. She became unable to venture far from the sofa physically or with her emotions. Her mind became bitter and angry with the unfairness of life, why her, what had she done to deserve this? By the time I had left for my gap year, the drink had insidiously taken over her life. Loosening her grip on reality and that of her tongue.

Car journeys became intolerable as she shouted and swore at the other passing drivers. The air inside the cramped interior was filled with obscenities she'd hurl at the other cars. For driving too slowly, turning without an indicator or an indecisive learner driver were enough to agitate her over-wrought emotions and bring down a rain of fury with her displeasure.

Oh, there were times when I would have done anything to change this world, to wave that proverbial magic wand and take the pain away, but that was mere fantasy. My mother had wandered so far down her own narrow and far away world it was crushing me in its exclusion. Although I understood my mother's undoing and the reason why she'd become like this. To live everyday under the rule of tyranny, to be the outlet of her misery and unjust poisonous words were in the end too much to bear.

I'd had to find a way to leave.

I glanced about me, suddenly aware of my surroundings again, feeling emptier than before, feeling sick. For now I'd been reminded exactly the extent to which my life had been lacking. I had been shown it, felt it and now I felt utterly and completely alone. I felt tears springing to my eyes. The memories still so sharp and painful, the feelings vivid and harsh, no longer blunted by the frozen numbness.

Jaya spoke from beside me. I'd forgotten he was there.

"You are honoured Alice, for you have been visited by the Spirit Keeper of this place."

Honoured! No, I'd been reminded how bare, how utterly crap my life had been. Whatever this thing was, it had shown me the truth. The one I had been unable to face.

"Spirit Keeper?" I replied puzzled, forcing myself to focus on his words.

"There's a Spirit being who resides here. Over the surface of the world there are many sacred places. Energy vortexes which rise through the Earths crust from deep below, likened to the acupuncture points on a human body. Such is it's power and force it can amplify our own awareness and perception, heightening our psychic abilities. Tribes have worshiped in this place to honour it."

I was surprised by Jaya's words.

"What is a Spirit Keeper?" I said. My beliefs about such things meant it was hard to take Jaya seriously, but the sincerity of Jaya's reply had spiked my interest, and I could not immediately dismiss what I had just felt.

"It is one who guides and protects, all living things have one."

"All living things have one," I slowly repeated to myself. A memory flickering at the back of my mind.

"Humans have guardian angels, nature spirits for plants."

"But why does a place need one?" I asked curious now.

"The Earth is a living breathing organism like you and me. There are many places where there is special energy, the very same energy that drives our bodies and our Souls. Without these special energy centres, the world would not, and we could not, survive. It is important to protect these energies and help them in their processes. Here, the veil between dimensions is thin. It is why the Shamans come here for guidance, to access the information they require. Because of the very special energy of this place, a Spirit Keeper stays to protect it."

"Are there many these energy places?"

"Yes, and they are all connected by a network of channels, ley lines which carry this energy from place to place."

"Why can't other people feel it?"

"Some people can, you did."

"That was the spirit person?"

"Yes, you connected into the energy of this place and by doing that you opened a channel between you and the deity."

It was all confusing, that the earth had energy points like in humans, veils between dimensions, accessing information. What did the Shamans need to know?

"What does a place like this need protecting from?"

Jaya smiled that jaw dropping million dollar smile.

"There are dark forces all around us. Like the darkness in you Alice."

*How did he know that?*

"If I'm the antichrist then why tell me all this?" I retorted.

"Because the Spirit Keeper does not reveal itself to just anyone."

I stared back perplexed, not understanding.

"Why.......why did she reveal herself to me then?"

"That's what I would like to find out."

"I don't understand."

"Well, that makes two of us," he said catching one of my arms and pulling me onto his back.

Now I was more than confused. It made no sense to me. Why had Jaya brought me here? Why had I been visited by the Spirit Keeper or whatever it's name was? And why had Jaya been looking at me with such a strange expression? My original assumptions were on shaky ground. This was not what I had anticipated at all. There was something odd going on and somehow it was linked to me. Jaya had brought me here for a reason, of that much I was certain. I was beginning to understand his reasons for insisting I stay with him. He'd wanted to bring me here, to this cave, but why and what did it mean? Now I was convinced wherever he was taking me there was a purpose to that too. He'd changed his plan after the spear threatening incident and instead of taking me straight back to Chang Mai, he was taking me somewhere else first.

*Why?*

A shudder of trepidation spun through me, the unanswered questions trundled slowly through my head. Trying to second guess beyond this point was futile. I had no idea where we were headed, no idea the meaning to anything Jaya had just told me. My whole security blanket and original assumptions had been torn away because this whole situation seemed to uncomprehendingly revolve around me. Suddenly I didn't know whether to be thrilled or terrified.

No! I chastised myself for being so foolish. Remember, it was always better to feel nothing at all.

*About anything.*

# Chapter 9

# The Hidden Valley

We arrived at the exit of the cave network, the heat shimmering down to meet us. Jaya strode towards the open ledge beyond, over looking a new vista different from the one before. Instead of miles of jungle stretching as far as the eye could see, here a valley lay enclosed by sheer faced mountains. No gaps or plummeting passes interjected their pinnacles. The bowl created by their mountainous clasp effectively sealed the valley within their all encompassing embrace. Far ahead white tendrils of distant waterfalls fell in undulating feathery contrast against the dark stone. The green of the jungle vegetation staggered to a halt where the soil gave way to sheer grey rock.

It was simply beautiful. Like something out of a fairytale story book.

Jaya scooped me up in his arms and walked to the edge of the cave and began to descend a steep flight of steps carved out of the rock face. Eventually, after a tortuous downward climb we reached the valley floor and from here taking a well worn path threading its way through the trees beside a vigorous spring. In due course, Jaya lowered me to the ground and I knew it was time for me to exercise my puny legs again. My limbs, or what was left of them had almost halved in size since the injury and I knew it would take a long time before they returned to their former well muscled strength. In fact my entire body had somewhat shrunk. Since being in the jungle, my diet had either consisted of meat or fruit and roots, the three never usually coinciding in the same meal. Before coming to the jungle my body weight had never been a cause for any concern by any stretch of the imagination. Always consistently maintained at a steady level due mainly to my sporting endeavors, despite the fatty cholesterol laden fodder provided for me at home. Nevertheless, during these few weeks all superfluous flesh covering had melted away, leaving bones once hidden protruding sharply through my skin. My cheeks felt sharper too and more tightly drawn over my face and my hip bones, always a projectile landmark at the best of times, now stuck out jauntily through the fabric of my shorts. Soon I would have to find new ways to keep my shorts hoisted over my hips before they conspired to succumb to the enticement of gravity. My shrinking flesh was not in anyway due to any shortage of food, Jaya always made sure there was plenty to help aid my recovery. It was just that with no cakes or stodgy foods, sweets or chocolate that normally contributed to a large chunk of my diet, the clean, nourishing food I was now provided with was just another adjustment my body and metabolism needed to make.

"We will camp for tonight," Jaya announced as he gathered his things to hunt. I wondered what would be on the menu tonight. Parrot, monkey or maybe fish, berries or roots? I had lost count of the number of new foods I had eaten and some I didn't even want to ask what they were.

My new job was collecting sticks for the fire, giving me an incentive to walk. I knew it was Jaya's way of getting me moving. For being carried for such long periods of time did not necessitate much in the way of exercise. I had become adept at clinging and binding myself to Jaya's body and I couldn't help but think of all those other gorgeous native girls who had......done the same. The gentleness and assurance in the way he touched me lead me to wonder if he carried these attributes into the bedroom and if this was the reason for such confidence around women? I knew it was unforgivable to think in such a way and these thoughts were a surprise even to myself having never entertained such imaginings before. Nonetheless, my curiosity about this man had not reached any barrier. He was an enigma, a paradox, self contained in such a way, I wondered if he needed anyone at all.

Even Jaya's manners surprised me. Not just around me but in many ways. Like in the way he ate his food for instance. Chewing each mouthful slowly and without hurry. This was the way he approached everything he did, swiftly returning my thoughts to the bedroom daydreams again.

I remembered a teacher at school who'd had the sickening habit of rolling the food around in his cheeks, his mouth never quite closing. Leaving you in no doubt as to what he was eating.

Jaya never did that and more frustratingly never talked about himself. I knew nothing of his family, his home or even if he was married. I was ignorant to just about everything about him other than small habitual attentions he paid to his appearance. By now I knew the routine, the plaiting and braiding of his hair was slow and time consuming, but I never got bored watching. The way he carefully threaded the strands to sit obediently between his fingers and thumb, forming the neat patterns within the braid never failed to fascinate me.

It was disturbing how dangerously handsome he was and his effect whenever he came near. His looks would arouse even the most frigid of virgins, I thought and had certainly jumpstarted something within me.

I cursed myself for thinking in such a way. I didn't need anyone. I had to be cool and detached, like marble, impenetrable and frozen. I would never let myself get into situations ruled by my emotions. For they took you in a direction where it wasn't safe to go and that was far too dangerous and was never going to happen. I'd promised that much to myself.

*Not now, not ever.*


Over the last few weeks I'd gradually becoming accustomed to this new way of life. Jaya had me employed gutting and preparing any animals he brought back from the river or a kill while he set about making camp. The chore was at first so repugnant. Requiring me to pull the slimy red guts out with my fingers, but hunger soon solved this reticence. I became adept at building and lighting the fires, skinning an animal, cooking over an open fire. Learning by example and taking small pleasures in my new found skills.

At home, in my former life, I'd learnt most of my cooking skills when my mother was too drunk to make our tea. A task thankfully removed from her in an attempt to break the monotony of eating the cholesterol laden frozen pastry pies and oven ready chips, our staple diet at the best of times. I'd taken over many of the tasks my mother as a responsible adult should normally have performed. From a young age I'd learned to fill in the consent forms for school trips and pay for my own clothes with my paper-round and later the supermarket job. There was no money left over from my mothers wage packet to pay for those kind of luxuries.

As the years went by my mothers outlook narrowed. The routine of the household revolved around three things, food, alcohol and TV, and not particularly in that order of preference. My mother ruled the remote controls, breeding like rabbits on the side of the sofa. The hard drive of the DVD crammed with nature programmes or Countryfile, broadcasting their fresh faced enthusiastic presenters wearing their squeaky clean, brand new performance clothing, beaming out the beauty of the world and the wonders of all its inhabitants. Who only had to find sustenance and a mate to survive in the diversity of their habitats. A sharp contrast to my environment. Living with a mother who bitterly resented the past, brooded about the present, or agonized over the future.

The irony was not lost on me.

Because in our house there was a different kind of wilderness within and one that was far more difficult to survive.

*One that lacked any kind of nourishment at all.*

Stick collecting took far longer than I had anticipated, but I'd gathered a fair pile by the time Jaya returned. I was horrified when he showed me what he'd caught. Over the last couple of weeks I had flatly refused to eat any form of insect, but this new prospect for dinner brought a shudder of revulsion. Five small rodents dangling from his hand. He smiled at my expression.

"Nasty," I said curling up my lips in disgust. "Are they for attracting bigger prey?"

"You're a far better lure than any rodent!" he countered, getting down to the task of preparing them for the meal.

"You're not seriously expecting me to eat those."

"These rats live free in the jungle. They don't carry disease like their relatives in the cities."

"Yeah, but they could still be full of germs. I could die from rat poisoning!"

He smiled into his work ignoring me.

I carried on stubbornly. "They might have been eating rotten animals or living in faeces infested nests. I don't want to eat something that lives like that!" I said impetuously giving my ultimatum.

"You don't have to Alice," he replied quietly. "You don't have to eat anything I catch."

That wasn't the reaction I'd expected and it annoyed me how Jaya was always so reasonable with me. My silly comments never made any difference.

I turned away upset with myself and Jaya. He was right of course, I didn't have to eat anything he caught but there were some things that were literally too hard to swallow.

"Alice," he said calling me back. "I know how hard this must be for you, living like this. When I hunt I have to take whatever puts itself in front of me. I can't magic a meal to your liking out of thin air. Just try to forget everything from before, from your other life, for none of those things apply in the jungle." His eyes flickered over my face, searching for something before they slid away, but I couldn't work out what.

Later I helped Jaya pack up the little camp, kicking over the ashes then covering them with soil before he turned to me, his face suddenly deadly serious.

"Where we go now you must never tell anyone. I'm trusting you to keep your silence," he said bestowing me with more merit than I felt I deserved.

So, we were nearly there. Wherever that was. Perhaps there would be others, like Jaya. Christ, one looking like him was more than enough. Maybe there really was some kind of mutant tribe in these parts. Where people grew to unusual heights and beauty and would make me only too uncomfortably aware of my own awkward unattractiveness.

Jaya swung me effortlessly up into his arms as usual but this time I turned my head into his chest to hide my face, trying to calm the uneasiness I knew that was to come. The feel of his warm strong hands and the heat from his body while he held me tightly against his chest always pulled at something inside. It was the close proximity I found hardest to deal with. Being cocooned next to his body evoked responses I never knew existed, each time becoming a little harder to quell.

The heat had risen throughout the day, laden with humidity, it seemed far hotter than it had been at any time I'd been in the jungle. Jaya as always in tune with my thoughts announced.

"There's a storm coming, perhaps it will be here by the end of tomorrow."

"How bad do you think?" I asked not knowing much about the weather patterns of this country.

"Pretty bad, the rain is always heavy in these parts," he smiled that smile. I had to catch myself from softening under his scrutiny, or allowing myself to enjoy the glint in his eyes.

"Will there be a hurricane?" I asked, concerned now. Jaya laughed at my serious face. I could see he was debating how to tease me.

"No!" he said with a smile twitching over his lips.

"What's so funny? That was a very serious question!" I said.

"Its nothing," he said.

"You can't act all mysterious now, what is it?"

"You!"

"What do you mean, me?"

He looked down at me again.

"It's those blue eyes of yours, one minute I think they are like a cloudless blue sky and then at other times they're dark and brooding," I assimilated this information thoughtfully.

"What do you see in them today?"

"Today they're dark, something's troubling you."

"How can you possibly know that?"

"It comes from experience," he said gently. "What is it Alice? I can feel something's wrong."

I fell silent not trusting myself yet to speak or even how I could say it. I felt him waiting for my answer, not pushing. I knew I could not tell him the truth, half truth maybe or even a convincing lie.

"I'm scared." I eventually said.

## The Stone Circle

"Of what?"

"Everything, the thought of those men hunting us. Where you're taking me, its the unknown and........" Then shyly. "You."

"Me?" His surprised face looked down at me.

"I can't.......it's just........" I couldn't continue. He looked at me for a long time. I feared he would too easily see my feelings and the real fear which I kept hidden, but nothing happened as Jaya continued to walk as if I had said nothing at all. For a time at least.

"Have I given you anything to fear?" He asked eventually.

"Yes, when you attacked me with that spear," I said again.

"Apart from that."

"No. Its just I don't know anything about you. I've spent all this time with and you haven't told me anything."

"Do you need those things to know me?"

"It would help."

He tilted his head backwards to look up to the sky as if for inspiration and I suddenly realised he did not know how to reply. For like me, he held secrets and for whatever his reasons, he could not tell me.

"What do you wish to know?" he said eventually.

"Where you're from, how you learnt such good English, why you look so different from other Thai people."

"I will give you three answers and no more, okay?"

"Yes, but what if they don't answer my questions?"

"That's the deal, take it or leave it."

"So where are you from?"

"America," he said smiling down at me and I knew he was enjoying my shocked expression.

"That's why your English is so good!"

"Yes, and last question!"

"But I've only asked one!"

"It's two, last question!"

"What are you doing in Thailand?"

"I'm on a gap year like you!"

Much later, when his arms had grown tired and we'd stopped to rest, he asked. "So, do you feel you know me better or worse?"

"I feel I know you even less."

"Like I said, it's not the information you know about a person it's what's inside that counts."

"But that's the part you cannot see."

"Not necessarily."

He was talking in riddles, playing with me, I'd never liked puzzles. "So what are you doing here? Can't you tell me that at least." I said.

"Sorry, no."

"Why are you living in the jungle on your gap year, are you working on some community project or something?"

"Can't tell you."

"Have you come here on your own?"

"For an English person you're incredibly persistent."

"That doesn't say much for us Brits."

"Well, I've never met one like you, that's for sure," he smiled and I wondered what he meant by the remark, but I pushed the thought quickly away.

We continued on in silence for sometime. The path opened out ahead when Jaya abruptly put me down, no doubt to give me an opportunity to exercise my legs. He was very diligent in making sure I had frequent breaks to do so.

"Stay here," was all he said before striding away, the gloss of his hair catching in the sunlight with the rise and fall of his step, before disappearing behind a curve in the path.

That was strange, apart from leaving me to hunt, Jaya had never left me alone. I wondered what I was meant to do. In want of any other options, I made my way to the where I had seen Jaya disappear, settling myself beneath the trees to wait for him to return. I no longer wanted to venture any further, the heat and humidity had exhausted me. The hours of being carried, the heat from the time of day made me content to stay here and do absolutely nothing.

Under the tree, the heat and humidity made me drowsy. Despite the shade, trickles of sweat rolled down my spine and my skin prickled and gleamed with perspiration. It was too hot to think, too hot to do anything other than sit and watch small insects dancing under the canopy or the lime green leaves barely fluttering in the light movement of air.

I must have fallen asleep for I was suddenly woken by two large hot hands cupping my face. Jaya swam into view, crouching on his heels in front of me. He was not alone. Behind him several other natives stood stiffly. Staring at me with such cold intensity, a shiver of fear ran down my spine.

Crap.

# Chapter 10

# Other Natives

My eyes widened in shock with the unexpected company. I wondered how long they'd been watching me sleeping and suddenly I felt embarrassed to have been caught off guard while I slept.

*I should know better.*

The natives stood only as high as Jaya's shoulder, stocky, well rounded in build and compared to Jaya's fine attributes their features were course and ordinary. Their dress was different too. A mishmash of east and west, consisting of tatty trousers or shorts, braided hair and faded T-shirt's blaring meaningless slogans across their chests. Several wore the familiar leather strap slashing diagonally crossing their torsos, suggesting a similar origin to Jaya's.

They all had something in common I thought, as they stared at me coldly.

The oldest native with a pudgy face began talking first. The strange language guttural and throaty, interspersed with sharp clicking noises. Jaya replied in the strange dialect, it's different sounds changing his facial movements as the vowels rolled differently from his mouth. It seemed odd to hear him speak in another tongue and to be so completely comfortable with it when comprehension suddenly dawned.

*Gap year indeed.*

There must be something else going on here, something Jaya wasn't telling me.

Pudgy Face's eyes flickered over my body, his expression suspicious, wary, taking in the colour of my skin, my hair and the bandage on my leg. The conversation continued back and forth until eventually he came to crouch down in front of me. Clipping a brown finger under my chin and I suddenly knew what he was about to do.

Alarmed, I looked up at Jaya who only nodded I should comply, but this did not quell the apprehension beginning to twist inside. What if he didn't like what he saw? What if Jaya had made a terrible mistake in bringing me here? His gaze seemed to hold it's own gravitational pull, falling deep inside me, reaching, pulling, searching out my secrets. Stirring up images I never wanted to remember. Abruptly it stopped, his attention already elsewhere, this time my hair. I guess curls are unusual in a nation of the straight haired variety. All the more curious because now it no longer resembled anything close to being hair. He grabbed a handful behind my neck, twisting it carefully over in his hand before allowing it to float away. Coming to stand in front of me he gestured towards my leg.

"Open the bandage Alice," Jaya instructed.

I quickly pulled at the twine to allow the foliage to drop open, revealing a bright, red weal almost completely knitted together but for a few patches of weeping skin still gaping but clean. I'd been lucky to escape infection in this hot, sticky environment.

Pudgy Face covered the short distance back to the others who'd remained a comfortable distance away from me throughout the examination. Their cold, suspicious eyes had not left me for a moment, flickering back and forth over my body. A wave of apprehension shuddered through me when I noticed Jaya had became suddenly very still. An unusual uneasiness forming over his features.

*Obviously things were not going to plan.*

A quiet disagreement had suddenly broken out between Jaya and the natives. Their conversation had quickened, with quick fired responses shot back and forth. All the while Jaya's expression became increasingly worried with thick creases forming between his brows. For a moment I thought all had been lost when the conversation abruptly ceased, but all at once they started talking again. This time the tone had changed into something more easy. Until eventually the conversation stopped and all eyes turned ominously towards me. I felt the heat rise in my face under the scrutiny of their eyes before looking nervously at Jaya.

"They've made a decision," he stomach summersaulted. I could not tell from his voice or expression if this was good or bad.

"You can come with us," he said evenly, giving no hint of what had passed between them.

"That didn't sound like it went terribly well."

"No, it didn't."

I looked at him closely. "You're regretting bringing me here now aren't you?"

"It's complicated."

"What's complicated?"

"Finding you half dead, it wasn't part of the plan," he said looking down at me. "But I couldn't just leave you."

"What plan? You never said anything about a plan," I said accusingly.

Jaya looked at me thoughtfully. "You know how dangerous it is out here Alice. Just leave it at that."

"And you're stuck with me, or something like that?"

"It's complicated," he said again but with no hint of humour.

"Then take me back to Chang Mai. I didn't want to come here anyway," I challenged.

"It's too late for that."

"I don't want to cause any more trouble."

"Your not causing any trouble, it's me who they're not happy with!"

"Who are these people?"

"Natives from a tribe called Sanuri."

"They didn't look very happy to see me. Am I unwelcome here?"

"You will be fine, they mean no harm."

I glanced over to where they still stood glaring at me and I knew this to be untrue.

"But somehow you won them over. Was it your charm or wit?"

"Neither," he said holding out a hand to pull me up and swung me onto his back.

We headed off in silence in single file. The path twisted and turned through the trees and undergrowth. The heat of the day had intensified and a hushed expectant silence descended over the jungle. The air felt hot and oppressive and laden with humidity, causing my T-shirt to cling to my chest and half moon crescents formed under my arms.

I felt nervous about this new turn of events, hating the unknown and of being kept in the dark. As was my custom when situations became stressful, my attention would turn to my hair. It had become a way of diverting my mind away from more stressful circumstances that frequented my life and now was no exception. The humid dampness had calmed the fluffy, candy floss cloud into a more restrained lank and stringy affair. At least the other natives didn't know any different in how I should look and neither did Jaya. Ever since I had known him I'd looked this way. Scruffy and unattractive.

*But when had I looked any different anyway?*

The tedium of walking for so long struck numbness through my body and the heat sapped what was left. The sweat dripped down my back and sides, collecting in pools inside my bra adding to my discomfort. Soon I lost interest in my sweaty discomfort switching my thoughts to something infinitely more enjoyable. Jaya, who was diligently focused on the task in hand, avoiding the tree roots and rocks over which he carried me. I concentrated on his arms. So golden brown next to my creamy tan colour. The veins standing proud of the tendons and muscles contorting under the effort to support my weight. The dusting of fine hair hardly noticeable, the luster of his smooth skin glistening with the heat. I'd noticed before how his hands bore broad palms and long fingers, the nails with their pale half moon crescents so milky in colour next the darkness of his skin. This was just a microscopic portion of the sum total. A pinhead compared to all the other captivating parts I enjoyed looking at.

If Jaya could be likened to a food, I mused, then undoubtably he'd be a banquet.

Suddenly, through the sultry air I caught the scent of wood smoke. We must be close to our destination I thought.

Biting my lip nervously I scanned the trees and bushes where the path began to open up. Elevated wooden stilted huts half hidden swung into view as the trees grudgingly gave way. Their roofs were layered with a long thatching type of material above open glassless windows interjecting their sides. Small brown figures moved slowly between the huts, going about their chores unaware of our imminent arrival. Suddenly I felt shy and self conscious. What would they make of a Westerner coming into their camp? Would they be angry and disapproving like the others had been? Probably, I thought, just as a loud whoop rang out from our group in greeting. Ahead in the camp, faces turned in our direction and an answering long whistle came in reply.

Jaya gently lowered me to the ground, his attention now focused ahead.

"Walk now." He said in a distracted manner as he stepped past me to catch up with the others. I wondered if they felt the need to preempt my arrival, to warn the villagers of my approach. My pace was slow at the best of times but now I felt reluctant to continue, unsure of how I would be received. Perhaps it would be better to hang back until they'd had time for their reunion. Besides, from here, I would be able to better assess their mood.

I watched as the villagers swarmed around the new arrivals, petting their faces in greeting and stroking their arms. Smiling and laughing with the exchange of words.

Suddenly from the far end of the village, I caught the movement of someone running towards the gathering. A slim young woman with long dark hair fanning mane like out behind her, was working her way through the crowd and then heart-stoppingly, straight into Jaya's arms. A spasm of shock ran through me. Their embrace seemed so intimate, so loving as they wrapped their arms around each other and swayed in each others arms. Then, the look on Jaya's face, the joy in hers. Everything stopped, time stood still, as I watched their microscopic universe. The small caress of Jaya's hand on her back, the way she leaned her head into his shoulder. Jaya had never mentioned a girlfriend or wife, but then he'd never told me anything about himself.

Apart from being an American on a gap year, I thought sourly, but that didn't break the leaden feeling I now felt in my heart.

# Chapter 11

# Layla

I flopped to the ground not wanting to see any more, but the image of Jaya in the arms of the girl would take more than just doing that to erase. Because now something was twisting inside, something alien to anything I had ever felt before. How stupid, how warped my sense of proportion and reality really was. How inexcusably idiotic I had been to imagine anything else in Jaya's kindness and concern.

I looked up again. I wanted to get a better look at Jaya's woman as means to tormenting myself. To compare myself to what I was not.

Yes, there she was and only one word that could describe her. *Exquisite.*

Her body was long and slim with just the right amount of roundness and curves. Her long dark hair cascaded around her beautiful face while the white teeth flashed at regular intervals. How could anyone compete with that I thought? No wonder Jaya's eyes had never strayed from her face since their reunion. How could any man not want to gaze at her for eternity? My foolishness swarmed over me. I pulled my hands over my face as if the gesture could erase the image. I'd seen enough to realise my idiotic wild imaginings were based on mere fantasy.

I picked at the stringy grass beneath me, tearing it angrily in clumps, only to throw it away again unwanted. I cursed myself. How utterly stupid I was, how ridiculously dumb. I'd worked hard to uphold the ice queen exterior yet now I was acting like a love sick teenager. What on earth was going on?

I'd always been good at pushing away feelings and unwanted thoughts, but that had been before Jaya came along. I'd been justly cynical about the world before I'd come here. I'd never thought there'd be any possibility of a relationship or even eventually marriage. My role models and experiences up to now had given me little in the way of enthusiasm to aspire to those ambitions.

*I was only deluding myself to imagine otherwise.*

My life had never resembled the fairytale lives we were drip fed on TV, the homely atmospheres and doting parents in happy families. My world was poles apart from that kind of fantasyland. At least my cynical approach saved me from hoping for anything more. I wasn't stupid enough to believe otherwise.

*It was just the other poor bastards that hadn't worked that out yet. They were still living the illusion of a happy-ever-after.*

Anyway what did it matter? There was never going to be anything between Jaya and me. My imaginings were pure fantasy. The daydreams of a frigid, remote, unemotional person too far out of any spectrum in which Jaya would be interested. I looked down at myself, seeing myself as if for the first time. The tatty clothes, ripped and torn, the feeble legs still bearing the yellowing bruises. The cloud of fluff that was now my hair batting uselessly against my cheek in the light breeze and catching on the wetness which now streaked down my face.

There was only one word to describe me.

*Pathetic.*

I wiped the tears from my face, they would only add to my humiliation, because now Jaya and his girlfriend were approaching.

"Alice, I want to introduce you to Layla," he said. I didn't pull the candy floss out of my face this time. Giving me some measure of concealment from their critical stares. So this was Layla, even more beautiful close up, achingly so.

*Cow.*

She was dressed in western style clothes but adorned with colourful beads. Jewellery dangled in numerous strands from her neck and matching beaded bracelets from her wrists. Large liquid brown eyes held a softness of expression as they examined me with a friendly expression.

*A shame I could not feel the same.*

She lowered herself gracefully to sit beside me. Maybe Jaya had already told her things about me. That now, I was an object of curiosity having spent so much time with her boyfriend.

"I hear you hurt yourself," she said in a friendly warm tone, the perfect English making me suspicious immediately. She glanced down at my leg as if she already knew where my injuries lay.

"Yes I did, I fell into a river and luckily Jaya found me," I replied. She smiled a perfect smile and glanced tenderly at Jaya who'd joined us on the grass.

"Jaya is very good at finding things," I noticed a silent look passed between them. "And you are getting well now I see." She continued as she examined the foliage bandage covering my leg.

"Yes, and I'm very grateful to Jaya for looking after me."

"You're welcome," he said looking up at me through his long lashes.

God, I had to get over him or this was going to kill me. Tearing myself away from his gaze I turned my attention back to Layla.

"Is this your home?" I asked.

"Sanuri." She said the word proudly. "This place has not been discovered by any outsiders, until now!"

"I've hardly discovered it," I muttered looking at Jaya.

She smiled at me again. "Nothing much happens around here so it will be fun to have you here." Her enthusiasm touched me. Her assumption that we would automatically be friends, comforting. It was there for the taking if I wanted it.

"Where are you from?" She probed, and I explained about my gap year and the disastrous trek where I had fallen into the river. While I talked I noticed the dreamy look in her eyes, as if she was not really listening but thinking of something else entirely. Maybe she wasn't as bright as I'd though at first. My spirits rose a fraction at the thought.

My explanation had wrought a pained expression to her face and I immediately regretted being so crass.

"You're a fighter," she stated matter of factually. "Let's get you cleaned up and feeling better." She grabbed my hand and pulled me to my feet, dragging me towards the village while I hobbled behind. I glanced back towards Jaya smiling down into his lap. Something had evidently pleased him.

I felt conspicuous hobbling beside Layla. Not only was I considerably taller than her but my dirty clothes and white skin shouted foreigner from every inch of my body. People watched our progress through the village and I suddenly wondered why I had ever thought I had wanted to come here at all.

*Everyone must hate me being here, I thought.*

I glanced furtively at the girl beside me, watching her graceful fluid movements next to my jerky lameness. Jaya had chosen well, there were no other native girls in the village that touched her good looks. That was hardly surprising, there were no other men who matched Jaya's either.

We arrived at a pool at the far side of the village. Women sat at its sides washing clothes while others bathed. Layla began removing her dress, tossing it aside. I glanced round worriedly.

She smiled easily. "Men are not permitted here, they have their own pool."

Her remark was all the encouragement I needed, as I hastily stripped down to my underwear before stepping into the deliciously cool water to wash away the sweat and grime. The fresh water livened every nerve ending helping me forget what had just passed before. Including the watching native women probably fascinated by my white skin and giraffe like long body, I thought. I stuck out like a sore thumb around here and I hated that.

I floated on my back allowing the weariness to wash away and tried to make a plan. If this was how it was going to be then I had no option other than to accept the way things were. I would continue as before, admire Jaya from afar, nothing more, nothing less. I had never made any assumptions regarding anything happening between us. My admiration had always been a oneway street. To think anything else would be completely outlandish. I had decided long ago not to get into the merry-go-round of dating, because ultimately it would eventually lead to something else. There were certain prerequisites required in any relationship and I had none of the right attributes to offer. Besides, there were no redeeming features about me that would add anything beneficial to the human species. It was best for everyone's sake to keep myself to myself to avoid any disappointment.

Thankfully Jaya had appeared unaware of my hidden admiration for him. I had been careful in keeping my gawking to a minimum. It had been hard to hide because Jaya had become like an addiction. Every moment I spent with him was like getting that hit a junky constantly craves. The fact that Jaya was with Layla did not fundamentally change anything. It would continue to be as it had always been.

*My fantasy.*

Layla joined me at the poolside.

"Alice, wasn't that great?" she giggled.

"Yeah," I said taken a little aback by her enthusiasm, she must do this everyday.

"So how was your time with Jaya?" she asked with such an engaging smile I wondered how anyone could refuse her anything.

Then I put up my guard. Was this was a trick question? How could I tell her I'd been attracted to her boyfriend?

*Still was.*

"He looked after me very well," I said carefully.

"And?" there was an expectancy in her eyes I could not work out.

"He's not exactly chatty."

"Are you saying your time with Jaya was dull?" she said with an amused expression.

"Not exactly dull, he didn't say a lot that's all."

"I'll have to speak to him, he takes things far too seriously. He needs to lighten up a little," she said with a light dancing in her eyes and leaving me wondering what on earth she meant.

Later, after we'd redressed she turned her attention to my hair and clothes. I shifted uncomfortably under her stare, making her laugh.

"We're going to have to do something about this attire," she said. "And your hair I think!" She said lifting the wet clumps and suddenly I was glad to have someone on my side. Who understood what it was to be a girl. I had never been fashionable or taken much notice of my appearance. Lack of money had been the root of all that. But there's a difference between indifference and looking cringeworthy. Of course, I was under no illusion how I'd pale into the background standing next to Layla and Jaya had already made his choice. Besides, her generous nature was already warming the iciness inside me.

"You think you can do something with this?" I said in surprise, lifting up some bedraggled wet strands.

"Come with me," she commanded, looping her arm through mine, pulling me in the direction of the village. We arrived at the largest hut. Round tree trunk steps lead steeply up to a small veranda and, from here, giving a commanding view over the rest of the village. The hut had a solid feel to it, ruggedly made from roughly hewn planks and small round tree trunks. The carpentry was rudimentary but effective in making it fit for purpose. Aesthetics aside, I was glad to be under a roof for the first time in weeks, with a storm brewing I was grateful to have shelter from the impending elements.

Taking a moment to adjust to the gloom inside, the interior was surprisingly homely. The wooden floors and walls were adorned with large rugs, crafted in striking colourful patterns. An assortment of wooden stools and chairs hugged the walls and various cooking utensils and wooden crockery were stacked in neat piles.

Layla pulled me into another room further back which I assumed to be the bedroom due to the rolls of bedding laying in the corner. Space must be at a premium here, I thought. Against a windowless wall hung her compact wardrobe. An array of colour and texture so different from the meager content of my own wardrobe back home.

"Here, try this on," she said, throwing across a tan coloured dress made from a loose weave. Taking off my old T-shirt and shorts I tugged the garment over my head allowing it to slip to just above my knees. It was too tight, my breasts and hips strained suggestively against the fabric and accentuated the dramatic dip into the curve of my waist. Layla covered a giggle.

"The men would love you in that," she smirked. "But here, try this one on instead."

Eventually she found a rather less revealing dress. Its v neck sat comfortably above any cleavage and skimmed over the curves of my body. It was perfect.

"Okay, now lets have a look at your hair. Come and sit."

She began playing with the strands with a look of concentration, gradually teasing out all the tangles.

"Have you ever used wax on your hair?" she asked.

"Wax, the same as in candle wax?"

"Kind of, but I'm talking of bee's wax, we collect it here in the jungle. It's useful for a number of reasons. We use a softer version that's easy to apply to hair, to condition and give shine. The heat and humidity is very drying for long hair and hair like yours."

Her confidence was infectious and under it's unrelenting flow, gradually began to make me feel more comfortable.

*And hopeful.*

There were no judgements or criticisms, no catty remarks or put downs, just easy conversation as if we had been friends for years. There was nothing pretentious about Layla, no vanity or egotistical preoccupation. Nothing manufactured in her manner despite how stunningly beautiful she was and soon my shyness began to dissolve.

Only a little, because Layla simply seemed too good to be true.

*There had to be a catch.*

Oh yeah, she was with Jaya, I reminded myself.

Layla's gentle hands tugged through my hair dipping them occasionally into a bowl beside her. Eventually she finished standing back to survey her handy work.

"Do I look as good as you now?" I joked suddenly embarrassed for her. It was always going to be an impossible task.

"Alice you look just great, wait until I can show you!"

"Yeah, right." I muttered under my breath.

"Alice, you look beautiful, trust me," she nodded as if having to confirm the notion to herself.

"Anyway, we'll get Jaya judge the result. He's a man after all!"

She fished around for something behind me.

"I wish I could show you properly but I only have this," she pulled out a broken jagged edge of a mirror only just big enough too see a portion of my face at a time. I surveyed the image doubtfully, was this beautiful? My hair had been fashioned into thick locks of spiraling curls that draped gently onto my shoulders. All signs of frizz had vanished. The hair that now shone back at me looked as if it belonged more in a magazine advertisement than in real life. It was shiny in a way it had never been before. Softly framing the angles of my face and drawing attention to the other features I'd never really noticed before. The square jaw and prominent cheek bones, the large blue eyes fringed by long dark lashes and the freckles I had always hated sprinkled over my nose. I hardly recognised the person that shone back at me. Somehow I looked more in focus, sharper, the features accentuating and complementing each other.

"Well?" Layla said smugly when she saw my astonished expression.

"Amazing!" I said patting and pulling at the curls

Lalya held up a pot of wax. "Well, this is your abracadabra!" She said grinning at me.

"Come, we'll show Jaya."

I suddenly felt apprehensive. Before, I had been a disheveled, frizzy invalid, easy not to notice, but now Layla seemed to think my transformation warranted a reaction.

Anything that drew attention to myself made me cringe inside, I actively sought ways to blend chameleon like into the background. Nonetheless, my abnormal height and curly hair had always given me away. People seemed inordinately interested at staring at my freakish attributes. I had tried to become numb too their critical glares, in fact numb too everything around me and in some ways I thought I had succeeded.

Layla disappeared, leaving me to play with my newly obedient curls when a new thought began to crush me. What if Jaya didn't like what he saw? That was silly, I told myself, there'd been nothing to commend me before. Anyway why did it matter? He was with Layla anyway. What if Jaya and Layla started holding hands or kissing? How was I going to react to that? As if on cue I spotted them through the window returning to the hut. Leaning in together as they laughed at some private joke causing my heart to lurch and my mouth to suddenly feel dry. Layla talked excitedly, Jaya looking down at her appeared to be unaware of anything else other than her lovely face smiling up at him. I suddenly felt foolish to have imagined Jaya would find me attractive, there could be no other woman he could possibly have eyes for than Layla. She was simply too beautiful. Standing next to her would be like rock being compared to a flawless diamond.

I retreated into the confines of the hut, the darkness suddenly my best friend.

"Alice what are you doing in there? Come right out!" I heard Layla call out in her sing song voice. "Alice?"

I hesitated a moment before reluctantly walking into the light, watching anxiously for Jaya's reaction. The silence stretched out for far too long, hanging heavily in the air. His eyes had swept casually over me, taking in the new dress, my face, the hair. It seemed to take forever, oh God.

"It's a good sign Alice if he can't find anything to say!" Layla said fluttering around me to adjust some curls. I felt a flush beginning under the scrutiny of his gaze, not knowing quite what to make of Jaya's silence. He glanced at Layla before returning his gaze to me.

"You look wonderful," he said eventually. I laughed stupidly, suddenly embarrassed, trying to deflect the attention away from myself.

"Yeah, well, Layla's done a good job with a hopeless project," I scoffed, suddenly feeling bad because of Layla's crestfallen expression.

"Don't you have any idea how lovely you look," said Layla.

"Well, always being average, means I've never really bothered to look in the mirror that much." I looked down at my hands when the silence filled the room again. Examining my ragged nails I continued. "But I can see you've managed to improve things, I look a great deal better than I did, thanks."

I heard Jaya's weight shift before speaking in a low husky voice. "Alice you're far from average."

"Anyway why does it matter," I rushed on. "Looks are only skin deep, we're in the middle of the jungle, who's going to want to look at me anyway." Again, the silence stretched onwards.

"Looks are important, only because you should take pride in your appearance, to acknowledge this part is also who you are. It's not vain or self centered it just being you," Layla said.

"What about the inside, doesn't that matter?" I said, thinking of the ugliness that lay deep within.

"Of course it does."

"How do I make that feel good then?" I said without thinking, regretting my words immediately.

"Is that how you feel inside?" Layla said gently.

I cringed inwardly, suddenly wanting the floor to swallow me up. How could I have been such an idiot?

"It's just been a long day," I said, and it had. With Jaya disappearing and then returning with the natives, being brought to Sanuri, the attentions of Layla. I was overwrought but that wasn't what had triggered my outburst. It was Layla's kindness which had edged open the door.

Layla was still looking at me in surprise and Jaya, Jaya continued to stare at me with a curious new expression. I tore my gaze away to sharpen my resolve, this was never going to do. I was a plane Jane, always had been, always would be and nothing anyone was going to say or do was ever going to change that. This had all been a waste of time and I suddenly felt sorry for Layla having tried so hard. She'd done her best with a hopeless project.

"Cinderella shall go to the ball," he said magnanimously, smiling that smile, holding out his hand in a courtly manner.

"I don't see my carriage awaiting." I quipped.

"Who needs a carriage?" he said. "We've already walked miles through the jungle without one!"

"Ah, you're giving me a little credit I see, you said *we*."

"A figure of speech," he looked thoughtfully at me for a moment.

I bit my lip nervously. "Before, you said you could see me. What did you mean?"

"I saw who you are."

"And what have you found out already?"

He gave me a dark look causing my heart to kick up a notch. "That you don't like eating rodents!"

He stepped back to consider me for a moment and suddenly I was lost in the liquid brown eyes hypnotising me. Casting their spell. Making me forget the other Universe I'd inhabited moments ago.

"I never realised I was carrying such a siren for all that time," he said as I noticed the golden flecks in his eyes dancing, then a ghost of a smile twitched over his lips.

Stupid! I should have known it was all just a joke, that I was like something a cat would toy with until it got bored, and what must Layla be thinking of this flirting, standing so silently behind Jaya. How could she bear it? But I was too distracted by the way Jaya was staring at me through his dark lashes to guiltily linger on the thought for too long. There was something different in his eyes, something I had not seen before, almost like..........

I immediately pushed the thought away, impossible! Only, the burning expression in his eyes told me something else entirely. Something I had only dreamt about in my fantasy, but in reality, had never wanted to happen.

Cold panic ran through me, until I remembered he was with Layla, and this fact alone suddenly allayed my fears. What was I thinking to have imagined anything else? Yet, a tugging uncertainty nagged at me, pulling up something deep within, flagging my inner most fears.

I knew then I couldn't take anything for granted. I had to keep up my guard.

# Chapter 12

# The Storm

The dark and ominous rain clouds brewing throughout the previous day had finally given way. Torrents of rain pelted heavily from the dark skies, while lightening flashed in huge electrical bursts across the mountains, the ringing peals of thunder echoing around the valley. None of that bothered me. It was the wind that scared me, violently shaking our hut, swaying and lurching under each onslaught. Whipping gustily through the open windows where the roof's overhang could not contain the near horizontal torrent.

Jaya and Layla were still sleeping, but then I remembered, they probably hadn't seen each other for a while. They'd most probably be getting down to doing other 'stuff.'

I looked through the glassless window, watching the rivers of brown muddy water flowing past the long stilted huts, collecting in pools around the poles. The ground below so tinder dry yesterday had now become one large muddy puddle. Compared to the thunder storms in England this was a monster. Even the slanting rain falling in sheets seemed to be different.

I rose silently, changing quickly before creeping quietly out into the communal room. I wanted to catch a few moments to myself before the quiet was disturbed by the others. I was struck by the disproportionate size of the hut Layla and Jaya had all to themselves. Far more than they needed for just the two of them.

I sauntered over to look at the eight or so woven hangings lining the walls of the room. Their large colourful presence breaking the monotonous dark brown of the wooden slats within the interiors gloom. The weavings looked old, some badly frayed at the edges but the colours still remained true. Shining out into the room with striking vibrancy and drawing the eye to circumnavigate the intricate patterns. Then, something caught my eye, something I hadn't at first noticed. A symmetrical pattern had begun to form before my eyes and as I looked closer I could see amongst the random swirling patterns a regular uniform evenness to the design. I stared intrigued before moving onto the next weaving. Another set of swirling patterns, again the same design, almost hidden, formed within the chaos. Eventually I found all eight rugs contained the same patterns and images. Strange, I thought, what did they mean? Nothing presented itself as an answer and I soon became bored and returned to my bedroom.

There was something else I wanted to look at.

Glancing into the jagged mirror Layla had leant me propped up on a sill, I wanted to check on my hair, to see if it was still behaving in a subdued manner. Yes, the sleek coiled tendrils still hung attractively onto my shoulders, showing a restraint I'd never seen before. Examining my face again I noticed how my eyes seemed larger than before perhaps because they weren't hidden by a crazy fluffy fringe. The curls coiled delicately around my cheeks and framing the strongly set bone structure. My skin tone had changed too, now a creamy golden colour, a definite improvement to the usual persil whiteness. Especially for my legs which suffered in the damp winters cold and taking on a mottled corned beef appearance beneath the minuscule gym skirt.

I shook my head at the memory of Layla's and Jaya's well intended compliments. Impossible! I knew they were just being generous. Well, they'd soon find out that I didn't need flattery, I was too self contained to require that sort of thing. Satisfied with my own opinion still intact I turned to find Jaya casually leaning against the doorway to my room. Arms folded over his chest and looking every inch a sex God.

Christ! I jumped, guilty at my supposed vanity and my feelings now exposed. How long had he been watching me?

"I didn't hear you," I said embarrassed, nervously combing back a tendril from across my face. The movement seemed to remind him to look at my hair. Sweeping over it fleetingly with his eyes, then down over my body then back to my face.

"Still looking good!" he said as a smile played across his lips. "Did the storm wake you?"

He looked so startlingly handsome in the half light, shadows cast against his face accentuating the angles of his face. His tall frame almost touching the ceiling of the hut.

"Yes," I replied, feeling a flush beginning under the intensity of his scrutiny. "And I'm not used to living in all this luxury!"

He snorted. "I'm sure you'll soon get used to it."

"Perhaps," I said vaguely, looking out at the rain.

"Would you like a drink? Tea, coffee?"

"Isn't it too wet for a fire?"

"No, I've got a gas stove," he said smiling at my shocked face. As I remembered all the fires we'd made from scratch! All this time it had taken to get them alight and he'd had a gas stove! Meaning he'd have matches as well.

"You had a stove?" I said coldly.

"I use it only when I have to, replacement canisters are a little hard to come by and it's not as much fun. I liked it better when you thought I was a real native and building fires was part of the illusion!"

"You think I enjoyed hobbling about getting sticks for the fire when my leg hurt like hell?"

"Well you didn't have much else to do," he said, the teasing tone now back in his voice.

I changed tack. "But aren't you a real native in your own country, you know, an American Indian?"

He looked at the floor before replying. "Yes I am from that heritage and so is Layla."

"So what are you doing here so far away from your home, living with these people?" he question had been burning since yesterday.

"Like I said we're kind of on a gap year. Every few years the native tribal leaders from all over the world gather in a native convention. Many things are discussed, world pollution, encroachment on their tribal lands, world events, you get the idea. We were invited from America to spend time here for many reasons but mainly to help them understand about Western ways. These people have little understanding of the greed and lust for money that has consumed the West. The destruction of family values, the selfishness, corruption and wars are all utterly inconceivable here."

"They need you to tell them? Don't they know already?"

"Living in America as an indigenous tribe which has been persecuted over the years means we understand only too well what can happen."

"Is their way of life threatened?"

"It could be."

"Why couldn't you tell me all this before? Why all the secrecy?"

"Because I had to be sure of you, these people want to protect their way of life. They don't want Westerners here or anyone who might threaten it."

"Then why did you bring me?" I said bluntly, noticing how he suddenly looked uncomfortable.

"This place will give you the time to heal, away from the dangers outside the valley," he nodded his head in the direction we had come. "In any case, I had to keep you in the dark because we were being followed for quite sometime. The drug runners were hot on our trail and I did not want you to be concerned. Not after I'd seen how easily you became frightened. What if they had captured you or me? It was better for you not to know anything, because in the worst case scenario you would have had nothing to tell them." His words jolted a shock wave through me. We'd been followed by drug barons who'd been close enough on our trail for Jaya to worry about them.

"So what are you doing scurrying about the jungle like that? Isn't it safer to stay here?"

"We like to know their whereabouts."

"So you're like the Lone Ranger?" I said and he laughed.

"Kind of."

"How far did they follow us?"

"I'm not sure, but I left them loads of false trails while you were sleeping or when I was away hunting. It fooled them for a while, but it got a bit too close to call towards the end." He said with a satisfactory look.

I shuddered at the thought.

"What would they have done if they'd caught us?" I asked holding my breath as I waited for his answer. He hesitated a fraction too long before he answered.

"They would have extensively questioned us."

It sounded like a shortened version to me but I did not want to know any more details.

"What do these men want Jaya?"

His face darkened before looking away. "They're suspicious of anyone in their territory. Mostly they want to keep out the competition." I waited for any more, but Jaya didn't continue.

"Aren't you afraid of putting yourself needlessly in the path of danger, when you could stay here in safety?"

"Yes and no," he said seriously but there was something in Jaya's expression which switched on a light bulb.

"You enjoy it don't you?" The realization dawning on me, the cavalier in him meant he could not resist the challenge of pitting his skills against theirs.

"I can't deny it, but it does come with some benefits like rescuing an English damsel in distress from raging rivers and near death injuries." He grinned, enjoying himself now. "You were my greatest test yet, carrying you for miles, tending to your wounds and escaping from the men who hunted us all at the same time!"

I was stunned at his reply and retorted hotly with unexpected emotion. "So that was all I was to you? A challenge, so that you could congratulate yourself later over your expertise and gallantry!" The words had shot out of my mouth before I could stop them. I saw the look of surprise in response to my angry outburst and suddenly I feared I had revealed too much. Nothing good could come from him knowing anything about my feelings.

Jaya's mouth opened to speak just as Layla appeared brightly around the door frame.

"Good morning! Wow, we're all looking so serious this morning. Faces as long as a wet weekend! Would anyone like some tea or coffee?" she asked as her hands slipped round Jaya's waist from behind, the backwards hug making me feel uncomfortable and suddenly I felt like I shouldn't be here at all. Wishing more than anything Jaya had taken me straight to Chang Mai after all.

# Chapter 13

# The Elders

A meeting had been arranged for today so that I could meet the Elders. I was nervous, not knowing what to expect but still wanting the encounter out of the way. If I was to remain here in Sanuri I would need the blessing from the tribal leaders. My surprise arrival had already caused quite a stir amongst the villagers and not all reactions had been favourable.

The natives who'd first escorted Jaya and me into the village had not been welcoming nor thrilled whenever I encountered them within the village. I was an unknown stranger in a place they wanted to keep secret and I couldn't blame them for their cold responses towards me. Now I was here, I was at a loss to understand this strong desire to keep Sanuri secret because to me, there didn't seem to be anything remarkable about this place at all. Yes, their way of life appeared to be simple and easy but why they shunned any interaction with the Western world seemed strange. Especially when there were certain items of equipment which would greatly ease the burden of their chores.

The meeting had been scheduled to take place sometime in the afternoon. Time seemed to hold little meaning here in Sanuri, arrangements were loosely adhered to and nobody seemed bothered by the lack of organisation. Not like back home where time had become another pressure to stress over. Being late for school or gatherings with the relatives was looked upon by my mother as a mortal sin and I had learned early on, never to ever be late for anything. It wasn't worth the haste.

Jaya told me meetings were normally held out in the open, but due to the torrential rain outside a change of venue had been decided. Namely within this hut. Until that time the whole morning stretched ahead of me and the worry now weighed heavily on my mind. Now that I knew the dangers lurking outside the mountain walls of this valley, getting to Chang Mai had substantially lost its allure. I needed to stay here.

For a while at least.

To pass the time Jaya, Layla and I sat out on the sheltered small verandah over looking the village. The storm still raged as powerfully as before only now the rain had let up a little.

"Are there many people who live in Sanuri?" I asked. I had not seen many natives, the village as far as I could tell held only a dozen or so huts.

"There are around a hundred or so, many of them don't live in the village itself and are spread out over the valley."

The few natives I had seen were mainly women and children going about their daily chores. The pace of life here was very slow, people never hurried. The lack of electricity and running water and the need to cook everything over an open fire, apart from Jaya's little gas stove of course, meant everything took much longer. Layla and Jaya must miss the comforts of home back in America. Their friends and family so far away. The insular nature of living their lives within the confines of this valley must create limited conversational topics. My arrival here in Sanuri for Layla, must feel like Cinderella had come to town.

"Don't you miss home, your parents and friends?" I asked.

"Yes, I do," replied Layla no longer looking wistfully out the window, the darkness of the room casting a dull light over her face.

I turned my attention to Jaya.

"Do you think the natives hate me?"

He laughed. "No not really, but you've created quite a stir. They like having a bit of eye candy around. I think they've grown bored just looking at Layla lately!"

"So what part of America are you from?" I asked.

"We belong to the Crow tribe in Montana, big sky country." Jaya said and I saw the twitch of the lips and knew what was coming.

"Does the rain make you feel at home?"

"This isn't rain, it's a tap turned on."

"But in England you get lots of rain, especially around the time of Wimbledon tennis tournament!" he teased.

"You watch that? England does have sunshine you know. Cricket and tennis are national sports they'd never be played if it rained all the time," I retorted.

"I thought rain was an integral part of playing, dodging the showers by going in for 'tea'?"

"Its not all cucumber sandwiches and Pimm's you know."

"Isn't it?"

"I bet you never even watch cricket or Wimbledon."

"Like you said, you don't know anything about me!"

I relented slightly then. "So do you play any sports back home, or was practising being a boy scout in the great outdoors too inviting?"

Over the course of the last few days I'd begun to find a certain amount of enjoyment teasing Jaya now that he'd become more relaxed.

"Baseball and American football are American's pastime, everyone plays them." He replied.

"Even on the reservation or do the drumming and dancing lessons get in the way?" I said trying to keep a straight face.

"Those too!" I caught the look, as he brushed his hair behind one shoulder. "Seriously though, we do learn a lot about our heritage. The different tribes that populated America before the white people came."

"Do you still have names like Broken Arrow or Strong Bone?"

"Yes, we have two names, one for the tribe and one for everyday use."

"What's yours?"

"Tocho," he said. "It means mountain lion."

"Why be named after an animal?"

"It's our totem. It helps us take on positive attributes of an animal. Like a bear would give strength and courage, a deer being swift and sure footed. The Crow people and many other tribes believe different animals have special significance. Each have their own innate qualities which we copy to help us to bring those qualities into us as well."

I snorted. "Really?"

"And when we cross paths with a certain type of animal they hold even greater significance."

I stopped my taunting for a moment as a sudden thought came back to me. Our small terraced three bedroomed house fortuitously backed onto hay fields. Beautiful in spring and autumn when the early morning mists hung softly over the grass. The beauty of the rosy glow of first light was not lost on me as I'd set off for my paper round, but I'd never had time to linger and watch its beauty. Later, in the September before I came away I'd seen a white fallow deer grazing in the heavy dew laden field. An ethereal vision merging with the ghostly misty tendrils. A notable appearance if it had only happened once, but that had not been the case, appearing with persistent resolution everyday for several weeks. I'd thought nothing more of the incident until now.

"What about white deer?" I asked.

"Have you seen one?"

"Yes, just before I came away. Early in the morning it would wander right up to our garden fence."

"Male or female?"

"Male," I said remembering the tell tale tuft of hair on the deers belly.

"Ah."

"What?"

"It's a message."

"A message?"

"Our forbearers considered white animals to be of great importance. A sign of great prophecy. Elders would meet to discuss their meaning. Traditionally deer have been a symbol of the great spirit and a sign of the sun. The antlers symbolizing the sun's rays. The shedding and regrowth of the antlers represents regeneration, cycle and growth. Deer also represent great sensitivity, being alert and always aware. Seeing a white deer is a powerful sign and a message you are on the path of change and expansion. To 'get ready' for what is to come. Added to that is the male energy meaning longevity, abundance and endurance. Perhaps the qualities you need for the times to come."

"Animals can mean all that?"

"Not all animals, they all carry different messages."

"That can't be me," I said almost to myself.

"You're very fortunate to have been given this gift. More so for the length of time the deer waited outside your house so that you could hear its message."

"Animals don't do that."

"Animals are guided just like we are, who are we to question why or how?"

"You believe all this stuff?"

"It's my heritage, its what we believe. By watching the world around us and reading the messages given to us is how we have come to understand the world around us. It has made us who we are."

There was nothing I could say to that. To argue against the beliefs of multiple generations would be futile. Besides, their faith in these messages was impressive and certainly persuasive, but I seriously doubted the meaning of the white deer could ever have any meaning for me. It had to be a mistake.

The sound of numerous feet hitting the creaky wooden steps announced the arrival of the tribal Elders. We stood to greet them.

Five elders filed into the communal room each nodding at Jaya and Layla then gravely at me as they passed. Their faces blank and unreadable, a sudden twisting sensation curled in my stomach. We followed them in and joined them on the floor of the hut. All but one wore weather beaten faces, their wrinkles etched deeply into the skin like tanned old leather. One Elder was completely bald. His head was as brown and shiny as an autumn acorn. Each wore a thin woven shawl draped over one shoulder, an item I assumed denoted their status. Numerous long colourful beaded necklaces and bracelets swung loosely about their bodies. I had a sense they'd taken great care in their dress and appearance.

Silence fell over the gathering as all eyes turned towards me. Assessing my appearance, my clothes, my hair, then staring fixedly into my eyes. They were looking into my Soul already. A quiver of trepidation swept through me. Supposing they did not like what they saw, supposing they found what really lay beneath. I tried to remain still and calm but my heart had kicked up to a galloping pace and I felt the sweat prickle over my body. The scrutiny was only what I'd been expecting and I had to keep my composure.

My attention was drawn to the youngest of the Elders. His age was hard to gauge but I noticed the intensity with which he stared at Layla, but then who wouldn't want to look at her forever?

Eventually the silence was broken by the Elder sitting directly in front of me, giving off such an aura of quiet authority I assumed him to be their leader. He directed his speech in the strange clicking language mainly towards Jaya and Layla but occasionally his discourse was aimed at me.

Jaya began to translate some of the proceedings.

"They wanted to hear your story directly," Jaya said turning to listen to the Elder continuing to speak.

"They want to know how you happened to be on the trek and what region you'd been walking in."

I felt my throat turn dry, I hated talking in front of people. Concentrated stares fixed unwaveringly on me had always made me feel nervous. I remembered in school how we'd been encouraged to give little talks in front of the class about a favourite subject or project. I'd never been any good. The words sticking in the back of my throat and never seeming to come out in the right order. Now was no different. My confident banter of only a few minutes ago had withered away under the onslaught of their stares.

Haltingly, I told them about how I had come to be in Thailand, my gap year and then booking the trek in the backpacker's 'Changs'.

"Did you tell anyone you were going on a trek?" Jaya said.

"No, no one knows I'm here."

"What about your family?"

I looked at Jaya questioningly.

"They want to know about your family."

Did I want to tell them my sad little sob story? An alcoholic mother who'd hardly noticed my presence, let alone my absence? The brother who had moved out to escape our mothers intoxicated ramblings and rantings. The death of our father.

"I have a mother and brother, but my father died sometime ago," I said.

Jaya paused briefly before relaying my reply as if the news surprised him.

The Elders were talking amongst themselves, discussing my story I supposed. I waited, fiddling nervously with the beads on my dress.

"Who were the trekking leaders?" Jaya asked.

"Bing and another called......" I thought back trying to sound the name in my head," the other was called something like Alak I think." Jaya was already relaying the information and I could see the news interested them.

"Did they stay with you throughout the trek?"

"I was only on the trek for a couple of days, I'm not sure ........." I thought back. "Yes, there was one night when one only one guide was with us. I hadn't thought it unusual at the time and I wondered what they found significant about this information.

"What was the planned itinerary of your trek?"

"First the waterfall, then we were due to spend a couple of nights with the 'Karen' tribe, but I never made it that far."

I knew that my disappearance within the backpacking community would become a local legend, bad news always hung about like the stink of smelly socks.

The discussion continued for sometime. I could see Layla and Jaya's focus on the flow of the conversation, the conferring sent back and forth, and I could only watch the proceedings anxiously.

Finally Jaya turned to me to translate.

"Alice, the Elders wish me to tell you that your arrival here has certainly caused much concern within the community but they wish to welcome you. You can stay. They only ask you do not to venture any further than the outskirts of the village unless you are accompanied. They have cast Layla and me as your minders while you stay here. Layla and I will show you what they mean later. This village, this valley must remain a secret, this is more important than you can ever know. Can you agree to this?"

I looked around the circle of serious faces waiting expectantly. What would they do if I said no, I thought distractedly?

"Yes," I said wanting their attention to be directed away.

Everyone's smiles suddenly lit up the room before Layla rose to her feet and disappeared into another room. The meeting was over but nobody left and it was not until Layla returned with a tray of refreshments I understood why. The atmosphere had changed into a more relaxed affair. The Elders once so stiff and upright now lounged on the hut's floor talking and drinking amongst themselves. I saw Layla being monopolizing by the younger looking Elder, now up close even more surprisingly youthful in appearance. His skin smoothly taut over his cheeks and neck, the hair a dark brown and not showing any signs of greying. He did not look the same as the others in the tribe. Taller and with more Caucasian features, he acted differently too. Layla seemed to encourage the attentions of the man at times placing a light hand on his arm or laughing at some funny witticism. I could not understand these American Indian Crow people. Their need to attract and enchant the people around them and then to enslave them with merely a look or a touch was perturbing. Couldn't they be satisfied with the partner they already had?

Looking away from their conversation I was met by the eyes of Jaya staring intently at me from across the room. How long had he been watching me watching Layla? I noted the strange quality to his eyes and behind them, a burning intensity I could not fathom. What was he thinking now? I flicked my eyes away to gaze out into the storm still furiously battling the elements outside. Water fell in sheets from the roof and no one seemed inclined to leave the dry interior of the hut. Already the temperature and humidity had dropped considerably since the storm had started.

Jaya crossed over the hut to join me.

"Hey," he said easily as he sat down beside me.

"Glad that's over," I said. "What would have happened if they hadn't wanted me to stay?"

"I'd have to take you back."

"Wouldn't it be dangerous?"

"Yes."

"Let me guess, you'd enjoy it."

"In a nut shell."

A silence fell between us.

"Thank goodness it's cooler," I said eventually. "It's been so hot I thought my brain was going to fry."

He smiled. "I guess it has been a little on the hot side."

"What's it like in Montana? Is it hot, cold, rainy?" I asked not knowing anything about where Jaya lived and then feeling suddenly so typically English. Always obsessed about the weather.

"It can be hot but the air is dry, not like the humidity here. We have the plains but also mountains and a tremendous amount of plant and animal life. There is some rain but the mountain ranges block much of the moist air coming from the Pacific making for a drier climate. In all, its a very pleasant and beautiful place to live."

"I didn't ask for the entire geography and weather patterns of the place!" I teased.

Non plussed he asked me, "how about Harpenden, do you like it there?" I was surprised he'd remembered the name of my home town but I was soon to realise there was very little that Jaya missed.

Yet, what could I say about it in comparison to the near perfect sounding Montana? Harpenden with its fancy boutique shops and numerous alfresco coffee bars, the high street littered with historical pubs. The narrow greens in front of the stores and tree lined residential avenues mingled with large Victorian houses owned by wealthy bankers or lawyers. The yummy mummy housewives swanning around in their huge flashy 4 x 4's. The cliche social scene. Did I like it there, would I choose to go back after completing my degree at University? Most of my friends talked about leaving and living in London once they'd got jobs or finished Uni like me. I knew most of them would probably never return, following the bright city lights for pastures new. If I decided to return home would it ever be the same? Probably not, it would be like staying on when the party had left town, empty of all my casual acquaintances and the superficial life style I'd thought I'd once enjoyed. And what of my mother? Would I want to return to the depressing family home? Back to a house far too small and in desperate need of redecoration. With its mustard, yellow swirling patterned carpet, the dirty brown, shiny lounge wall covering, the donkey chip wall paper lining the walls in the characterless rooms. The furniture from the old house too large and out of place in the small sized rooms. The 1970's kitchen, too tiny for even a washing machine and over crowded as soon as you entered it.

This had been the unhappy house we'd moved into a few years after my father had died. Leaving behind the bitter sweet unbearable memories of the house my father had worked so hard to provide for us, when my mother could no longer pay the bills for the large family four bedroomed house on her stingy secretarial wage. The wage now mostly wasted on nonessentials like cigarettes and booze, leaving little left over for anything else.

"Alice?" Jaya's voice brought me back to the present, he was looking at me, waiting for my answer while I'd drifted away into my yesterday world.

"Harpenden, you know the usual, houses, shops, people."

"Can't you do better than that?"

"What do you want to know?"

"Something interesting about the place."

I thought for a minute then suddenly feeling mischievous. "It's a very pleasant place to live. Affluent, nice shops, easy commute to London. There used to be an open air swimming pool. We'd go skinny dipping after the pubs had closed for a laugh on a hot summers night!" I smiled at the memory, remembering the rush of scaling the high metal fence to get in. Delinquent behaviour by smart Harpenden standards, but the thrill drew us back to do it again and again. Never doing any harm and invariably joined by the hoards of others after the same fun.

Jaya laughed in mock, shock. "You English girls! I always thought you were brought up to be more modest and mind your P's and Q's!"

I snickered. "Yeah, we did have to in the swimming pool!"

We laughed. "Well Alice take your pick, there are plenty of pools around here to go skinny dipping in! I'd only be too glad to show you where they are!" he said grinning at me.

"What about Layla, would she come?" I said playing along.

"She swims naked anyway, it wouldn't be such a thrill for her!" Before I could think of a clever reply we were joined by Layla and the young elder.

"I want to introduce Chana to you Alice," she said. "He's been helping me with some interesting research.

"Hi," I said but received no such greeting in return. I felt the sweep of his stare and noticed a hard look behind his eyes. He didn't like me, that was obvious, but for what reason I could not make out. I was relieved when eventually they drifted away again because the conversation had been so stilted.

Jaya lead me away towards a quiet corner at the back of the hut. A serious expression cast over his face. What now? He dropped his voice low so only I could hear.

"Alice, you said you didn't want to go home yet, because of your home life."

"Yes," I said slowly not sure where this was leading.

"I don't want to seem like I'm prying......." He looked down at me with such intensity I thought my heart was going to stop. "Secrets have a habit of eating away at us inside.......If you ever want to talk.............I'm here." He left the remark hanging but I already knew the world would have to stop spinning before I would ever tell him anything.

*Especially because of him.*

I countered. "And you'll tell me your secrets as well?"

"They're not my secrets to tell."

I changed tack. "What did you mean when you said the Elders wanted you to show me something?"

"Yeah, I'm going to be your teacher," he said grinning, enjoying my dubious expression.

"The Elders wish you to learn something while you're here."

"Hope it's not all chanting and clapping hands, I find that stuff really boring!"

"So you've done it before?" he said raising his eyebrows.

"Yeah, back in primary school in hymn practice."

"Well, I think you'll find it a lot more interesting than you imagine."

I looked up at him with a teasing expression. "As long as it's not weird and doesn't cause any long term injury." I quipped, enjoying myself now. "You natives have strange beliefs. Spirit keepers, animals bringing messages. Next, you'll be telling me you can bend metal spoons with your mind!"

He smiled. "You're much closer than you think Alice."

"Am I?"

"When the weather improves I'm going to take you somewhere, just you and me," an involuntary electrical charge swept through me at the thought.

"Take me where?"

"It's a very special place," he said as a smile twitched at the corner of his mouth.

"Not a skinny dipping pool?"

"If that's what you want I can always change my plan!"

"You were just waiting for me to say that!"

"Was I?" He grinned.

And Layla won't mind us skinny dipping alone together?" I said guardedly.

"Layla's got other things on her mind," he said, his expression darkening as he glanced over to where she stood. Abruptly he walked away leaving the remark hanging in the air behind him. I looked after Jaya more confused than ever. I knew he was teasing me but still I wondered at this man.

*Who talked with his eyes and deceived me with his words.*

# Chapter 14

# The Pool

A new day and a new quandary. I wondered what new perplexities would manifest in this one. For over the last few days I'd been living in Sanuri I'd become increasingly confused by the conflicting messages Jaya was giving me. Whenever he was with Layla the looks and manner between them left me in no doubt as to their affection for each other. Yet, when he was with me his demeanor changed. I often caught him studying me in a way that seemed different from before. He lingered in the hut for longer than need be if I happened to be alone. Which was often because Layla disappeared for long periods at a time. The careful politeness had changed to a more open approach about himself and Sanuri. I puzzled over this new behaviour but could not fathom any answer.

I could still smell the dampness of the earth as it rose from the drying ground, its scent was still pungent, even though it had been several days since the storm had passed. The sound of early unfamiliar bird song echoed through the valley accompanied by the customary drone of insect activity. I lay still, drinking in the sounds and smells of the jungle enjoying this new experience. Grateful at my good fortune to be here at all when I had so very nearly died. Time was all I needed to make a full recovery and already the yellowing bruises on my legs had now all but faded. The scab covering my gashed shin had grown smaller by the day and yesterday all last remains had finally fallen away. I could now largely walk unaided. A faint limp now the only evidence of my injuries and I knew my time here would soon be at an end. The Elders had generously given me their consent for me to stay in Sanuri until I was fully recovered and that time was fast approaching.

"So what's an average day here in Sanuri?" I asked one morning.

"Find wood, find food, eat, sleep," he'd said over his banana at breakfast.

"That sounds exciting."

"And you wonder why I scour the hillsides for drug runners?"

"How often do you go?"

"Several times a month, it depends on the season."

"Shouldn't you be heading off again soon?"

"I have a new job."

"What?"

"Keeping you out of trouble!"

"I'm trouble am I?"

"Yeah, from the moment I found you!"

"Perhaps you should have left me to die after all then," I said tartly.

Jaya gave me a hard stare making my heart skip a beat. "You know I couldn't do that."

"You've gone to so much trouble for me, why?"

He fell silent looking into his hands. "What else could I do?"

"Taken me straight to Chang Mai."

"That would have meant moving through the drug lords territory. Not a good idea."

"So instead you've brought me to a village where everyone hates me. I think I would rather have taken my chances."

"And risk getting caught? Alice you have no idea what these men are capable of."

I fell silent for a moment.

"Originally you were going to take me back. You had no intention of bringing me here did you?" I pressed.

"Yes."

"So why?"

"Because Alice there is something......." He paused before continuing. "Something about you and I don't know what it means. When I threatened you with the spear your hair fell away from your neck revealing an odd looking mark just beneath your hairline. It reminded me of something I'd seen in Sanuri. Something which the Elders confirmed to be an insignia of artifacts here and similar to some of the drawings back in the caves. I wondered if you would recognise them but you seemed to be completely unaware of any connection to the symbols and the mark on your neck. It cannot be coincidence, finding you like I did, the mark. That was why I brought you here and that is why you have been allowed to stay."

I stared at him horrified. Something different about me? Well, he had got that much right but not in the way he meant. I touched the back of my neck, feeling for the location of this strange mark and began to laugh.

"You brought me here because of a mark on my neck?" I said but Jaya didn't reply.

"It's just a birthmark I've always had it."

"It's not any old mark."

"And the Elders allowed me to stay because of it?" I said beginning to laugh again. I had never heard of anything so ridiculous.

"Yeah, something like that."

I looked at him seriously. "I'm afraid you've been short changed, there's nothing special about me Jaya, this is all there is." I said spreading out my arms and smiling, but Jaya didn't seem to get the joke.

Jaya looked down into his hands for a moment. "There is something special about you Alice, it's just you don't know it yet."

I snorted. "Well I'll be waiting for eternity to find it."

He leant back considering me for a moment. "You're not like anyone I've ever met before."

"Is that a bad thing?"

"It's a compliment!"

A compliment! It sounded as if he was saying I was weird or something.

"What happened to you Alice?" he said, his remark took me by surprise. No one had ever been so direct. Usually I'd pushed them away before that happened. Of course I often saw it in their eyes, the confusion when I brushed them off, or coldly elbowing them away when they got too close. That was my self defense mechanism coming into play. I could not afford to let anyone get too near.

For a moment I could not think how to answer. I never usually divulged information about my family, but something in Jaya's eyes stopped me from sidestepping.

"Growing up without a father wasn't easy, life was hard."

"No, that's not it. There's something else, I see it in your face sometimes. A sadness or a disappointment or something."

I stared at him perplexed, he was closer than he thought.

"Life doesn't always turn out how you think," I said remembering there had never been a happy-ever-after for my family. That was why I tried never to dwell too long on the past. It didn't do any wonders for stoking any happy molecules. "And yeah, you could say life has been a disappointment. Crap happens. Things were never the same after my father died." *Biggest understatement of the year, or decade for that matter.*

A silence fell between us, but I had been expecting it. Talking of anything closely relating to emotions always scared blokes, I'd seen it in my brother Harry. They just didn't know what to say. Then Jaya surprised me.

"I lost a sister a year ago," he said. The expression on his face did something to my heart, pulling at something within.

"She disappeared one day, vanished. No one ever saw her leave. She left no note, there was no phone call, nothing. We searched for her for weeks but nothing turned up. The hardest thing is not knowing how or why she disappeared or whether she's still alive. At least when someone dies it is final, but my family are left with always wondering what had happened to her."

"That's terrible."

He nodded, looking into his hands again.

"Were you close?"

"Yes, the whole family are tight. She was my big sister, always looking out for her kid brother, always at pains to teach me the subtle meanings of life. She helped raise me and when she vanished she left a huge hole in my life."

I nodded, understanding completely. When my father died, it had felt like a crater.

"So what sort of things did she do."

"She helped people. She was one of those people who would always be there when you needed them. She was good at beading. It's an American Indian craft. She made this bracelet," he held up his arm so that I could get a closer look. It was really beautiful, mostly turquoise with intricate diamond shapes woven in.

"My father felt her absence the most. He still calls the local police once a week for any news."

"That's awful."

"Yeah." Jaya looked up at me. "What about your father? How did he die?"

"Heart attack. It's a family trait on the male side."

"What was he like?"

I took a moment before answering. In truth it was hard to really remember. "I was ten when he died, my brother twelve. He was a very active man, always working, a keen cyclist and according to my mum really good looking." I smiled sadly. "It was tough when he went, it felt like someone had ripped my skin off. I can't really explain it but our lives were turned upside down. We muddled through, but none of us were the same afterwards. That's what grief does to you. My mum couldn't cope and became an alcoholic and my brother escaped as soon as he could."

"And you were left to deal with your Mom on your own."

"Yes."

"That's tough."

"Yes it was. It's why I had to leave home in the end, why I went traveling."

"Did your mum take out her grief on you?"

"It wasn't grief, it was the anger. She became bitter to everything in the end. Nothing made her happy. She turned inward and when she did surface it was only to criticize my brother and me."

"How did your brother take it?"

I thought back to how Harry had been after our father had died.

"It was pretty bad for him. He'd just begun to get to know our dad. They'd go off cycling for hours, spend time cleaning and repairing their bikes. When he died Harry was left without a role model or someone who he could really relate to. He and our mum clashed over just about everything, they didn't really get on much even before our dad died. My brother couldn't handle our mother giving up when she still had us to look after. So as soon as he was eighteen he left and moved into bed and breakfast accommodation. Supported himself with part time work to get himself through college."

Jaya nodded. "It's been tough."

"Yeah, you could say that," I said smiling weakly.

We stared at each other, a mutual understanding passing between us. Each recognising the others grief and suddenly there was nothing else to say. Sometimes, some things are beyond words and only silence is needed to fill the space. And so we sat, each separate in our thoughts and memories of another time, but somehow still together. The wall with which I'd managed to keep other people at bay was beginning to crumble and with only a few simple words, but nonetheless potent. Sharing our sad stories had made me feel less alone and somehow comforted. Here was someone who had suffered too, who knew how much it hurt. I looked at Jaya from under my lashes feeling something moving in my chest. Before I had known Jaya, I had been unemotional, dead inside, enabling me to safely navigate through life without falling into the snake pit of hurtful emotions. Now a whole wealth of different sensations moved through me. Strange all the more because I hardly knew what they meant. All I knew was that I felt Jaya's gravitational pull as keenly as a rock falling to the earth, but why? Especially when boys or men had never owned any part of me nor made any impression. Yet, there was something about Jaya I could not dismiss or ignore. Was it his looks, the smile, the body? Who knew? I certainly didn't. Yet, it was still unsettling for someone like me.

Layla had remained in the hut with me this morning, Jaya had gone to find food and the two of us were left alone together for the first time for a few days.

"So do the Sanuri people grow opium like the other hill tribes?" I asked.

"No, they don't use opium for medicinal purposes, they use other methods to heal," she said.

"I thought all hill tribes within the golden triangle sold opium to supplement their income."

"The Sanuri people don't have much contact with the outside world and they wish to keep it that way."

I remembered what Naomi had told me about the drugs trade before setting off on the trek. The opium business was considered very lucrative and the hill tribes competed with each other to produce the purist opium, because it yielded a greater price. Dealings with the drug barons could be very volatile and could quickly get out of hand. Killings were not unheard of and making such transactions were tricky and unpredictable. I wondered if this was one of the reasons why the Sanuri people desisted from any dealings with it.

Layla continued. "And the same goes for the Berel fruit. Hill Tribes use the Berel fruit like the West uses cigarettes. The Sanuri people consider the unnatural high to be unnecessary."

I had noticed the wide spread use of Berel fruit throughout the regions I'd travelled in Thailand but most notably in the northern territories. The red stained teeth and mouth easily denoting who partook in the habit. The berry was rested between upper and lower front teeth and sucked. The acidity slowly etching the enamel away and leaving a tell tale arch in a users front teeth.

"So what do you do back home, do you work?" I asked.

Layla smiled. "In someways you could call it work. My grandma teaches the art of bead work, a tribal tradition we're determined won't die out. So many old ways have been lost and we're trying hard to keep the ones we still have alive. I'm also involved in learning the history of our people. Not just about all the other Native American tribes who existed in America."

"Wow."

"It's a huge responsibility."

"Did your father mind you coming here?"

"No, he was the one who suggested I came."

"But how do you keep in contact with your parents? Surely they would want to know you're okay."

"They know I'm fine, we send word back to them every now and then."

I thought of Jaya and wondered if his frequent trips outside the valley were more than just to keep track of the mercenaries.

"What about you Alice? How have you found your time here so far?"

"Good. Interesting. Slow!"

Layla grinned. "Yeah, nothing gets done quickly around here, but you soon get used to it."

I already had, I thought. The thousand mile an hour life I lived back home in comparison to this, now seemed utterly ridiculous. Here the community prospered by helping each other and sharing difficult chores. Something which rarely translated into the Western world.

"Do you like it here?" I asked in return.

"Yes, but there's not much to do. I miss my family and friends, your arrival here has helped."

"I don't think I deserve that much credit."

Laya looked up and was about to say something but then we heard Jaya call up from beneath the hut.

"Time to exercise those lovely legs of yours Alice!"

I looked out of the open window to see Jaya with a small knapsack slung over his back beckoning me to come down.

"Layla do you want to come with us?" I asked, unsure if Jaya had already asked.

"No, I've got too many things to do, go and enjoy," she winked as I turned to go.

We headed away from the village, the path becoming narrower as we progressed and appeared to be hardly used. My leg, although much stronger still hampered me, but Jaya only slowed his pace to match mine unperturbed by my sluggish progress. Taking a sideways glance, I could see him walking happily beside me. Content to stroll in companionable silence with just a small smile set to his lips.

The flat path gently meandered under the trees.

Our foot steps quietly fell on the brown earth, the only sound in the heat of the day. Since yesterday, Jaya had re-plaited his hair with a different combination of colourful beads, reds, yellows and blues shone brightly against the dark glossy hair. Two thin plaits began either side of his parting and were pulled neatly behind his head to conjoin into one and here, secured with a hairband. The new look showed off his features in a different way and hard as it was I resolved not to stare at him.

We passed through a variety of different landscapes, sometimes rocks fringed the path, at others the vegetation became dense and impenetrable allowing us to only walk in single file. I drank in my surroundings, the vegetation so lush and ripe, the shafts of light slicing through the canopy and the heavy scent of the earth. It was beautiful.

Jaya ahead of me stopped abruptly.

"I hope hope you're not scared of spiders," he said looking at me.

"Why?"

"There's a massive one over there." He pointed towards an expanse of silk spanning at least a meter wide across the path. The leaves by which it was attached were enshrouded within a veil of fine gauze. An enormous spider sat within the centre, the intricate web's filaments fashioned in perfect symmetry. I recoiled involuntarily, spiders had never really scared me, until now. The proportions of this one were just like every other creepy crawly in this place, enormous, and I didn't like the look of it.

"Yeah it's best to keep away, this one eats small birds if it gets the chance and can give a nasty bite!"

"Of the feathered kind I gather?" I said making Jaya laugh, "It's big or is that normal for this country?"

"It's big."

"The web is enormous," I said.

"In someways it's like the web of life."

"The web of what?"

"The interconnected web or matrix we live in." He paused. "Indigenous tribes all over the world believe in a matrix of energy connecting each and every living thing. Some call it Divine Intelligence or Oneness, others call it God. It doesn't matter how we perceive it because we all live within this energy field. We're all connected in ways we can't even imagine."

"We were talking about a spider moments ago and now were discussing the workings of the Universe?"

"It seemed a good opportunity to slip it smoothly into the conversation!"

"Why?"

"This is was what the Elders wanted Layla and I to talk to you about."

"And a spiders web is going to explain it all?"

"Kind of."

"You brought me here just to explain to me about the Universe?"

"Life sucks doesn't it?" he grinned at my dubious expression.

Jaya continued warming to his task. "Everything is made up of energy. Everything. The soil, the leaves, the rain. Energy moves through all things. It is absorbed into and drives our bodies, connects us to the matrix and in return our thoughts and emotions influence the matrix. You remember how you felt in the cave?" Continued Jaya, even though he must have read the expression on my face. He stooped to pick up a small stone from the path rolling it around over his palm. "Energy is in a constant flux, it never stands still. It is like billions and billions of threads sewing us all together in an intricate design which is always changing. Like the spiders web for instance. Only it is a trillion trillion times bigger and in 3D!" He paused for effect. "Each thread is influenced by other threads around it and because of this they are always in a state of flux or growth, nothing ever stay's the same, it can't. Just like a guitar string can cause the strings next to it to vibrate, so do we. We are those threads or strings, as are all livings things." He swept a stray hair away from his face. "Think about when you are with a happy person, after a while you become happy. Spending time with someone who is depressed you soon become depressed. If someone becomes angry with you, you feel angry in return." He looked at me questioningly to see if I understood, but I'd already grasped the concept and nodded.

"If we have such power to influence the people around us doesn't it follow we have great influence over our environment and all things around us? Doesn't it mean we have the ability to also change the place in which we live? Our environment changes the way we feel and we change the environment with our thoughts and feelings too. Like happy people will make a happy home, depressed and sad people will create a sad and depressing atmosphere."

I thought of the house I called home back in England, the heavy smog like atmosphere which drained every shred of happiness as soon as you entered it and I knew Jaya spoke the truth.

We walked around the enormous spider's web and continued on the path.

"You said we influence our environment, do you mean everything?" I prompted.

"Yes, the earth is a living breathing organism and has it's own energy field. There are now instruments that can measure this energy and the changes in it. After 9/11, the collective human emotion of grief caused changes in the earths magnetic field. At first the scientists didn't know what to make of these changes and for a long time they couldn't believe it but soon came the realisation that emotions and thoughts are energy too and can influence, as I have said, everything around us. The huge out pouring of grief was collectively so powerful, it changed the earths magnetic field."

"How do you know all this."

"It is what has been known by indigenous tribes for centuries, science is just beginning to catch us up. Scientific organisations such as Nano technology are exploring these new concepts. Greg Braden, a renowned scientist and author also speaks of this phenomena. He talks about how feelings of gratitude, love and appreciation are generated within ourselves, and that heart based living can then affect the Earth's own magnetic energy field. Native people have known our emotions can affect the earth for millennia."

"Do you think we're killing the earth?"

"Yes. We've become like parasites but not ones that are beneficial to our host. We take without respect or gratitude, we infect without clearing up our mess."

We fell silent as we walked on. Jaya had opened up a whole new area to contemplate, and now a whole swath of thoughts swam inside my head as I tried to compute this new information. I knew all the arguments against polluting our environment, it was logical we should look after our planet. Yet, I had never considered how inextricably linked we were to each other. I'd never given any such notions a second thought. Each of us a thread in the woven fabric of life?

Did that mean I infected everyone around me with the darkness which lay inside?

*I hoped not.*

The path began to open out ahead as gaps in the trees indicated we were coming to a clearing. We entered a small, beautiful glade filled with long yellow grass swaying gently in the light movement of air. Haphazard butterflies fluttered above long stemmed flowers while the glade imparted an ambience of calm and stillness. A far cry from my heart doing its usual somersaults whenever Jaya came near. Knowing he was with Layla in someways had made it easier to be with him, because now, I no longer worried that anything could happen between us. Admiring him from afar was indulgent I knew, but I yielded to it nonetheless. Jaya was now unattainable and beyond reach, my imaginings just an illogical fantasy. Yet, this I reasoned, was what make believe was all about. To daydream about the impossible. A place I was all too familiar with, having frequently withdrawn to this location during my younger years.

We sat down, surrounded by the tall grass creating our own mini Universe within. I watched the small creatures crawling about their business. Their whole world contained within this small circle and now my whole world too.

Jaya lounged backwards resting on his elbows the taut muscles in his torso outlined against the golden brown skin. He never wore any clothing on his upper half except on the chilliest of mornings.

"You're wondering why I've brought you here?"

"Why have you brought me here?"

"To show you life.

"Life is everywhere."

"Yes, but out here you can feel it more easily and not be distracted," he said.

I looked at his handsomeness and knew this to be untrue.

"Look around you Alice and what do you see? Look at the life which surrounds us."

I looked around me taking in the trees and bushes, the frenetic quality to the insect life that buzzed around us. It all looked the same as it had yesterday and the day before.

"Keep looking," he encouraged.

At first I couldn't see it. I'd always appreciated a beautiful view or a pretty flower but I had always taken nature so much for granted. It was just that it was always there. Outside the window or wherever I looked, so much so I'd forgotten to really see it.

"What am I supposed to be looking at?" I said keeping my eyes carefully averted from Jaya.

"Life, look at the life."

I tried again and slowly I began to grasp the enormity the life on this planet, nature and all it contained. While we huddled in our warm dry houses, the animals, birds and insects were still here. This was where they lived, living out here in nature, rain or shine. The very nature we built our houses on, on which we drove our cars. Following its own innate cycle of life and rhythm, right before our very eyes and we hardly noticed. Only paying attention when the leaves had gone and the starkness of winter chilled our bones. Only then did we regret the warmth of the summer having passed. Noticing nature when we became inconvenienced by the rain or snow or the freak flooding rivers invading our homes or blocking our roads.

Killing a rabbit or bird while speeding in our cars, only then did we look up with regret. Only then taking notice of the tangle of blood and fur left behind on the tarmac, but never stopping, never thinking it was more than a little sad. No more than a small inconvenience to our journey and momentarily regretting our carelessness.

When had we forgotten to appreciate the others we shared this planet with, now rendered little more than a nuisance to our own existence? When had we forgotten and taken charge of our heritage which we now held within our reckless and uncaring hands? When had we become so selfish? We not only treated the Earth and animals with disrespect, we also treated each other like this. Our own kind, our brothers and sister's who walked the same path as we did and yet with them, we are the cruelest of all.

The wars, the revenge and jealousies overshadowing the goodness that lay hidden within our souls. Our lives too busy with things more important. Turning our backs on what we did to the world, how we vandalized and abused it. The damage always some other person's problem, not ours. Divorcing any personal involvement in looking after the very thing that gave us our sustenance, our way of life. We'd become too blinkered to anything else other than the pursuit of wealth, the fast car, the fancy house, the instant gratification of sex. Our voyeuristic world we now viewed through a television set or computer screen, severing our links to everything that was real. Our lives had become so far removed from nature we'd allowed mania to take over instead. So encumbered with stress and toil we had no room for anything else, and sadly this was what we believed to be our choice. That this was the way it was supposed to be.

How ignorant I'd been, only thinking of myself, and too wrapped up in my own life and my own problems to notice anything else beyond. Here I'd sat surrounded by the incredible diversity of life and I had hardly noticed, hardly been aware.

*Until now.*

Jaya was watching me with a softness in his eyes. How long had I drifted away on that thought train?

"Wow," I said.

"Yeah. Here, living so close to the earth makes you appreciate the rhythms and cycles, the Earth and everything in it."

"Why do we forget?"

"It's human ego, we think that by fighting our way to the top of the food chain we are above everything else. With the advances in science we can manipulate nature to the way we want it to be, play God with the genetic codes, mould the world into something for our own convenience. We must not forget our roots, the Divine aspect of ourselves and nature, the essence which threads it's way through all things. We are just another cog in the wheel creating the tapestry of life. Each creature and plant needing the other by which to survive, but somehow we think we have removed ourselves from this web. Have risen above our animal nature."

I thought about my mother's hate for wasps, seeing no point to their existence at all. Making jam jar traps in a bid to get rid of them or squashing them behind a newspaper against the window pain if they happened to get into the house. How in an attempt to remove the nuisance of scores of ant colonies building homes in our garden, she'd attempt to eradicate them by pouring boiling hot kettles over the nests, as if just washing away some troublesome dirt. It had made me sad watching her, even as a small child.

"How do you account for eating animals if you have to respect them," I said. "You can't have it both ways."

"The animals who live free in the jungle have a good life and we're always thankful to them for allowing them to be our food, we only take what we need. With modern farming practices the dignity of the animal has been taken away."

"This is getting depressing."

"It is depressing but it's important," he pressed on. "Factory farming, chickens kept in cramped cages too small to even stretch their wings, living their whole lives just to produce the egg to eat for your breakfast. A calf taken away from its mother just hours after giving birth, just so we can drink milk in our tea or coffee. The barbaric way we slaughter whales, the pregnant horses who are chained up for their entire lives to extract estrogen from their urine to make hormone replacement drugs. The bears in Russia milked for their bile, again for medicinal purposes to name but a few. We pump them full of growth hormones to shorten their growth time, antibiotics to protect them from the diseases they're prone to from being kept in confined spaces. The thousands which die needlessly every year in scientific experiments or for cosmetics companies, testing some new wonder product that will make us look ten years younger. These animals suffer and die all in the name of vanity. How is this respect for animal life? Animals have been side lined, become inconsequential, merely something that gives us food or to experiment on. The twenty first century, with all the advances and improvements to our world, you'd think we'd use this knowledge to treat animals better like we do ourselves. How has the technology benefited the animals in our care? We've simply used it to enslave them even more in an effort to cut costs in the quest for profit. We think ourselves superior in intelligence than to animals, but are we when we treat them like this? We believe they don't have the same complexity of emotions as we do, but ask anyone who has owned a pet and they will tell a different story. Animals have enriched our lives now and in the past, guide dogs, horses, cats. They teach us what it is to be loved unconditionally, loving and accepting us for who we are, not for what we're not. Animals and the environment suffer because of our ignorance, because we are only interested in money and now we have closed our hearts and minds to their suffering." He stopped suddenly catching himself after the tirade, a subject obviously close to his heart.

"It's the same for the environment. Thousands of species become extinct every year because their habitats are lost through deforestation. For housing, roads or for grazing, such is our thirst for eating meat. Perversely we infect the land and water, we need to eat and drink from. Causing the fish to mutate or die, contaminating the soil with insecticides and fertilizers. Fossil fuels polluting the air we breath, chemicals from factories, human waste pumped into the sea allowed to infect the earth with their toxic waste. The plundering of the earths resources, the dumping of radioactive waste, the untold damage we do to the delicate ecosystems. There are so many aspects to the destruction and we do nothing, thinking our planet is a never ending bountiful cache. Believing none of these things will cause any lasting harm. But the human race does not understand the naivety of treating our planet like this. We are all connected by the matrix, what we do to the earth and each other we do harm to ourselves. The closed mindedness of what is happening and the total absence of any thought or compassion bodes badly for the human race. What we have done in the last hundred years alone cannot be endured for much longer, something has to give. It's up to us, each individual to take care of the world. We cannot leave it all to the governments, not when they are lobbied by wealthy corporations and businesses to lever some influence in legislation beneficial to their own causes." He sat up no longer an image of calm.

"Individually we're so small and insignificant, how can we do anything?" I said.

"That's what everyone thinks but we can change things. Change happens by osmosis. When a critical mass reaches a certain point. When a certain number of people believe in the same thing and want the same thing, then we can demand change. Then change will be unstoppable," Jaya smiled that smile distracting me from my thoughts of doom and gloom.

"Enough of all that, come on, lets do something less heavy," he said, pulling me unsteadily to my feet. Balance was still a problem but Jaya only grinned widely as if this pleased him, encircling my waist with his hand.

He led me to the far end of the clearing, his hands softly burning me under his touch. I was all too aware of the bump and touch of his body as he fell in step beside me.

We reached a large dark pool hidden amongst the trees, fed by one of the numerous streams traversing the valley floor. Up ahead a thin waterfall fell from a jutting ledge, disturbing the otherwise tranquil atmosphere. Large brilliant blue dragonflies darted here and there stopping suddenly to hover just above the water's surface. Ferns hung waving in the light movement of air while the surrounding trees and bushes shielded the pool giving a sense of privacy and seclusion.

"Skinny dip?" he said looking down at me again with a teasing smile.

"You just want to see me naked!"

"Yes!" he said in mock seriousness before seeing my disquiet. "Just a swim Alice. If it makes you feel any better I'll keep well away!" he said turning round to allow me to undress.

"I'm not taking all my clothes off!"

"Coward!"

"Sex maniac."

"Namby-pamby."

"Shallow person with weird braided hair."

"Kinky."

"You said you wouldn't call me that anymore!"

"Yeah sorry, it's just your hair, I couldn't help it!"

I didn't bother to wait for his reply because I'd already undressed and had jumped into the cool refreshing water below me. Heading out into the middle of the pool I vigorously kicked my legs to reach the centre first, hearing behind me a satisfying splash as Jaya entered the water after me. A thrill of excitement ran through me as the cool water enlivened my body after the heat and humidity of the outside air. When I finally looked behind me the water was empty, not even a ripple or air bubble denoting where Jaya had gone. Suddenly I knew what was coming, but I screamed anyway as I felt him grab an ankle before surfacing inches in front of me grinning.

"I'll give you a five-second start.......one, two, three...."

"Hey......." But I decided to dive away anyway kicking as hard as I could. Swimming had never been my best sport but I could do a pretty decent crawl when I put my mind to it. I drilled through the water trying to put as much space between us as I could, my bad leg no longer a hinderance in the weightlessness of the water. Then I heard a shout as Jaya signalled he was after me. I drove my hands deeper, kicking harder and finally gasping for air, I made it to the waterfall first. Sliding behind the thin curtain of water in a poor attempt to hide, I giggled when Jaya joined me almost immediately. He pulled up beside me then wiped his hand backwards over his head to pull away the dripping strands. The already dark hair now jet black and stuck flat against his head.

"Not bad for an invalid!" he said laughing, blowing the last of the water from his nose.

"So, do you bring all the native girls here then?"

"Only the ones who I think will want to skinny dip!"

"They're a bit thin on the ground around here I should think."

"I'm working on it."

"A guy with your looks and charm......?"

He grinned. "You fell for it didn't you?"

"Did I?!"

"Anyway what's wrong with looking at a beautiful naked body?" he said and I suddenly thought how could I answer him when I found *him* so mesmerizing to stare at? That was different though, he was undeniably good looking.

"So are there many places like this around here?" I said changing the subject as smoothly as I could.

"Some, but not as beautiful and secluded like this," he looked away from me. "Over there you can sometimes see a troop of visiting Gibbons." He pointed. "It's very peaceful here. Sometimes when I let my mind drift away I can almost imagine I'm back home with my parents, back on the reservation."

"Do you miss home?"

"Only when I let myself think about it and I haven't had a Macdonalds for ten months!"

"I thought as much, the need to eat burgers is written in the American DNA!"

"Sure is!" He smiled reaching up to hold on to a rock beside him.

"You could change that, you could leave."

"We can't yet, not while the Sanuri people need us."

"Surely ten months is more than enough time to educate them about the dangers of the Western world?"

"It's not as simple as that, Layla had become more...... immersed in the place, she wants to stay longer."

"Why?"

"She feels she's helping these people."

A silence fell between us while Jaya studied my face in a way I'd never seen before. I was suddenly all too uncomfortably aware of his closeness and in the way he leaned in towards me. Somehow different from when he carried me all those moons ago. I liked it better when it was only *me* admiring from afar I thought, as I noticed a new light of something shining behind his eyes.

And suddenly he was so close, so very male and if I was really honest with myself........

*It scared the hell out of me.*

139

# Chapter 15

# Village Meeting

The next day a village meeting had been arranged. Word had taken a few days to reach the furthest settlements in the valley. The Elders considered it necessary to inform all the Sanuri people I had been invited to stay.

For my own safety.

Strangers here were treated with a mixture of suspicion if not aggression. To be known by the community would mean I could wander the village and surrounding area without any danger to myself and this I welcomed because I hated any form of scrutiny. *Although it came with the territory of having unusual hair.*

I followed Jaya and Layla as we walked to the communal seating area in the middle of the village to wait for the meeting to begin. I ambled behind them as they walked with their arms wrapped around each other and talking so only they could hear, verifying my suspicions. Jaya's hand caressed the small of Layla's back in small circles and she in turn responded by leaning into him. The looks and smiles between them confirmed to me the depth of their relationship. So why did I feel a disquiet about the way Jaya behaved in the pool yesterday?

I knew why. Attractive people had a tendency to play on the emotions of others, knowing their power and drawing you in. Jaya and Layla were no different. The perfect couple, beautiful, charming and here in Sanuri, like film stars on location. The undulating green of the jungle and the plainness of the other natives only serving to accentuate their glamour.

Lowering myself onto a log next to Layla I watched as people began to gather nearby in the early evening. Perhaps more than fifty people stood scattered around in various sized groups, talking, laughing, exchanging greetings with perhaps a relative or an old friend. Others glared in my direction with such intensity it made me shiver. I looked down at my hands instead. I did not want to appear too confident or bold. Humility would be the best course of action. I noted how my fingernails were still ragged in the absence of a nail file. My old nail scissors had survived the river, but had been too blunt to be of any use.

The Elders eventually arrived. Filing into the circle of logs, adjusting their shawls and jewelery as they sat glancing around the gathering briefly. My anticipation and nervousness began to spiral rapidly. Crowds always made me uncomfortable, especially when they were all staring at me. I felt Layla's hand grasp mine and suddenly I was grateful for her support. Somehow she understood my agitation.

Finally the meeting began. The Elders each spoke in turn, glancing around the gathering as they did so, there voices steady and confident. My fingers on my free hand found the beads on my dress to play with, distracting me from the intensity of stares. They were all looking at me now.

*Crap.*

They scrutinized my face, my hair, every part of me, my skin crawled under the onslaught. Occasionally someone would speak from the crowd, presumably to ask the Elders a question. Speaking fluently and with confidence, Jaya also took it in turns to address the crowd and I wondered if he was used to speaking in front of people. Finally he rose, beckoned for me to do the same and walked us into the centre of the gathering. Pulling me tightly into his side as his arm came to circle my waist. I understood it was a gesture to show the villagers that I was with him and I was nothing to fear. I leaned into the warmth of his side. Aware of the lovely woody scent and feeling the reverberation of his words through his body. Jaya turned us slowly to meet the gaze of the villagers while he spoke, and slowly their expressions began to change. The suspicion and dislike had begun to be replaced by curiosity and interest. Jaya looked towards the Elders who nodded at the unspoken question.

"Alice, there is just one thing the Elders ask of you to be fully accepted here," I looked at him puzzled. "They wish to see you."

"But they can already see me," I whispered back.

"No, they wish to see *you*, who you are inside. Show them they have nothing to fear."

"How can I do that?"

"Just let them look into your eyes," he gave me a quick squeeze when he saw my worried expression.

"It's okay, there's nothing to be afraid of," then he spoke even lower, so only I could hear. "I've already seen for myself, you have nothing inside they'd dislike," he smiled when he saw my look of disbelief before manoeuvering me to stand in front of him by grasping my shoulders.

"This is Alice," he said loudly from behind me. I nervously looked towards the villagers, seeing an expanse of brown faces staring back. Did they see a frightened gawky girl, the ugliness she felt inside? Did they see the horrors, the secrets I'd kept hidden for so long? Turning my face bravely to meet their stares, I pulled at the cloak of invisibility. The impenetrable wall which had served me so well in the past. I looked but didn't see, staring impassively, vacating my being. Floating away and curling within myself beyond the reach of their prying eyes. To hide and evade, to conceal this one last piece of me.

Their eyes fixed onto mine as they stared intently into me, their glares holding a different quality to earlier, one I could not quite make out.

Jaya turned me slowly for all to see. I tried to keep my eyes from lingering for too long. Trying not to see. I felt Jaya watching from behind, the Elders watching, the villagers staring and suddenly I felt too hot and dizzy as if being held under a spotlight. What did they see, what had they found? This time there were too many to hide from. The situation was slipping away from my control as if I was losing my balance. The strong persona and facade I maintained so vehemently was about to fall. The confident veneer I brandished so expertly was now revealing a hole. The villagers had found the place I had fought so hard to hide. Pulling it upwards, pulling it free. Suddenly I was spinning away from myself, careering through the memories. The terrifying, powerful emotions I wanted to hide from now tore through me unchecked, swamping and engulfing, like a blocked drain finally being cleared. The first sob escaped and then the tears finally came, but were no longer enough to clear all the hurts and heartaches of the past, the pain and the horrors which lay within.

*They were too late for that.*

Yet, still they came, like a thundering river of emotion, pouring from my heart and Soul. The locked away unbound memories finally tumbling from me. Everything became a blur as the memories unhinged all remaining self control. The villagers had found what they sought, the door to things too dark to reveal, even to myself. The brave face, the shop window was only a lie, now I was being shown who I really was. A person I hated above all else. A weak and pathetic coward, a human tarnished forever.

Suddenly I felt Jaya's arms close around me and pull me within the safe confines of his arms, rocking me as I continued to cry. The flood gates were well and truly open, raking through me so forcefully I gasped for breath between sobs. Leaving me helpless and weak in their wake.

This was how we stood as time passed unnoticed. Until finally the shaking began to subside and the sobs fell quietly away. Leaving the reopened scar inside me once more in need of healing. Under my cheek I could feel Jaya's chest wet and slippery, and I noticed for the first time how his hand stroked my hair. The protective way he held me as he cradled me in his arms.

Eventually, when I raised my face I saw we were standing alone under the dusky light. The last shades of daylight fading as darkness drew itself softly around us.

Jaya looked down at me with concern before raising a finger to wipe away the last of the tears.

"I'm sorry, I...." but before I could finish he interrupted.

"There is no need to apologise. Nothing to be sorry for," he looked at me in a way to give weight to his words. "Okay?"

I nodded and then looked away as the embarrassment replaced the tears.

"I think you could do with a coffee or something, come, we will go back to the hut," he lead me by the hand before replacing it with one circled around my waist. I was grateful he did not press me. The emotions were still too raw and close to the surface and I feared I would all too easily succumb to their power again.

We walked slowly back to the hut. I could feel the warm strong fingers through the thinness of my dress. What must he think? What must the villagers think? I was a flaky, an idiot and now whenever the villagers saw me they'd think of me as that poor emotional foreign girl, crying when ever they looked at me.

*I was an embarrassment to Jaya and myself.*

He sat me down in a place so that I could watch him make coffee over his little gas stove. Lighting a few candles to give some light as he did so. I was relieved to be in the relative comfort of my own space. Away from those prying eyes who'd extracted my secrets disconcertingly easily.

*When all this time I'd thought them safely hidden.*

I shivered at the memory. I had never thought my defence mechanisms could ever be breached and now suddenly I felt naked and vulnerable.

Jaya brought a steaming cup of hot black coffee and placed it in my grateful cupped hands before lowering himself beside me. Taking a side long glance over my face to check I was still holding it together. Probably regretting he'd ever brought me here now, I thought.

"There's a lot going on in there," he said eventually. Not as a question but a statement of fact.

I nodded, there was no point in denying it.

He looked at me carefully as if accessing me for the first time as I took a sip of my coffee. The warm familiar taste soothing my tight throat and allowing the lump to subside a little. I didn't dare look at him.

"I owe you an explanation.....after behaving like that." He waited as I fiddled with the cup, disgusted with myself all over again to allow this weakness to show.

"My life hasn't been all that easy. Everything inside is....... private. I've never wanted anyone to feel sorry for me or know.......and when all those people wanted to look.....and see......." I had to stop, the lump in my throat was back causing the words to get stuck. Jaya waited for me to continue but when the silence lengthened he spoke softly.

"If its's too painful you don't have to tell me," I sneaked a glance. The golden brown flecks in his eyes caught in the candle light and their softness of expression almost made me want to cry again. I'd found it was always harder to stay strong when shown any form of kindness.

"I......" the shaking had begun again and I had to swallow to gain control over my voice.

"You've been so incredibly kind to me Jaya, I really don't know why. Rescuing me from the river, helping me to get better, bringing me here," I continued to look down into my cup.

"Why? Why bother with someone like me?"

"You don't know?" I heard the surprise in his voice.

"No."

"Haven't you noticed anything Alice?" he said with a faint smile to his lips. "Haven't I given you more than enough hints!"

I looked up at him puzzled.

"I was waiting for you, waiting for a sign you liked me in that way too!" he said in sudden seriousness.

"But you and Layla?" I pressed, not really a question but one he answered anyway.

"Layla came with me from our reservation back in Montana, really just to keep me company. It's a long way from home and she felt I'd need her support and thank God she did, I would be lost without her here," he spoke with such affection in his voice as I became even more confused.

"Layla's so beautiful, smart and loving, how could you want anyone else?" I said before registering the look of shock pass over his face. Then he laughed, a deep belly laugh as his head rocking back on his shoulders and it was a few moments before he could answer.

"You think Layla and I are together, a couple?" he laughed again seeing my surprised expression. "Have you not guessed? Layla is my sister!"

Then the world stood still, motionless, no movement, not even a breath or a blink of my eye as the astonishing information reeled itself inward.

".....Your sister?"

He laughed again "Yes!"

My mouth hung open, they weren't together, they were brother and sister!

"You sleep in the same room," was all I could only say, as if this was a defense to my assumptions.

"Yes, because we wanted you to have some privacy, due to lack of it after I had found you. We wanted you to have some time on your own so you could make some adjustments to your life here."

Suddenly the absurdness of what I had assumed made me giggle and Jaya laughed with me too. Until the giggles turned to roars, clearing all last remnants of tension and sadness. Finally we stopped and smiled at each other.

"I can see how it must have looked to you, we're very close, she's a great girl my little sis."

"Yes, she is," she said remembering the saucy wink when I'd left for my walk with Jaya only yesterday. She must have perceived how Jaya felt, perhaps even knowing he'd make a move on me. Then I recalled how Jaya had leaned into me when we'd talked behind the water fall, the strange intense looks, the lingering hands on my body. He'd been giving me signals I'd not even really noticed while waiting for a sign from me. I pulled my hands over my face as if I could wipe away the embarrassment. Then I remembered, it could never work.

"Jaya look at me, my frizzy hair, the big nose, freckles, the ugly eczema!" I held my wrists up for him to see the evidence. Showing him all the unattractive parts of me.

"Alice I have seen nearly every part of you and it all looks perfect and beautiful to me!" I blushed at the thought. I looked into my cup.

I looked into my cup perplexed. "I'm bad news Jaya, believe me."

"Maybe, maybe not, but I'll be the judge of that. Alice look at me," he hooked a finger under my chin to turn my head towards him so that I could no longer avoid his eyes. The eyes which were melting me under their gaze.

"I've been fighting this too, but in the end I decided life isn't about standing in the side lines and wondering. It's about taking opportunities that shouldn't be missed. You've come into my life and I can't deny how I feel anymore. I've realised I would be a fool to do so. It's probably not the best timing in the world but what the hell, it's life."

"You've been fighting it?"

"Yeah. All the way."

"You still want this, even after what you saw..........?" I couldn't finish.

"Yes."

"Why?" I said in an attempt to delay. I had to find time to think.

Jaya smiled gently. "I thought you would know why." I shook my head hardly able to believe this new turn of events when only half an hour ago I'd dissolved into the most pathetic and stupidest of girls. Now with this man who I'd admired from afar, declaring his inner most feelings for me, I wondered how I would have the strength to resist him for much longer.

"You're strong and humble and you don't take anything for granted and look at you."

"What?" I said dumbly.

"Christ Alice! Haven't you ever had a boyfriend?" he voice broke through my thoughts.

"No, the boys back home are........well annoying."

"Could you perhaps think of a reason why they would want to be annoying?" he was smiling at me now, waiting for me to understand.

"Oh well, if I have to spell it out for you... Alice you're beautiful."

I stared at him perplexed, before looking dubiously down at myself, but it all looked just the same as the last time I'd looked. Was this beautiful? I couldn't doubt the sincerity in Jaya's eyes or his words but I'd never considered my unusual features to assemble into something beautiful. If this was beauty, it was only skin deep. Jaya couldn't possibly know the extent to what lay beneath the exterior.

*This mangled inside part or me.*

How could he possibly still want this if he knew? This ugly part had been left to fester for too long and I feared it was too late for me to change.

I could feel Jaya looking at me before he continued.

"Have I said something to upset you, is that why you won't look at me?"

What could I say to him? That there were things I could never talk about, never reveal to anyone? Suddenly I felt bad for him. I was making this really difficult for him and myself. I had to end it quickly. It would be best for both of us, before it was too late, the fantasy could never live up to real life. Yet, the words would not come.

"Is there someone else? Someone waiting for you back home?"

"No, there's never been anyone like that."

"Talk to me Alice, what's wrong?" he saw me hesitate and pressed on. "The other day, when I frightened you with my spear. When I looked into your eyes, I saw some of what you showed out there." He tossed his head in the direction of where the village meeting had been held.

"Oh."

"I know you've been hurt in some way, there was a darkness inside I couldn't make out," he saw my confusion, how could he know? As if he'd read my mind he carried on.

"The Sanuri people use a special technique to look into a person, to see what lies inside. It's served them well in being able to know who to avoid or who to fear. They've taught me a little of how to do this but I'm not as good as they are."

Thank God, I thought.

"Is it so terrible?" Jaya's eyes flickered over my face. "Wouldn't it be better to share it and let it out?"

"I don't know, why would you want to know anyway?"

"Because I can't bear too see you suffering Alice and I want to help you."

Silence, but only outwardly. My heart hammered in my chest while my panicky mind ran through the options.

"I've never told anyone.........about my past." I eventually said.

He waited.

"Don't you see, it's the past which has made me ..... what I've become," the words had come out in an almost desperate staccato.

"Are you afraid of what I'd think?"

I nodded feeling the fear bouncing in my stomach.

He looked me squarely in the eyes. "I'm not here to judge or criticize you. No one should have to suffer, especially not alone. I want to help you Alice if you would only let me." He took my hand while burning me with such a look of sincerity I felt myself wavering, but still I hurled more obstacles.

"Jaya look at you, you could have any woman you wanted, why waste your time on me?"

"I wouldn't be sitting here if I thought I was wasting my time and I don't want just anybody."

Silence sat between us, again. I was frightened to speak, to show my true feelings or let the buried agony be revealed. It was all I could do just to keep myself together under Jaya's melting gaze.

I felt a shift in Jaya before he broke the silence.

"You like me too don't you Alice?" he said quietly. "I know you do."

I cast my eyes away before they could tell him the truth, but it was too late.

"I see it in your eyes. So why can't you let me in?" he said so gently I felt myself shudder under the unrelenting onslaught of such kindness, but when eventually I managed to meet those beautiful soft brown eyes I could feel something changing inside me. Maybe there was hope. Maybe this person who had never given me any reason to doubt him, could help me.

Looking at Jaya now I was suddenly grateful that he cared so much. I wondered if I could climb over that final frontier and tell him my inner most fears. What if I did, what if I didn't? Either way I could be making the biggest mistake of my life. I couldn't know, having kept it so closely hidden, no one out side of family had ever known, making it difficult to gauge how he'd react. I had wanted this hideous event to be kept secret because of the shame cutting deep inside. Now, Jaya was offering me a choice when I'd never thought there to be one, but nonetheless it was still hard to make. Opportunities like this didn't happen everyday and I knew deep down I might never have this chance again. Not with someone like this.

I felt the familiar fear tighten in my stomach. It was always like this, the apprehension quashing any initiative, preventing me from taking a chance. Yet suddenly, I knew I couldn't keep living my life like this, fearing everything, keeping myself locked away. I had to try to get over it and maybe with Jaya's help there was finally hope.

I was frightened when I reached out to clasp Jaya's hand. Feeling the emotions threatening to overwhelm me again as they foamed underneath. The voice in my head telling me I shouldn't do it, I was stupid to even try.

But somehow I gathered myself together and hoped with all my heart, Jaya would still feel the same about me afterwards.

*When he knew.*

# Chapter 16

# The Shadows Come to Light

I looked at Jaya cautiously, not knowing how to begin or even if I could. All the layers I'd created to hold this tightly within were making me hesitate. The words just didn't want to come.

"What is it?" Jaya said trying to read my expression.

I stared at him unable to speak, rendered mute by all the years of suppression and fear. I fought for control and to conceal the quagmire of emotion threatening to bubble upwards.

I had to tell him, there was no doubt about it. Otherwise I doubted I would ever have this chance again, but trying to form the words would take more than just willpower.

*It would take all my courage too.*

"I have to tell you something." I managed eventually, looking down nervously at his hands. Wondering if in the space of the next twenty minutes it would all be over.

*Before it had even begun.*

Yet, something inside me wanted to try.

I looked into his eyes, studying the concerned expression spreading over Jaya's face, the candle light casting shadows over the planes of his face. His gaze held no judgement, only kindness and this gave me all the strength I needed when I took a deep breath and began.


The summer after I'd turned sixteen Harry had organised a holiday for some friends. The destination was Wales and I was surprised when he asked me whether I wanted to go too. Although I suspected it was more to do with the fact my best friend Georgia, now his girlfriend, was going as well. Despite my pessimistic concerns, any chance to spend time with my Harry I jumped at. Somehow always looking to heal the continent size gulf created in our childhood and maybe this was his way of mending it too.

The six of us stayed in a rustic cabin on the outskirts of town in a beautiful wooded campsite next to a fast tumbling, cascading river. I'd thought it to be tranquil and green, a haven from our other life.

Our mother although at first perturbed by our sudden desire to get away from the cramped and emotionally confined home, had eventually agreed. Probably more than a little relieved to have us absconding for half a dozen days. For now she could drink and smoke to her hearts content and without a disapproving audience.

Wales that week was sunny and hot, a miracle by any standards. We went to the beach, growing our golden brown tans daily, playing football and Frisbee and swimming in the murky freezing cold waters with the jelly fish. We visited Bangor castle and climbed Snowdonia, playing snooker in the pub of an evening and generally a very good time was had by all.

That was until the very last night of the holiday.

How do you explain one moment in time, one bad decision which acts as the pivotal point that changes the rest of your life forever? Sometimes your whole life comes down to such a moment. Its repercussions reaching far into your own life, not only your own turning point, but also for others who'd had to share it with you. That night was one such moment, as all good sense and instinct for caution had fled to happier hunting grounds as we strove to let our hair down and to enjoy the last night of the holiday.

When my innocence to the workings of the male mind and motivations caused me to make the most terrible decision of my life.

When a troubled past became wrenched into a future of crippling torments.

Even a small thorn can cause a festering wound, gnawing away at the healthy flesh until all that is left is putrid and rotten, but mine was not a wound that could be seen. It was hidden but nonetheless septic and I doubted if anything could ever heal what had happened to me. Because since that moment I'd become disfigured, in mind and in my body and now I wanted only to merge into the background, to be camouflaged. For here was the only place I felt safe, away from everyone and everything that could hurt me.

Afterwards, the only way to conserve the very thing that kept my heart beating, my body waking every morning was the knowledge I could survive, but in a different way from before. Knowing deep within I was now unlike other people, something had been changed forever. A large chunk of my Soul had been taken from me and what was left had become a mere shadow of what I'd been before. I'd been irreversibly altered and the only way to live from now on was to shut everything out, hide within the safe confines of my being and endure the pantomime of life, by simply existing.

We were in the bar at the campsite when a reasonably good looking man started to chat to me. Not a local I deduced from the subtle twang of his northern accent which accentuated his otherwise bland voice. I was flattered he'd taken any notice or bothered to talk to me at all. Men usually left me alone in the pubs back in Harpenden, but I'd always had a sneaking suspicion that my brother virulently warned his mates or anyone else for that matter, from chatting me up.

"Hi," the guy said. Now I saw his appraising stare, the once over sweep of my body, no doubt about it.

"Hi," I said in return, amused he wouldn't know he was hitting on a sixteen year old although I knew I looked a good few years older.

"What pretty blue eyes you have, dar'lin," he said in an attempt to flatter me. "Is that a ladder in your tights or is it the stairway to heaven?" he said in a well practised voice, grinning from ear to ear, and very well satisfied with his clever remark. I blushed, I wasn't used to such a lewd remark so early in the conversation or any conversation with an older man for that matter. I considered going to join my brother, to get away from this man. Sex was obviously not far from any braincells, or the other department for that matter, better to avoid him.

Turning to leave and picking up my depleted drink from the bar I made my escape.

"Hey love don't go, I was only joking. Here, let me buy you another drink, what'll it be?"

I hesitated just a second too long. Money was always a bit on the scarce side, my holiday funds were nearly at there end and wouldn't go as far as buying anymore rounds. I knew it was bad but the appeal of a free drink stalled my escape. I reasoned I didn't have to sit with him for the whole time. I could always excuse myself later after an acceptable amount of time.

"Yeah you can buy me a Bacardi and coke please."

Alcohol really wasn't a problem to me, I'd been drinking it in pubs for years and if I'd really wanted to get drunk I could easily syphon off my mothers stash of alcohol. But I didn't want to be like her, or use alcohol the way she did. Being around a drunk long enough had taught me there was nothing pretty about slurring your words, staggering into bed or not making it to the toilet in time. When most parents were probably watching their teenagers for any signs of smoking or the whiff of alcohol it was me watching my mother embarrass herself at every turn.

I sat back on the bar stool glancing down at my tights to see if there really was a ladder in them.

"So..... what brings you here?" he said.

"I'm here with some friends and family," I replied, being polite. "You?"

"Oh, I'm just down this way for some business, will be back home in a couple of days, just a flying visit. What's you're line of work?" He said leaning in towards me, glancing down at his drink, but I could have sworn he had tried to look down my top. I brushed the thought aside, pleased and flattered he thought me old enough to be working and decided to play along. I wasn't going to ever see him again was I?

"I work in one of those London banks," I quipped. "By the Justice Courts." Remembering where one of my friend's brothers worked up in town.

"Nice," he replied. "Pays well?"

"Well, I don't think you're ever paid enough are you?" I laughed in what I hoped was a sophisticated way, feeling quite grown up, having drinks bought for me and pretending I was much older than I was letting on. Although I'd never normally

choose to spend time in his company, I was getting caught up in
the play acting, it was fun for a moment or two.

"By the way my name's Jake," he held out his hand for me to
shake.

"Alice," I replied, placing my hand in his, surprised when
he raised my hand to his lips, but then I was only sixteen.
I wasn't used to this sort of attention.

"Pretty name, suits you," he said. "Did I tell you I'm in the
music business. Come down for a few meetings with EMI's top
nob's, staying in a really plush hotel down the road. Perhaps
you know it, called Spring Bank, really luxurious. Lot's of posh
furnishings and the most enormous king size bed I've ever slept in."

"Sorry, I'm not from around here."

"Where've they been hiding you then? Do you dance or sing?"

I shook my head.

"Pity."

"Do you....sing or anything?" I was curious now. Was he
famous?

"Na, I've just joined the company, just peddling paper work
and that sort of thing," he continued. "Just come down to talk
about some promo videos for the tour."

"What tour?"

He smiled. He'd slung the bait and I'd taken it. "Do you
know Usher? He's down here to do some kind of dance video."

"Usher is here, in Wales?" I could scarcely believe the American
was here, I'd always loved his R & B music and the fabulous dance
routines.

"Yeah, til the day after tomorrow," he looked at me." Do you
like his music?"

"Yeah, it's the best....." I stopped, suddenly wanting to get
back to Harry. "Anyway Jake, I have to go, thanks for the drink."
My drink was finished, there was no longer anything to keep me
sitting here. "I'd better get back," but before I could get away he
threw one last rope, one last lasso that reeled me in like pulling a
diamond ring through soft butter.

"I'm meeting up with Usher later, got some promotion stuff
to talk to him about. Fancy coming along? I could introduce

you........" he left the remark hanging waiting for me to take the lure, he didn't have to wait long.

"Usher?" I repeated to make sure.

"Yeah, he's in town, they're shooting the music video tomorrow. Not the one that goes with the album but the one for the tour," he added, seeing he had my full attention now.

I had to admit I was impressed. This guy looked the last sort of person to be in the music industry. His clothes were too straight, nothing fashionable or rock star about them at all. The parting in his hair, the slight sprout of nasal hair, nothing sharp or trendy about him that was for sure. Wasn't the industry supposed to be over run with people mimicking rock stars? The celebrity *look* rubbing off like grass stains on the wannabes.

"So, are you coming then?" he said pressing me, seeing his advantage, noting my interest.

Usher was only down the road, just a few miles from here I thought forgetting my misgivings! I refocused on Jake.

"I'll just go and tell my brother where I'm going, be back in a sec," no need to tell him I'd be asking for permission.

Finding my brother at the far end of the bar I could see he was already half cut. The three beers he'd already imbibed working their influence on the slightly glazed eyes and the too ready laugh.

"Harry, do you mind if I go out for while with Jake, he's in the music industry. I'll only be gone a couple of hours, just down the road," my mind quickly galloping ahead to the meeting with Usher. The girls at school would be so jealous! I quickly looked in my handbag to see if I had my phone, I wanted some photo evidence to take back with me. Harry turned to face me, the laughter dying from his lips as he peered at me through glassy eyes.

"Going? Going where?" he said, not yet drunk enough to be completely unable to understand.

"I've met this guy, he's going to take me to meet Usher, who's just a few miles away, he's their manager!" I added trying to add weight to the argument only the alcohol had already done most of the work for me. I didn't have to try too hard.

"Ppppppleeeaaaassse, oh Harry please, please, please," it worked, he nodded turning back to our friends, but I had already dashed back to Jake before he could change his mind.

We walked out into the cool fresh Welsh air and got into his rather old looking Vauxhall Omega. A bit battered for someone who must earn a pretty good wage I thought, but before my mind could dwell on such things I was already ahead of the game. Imagining what Usher would be like in the flesh. I saw it in my mind, Usher leaning into to kiss me on the cheek as I was introduced, or how I would sit in the back ground listening to their meeting or watch the rehearsals. My heart raced as I daydreamed of the evidence I'd capture on my phone to show to everyone back home, of being just a few feet away from Usher! Just as my mind began to focus on the world outside the window again, I noticed we'd slowed down and then stopped in a deserted pitch black field. Jake turned off the engine. Silence. He turned to me, a slightly rueful expression on his face.

"I thought we could just get to know each other first, you know, before introducing you cause I know I won't have a chance in hell once I've done that," he laughed nervously, playing the poor me gag.

"Have hard enough trouble getting any attention as it is," he muttered under his breath looking at me with a new manic expression on his face sending a deep chill of fear through me.

"Come over here then won't you? A bit closer so as I can see ya better," his hand reached out and yanked me over to his side of the car, no gentleness implied. He forced himself on me then, his lips sucking at mine as his hand groped painfully on my breast. I tried to wriggle free, batting and pushing him uselessly with my palms, but he was too strong and heavy. The awful truth of what lay in store for me surfaced, I'd fallen for his story and now I was alone without my brother to protect me and it was all my own stupid, stupid fault.

Finding his movements constricted by the confines of the car, he opened the car door and pulled me out with him. Fear began to quake through me, then the shaking began. I'd always thought I was a strong kind of person having lived with an alcoholic for all these years but now I was becoming a person I did not recognise.

Fear, fear, fear tore through me even as my mind frantically fought to plan an escape. Running would be impossible in these shoes and even if I found the time to get them off I did not think I would be any faster than a grown man.

I had to fight and get away. Somehow.

We wrestled with each other, he trying to force me to the ground while I kicked out at his groin and screamed as loudly as I could, but my knee had fallen someway short so instead I tried to pull free, trying to make my escape. Only somewhere deep inside, I already knew it was too late. I was merely prolonging the agony.

He grabbed hold of a handful of hair and roughly yanked my head, pulling me painfully backwards.

"If you scream again, I'll kill you," he growled. "There's a rock over there and I'll use it." The threat and tone in his voice and the vice like iron grip with which he held me meant I believed him. My stomach lurched with nausea at what lay before me.

"So shut the fuck up if you know what's good for you."

This person no longer belonged to a species I recognised, he'd become a creature of the most base of instincts. A monster not a man, predatory and vicious, taking no care not to hurt me.

And so there comes a moment when we divide into two types of people. The one that stands and fights, kicking and screaming until the last with every once of strength, or the other kind of person, as if caught like a frightened rabbit in a car's headlights, unable to move, unable to do anything other than watch the horror of the unfolding subsequent events that follow.

I fell into the latter, enduring the pain, the horror, the agony of such violence. The degrading performance I had to partake in for his own gratification. My body and mind shut down into survival mode, I lay still and retreated inside. A place I'd gone many a time to escape my mother. Only this time it was different. I screamed silently from every part of my being, I was being broken, torn apart and finally reduced to nothing.

*I was nothing.*

I was being defiled and shattered into little pieces in the most effective and brutal way possible. I was disintegrating, fragmenting, coming apart and I knew I would never be the same afterwards.

How could I be?

Something was being taken from me, my innocence and the true light of my Soul, reduced to a mere fraction of what once had been.

How stupid, how pathetic and cowardly I was, no wonder this had happened to me, this was only what I deserved.

Afterwards, as if guilty about what he had done, he dropped me back to the holiday village entrance before spinning away in his clapped out old Omega. I noted dully one of his rear view lights wasn't working properly. There'd never been any intention to meet Usher, it had all been a lie and I'd been dumb enough to believe it. Stupid, stupid, stupid. I looked down at myself seeing the drops falling from my eyes in the dim light. My long pencil skirt I'd made in needlework was ripped and stained and I had lost one of my shoes. There were bruises forming on my arms but that was nothing compared the pain coming from between my legs.

Trembling, I knocked on the locked door of the cabin. I didn't have a key, it was late and I'd been locked out. It was then I finally collapsed in a heap of chaos, the sobs erupting with such force I could not breath. The shaking so violent I slid to the ground when my legs finally gave way.

The aftermath of shock wound its way through me, snaking and sliding into every part of my being. I'd been changed, forever, and I wept for this lost part of me.

My brother, not knowing what else to do with me took me too the local hospital late that night. The staff informed the police immediately and without our knowledge. They were duty bound, it was standard procedure. Despite it all I did not want any fuss, or pity, because already the shame was too deep. I didn't even want the police involved, I was too humiliated and horrified at what had already happened. To have gone through this once was bad enough but to share my shame with others made it all a million times worse. Especially not my mother. She had so many other worries, I could not wave this in her face as well.

I wanted it all to go away, to forget as soon as possible. Not look at the faces of concern and pity.

Now it was all too late, never to be undone and never to be forgotten.

After the embarrassing police examination and the swabs taken, we were allowed to leave the hospital and leave for home. The police phoned ahead to our mother to tell her that her sixteen old daughter had been sexually assaulted.

*Oh, the shame I'd brought upon this family.*

For a time afterwards, it was as if my mother had had her sights reset, rising to the severity of the occasion. Lifting her out of the mental smog that mostly occupied her mind these days. Showering me with an almost embarrassing amount of compassion and love, all the more noticeable having been absent for so long. She stayed with me, making sure I wasn't alone, for this was when the horror and the nightmare memories would return. Between my mother, Harry and Georgia I struggled through the first few days with their help. All I did was cry or sit mute in front of the television. My mother said it was the shock coming out and not to worry, just go with it and let it all out, but I often wondered when it would ever stop.

Gradually life got back to normal, my mother told the police we would not be pressing charges. With no witnesses to cast the vote in my favor, it would be only my word against his. Not good enough to win a court case and my mother did not want me to go through the trauma of a court case so close to my A levels.

So I'd buried myself in homework and school, the friends from the pub never visited or called to discover the reason for my absence. Nor did my school acquaintances ever question why I never went bowling anymore. I retreated into my own small world, too afraid to spend too much time alone, yet too withdrawn to be able to make any sensible conversation either. Until the new term of sixth form started, heralding the end of the long hot summer and my days slipped back into a comforting routine. Lengthening the distance from the awfulness and horror of the rape that had devastated my already fragile and torn apart world.

I often wondered when I would ever get over this monstrous act, for it had cast a shadow over my soul, the light eclipsed by the repulsive feelings I had for myself. My stupidity at bringing this upon myself and everyone else who'd had to suffer with me. The guilt knowing how my brother Harry had felt so responsible for not protecting me, his anguish and distress of not stopping me leaving the pub and since that abhorrent night he'd barely touched any form of alcohol. The anger and disgust he felt for the person of the same gender lacking any moral fibre. How he'd wanted to lay into this monster and hit him where it hurt most. Then there was my mother. How she berated herself for what had happened to me. The empty shell she saw in those first few days after, the total chaos of the emotional heap of trauma that lay crying on her bed.

My best friend Georgia would come and visit and spend time just sitting by my bed holding my hand. Talking about what she had been doing as if I was a sick person laying in a hospital. While my mother would hover, glass in one hand, tranquilizers in the other looking anxiously for any sign of improvement. Now all they could do was to hold me in their arms. For there was nothing to say, nothing that could make the pain any better or to take it away, nothing that could change what had happened.

Time passed and the rawness of emotion gradually healed, pulling together, leaving an ugly scar inside me, one which doubted would ever allow me to live a normal life again. The traumatic events were too powerful to bury this time as I had done with my fathers death. The repercussions meant I would never entertain the idea of a boyfriend when all the girls at school had one following them about, doe eyed and puppy like on their heels. My being became distant from the world, hardly noticing the bustle of life around me, hearing the conversations, not really part of what was going on, but not absent either.

Then there were the rumours at school I was a lesbo, that I fancied women instead, but no one actually said it to my face. I only heard girls discussing it one day in the school corridors when they thought I was somewhere else. The knowledge that this was what people thought of me did not surprise me. I had shown no interest in the boys, merely enduring their presence with as much enthusiasm as a visit to the local museum. I never noticed the scrunched up balls of paper flicked at me behind the teacher's back, or reacted to the prod of a ruler. I merely continued to concentrate on the class in hand, absorbing myself to the extent that I did not have to think of anything else. I'd shut myself away to keep everyone out and to keep the pain inside. Safely away from the bullies, the criticisms and laughter, so no one would ever know that another large chunk of my soul had been chipped away forever.

This was when I finally began to hate myself, the ugliness I felt inside, nothing to what I'd felt when my father had died or the unbearable home life. Now the shame had triggered the guilt, the guilt triggering inadequacy in letting this happen to me and finally the self hatred and loathing at what I'd become had really taken hold, reducing me to feel worthless and valueless in every way. I had thought in time the wounds would heal, the fears and terrors, the hateful feelings I had for myself would recede in time. Now I felt the emotions as raw and real as they'd been those two years ago and I knew now nothing had changed.

My face felt wet. Large blobs of tears loomed in my line of vision as they still hung as if suspended by impossible glue to my eyelashes. Blinking, I watched them fall into a small dark patch in the lap of my dress creeping ever larger. I shuddered involuntarily, the memories were still so vivid from not so very long ago, the pain still cutting deep inside. Picking holes in the scar I'd thought to have healed. The buried emotions had remerged, lawlessly igniting the oil of my pain as they blazed searingly and out of control. Now there was nothing I could do to stop them.

I was too afraid to look at Jaya, too afraid at what he must think of me. This vandalized and disfigured person that sat before him.

*How could any man want this?*

I hung my head, the self loathing was back. I'd made a mistake. I should never have told him. What was I thinking? The silence told me everything.

Suddenly I felt his arms wrap around me, pulling me softly into his body, wrapping me into him. The light touch of his lips as he kissed the last remaining tears from my face became too much again as the sobs once again racked my body. The kindness I'd craved overwhelmed me, making it impossible to keep it all in anymore. He just held me, allowing me to cry myself out and it was enough that he did so for the luxury of being held within the circle of his arms was more than enough comfort. Gradually, as my breathing returned to normal and as I lay quietly in his arms, I noticed how the thin blue veins stood proud. Weaving an intricate pattern over the top of his hand. I took a finger and lightly traced their shape as they ran into his arm before disappearing beneath the lovely smooth honey brown skin, turning a deeper shade of gold in the muted light of the hut.

We lay like this for a long time, neither of us speaking, it was just enough to be held like this. Hearing the beat of his strong compassionate heart and feeling the safety within the circle of his embrace. Night had long since arrived, throwing the hut into a velvety darkness while the noises outside had dissipated a long while ago replaced by the reverberating hum of crickets.

"Let's get you to bed," Jaya murmured softly into my ear, pulling me to my feet while his arm circled my waist to steady me. Leading me to my room he lowered me gently down on to the thin mattress. Suddenly I felt exhausted, aware for the first time of the rawness of the day and suddenly I was afraid. Knowing the nightmares would return tonight having raked up memories of the past.

"Jaya....stay," I whispered half afraid he would make his escape, even now. Wanting so much to feel the closeness of a few moments ago, still feeling so vulnerable. I didn't have to wait for an answer before I felt the weight of his body sink into the bed next to mine before pulling me close into the warmth and safety of his arms once more.

As our breathing slowed into a steady rhythm I could only wonder at this man. His compassion he'd shown towards me, his desire to comfort me. There had been no judgements or repulsion, despite what he knew.

Inside, I felt my heart begin to edge open, wanting so much to trust in something, someone. To believe once again in the goodness of the human Soul. Everything I needed from now on was right here, right now, but still a nagging thought tapped away in my head. Not only a thought, but a knowing deep within. I'd learned the painful way in my short life, nothing could ever be relied upon. How could it be? When all that I had loved and depended upon had been taken from me.

Nothing ever lasted, nor would my time with Jaya. I could no more trust in him for fear he would also disappear from my life. I was in the jungle for Christ sakes. Jaya had never planned for me to remain here for very long anyway. This was just an interlude before I returned to my real life in England.

It was still just a fantasy.

Me and Jaya.

It could never work, not in a million years and I'd rather eat cold vomit than allow myself to be hurt again.

Yet, everything was different with Jaya. I'd never felt like this about anyone before. I didn't know whether to laugh or cry, such was the irony of the situation. What were the odds in finding such a person in a jungle miles from anywhere? When after all this time I'd just found what I'd been searching for and he'd look beyond the blemishes and want me still?

Suddenly I knew, I'd been kidding myself to believe there was hope. The odds of such a relationship surviving were next to nil because of the impossible juxtaposition of our cultures and homes. How could life be so cruel?

I knew why.

Despite all the wistful imaginings, I was better off on my own than to risk the disappointment and the wrench of separation.

*Because nothing ever lasted and forever was always a lie.*

# Chapter 17

# Alone

I slowly awoke to the sound of early morning bird calls. It was dawn, the rosy light filtered into the gloom of the hut but not enough to wake me fully. Contentment flooded through me as I remembered Jaya had stayed with me last night. Holding me close when the tears had revisited and the quagmire of emotions had still fought for control even while I'd slept.

When I next opened my eyes, emptiness gaped around me. The ruckle of bedcovers next to me the only evidence of Jaya having lain with me during the night. I strained for sounds of tea being made or for any familiar movements within the hut but there was nothing. Only silence filled the hut.

*Deafening silence.*

I wondered vaguely if Jaya sat out on the little balcony waiting for me to wake, but my mind was still too exhausted from the revelations of only a few hours ago for me to coherently wonder for long.

Time had moved on swiftly. The pinky soft light had been replaced by the hardness of a midday sun, slanting brilliantly through my small open window. The hot outside air now pervaded and warmed the chill of the hut where not so long ago I'd lain warm and snuggled within the circle of Jaya's arms. With difficulty I pulled myself fully awake, realising suddenly it was still much too quiet. Usually, at this time of the morning the sound of heavy steps on bare wood would normally be heard intermittently within the hut, or there'd be the sound of talking. Now there was nothing.

*Where was everyone?*

It was likely Layla had already left to do whatever she'd been working on these last few days with Chana, the young Elder. But Jaya? He never left the hut without saying goodbye. Even if he sat out on the balcony before I'd risen I'd usually hear the occasional call or greeting from the villagers as they passed beneath the hut.

I waited longer, feeling the growing heat already drawing a light sweat to my skin but inside a chill had begun to take hold. Jaya was no longer here. He had left me.

*Stealing away like this what did it mean?*

The notion stung me, but I tried to push the uneasiness away. It could not be possible, not after last night.

Not once had Jaya shown any sign of the repulsion I'd expected, even after I'd finished my hideous story. Now within the deafening silence of the hut, a creeping realization hit me. Perhaps Jaya really had gone because of what I'd revealed, or he'd gone because he'd realized his mistake. I was no longer someone to admire. Maybe he'd hidden his true feelings well. Maybe this was the reason he was no longer here.

The comprehension hit me with such force I doubled over on the bed. A hurricane of emotions swept through me, paralysing all other thoughts.

No! This could not be true, Jaya would never do that. Last night he'd told me of his feelings for me, how he wanted to help me. He would never have stayed with me if he'd been waiting to escape.

Then a new thought hit me.

*If he'd gone because of what I'd told him, what was I going to do if he did not come back?*

The day dragged itself into afternoon and a gnawing hunger turned to nausea. The sickness not only in my belly but also in my thoughts.

*But how could I blame him for leaving me?*

It had only been what I'd expected. I'd known all along what had happened to me had tarnished me forever and to have imagined anyone could overlook the damage was too much to expect. When I'd taken Jaya into my world, when I'd felt the first stirrings of any real emotion in my heart I'd known it to be a risk. At least I'd tried, at least this was not something else to blame myself for and regret for the rest of my life. I'd always known people could never be relied upon. That in the end they always let you down. I'd tried never to have any expectations in others for this very reason. For then, how could I ever be disappointed? Now

I only had myself to blame in hoping Jaya had been different from the rest. Life had never been fair or just and the scars inside me were simply too thick and ugly to love. The outside chance Jaya had been able to look past my defects now seemed such a distant hope. As if in what I'd once imagined, once hoped for, was now being stolen away.

Fighting back the panic I considered other options, other reasons why he was no longer here. I could think of none at all and the growing disquiet became a corkscrew of inner torment.

I should never have let him in. I should never have imagined him to be some sort of proverbial shining knight coming to my rescue. Men like that just didn't exist.

A deep loneliness swept through me. There was nothing in my life, nothing worth living for, I knew that for certain now.

My life was empty, hollow, worthless and it had taken Jaya to finally show me this glaring truth.

The tears prickled as the desolation racked through me. Hating myself all over again, loathing what I'd become. Self pity had never been a storyline I'd wanted to follow but now I wallowed in its embrace. Nobody wanted me, no one could really see me. Not the real person who lies underneath waiting to be discovered. The one obscured by all the crap.

This had never been the way I wanted to live. I'd come to this Godforsaken part of the world to unearth the real me. Find out who I really was, not to continue living in a virtual prison of my own fears and traumas. I'd been mistaken to think a new environment would dissolve these walls and now I realised I carried them inside. I couldn't escape who I was or what I'd become. Nothing would change what had happened to me.

*I was still the same as before.*

Only now I was lonelier and loathed myself even more. This gap year had been a dead end, there were no new inroads to finding the real me. Only reconfirming the well worn routes of feeling worthless in every way.

I rolled over burying my face into the bed covers. Feeling the wetness spreading slowly beneath me and the shaking that rocked the bed, never feeling so alone.

Eventually I wiped at my face angrily. I had to get a grip. I couldn't fall to pieces now. I had to find some thread of inner strength or my life would continue to be as intolerable as it was now. Whatever the reason Jaya had gone, I had to get on with life, even if I'd never know the reasons why he had done so. For how often do we have the luxury of knowing how we repelled people? My existence until now had never revolved around other people and now after this small blip it would return to the normality of my former life. I knew it would be all to easy to do so once I regained my self control. To feel nothing had been a well worn road over the years and soon it would be just as it had been before. Now I had to deal with the panic which bubbled cauldron like beneath the surface. The place where my fears and phobias had always lived. I tried not to listen to the nagging voice telling me I'd never been good enough for him anyway. Jaya had always been way up higher in any galaxy that I could hope to orbit. Why would he want someone like me anyway? Why had I ever thought he'd been within my reach?

Time dragged on and eventually I got up, more to distract myself than anything else. Dejectedly I made my way onto the small balcony to watch the slow motion life out here in the village. The pigs and chickens roaming freely beneath the huts, the villagers worked in small groups sharing their chores. The small children wearing only T-shirts to their waists, as brown as acorns playing in the dirt. Their naked little brown bottoms peaking beneath their shirts so cutely gorgeous for a moment I became engrossed enough in their game and I lost myself for a few moments. The scene was one and the same I'd watched every day here in Sanuri. Nothing ever changed here, nothing seemed different or out of the ordinary.

*Only I had been altered.*

Suddenly a distant movement caught my eye towards the far line of trees. I could just make out a brown figure running towards the village. Recognising almost immediately the distinctive racing gait as Jaya sprinted towards me as if every moment counted. My heart summersaulted in apprehension while my stomach recoiled inside me. Tightening into a knot when I saw the strained expression upon his face. He looked angry, his face dark and distorted reminding me of that other time when he'd threatened me with the spear. He bounded up the steps taking two at a time before stopping suddenly in front of me. His chest heaving, the beads of sweat on his skin glistening in the bright sunlight. I noticed the fast beat in his neck, the jaw muscles clenching as he stood looking down at me, as the strength of emotion pulsed through him. Even in anger he was captivating to look at. So much so I involuntarily stepped backwards too afraid to hear those words I knew he was about to say.

"Alice I have to go, to leave now," he said in a breathless voice. "I'm sorry."

Yes! Of course he would not want to spend any more time here with me than he had to. Leaving immediately would be best for both of us. A clean cut would hurt the least and heal the quickest. He moved quickly past me, disappeared into the back room he had shared with Layla. Appearing minutes later with a rucksack slung over one arm and various other implements he had carried with him on hunting trips. The spear and hunting knife tucked into the leather strap hung diagonally from his shoulder. The water pouch at his hip.

He was leaving, that much was clear.

He'd gathered all his belongings and was not intending to return.

My heart died then, as the last thread of hope shriveled to nothing. He was going, really going and not even an explanation or reason to give me. Knowing I would have to live with my foolishness all over again.

He turned to me finally, the agitation and impatience to leave written all over him. Looking down at me briefly, looking into me for one last time. The words he could not say blazing in his eyes.

"I have to go Alice. I must go. I'm so sorry...." He trailed off, his eyes had become dark and distant and a new hardness had formed over his features.

I nodded mutely unable to speak, fighting back the urge to cry, pushing the tears away until he'd left. Suddenly he was gone, leaping away down the steps and running back towards the direction he'd come without even a backward glance.

*Putting as much distance between us as he possibly could.*

I sat back numbly hardly believing this fresh twist which now stabbed deeper and sharper than anything else. My mind grasped at what had just happened. When I'd still clung to some distant belief I'd been wrong. I'd been too dazzled by his false compassion, the kindness and consoling words.

Stupid! Stupid! Stupid!

I sat dazed, not noticing the flow of life continuing around me. Pulling at the numbness to reinstate itself, the feelings to harden. Until finally, I twisted myself back inside. Curling myself away deeper than before. From the remembrance, the love lost and then eventually away from myself.

Time had sneaked past me unnoticed and with a rush I realised the lateness of the hour. As if waking from a bad dream I sat in an exhausted stupor and slowly began to face my options. Clearly I was no longer wanted here and surely the only decent thing would be for me to leave and find my own way back to Chang Mai. Jaya would not want the burden or the reminder of me if I remained here. It would be best to go for everyone's sake and to leave now. I was now an unwanted guest having long over stayed my welcome and it was time to go.

I reasoned the journey to Sanuri could not be that hard to retrace. The only hurdle I could foresee would be the exit from the caves. I remembered a labyrinth of passageways through which Jaya had expertly navigated.

Would I be able to do the same?

Once I'd left the cave, would I know which direction to take? Of course, every milestone had been noted in conjunction with my study of Jaya. The boulder on which he sat and braided his hair, the paths over which he carried me, the trees under which we rested and all the while the feel of his hands on my body. Each had irrevocably burned an image I now wanted to forget. Every landmark holding painful memories. Memories I could no longer take pleasure in like I had done before.

Once I'd found my way back to the waterfallI the path would be a well worn tourist track and would lead me back to where the trek had first entered the jungle. If I was lucky, I might find a new trekking group.

Feeling stronger by the impetus of having made a plan, I set about packing the few things I still owned into my rucksack. I took off Layla's dress and laid it neatly on her bed. Redressing in my clean but faded shorts and T-shirt. Lastly I grabbed some dried food and a few other edible items to put in my rucksack for later.

I looked around the confines of the hut one last time before stepping down the stairs as relief flooded through me. Soon this whole place would be out of sight as well as out of mind.

*I had made sure of that.*

I headed out of the village and towards the caves ignoring a nagging feeling of doubt to the hastiness of my actions. I pushed it aside, Jaya had made it clear he was leaving. He had not wanted me with him and he'd removed all his belongings from the hut. I knew he wasn't going to return.

The heat from the day was still stifling, hot jutting rocks fringing the path still shimmered and glared with white intensity. I wiped my brow, the anticipation of leaving had propelled my hasty walk up the narrow path drawing the sweat faster and more heavily than usual.

I reached the entrance of the cave as the sun began to slip behind the trees, knowing I did not have long before the light finally faded. Perhaps I should wait until dawn. No, I wanted to leave the valley tonight. Somehow it felt important to do so.

*To sever all links to what had been there. To put a barrier between myself and Jaya.*

The damp cool cave air hit me almost at once. Compared to the hairdryer heat from outside, the coolness brought a welcome relief to my scorched, sweaty skin. Navigating my way into the cave's recesses, the array of different tunnels brought a fresh bout of panic. Exploring each one would take time I did not have and I didn't want to get caught in the pitch black when the light finally faded. Eventually, after following several dead ends I found my way into the interior of the huge cave. The large round hole in the roof still brightly lit the gloomy interior just as it had the last time I'd been here. Only now the light slanting down to the cave floor was golden and cast a luminous glow throughout the chamber. The memory of the odd sensations of my last visit brought an involuntarily shiver over my body and pulled a profusion of goosebumps to the surface. The cavern once full of a strange electric presence now only seemed hollow and empty.

*Like I did inside.*

Perhaps it needed Jaya's presence to jump start this place to life. Like he's done once with my heart. Well, that was never going to happen again.

Not after this.

I systematically began to search the contours of the cave for any sign of an exit. The cave was larger than I'd thought at first. The shadows hiding many nooks and crannies. I moved on to the smaller cave, probing every section with increasing frustration as I reached each dead end. Light was fading, as was my hope, all available options diminished with each exasperating moment. Finally, I arrived at the last section of the cave, spotting a thin gap I'd missed at first. A vent, just large enough for me to squeeze through had been hidden behind a jutting rock. Cautiously I edged my head through the opening. I could feel a faint movement of air, this must definitely lead somewhere I thought. Hesitantly at first, stooping low, I crept forwards into the blackness. My footsteps echoing in the small space drawing a claustrophobia I had not felt since leaving the little house back home. The tunnel was pitch black, only the fading glow of the cave behind me lit my way. I was deep within the belly of the mountain. I tried not to allow myself to imagine the millions of tons of rock which lay over my head. I could easily die here and no one would ever know.

I was only alive because of Jaya.

*But inside I was dead.*

Eventually a faint glimmer of light glowed up ahead drawing me onward until I came to the exit cave and beyond the dimming world outside. It seemed as if I'd entered a whole new world. A brilliant red and gold sunset lit the magnificent panorama stretching as far as the eye could see. It was beautiful, too beautiful. A pang of fresh regret dragged through me. Wishing suddenly I'd never survived the river, never been found by Jaya, never known to hope for anything more than the monotony of only existing.

*And now it was too late.*

My heart would always remember the spirit keeper's love I'd felt in these caves, an emotion I'd long since forgotten. Buried with all the other debris of my life as I would also bury the memory of Jaya. My love for Jaya had been ignited by the spark of hope. Hope I could be loved after all. Hope that despite who I was and what I'd become I was worthy of another's affection. Now all those aspirations lay in tatters around me.

*Fool. To have believed I could be anything more than this.*

A staircase honed from rock lay before me, stretching away upwards presumably to the ledge where Jaya pointed out Thailand's geography. Climbing upwards, I took one last glimpse back towards the direction of the caves. Knowing I would never see this place again, nor did I want to. All my hopes had been erased in this blighted paradise, leaving me hollow and spent. I had tried, I had bared my Soul and revealed my inner wounds and afflictions. Serving only to repel and repulse Jaya's good opinion.

With every fibre of my being, I vowed to erase every memory of Jaya and Sanuri's secret valley from my heart and Soul forever.

Because if I didn't, I knew I could no longer live by only existing.

I would no longer be able to live at all.

# Chapter 18

# The Drug Runners

Early the next morning I left the little camp I'd made the previous night when it become too dark to walk any further. I'd made steady progress through the jungle since leaving Sanuri. The sun arcing through the sky became my only indication of the time of day. Not that it mattered that much to me, the numbness inside had taken the place of even caring.

Besides, my journey could not be measured by time, or distance, only by the duration it took to forget. The beat of my feet on the track knew how the fragments of my heart lay unhealed and festering. Each step like healing balm, helping to freeze out the old ache of loss.

I stopped whenever I could to refill my water container in streams and to bathe my hot grimy feet in the cool waters. I calculated roughly, the journey would take me around five or six days. Jaya had carried me for roughly that time scale, but that was if I didn't get lost in the meantime.

The need to be vigilant for the sight and sound of the drug runners worried me. The rape had left me cautious when traveling alone. Back home, I'd always made sure I carried a sharp nail file at all times. Now I had nothing with which to protect myself apart from a stubby, blunt pair of scissors. No more use than a wet paper bag on a windy day. The violent men Jaya had talked about would stop at nothing to guard their interests or their territory.

I tried to recall how Jaya had taken steps to conceal our journey to Sanuri. Remembering how he'd watched for a broken twig or an imprint in the track. I stopped to pull some twine from a nearby tree and tied back my hair. Keeping to walking on the grass beside the sand and shingle path wherever I could. It would be impossible to completely avoid leaving a trail, but all the same I might as well try to avoid doing so.

I recognised plants from which Jaya had torn leaves to eat, following suit by breaking bunches of foliage further back from the path to put in my bag to eat later. Since leaving the village I'd hardly been hungry, but I knew the lack of food would be a problem over the next few days. I had to stay strong if I was ever getting out of here alive. I chewed some tasteless leaves, hunger would be my constant companion over the following days, but I didn't mind because it provided a means by which to deflect my thinking away from other, more hideous thoughts.

Night time came quickly once the sun had dropped behind the mountains, the jungle became quiet as if in hushed anticipation of the night to come. The dampness of the air and the chill descended with the dwindling light. Biting coldly at my skin until I eventually fell into an exhausted sleep.

I woke to see the rose coloured sunrise beginning to lighten the dark end of the sky, midnight blue drifting into turquoise then gold. Thin clouds strung lazily across the sky, serving to catch the majestic rays.

Taking a swig of water and brushing the last remaining leaves and wood mulch from my clothes, I retraced my steps to the path. Glad of the light blanket which I clasped tightly about my shoulders in the chilly air. I hurried to keep warm, watching the vapor spew from my mouth with each breath, stealing into my hair and catching like jewels in the rebellious curls now coming adrift away from Layla's loving attentions.

I concentrated on my feet. The mornings were always the hardest when trying to forget the past. Preventing painful memories had become a daily struggle over the years and now was no exception. I focused on each footstep, the rhythm helping to steady my mind and thoughts. A welcome relief from thinking or feeling. It was the way I wanted to be from now on.

The morning passed into the afternoon until my newly healed leg began to ache along the scar tissue, still unused to any excessive form of exercise. Under Jaya's attentive doctoring the scar had knitted together well. A red weal of skin was now the only evidence that remained, but still it troubled me at times. With regret I knew it would be impossible not to remember Jaya everytime I noticed the scar. Yet, some things are not so easy to erase. Like the feel of his gentle fingers brushing my skin, or the way he had held me in his arms.

Night time came and went much the same as before, only tonight it was much colder. The chill seeping into my bones and inner core, allowing me to sleep only fitfully for short stretches of time. Eventually, I gave up just as the dawn began to creep slowly over the sky. Gathering my few belongings, I returned to the path. My mind felt stale and weary and my body badly needed a bath but these were minor afflictions compared to what lay inside.

Yeah, I thought, this is about as good as life gets, being numb, feeling emotionally dead. The trick was not to dwell on the crap because then it only got worse. Shoving painful emotions away had always been easier than confronting them, and lets face it, there wouldn't be anything more in my life to feel excited about. Not after this. It would be pale in comparison, grey when there'd been colour, starvation after the nourishment. Now there was nothing, void, only emptiness within. Nonetheless, I feared this wound to be one that would never heal completely. Spiking my consciousness whenever I least expected. I had to be careful with my thoughts because they never had any care for my feelings, roaming my mind at unexpected moments if I did not prevent them.

Suddenly, through the air I smelt the distinctive aroma of burning wood smoke. I stopped abruptly to locate from which direction it had come while my heart picking up a notch in my chest.

*Up ahead and slightly to my left.*

I strained to catch any movement or sound as I glanced quickly around me.

*Had I been seen?*

All the same I took several swift strides to step off the path to conceal myself behind some thick foliage. This was what I'd feared. Other people crossing my path before I reached home and safety.

Crap. What was I going to do now? Should I move towards the smell of smoke? Could it be other natives or the drug lords? Either way I knew it would be better to avoid them. Then

I remembered something Jaya had said. 'It was always better to know where your enemy lay as a point of reference from which to orientate.' With a sinking feeling I knew he was right. I had to find out who was responsible for the smoke, their exact location and then give them a wide berth.

Hesitantly I moved forwards, deciding to approach well away from the path. The uneven ground strewn with rocks and fallen branches impeded my progress significantly, taking me far longer than I would have liked to locate their exact position. The woody scent gradually grew stronger, I must be almost upon them I thought, then moments later I picked out the sound of voices from up ahead. The last few meters I moved slowly, edging forward in a commando crawl and coming to a ledge overlooking a small camp. Two men dressed in western clothes were drinking from steaming cups in front of a fire. Their faces concealed beneath baseball caps, giving me no clue to a rough country of origin. Were these the drug lords? One man prodded the logs, sending sparks flying, igniting the flames to blaze more powerfully against the dull light.

I scanned the camp quickly for others. As if on cue another emerged from behind the trees, wiping his hands on his trousers. Then another to my left, replying to one of the men who sat beside the fire. I took in the rucksacks made from camouflage fabric, bed rolls sat neatly beside them, a pile of wood stacked near to the fire. Obviously they were planning to stay for a while. I watched the activity or lack of it for some minutes. The men looked powerfully built and well organised. If these were the men Jaya had feared I should leave now and get away from here as fast as possible, but then the sound of a scuffle reached me from behind the trees. Someone was groaning in such a way an involuntary shiver ran down my spine. A very bad feeling was forming in the pit of my stomach, because now I had spotted the guns. Rifles and other firearms I could not identify sat next to the individual bed rolls, boxes of ammunition lay nearby. Every instinct told me to run and as fast as I could, but the sudden jagged movements behind the bushes caught my attention. A struggling man was pulled into view. The bruises had formed darkly beneath his golden brown skin. The long braided hair now hung in disarray, tangled, undone and once his crowning glory. I watched in horror when I saw the ugly bloody wound at his temple, seeing him suffering under their cruel and brutish hands. For it was Jaya who they dragged towards the fire. Jaya who only two days ago I'd thought I'd crashed and burned, now being punched and kicked to kneel in front of the men beside the fire.

I tried to ignore the way my heart kicked off as a full spectrum of emotions swept through me in rapid succession, horror, shock, fear, relief, joy, guilt, anger, worry.

Jaya had been captured after ten months of evading these men.

The men he feared.

What had he been doing in this part of the jungle and why so far from Sanuri?

He had wanted to leave Sanuri quickly, of that much I was certain, but now I doubted those reasons had anything to do with me. The comforting thought suffused through me. I would cling to that, for now.

Another man came to stand beside the others, smoking, dressed in combat trousers and bomber jacket. Yet, this one wore no baseball cap and I could clearly make out his features. The shock of recognition hit me like a juggernaut deep in my stomach.

Chana!

His appearance was a far cry from the humble native garb he wore in Sanuri.

My mind fumbled with the information. Jaya captured, Chana here, staring at Jaya as though he'd found dog shit on his shoe. He crossed the distance between them to loom over Jaya.

"Ah, Jaya, what a surprise this is."

I recoiled at the sound of his voice now heavily laden with an American accent.

Jaya merely ignored him and continued to stare at the ground.

"I can assume then, that you've been spying on me?" Chana said staring steadily at Jaya. "Of course, it was only natural considering how protective you are of your lovely sister. I bet you hated me stealing her away from you all the time," Chana said and then he added. "She was very willing."

Jaya looked up with anger in his eyes.

"So are you going to tell me why you're following me?" Chana waited expectantly, but when none was forthcoming he continued. "Tell me?" he said almost pleasantly. "Who's your contact?" Chana spoke almost gently but I could hear the underlying edge in his voice.

"Who the fuck sent you?" Chana said menacingly, causing my hand to involuntarily cover my mouth.

Still no answer. Chana's jaw began to chew in frustration as he seemed to consider his next move. I didn't have to wait long before he suddenly slapped Jaya hard across the face. Such was the force he almost toppled over, reeling like a wooden top.

"And what about that other bitch you brought back to Sanuri? How's she involved?"

"She has nothing to do with this," Jaya answered gruffly.

"Yeah, and where is she now huh? She's no longer in Sanuri. How did you get word back to her so quickly? Shame, I was looking forward to seeing more of that one."

Jaya remained silent but I could see the news interested him.

"Am I going to have to use force to get you to talk?"

One of the men stepped forward and yanked Jaya's head backwards and suddenly a knife was flashing at his throat.

"Just a word from me and he'll kill you, and what use will you be to your sister if you're dead?" he said smiling. "Of course, maybe I could get her to talk once I've woken her up."

"Don't touch her," Jaya said horsely.

"Oh but I will, and I'm really going to enjoy that part, believe me."

"Please, don't touch her."

"Then talk. Cooperate."

"Then you'll kill me," Jaya stated matter of factly with no hint of emotion.

"That depends on you and Layla. I need information. I made very sure to keep myself under the radar, but that was before you and your sister came along. Starting to ask questions, snooping around, making life difficult for me. Everything was running smoothly and for such a long time too. Maybe I got a little complacent, made a few mistakes. It's unlikely of course. I'm very careful. That's why they employ me. It's the attention to detail they like." Chana stared intently at Jaya. He nodded at the man holding the knife. I watched in horror as a trickle of blood ran down Jaya's neck.

"TELL ME," he shouted, his face contorting with rage while the cords in his neck bulged clearly visible.

Jaya coughed and spluttered. I could hardly bring myself to watch while Jaya's life was being held by a thread.

Finally he spoke. "My sister," he choked. "She worked as a contractor for the CIA."

"Layla?" Chana spoke as if he was surprised.

"No, Kara."

Chana regarded Jaya with a look of astonishment for a few moments and motioned for the knife to be released form Jaya's neck.

"Kara?" He said slowly as if he couldn't believe what Jaya had said.

"Yes."

"Go on."

"I don't know any details," Jaya said defiantly.

Chana suddenly looked bemused. "You don't really love your sister, do you?" he bent his head very close to Jaya. "I've never screwed information out of a woman before but there's always a first time. There's a number of others here who'd really enjoy helping me with the task. Should take a hell of a long time."

Jaya's head snapped up, a look of pure hatred forming over his features.

"Oh of course, where are my manners? You'd like to watch too. That can easily be arranged."

Chana fixed Jaya with a vindictive stare.

"Bastard."

Chana just smiled, enjoying Jaya's torment.

"I've been called far worse," he said dismissively.

Suddenly Jaya's whole body seemed to deflate, as if all the stuffing had been taken out. The angle of his jaw, the droop of his shoulders told me he could fight no longer.

"So, lets get back to the question. How did you find me?" Chana said, looking expectantly at Jaya. There could be no more pretence from Jaya, not if he wanted to save Layla from a hideous fate.

"There's not much. Kara came to me scared. She'd uncovered something at the CIA, a huge conspiracy and with it a name. That was all. She seemed really frightened but wouldn't tell me anymore. She said it would endanger me too. Then a few days later she disappeared."

"And? What then?"

"The police dug nothing up. So I started looking into the name she'd given me. Started asking around. As luck would have it I discovered some information that lead me to Sanuri after attending the tribal convention a year ago. Fortunately for you haven't changed your code name, Chana. That was a huge, fucked up, monumental mistake," Jaya said triumphantly. Chana glared at Jaya. "The Sanuri Elders invited me here when they discovered what I was searching for. A motive for my sister's disappearance and the name Chana roused their suspicions. For a long time they'd been troubled by your behaviour. Disappearing for long periods of time, smoking western cigarettes, not acting as they'd expect a Shaman to behave."

Chana turned away. "So why did they let me stay?"

"How best to watch your enemy than to keep him close to you? We've been watching you for a long time but never had a link, although we had a good idea what you were up to."

"Yeah, and what was that?"

"The drugs trade. Layla took her chances to follow you when I was otherwise distracted. I'd told her not to do that on her own." Jaya said shaking his head.

"Yeah, I've already discovered your sister has trouble doing as she's told," said Chana nodding conversationally in agreement. "So, you travel half way across the world to find me, then what?" He almost smiled but the line his mouth turned into was more of a grimace. "The trail ends here, you're wasting your time."

"I want to know what happened to my sister."

"Oh, so demanding and in no position to bargain for anything," Chana mused. "Do you think I care a fuck what happened to your sister? That's the least of my concerns. Just consider she's probably dead. Right now I'm only interested in who else knows about this." Chana seemed to be talking more to himself than Jaya. "What else do you know? What else aren't you telling me?"

Jaya remained silent.

"Oh don't hold out on me now, there has to be more. You wouldn't be here otherwise. Your sister disappeared, you found a code name, you want to know how it all links, join all the dots."

"Yes," said Jaya simply.

"And why the fuck should I tell you."

Jaya remained quiet.

Chana stared at him for a long time. "Tell me the rest of your story."

Jaya looked up this time before speaking. "You're operating in the Golden Triangle, only second in size to Afghanistan's opium production. It wasn't hard to figure out what you were doing or why you're here. You're camouflaged living with the Sanuri people. As a Shaman you can move about this region as you please without drawing attention to yourself. No one would guess you're responsible for the exportation of millions of dollars of drugs out of Thailand back to the USA. That this whole operation is orchestrated by the CIA. Because that's who you really work for isn't it? You're a federal agent, working for the American government. Making money out of these people who are so poor they cannot afford to grow anything else," Jaya shook with anger.

Chana regarded Jaya thoughtfully for a moment before turning and addressing one of the men, but I could not catch what he said. The other man left.

"Why not? America is almost bankrupt, why not make money out of a commodity that people want and bolster the economy at the same time? Would you deny people drugs that offer pain relief at an affordable price? Do you think you are doing the hillside villagers any favours by exposing us? This is what they want. To make money and earn a crust for their families, to put food on the table. I am only the middle man, putting together the two interested parties for mutual benefit. It's a win win situation and there is nothing you or anyone else can do about it because now it is part and parcel to the very way of life here. America supports these villagers by buying their valuable commodity, doing far more for these people than the entire Thai government and red cross charities put together. Who do you think these Thai people trust and turn to when the chips are down, huh?"

"What about the drug addicts? Opium based drugs are the largest growing substance abuse in the US and abroad. What about the pain and suffering these people go through, how it ruins their lives, wastes their bodies?"

"No one cares about them."

"No? My sister did. Alcohol and drug abuse are well worn roads in Native American communities. It's an easy way to forget how society treats us like second class citizens. Our values clash constantly with the American ways, causing low self esteem and that's just a small pocket of society. What about the other poor bastards who can't cope with life, who turn to drugs as a way of escaping?"

Chana waved his hand dismissively. "Drugs are a way of life, the whole fucking society uses them"

"It doesn't have to be like that."

"Yeah well, unless you're Jesus Christ, how the fuck are *you* going to help anyone?" he stared hard at Jaya then began smiling. "Haven't you worked it out yet? What this is really all about?"

Jaya shook his head.

"I guess it's not as obvious as I thought. This cheap opium is headed to one of the richest industries of the world and they're in the business of making money. Governments need power to control the masses, religion doesn't work any more as a means to control but drugs do. They dumb people down, stop them thinking too much. Helps governments keep control. Governments don't want any smart ass people questioning their every move, delving into their secrets, resisting new laws. No, and what better method to keep the balance of power in their favour than by dishing out drugs like dolly mixtures. Oh and if you think it's for our own good, the vaccines, the statins, then think again. Drugs aren't about curing anything anymore, they're about managing disease. They're not interested in making you better. Where's the profit in that for the pharmaceutical industry and their share holders? Governments and pharmaceutical companies, it's a marriage made in heaven."

"I don't believe you," Jaya muttered.

"You don't have to, it's already happening. They just want to keep you only mildly comatosed because then it won't affect the GDP."

"That's sick, I won't believe the American Government would do such a thing."

"Don't you? It's not just America. It's happening all over the world in developed countries. Countries where so many people have climbed out of the poverty trap they can start asking uncomfortable questions."

"And you're supporting all of it?"

"Doing this gives me a choice. Money talks," Chana looked at Jaya intently. "I've had to climb over a lot of people to make this kind of money and I'm not going to give it up without a fucking fight. Anyway, it's far easier than trying to earn a crust like the Sanuri Neanderthal natives hunting and gathering. We're living in the twenty-first century for Christ sakes and that neatly brings me to my next question."

Jaya looked puzzled.

"I need the code." Chana said.

"The code?"

"All this time living in Sanuri, I could hardly not find out. The Sanuri people's dirty little secret. What they've been trying to hide all this time. The real reason why they dislike having contact with the outside world."

Jaya remained silent, but the news seemed to trouble him.

"You are right. I was just keeping a low profile in Sanuri in the disguise of a Shaman. They bought that one didn't they? Fucking low life I had to put up with. Then it got really interesting, beyond my wildest dreams. I often wondered why the people in Sanuri never touched the medicinal benefits of opium. Why they always seemed so sickeningly healthy. But they use a different kind of medicine, don't they? They use a Stone Circle to heal themselves with. If I hadn't seen it for my own eyes I would never have believed it was fucking possible. Always thought that mumbo jumbo stuff was a load of rubbish. All those Jesus sandal wearing brigade, worshipping in Stonehenge on the summer solstice for fuck sakes. Seems they were doing something right for a change. Although the Elders never told me the code. I thought I still had time to figure it out, but that was until you came along. Seems there's far more to this place than I could ever have imagined. Just think how this Stone Circle and it's code are going to interest the pharmaceutical companies. Bet they won't want it left standing for long once they know."

"What makes you think Layla or I know the code?"

"'Cos I've seen the way those Elders regard you like you're bosom buddies. They don't fucking treat me like that."

I'm not surprised I thought.

Just then a movement caught my attention, from behind the bushes Layla was carried into view.

"Ah, here she is," Chana said in a voice that made my skin crawl.

Layla looked terrible. She hung from the men's arms as they dragged her towards Chana. Her head rolled on her shoulders. Her beautiful glossy dark hair now knotted and tangled and there was a large blood stain on her dress at the waistline. My heart contracted in horror. Was she dead? Then I heard a low moan escape from her lips.

"She's waking up, what fortunate timing," Chana murmured.

For the first time Jaya looked frightened. His expression became pinched, the worry lines creasing his forehead.

"Get some water," Chana instructed.

One of the men left, returning with a container of water. Without ceremony he threw it over her head. The effect was instantaneous. Layla's head jerked up, her soft brown eyes flung wide open in shock and suddenly looking too large for her face.

Chana walked forward. "Ah, glad to see you awake, you've been out cold for too long. I was getting a little worried."

"Leave her out of this," Jaya said gruffly.

"Ah, but I can't. She knows the Sanuri secret. She might know how to invoke the healing power within the Stone Circle and I have to have that information. I can't leave without it. Maybe the Stone Circle could be put to other uses, the mind boggles at the possibilities," he turned to stare at Layla.

Layla's head rolled on her shoulders, another low moan escaping from her lips. I wondered how long she'd been like this and then it all slotted into place. Layla hadn't returned to the hut that fateful night I'd bared my Soul to Jaya. Jaya having risen before I'd woken only to discover the hut empty of Layla's presence. Leaving quickly to search for her before returning to the hut to gather his belongings and prepare for a more extensive hunt. Two days she'd been gone, two days she'd been held by these men and now Jaya had been captured too.

The men who supported Layla in their arms stared at her in a way that made my heart skip a beat. There eyes were all over her with lewd intensity. I felt the all too familiar fear creeping into my bones and stomach.

"Layla?" Chana crooned. "Wake up my dear."

Layla raised her head a fraction, but the effort was too great.

"Fucking wake up," Chana shouted, roughly grabbing her chin to lift her face, beat. Their eyes only rolled in their sockets, her mouth slack and devoid of any expression. Chana turned away in frustration.

"Take her away," he said angrily before swinging to face Jaya.

"Tomorrow, if she doesn't tell me what I need to know, then you're both fucked."

He grabbed Jaya's arm and yanked him upright, pushing him beyond where my eyes could follow.

# Chapter 19

# Old Fears

I didn't even remember moving but suddenly I was sitting against a fallen tree trunk well away from the ledge. My heart thumping in my chest, feeling sick. The images I had just seen still playing over in my mind, the revelations crashing over me like a wave. Layla and Jaya both captured by Chana and his men. Chana disguised as a Shaman really worked for the CIA smuggling drugs back to the US with the full knowledge of the American government. The CIA was the government. Chana who wanted a code for a stone circle I had never seen or let alone even heard about. A stone circle which healed people.

Bloody hell.

Jaya had never told me anything of what I now knew. I'd believed his cover story in helping to educate the Sanuri people in Western ways to help protect themselves from the greed which consumed the West. In reality I realised, it was they who were helping him.

Everything was upside down, inside out. I couldn't formulate this new information into a coherent train of thought. The scale of corruption Chana had indicated left me breathless with its audacity. The implications almost unimaginable. That was hardly my concern right now. Not when Jaya and Layla were in the utmost of trouble.

More to the point what was I going to do? I couldn't go back to Chang Mia now. Couldn't ignore what my heart was telling me, couldn't leave Jaya and Layla to their fate.

*Couldn't, shouldn't, wouldn't.*

Yet, I was here on my own, with no weapons, no phone, no back up. Nothing of any use to counter five powerful trained professionals, with guns.

Panic pulsed through me, the fear rooted me to the spot, but I could not stay here, I had to move somewhere safer and try to make a plan.

Ha, a plan!

What plan could ever resolve this situation? It was an impossible task. Lille o'l me against all of those fit, 200lb professionals with guns. My heart sank, what was I going to do?

I crept away, heart pounding, finding some dense foliage within a bushy tree in which to hide. I pulled a shaky hand over my face as if this could wipe away the crazy spiraling fear which spun through me. The fear I knew so well, paralyzed every muscle, every coherent thought, rendering me mute and useless. What chance did I have of any rescue attempt feeling like this?

The men would be guarding Layla and Jaya 24/7 and would probably periodically make surveillance sweeps around the surrounding area. Was I far enough away? Was this a safe enough place to hide?

Yes, I thought so.

What if I returned to Sanuri to get help? That would take too long, a day and a half each way at least and Jaya and Layla would surely be dead by that time. And anyway, I knew Jaya would never have involved the Sanuri people in his own affairs for fear of endangering them too. For they had already told him of Chana coming to live amongst them and generously allowed him and his sister to stay with them. From the moment I had first met Jaya, he had vehemently protected them against any perceived danger, and particularly from me.

I wondered if Jaya and Layla were up to making an escape? They hadn't looked good. Layla's wound at her waist had looked serious. The extensive blood loss soaking into a sizable portion of her dress. Jaya's injuries had appeared more superficial. That was good. I couldn't drag both of them out of camp. Again the fear knotted in my stomach, my hands shook.

*Focus.*

I had to get a grip or I would never be able to do this. Yet every fibre of my being wanted to run, and get as far away as possible.

I tapped my head with the palm of my hand, think, think, think.

My only chance would be to make my move under the cover of darkness, yet now it was still only early morning. I had roughly eighteen hours to kill.

I looked about me, remembering Jaya's spear when he'd threatened me. Spotting some suitable trees I dug out my blunted scissors from my rucksack and hacked down two branches a meter and half long. Taking them back to my hiding place I began stripping the wood back to make a sharp point.

I hoped I would not have to use them.

Time dragged, I managed to pass some of the interlude by fitfully sleeping but never too deep for the nightmares to surface, I could not afford to make any noise. When afternoon eventually slowly slid into evening I decided it was time to change my position and watch the routine of the camp before dark. I needed to know where they held Layla and Jaya before I made my move.

I needed every advantage possible.

I ventured bravely forward, creeping low, stopping every few paces to stop and listen. My heart thudded too loudly, my breath coming in shallow bursts but I could not worry about hyperventilating now. I had to focus. I circled to the left of the camp in the direction I'd seen Jaya being dragged. Concentrating on every step, using every nerve, every fibre to sense ahead of me, beneath and around me.

Reaching an advantageous view point east of my original position, I spotted Jaya tied to a tree, but with no sign of Layla. His hands were pulled behind him and secured with thick rope. He leaned against the trunk with his eyes closed. The dried trickle of blood now lay dark and crustily against his cheek. Even from this distance I could see bruises formed under the golden brown skin, leaving a patchwork of dappled shadows interspersed with cuts and grazes. I felt my heart contract to see him in such a way. The dejected angle of his body and the hopelessness of the situation made me despair again how I was ever going to do this.

*Was there any point in even trying?*

Because in all likelihood I'd be captured too.

I watched the routine of the camp thoughtfully. Trying to work out a pattern to their movements, a chink in their armour. Something small enough with which to give me a chance. By twilight I knew the drill, the shift in patterns and when they took it in turns to pee. I knew where they stood guarding Jaya and from which angle I should approach the camp that night. I would only have one opportunity and if luck was on my side, I might even stand a chance.

The waiting stretched like eternity. Time dragging onward in the uncomfortable sweaty heat of the dying day. With each long hour my apprehension grew until it consumed me in gigantic proportions. The weight of what I had to do hanging heavily upon me. Would I freeze again as I had before? Would the fear be too much for me to think or act coherently? Now facing this new and frightening challenge I felt the debilitating weakness seep though my body and knew this was going to be one of the hardest things I'd ever had to do.

Making myself walk into danger.

*Because usually, I always ran away.*

I dragged my thoughts away from that dead-end train of thought.

In the past I had known enormous fear, a fear most people would never have to face in their own life time. The dark memory of it now, bubbled up like hot plumes of scalding hot air. I felt my mouth twist in self disgust. For Christ sakes grow a back bone I thought. Nothing had even happened yet.

What was the point in getting all panicky now?

I shoved the painful memories away and pulled another from the recesses of my mind. Thinking back to my childhood and my brother Harry. Harry who'd always appeared confident in every way except on Halloween when the fear of witches drove him into my bed at night. Landing a welcome punch or pinch just to tell me no teasing or telling allowed in the morning. At the time I laughed to myself at the absurdity of his fears, but that was before I'd known how fear eats away at you. Paralysing every genuine meaningful response that could save you. From the inside out, like swallowing a crocodile that tries to claw it's way out. Telling myself these fears were stupid and unfounded had never taken them away. Fears are not influenced by logic alone, in fact our brains are wired to fear. The proverbial flight fight mechanism designed to help us survive in dangerous situations. Yet, to counter such an ingrained subconscious behaviour needed far more weighty leverage to annul.

Leverage I was still unable to find.

It seemed strange looking back, remembering the different person I'd been before all the darkness had been infused into my soul. Fearlessly riding ponies a million miles an hour over Kingsbourne Green common or fighting with the annoying boys at school. Somewhere along the line I'd lost my way. Learning the world was a cruel and dangerous place, never to be trusted and everything in it was to be feared.

My deepest fears I'd hidden from, because they'd been too mountainous to climb, too astronomical to dare orbit and I knew even with just one glimpse they'd have the power to overwhelm me again. So I'd kept them safely padlocked away but still they came from nowhere, a void deep inside, a place I could never locate and thereby lock away. Yet, anyway, somehow, someway, I had to find those nerves of steel again because if I didn't..........

Suddenly I remembered something I'd read in school. We'd been studying the Second World War in History when I came across a passage quoting an army General.

'Courage is not a lack of fear, but an ability to face it.'

Did I have the courage to face mine?

The intense, lustful way those men had looked at Layla had rekindled the old terror. Let out all those monsters l had tried to forget.

I knew what I was about to face would take more than just willpower.

It would take every ounce of courage too.

Ha, courage. When had I ever owned 'that' in any great quantity?

# Chapter 20

# Rescue

Night time had long since arrived, covering the world in it's velvety blackness while the cold air bit at my skin. I hardly noticed. I was too tightly wound, too frantic with the adrenaline pumping scalding hot energy though my veins. My thoughts swung in circles, going over and over each detail until I felt my brain begin to ache. I felt like a rabbit on speed. Wired so high I jumped nervously at every sound or movement of the jungle, poised to run like hell if need be. I must not be discovered, must not make any foolish mistakes. I was Jaya and Layla's only hope.

I had to focus.

Taking a quick swig of water to try and calm my nerves and swinging my rucksack over my shoulder I began to move towards where I guessed to be the best position for me to wait. Close enough to be able to make a quick entrance into the camp, far enough away to remain safely hidden. The early hours of the morning would be my best chance to make my move. When the men would be in their deepest sleep. When they'd least be expecting any rescue attempt.

I crept slowly forwards. Jaw clenched, nerves jangled, muscles tightly sprung, every instinct telling me to run, run, run, to get away from this place while I still had the chance. Even though it was hours before I'd make my final move, I knew these debilitating afflictions would only get worse.

I stopped and waited every few seconds listening, looking, trying to keep my breathing steady and deep, my limbs from shaking. No, not possible, my body had other ideas. A remembrance of another terrible time, one which now flooded my mind with its horror. With effort, I pulled my mind back to the present.

Thankfully only a thin finger nail moon became visible just above the trees. A full bright moon would never have afforded me any possible advantage. The stars had begun to appear one by one, lighting up the dark end of the indigo sky. The golden glow of the sun now long since disappeared behind a distant hill. I watched this small reminder of the day slipping softly away. Until finally, the sky became solid darkness and the full cathedral effect of night diamonds shone clear and brightly against the velvety back drop. Darkness now enveloped the trees and foliage, engulfing everything within its gloom. Blotting out all the landmarks and any distinctive features by which I'd normally be guided. The growing blackness bringing with it a deeper dread. I shivered, pulling my arms around my body in a feeble attempt to hug comfort into myself. How I ached for Jaya. He would know exactly what to do. When to act. Say the right words to calm me.

How quick I had been to judge, how contemptible to have thought in such a fashion. I, of all people I who knew what it was to be criticized and judged unjustly. I, who knew the petty and narrowness of people's opinions.

And I had done just the same as them.

I did not deserve Jaya's good opinion or regard. I'd never been a worthy companion. When Jaya had travelled half way across the world to discover the reason for his sisters disappearance. When he raced to rescue Layla, saved me from dying by the riverside, he had shown his natural fortitude of spirit. His true worth as a human being. All I had done was run away, from home and all my problems.

How could I match such a man?

I couldn't. It was as simple as that, but I was sure as hell was going to try. Tonight I would finally show my metal, what I was truly made of.

Yet that was what I was really afraid of.

Yes, I was older and more mature than before but the violent ghosts of the past still haunted me on a regular basis, despite my carefully construed coping mechanisms. The very reasons why my hands now shook, my heart pounded, the moisture in my mouth had evaporated.

Facing fears was never going to be easy and I prayed I would be able to face mine.

When it most counted.

Because if I couldn't ........I felt the wetness on my face, the tears cold on my cheeks and wished for the first time ever, I was back in the safety of home with my mother.

*Because in comparison to this, she'd be a pussycat to deal with.*

The fire in the camp below still burned vigorously under the avid attentions of the two men huddling close to it's warmth in the descending chill of the air. Their faces illuminated by the flickering orange light silhouetted against the darkness. Until eventually, even these men retired to their beds. I'd noted their positions in the camp. Two slept by the fire, one near Jaya and no doubt Chana would not be very far from Layla.

How long should I wait? How would I know the best time to make my move? I knew my chances depended on the movements of one lone guard patrolling the area. Appearing at regular intervals after circumnavigating the camp. How far into the jungle he ventured I could not be sure, but he disappeared for at least five minutes at a time. This would be my only window of opportunity, my only chance, and within the next half hour I would determine all our fates.

I waited for the guard, there he was, melting out of the shadows, appearing again beside the fire to warm his hands. Then glancing about the camp with a bored expression before returning into the blackness.

All that lay between Jaya and me was a short expanse of open ground, football pitch size in proportion to my panicky eyes. First I would have to scramble down a short ledge. No sweat, that would be the easy part. It was the swath of open tundra that troubled me. Even in the dark I would be visible, the light from the fire carrying it's glow far into the night.

I waited for the return of the guard, then I would make my move. I grasped the small nail scissors from my rucksack in one hand, the roughly hewn spear in the other and groped my way down the steep ledge. Creeping low I scuttled across the turf. Fifty yards, forty, thirty, twenty and then I was pulling and tugging franticly at the tightly knotted ropes that clasped Jaya's hands and feet. Jaya moaned slightly, I cupped my hand over his mouth, willing him not to make a sound. Jaya raised his head fixing glassy unseeing eyes onto my face. Until his eyes locked onto mine, the shock of recognition registering quickly. He glanced down at my panic stricken arms tugging frantically behind him. With alarm, I realised the bindings were too tight to be undone quickly in the absence of light. I could not see how the ropes were knotted, I would have to use my blunted scissors.

Crap.

I hacked frantically at the threads holding the rope in one hand. It was taking too long. I glanced fearfully around me. No sign of the guard. Yet. That didn't mean anything, he could appear in seconds. I motioned to Jaya to hold the scissors while I slid into the shadows to wait.

Just in time.

The guard appeared almost instantly, staring hard at Jaya and then towards where I presumed Layla must lay. I noticed Jaya's hands continued to make minute movements before the guard eventually moved away.

Within seconds I was at Jaya's side, tugging, cutting, sawing. Each second felt like eternity, every moment filled with dread. Until suddenly, Jaya was free. How long had it taken? How long before the guard came back? I returned to the shadows too wait for the guards return. We wouldn't have time to rescue Layla as well in such a short time.

The guard appeared shortly and then finally left.

I scuttled back to where Jaya lay, pulling him hastily to his feet. A disquiet befalling me when I watched him sway unsteadily on his feet like a drunkard. Fear swept through me when I considered he might not be able to walk out of here. Jaya leant heavily on me for support, taking a moment to gain control over his beaten body.

Time we did not have.

Amongst the chaos of my mind I was struck by the reversal of roles. Now it was me Jaya needed, me who was saving his life.

Get a grip, I told myself, we still had to get ourselves out of here.

"Layla,: he croaked horsely, nodding in the direction I presumed she lay.

My eyes followed his gaze, just making out a motionless figure lying in the shadows. A quick glance around us told me the men were sleeping, we still hadn't been discovered. When I kneeled by Layla's side I feared she was dead. Until I saw the rapid fall and rise of her chest, the slightly dewy sheen to her skin. She was in poor condition and only a thin blanket protected her from the chilly air. Not nearly enough to keep her warm.

I suddenly felt Jaya stiffen beside me.

"Move!" Jaya whispered urgently into my ear.

We almost fell into a nearby bush just large enough to conceal our bodies when the guard reappeared. That was quicker than the last circuit, I thought. Supposing he notices the empty space where Jaya had lain? Because if he did.........I closed my eyes. I could no longer watch as the terror swept through me, we waited in agony. I jumped when I felt Jaya's hand on my arm.

"He's gone," he whispered. "Let's go."

By some miracle the guard had not noticed Jaya's absence, but I was in little doubt he would next time.

We were back beside Layla's side in seconds, both of us now panicky in our movements. The ropes binding Layla were easier, but still unravelled as if in slow motion. Jaya tried to scoop Layla up into his arms but was too weak, the beatings having taken their toll on those strong arms I'd known so well. Between us we pulled Layla's limp body onto my back piggy back style. From behind, Jaya pushing her against me to prevent her falling backwards. Clasping her legs tightly against me we shuffled into the welcoming shadows.

"This way," Jaya said pointing away to my left.

"We're not going to head for Sanuri?" I whispered.

"That's the direction they'll look for us first when they've found we've gone," he voice rasped. "We head towards the river."

"And then where?"

"Sanuri."

"But you've just said......."

Jaya cut me off." It's Layla's only chance."

Then I remembered. "The Stone Circle?"

"Yeah," he gasped, already out of breath.

"Christ," I muttered under my breath. Jaya was putting all his hopes in the powers of a stone age monolithic stone circle. As primitive as you could get.

Before tonight, I had never given a second thought to the remains of the Neolithic stone circles littered about the English countryside. I still wasn't prepared to believe something as prehistoric could miraculously save a persons life or even heal. Surely if they had such amazing healing powers we would never have forgotten their reason for existing.

Yet Jaya did believe and was prepared to head back to Sanuri instead of the nearest large town but what other option did we have? We were miles from anywhere, perhaps getting to Sanuri was our only hope.

We did not have much time to save Layla because now her skin burned hotly under my hands, slippery with perspiration, limp and lifeless. A shiver of fear ran through me. She could not, should not die. How could Jaya bear to lose another sister and because of the same poisonous cause?

I cursed through my teeth, the dread of losing Layla sharpening my resolve. We had to move and move faster, but Jaya's injuries prevented him from moving in anything other than a steady pace and even this was beginning to tire him.

My eyes had adjusted to the near blackness enabling me to pick my way through the scrub. The thin slither of moon dipped beyond the tree line at the light end of the sky, dawn was not far away.

In the distance the faint roar of water filtered through the air. The river was not far. A shiver ran threw me when I remembered my last misadventure I'd suffered at the hands of the ferocious water.

My thoughts returned to the camp we'd just escaped from. How much longer before our disappearance would be discovered? Surely not long, the guard would raise the alarm when he discovered Jaya and Layla were gone. We had made it this far at least. Further than

I could ever have imagined, but to out run fit well trained mercenaries with guns and torches would be near impossible. Not like this, not with the injuries Layla and Jaya had both sustained and not with the burden of carrying Layla between us.

Perhaps they wouldn't discover our trail.

Fat chance.

They'd looked well equipped, and probably possessed thermo-imaging equipment. If that was the case we wouldn't stand a chance.

A distant shout echoed through the jungle. Just as I had thought, our escape had been discovered.

*Too soon, they'd found out too soon.*

Panicked I tried to quicken our pace but Layla's dead floppy weight wobbled precariously. Besides, the breathing coming in rasps behind me told me we could go no faster.

How long did we have? How long before............. no, I could not think of such things. Focus.

I looked up at the dawn light beginning to filter over the dark sky, blotting out the stars one by one. Ahead, the sound of water had built in tempo, the river could not be very far. Yet it might as well have been a hundred miles or so, so slow was our progress. I turned to check on Jaya wishing immediately I hadn't. His face was contorted in pain, his chest heaving with the effort. Something turned over in my heart to see him suffer like this. I wished I could do something to help. Jaya nodded exhaustedly in the direction we'd been heading as he rested an arm against a tree.

"Just a little further," he said hoarsely.

"Is there a plan?" I asked, trying to keep the wobble from my voice.

He grimaced in pain before hanging his head wearily. "Yeah, the river, there's a raft. Following these people I had to plan for a worst case scenario. Over this region I've got many ways to quickly disappear." He looked up with a desperate expression on his face, his eyes flickering over Layla slumped over my back.

"No more talking. Go," he said waving me on.

The light had begun to strengthen, allowing us to progress more quickly but that also meant the mercenaries would be moving faster too. I pushed the thought from my mind, I had to concentrate on the now, be in the moment. I had been through the worst.

*Facing my fears.*

Now I only had to use my body to pit my strength against theirs.

Something I had done hundreds of times before. Winning races had not been about thinking or feeling. Only sensing my own ability, being in the zone, knowing deep within how hard I could push myself, pacing my breathing and heart rate to work hard but not exhaust. Until the very end. When the lactic acid burned in my muscles, my lungs screamed for air and my heart pumped wildly in my chest. The finish line in sight and then with one last push and I'd be over the line.

Victorious.

Now I concentrated on my breathing, following the intake of air down deep into my belly. Tension contracted the diaphragm and ribs, making the cardiovascular system work much harder than need be. I focused on my core muscles, alternating deep then superficial to work, enabling each set to rest and not over tire. Finally my legs. Throwing each leg further to increase the size of my step. Techniques I'd employed to win all my races.

An arena where I'd been good at winning.

*Because I was an expert at not thinking or feeling.*

We heard a fresh whoop echoing through the jungle much nearer than the last. Time was running out. They most certainly had tracking equipment. How else could they have followed us so directly? And why not? They worked for the CIA. When subterfuge is your way of life you'd use all the possible advantages that modern surveillance equipment had to offer.

A fresh bout of adrenaline propelled me forwards, we were so close to the roaring river. I could almost smell the water. Jaya stumbled behind, struggling to keep up, but I felt no slackening in the pressure against my back. I pushed on until the strain of carrying Layla for so long began to tell through my body. A painful ache from the healed wound on my leg started to spike through the bone. The sweat dripped from my brow and a weakness began to spread throughout my exhausted muscles.

"Left here," Jaya croaked breathlessly, pulling my thoughts away from my discomfort. Whatever I was going through, for Jaya it would be a hundred times worse.

I caught a glimpse of water through a gap in the trees.

We were nearly there.

We followed a thin trail hardly wide enough on which to walk but allowing a relatively easier access between the vegetation. Suddenly the jungle foliage fell away, the river stretched out before us, wide and flat but moving very quickly. The land gently swept down to a shingle beach and there in the shallows, half hidden behind some bushes sat the raft Jaya had spoken of.

Suddenly a burst of excited shouts erupted behind us, the mercenaries had seen us. Racing towards us with renewed fervor, thinking they had their quarry cornered and out of options.

We plunged into the water before clambering onto the raft. Jaya pulling Layla from my back before gently laying her on the wooden planks then drawing a knife hidden between the boards he hurriedly slashed the ropes apart. Almost immediately we were taken by the current, propelling us effortlessly down the curve of the river and out of the line of sight. Leaving behind only the sound of their angry shouts as the men reached the riverside we'd only just left behind and then the burst of desperate gunfire that followed.

# Chapter 21

# The River

For a moment I could not speak. All the breath and the last vestiges of energy had been wrought from me with this final effort. The horror of what we had just avoided sent tremors through my body. Jaya had sunk onto the planks next to Layla, his chest heaving, a tautness over his face. I shuffled closer, stroking back some stray hair caught across his face while grasping one of his hands with the other. I needed to feel some sort of human contact to comfort me after everything we'd been through. He opened his eyes, fixing me thoughtfully with those beautiful golden brown eyes and my heart began to suddenly ache for this man.

For what I had nearly lost.

"Thank you," Jaya said eventually, before closing his eyes and did not open them again for a very long time.

I glanced over to Layla who's chest rose and fell steadily. She was still alive. Just. But for how much longer? Would we be able to reach Sanuri in time? She'd been unconscious for several days according to Chana. What had they done to her to cause such injury? I remembered the small nail scissors I'd plunged into my shorts after sawing at the ropes. Pulling them from my pocket I began cutting a small hole in the blood stained dress at Layla's side. Gingerly I lifted the fabric away to reveal the true extent to her injuries. There, sat a neat hole, the size of a five penny piece. An ugly purple and black discolouration stained the skin around the edges. It looked like a bullet wound. I peered closer at the opening, but could see no sign of any metal. Gently, I turned her over as best I could to see if there was an exit wound. Yes there, the same discoloration sat around the small hole where the bullet had left her body.

At least that was something to be thankful for.

Looking at Layla more closely I noticed an odd hue to her lips, a tinge of blue. The skin covering her cheekbones seemed shrunken. Despite the tragic circumstances and her poor condition, these only served to make her look even more hauntingly beautiful. The features more defined and touching. I sat back, the worry replacing the fear. Jaya had known how to heal my injuries with his gentle administrations. I had no such knowledge or expertise to help Layla. We would have to wait until we got her to safety.

At least we had escaped, something I had never dared hope for. So much so, I had not even looked beyond the task of freeing Layla and Jaya.

My fears had seen to that.

What now? The landscape on the river bank all looked the same to me. How would we know when to stop?

I looked at Jaya sleeping, suddenly grateful to have him beside me again. He made me feel strong, safe, as if I could face the world without shrinking. His confidence in life rubbed off on me, something on which I had come to rely. The very reason I'd managed to spill out my miserable story when no one else had ever known. His nonjudgmental attitude had made me feel comfortable for the first time I could remember.

Without a doubt, I'd been caught up in Jaya's physical attraction. Now I saw past these characteristics. For what lay beneath were far more worthy attributes to admire.

I suddenly envied Layla. To have a brother such as Jaya looking after her. Loving her. For the relationship between Harry and I had never been an easy one. Stemming from the fact he had always felt second best even from the beginning. I knew it wasn't Harry's fault. Life's events had conspired to position me as the favourite within the family.

*When I had nearly died.*

Because when someone is very nearly taken from you, how much more precious do they become? Every moment from then on becomes a bonus, something in which to rejoice and so it was with me. Bizarrely becoming allergic to the bottled baby food with which my mother tried to ween me. The ensuing intersection followed by a coma combined with the doubtful odds of survival cemented my elevated status after the operation.

*How could anyone compete with that?*

Harry couldn't, for during that life threatening time of crisis, my mother and I had formed a special bond between us. One I at first took for granted, assuming with my young mind my mother bestowed my brother with the same quantity and quality of love. Later, the love triangle left in wake of our father dying brought to light what had been glaringly obvious to those around us. The disparity in how my brother and I were both treated. Yet, being the favourite had never been a title or status I had actively sought. Nonetheless, that never changed how my brother felt towards me for stealing our mothers love. Souring any good opinion of me or enabling any real love between us to grow.

In the beginning.

After our father died, my brother tried to fill our fathers shoes, trying to help, but our mother wanted no one to assist or challenge her decisions. They clashed like titans, more so when the steadying hand of our father was no longer there to keep the peace or to uphold the healthy dynamics of our family bonds. His death had thrown them awkwardly together, without the buffering interface of his presence to softened the impact. The invisible cords which connected us all were left dripping in disappointment and actively seething in their recriminations.

I knew Harry felt our father's loss perhaps more than any of us. A boy needs a father, a male role model and my brother had been left with nothing, the only point of contact was our mother and she threw these bonds away. Until the day came when my brother could no longer take the drunken rantings, the petty arguments or the belligerent attitude my mother mostly wielded these days. Inevitably pushing them further apart until they appeared to inhabit opposite sides of the emotional spectrum. Eventually Harry left the confines of the claustrophobic house for rented accommodation paid for by his part time job and to continue his education at college in happier solitude. An escape route I'd wished I could follow. I was only sixteen and I felt his departure like a blow in the stomach.

I'd thought family bonds should be strong like steel, but ours had been made fragile by the death of our father, until finally they shattered, like broken glass. The days that followed my brothers departure were empty and sad. My family had finally disintegrated around me, leaving only fragments of what had been before. Valueless to me in their isolation.

My mother had felt vindicated at first to have expunged the thorn in her side, but then the reality had eventually sunk in through the stupor.

This family was no more.

The sadness and heavy depression drew thicker within the little house, blackening her mood even further, driving her to drink even harder. A hurricane replaced the storm. Buffeting me from every angle, and I knew then I could not survive here much longer.

*I had to leave and leave soon.*

Only I was being held captive by my age.

The mother my friends had envied had been finally extinguished. Her laughter and cuddles now just a distant memory. The house became a stranger to happiness, as if a cold draught of ill temper blew unchecked through its innards, barren to any semblance of love or open displays of affection. My mother numbed the pain with the alcohol while I retreated from the world outside. Learning it was easier to cultivate the void inside in which to hide.

*Because there no one could hurt you.*


I looked down at Jaya still sleeping, he'd slept solidly for nearly an hour. I was beginning to worry about our whereabouts. I should wake him.

I gently shook his shoulder, watching with fascination how the long eyelashes fluttered like butterfly wings over his cheeks. Abruptly he jerked himself fully awake, wildly staring about himself in confusion.

"It's all right, we're safe," I murmured reassuringly stroking his arm.

"Where......?" he stared hard at the landscape moving swiftly past us before cursing under his breath. "You should have woken me sooner."

"I thought you needed some rest," I countered.

"That can wait, we have to get Layla back to Sanuri."

"You said that'll be where they look for us first."

"Yes, but we have to warn the Sanuri people before they get there and we have to get Layla to the....." he trailed off.

"You mean the Stone Circle?" I filled in.

"You know about that?"

"Yes, I heard Chana speak of it."

I looked worriedly at Layla. Over the last few hours she had not moved at all. Jaya followed my gaze, an angry expression forming over his features.

"Those bastards," he said bitterly.

"I'm sorry. I ....... distracted you."

Jaya fixed me with those golden brown eyes. "It wasn't your fault Layla took it upon herself to follow Chana and I didn't know he would make a move while you we're being the centre of attention." He said his brows furrowing. "I wasn't expecting you're reaction at the village meeting."

"Nor me," I smiled weakly. "Does it.......does what I...." Suddenly I could not finish for a lump had lodged itself in my throat and tears were springing to my eyes. Stupid! How stupid to get all emotional now, wanting to hear those words of reassurance that he liked me still when his sister lay next to us dying. I looked away ashamed.

"Alice?" Jaya said softly.

I would not look at him for fear he would see my neediness. I did not want that now. For how could he think of anything else other than getting his sister to the Stone Circle and saving her? How could I expect anything at all?

"It's all right," I said wiping away the tears. "It's just the shock coming out, I'm pretty crap in stressful situations."

"Pretty crap! I wouldn't say that, you were awesome, like a pro."

I shook my head. "You didn't see the volcanic shaking in my hands and knees. We were lucky, that's all."

"People make their own luck. Be proud of what you did."

"Believe me, I usually run."

"But you didn't. You rescued us when you could have saved yourself."

I looked down at my hands not knowing how to answer because in truth I couldn't believe I'd managed it either.

"I couldn't leave you and Layla. They were going to kill you both."

"Yeah, most probably. Yet you put yourself in danger to save us. That must have been a tough decision."

I thought back to before the rescue. In fact there had been no decision at all. I'd believed it to be the only option.

"You rescued me."

"Finding you beside the river did not present any danger for me," Jaya said simply.

"In the beginning."

"Yeah, is was a bit too close to call at the end but what you did was very brave."

"Why didn't you tell the Sanuri people where you were going?" I said changing tack.

"I wasn't sure who to trust."

"You mean, there might be others like Chana in Sanuri?"

"Something like that. If Chana can get amongst them so easily then maybe there are more."

"Are you sure? I mean, why would any one bother coming to Sanuri?"

"Sanuri has it's secrets. It creates curiosity not just from other tribes but also the drug runners. The Sanuri tribe are the only tribe in this region who don't grow opium for profit."

"Then how do they make a living?"

"Visiting Shamans from other tribes bring them gifts or money. The Stone Circle is famous in native communities for the special energy which resides here. Many come here to be closer to the earths energies, to pass into other dimensions."

"Surely its existence must be known to the outside world?"

"Yes, but not the true extent to what it can do. Westerners disregard the riches left to us by the ancients, viewing them as little more than primitive curiosities. No one in the West has any idea as to their purpose or what they can do. Yet Stone Circles can be found in almost all continents of the world, but we ignore them."

I didn't know how to respond to that so I asked instead. "Do you think Layla has a chance?" I said quietly.

"Yes."

"You seem so sure."

"I have to believe she will make it," he voice wavered and suddenly I was ashamed to have pushed him. I only wanted to fathom the extent of his faith in the Stone Circle.

"Sorry," I muttered. "I didn't mean to...." Jaya held up a hand as if to say it was okay but I knew it was a subject he did not want to discuss. So instead, I tried to distract him by prattling on about myself.

"You asked if the decision to rescue you and Layla had been difficult for me. All my life I've run from the crap. Thinking I was saving myself from more hurt, more trauma, but watching you, the way you live up to the mark, always facing your demons, living an authentic life and resolving your problems. When I rescued you both it was because I wanted to be like that too."

Jaya nodded. "Well you did that in spades. Even I would have had my doubts. What about now? Was it worth it?"

"Of course it was worth it," I said in surprise he could ask such a thing. "I could never have lived with myself afterwards if hadn't done anything."

"So it was guilt driving you?"

"No! Of course not! I did it for you and Layla," I said indignantly at Jaya's grin before he became serious again.

"And what of you Alice? What were you doing scurrying about the countryside when I thought I'd left you safe and sound in Sanuri?"

For a moment I could not think. Yes, I'd been trying to escape from Sanuri and from him, but he didn't know that, but I had no other explanation to give him.

"I........"

"Yes."

"I.........I thought you'd left me," I blurted out suddenly.

The stunned silence that followed told me this wasn't the answer that Jaya had expected.

"You thought I'd left you? After comforting you after the village meeting, staying with you all night to mop up your tears? Hold you in my arms when the nightmares revisited? That would make me a prize bastard in the least to have run from you then," he said indignantly.

"But I thought.........after what you knew about me......... I didn't think you would want me and that was why........." I looked down at my hands, willing them to still their shaking. I had spilled my deepest fears and I didn't dare look at Jaya incase of what I might see in his eyes. Disgust, anger maybe, but I hoped not pity. I could deal with everything else, but not pity.

I felt a slow flush beginning under my neck and then flaming over my face. Jaya had not given any sign he cared for me since the rescue, but then we'd had far more pressing problems to deal with. Escaping from Chana and his men, Layla dying. How could I expect anything more under such circumstances?

Suddenly Jaya leant towards me and sealed my lips with a kiss. A kiss so sweet and gentle I could hardly breath for fear of prematurely ending it. He pulled back to look at me and said.

"I don't care about the past. It doesn't change the way I feel about you, nothing does. I love you Alice and I'll be there for you in anyway I can. I only want you to care for me in return, if you can and if there's anything else that gets in the way, we'll work it out." He looked at me with such heart felt tenderness I became aware of an unfamiliar tightness crushing my chest. The words I had only dared imagine, had fallen so sweetly from his lips. I closed my eyes to squeeze away the moisture threatening to spill. Holding onto this moment to remember forever and finally allowing the rigid tension in my body to dissolve. I had expected the worst, but that only made this moment all the more wonderful. Jaya wanted me and not only that, loved me.

Again, Jaya's lips brushed against mine and this time the kiss deepened into something more. A restrained hunger unleashed a need so raw. The day's enormous tension had reached down to an untapped emotional resource or perhaps it was the culmination of all my innocent longings now transformed into something else. All I knew was this moment, consuming all others. My whole world existed in just this kiss. Everything else faded into the background.

Jaya's soft sensuous lips continued to move demandingly over mine. He was claiming me for his own, marking his territory and yet I felt his kiss reach down right to my soul. Awakening some dormant part of me. He had found me, found my inner most being and was now peeling back the layers one by one.

Eventually, Jaya pried himself away. "Sweet Alice, you have no idea how long I've wanted to do that."

"How long?" I said coyly.

He smiled. "Too long." He brushed away a stray strand of hair caught on my cheek. "How about you?" He asked softly.

"Ah, that would be telling."

"Then tell me," he said coaxingly.

Suddenly I was overcome with shyness. How could I say I'd been hooked from the first moment I laid eyes upon him?

"Like you, a long time," I hedged.

"How long?"

"Why the Spanish Inquisition? Isn't that enough?"

"No," he said simply. "I'm curious." He murmured, fixing me with his golden brown eyes.

"Why's it so important?"

"Why can't you tell me?"

I fell silent for a moment. "It's.........private."

"I want to know everything about you Alice. I want to know what makes you tick inside."

"Why would you want to do that?" I said warily, the old defences reinstating themselves.

"You fascinate me."

I looked for any sign of teasing in Jaya's eyes but only the soft expression shone back at me.

I laughed at the very idea. "Me? Fascinating? There are many other ways to describe me that would be far more accurate," I quipped.

"Well, that's for me to decide now," he said in an easy manner.

I stared at him perplexed unsure how to respond. I need not have worried because Jaya pulled me towards him, nuzzling his lips into my neck then nibbling my ear. Before pulling me into his arms and I only had moments to wonder before he kissed me again, if Heaven could get any better than this.

# Chapter 22

## Surviving

"We need to get into the shoreline otherwise we'll overshoot our landing," said Jaya, pointing towards a large rock looming out of the river way ahead. "We want to get just beyond that boulder." He pointed to a pole tied to the side of the raft. "Grab that will you." He said, while reaching behind himself to do the same. "Push towards shore, not enough to make us spin."

I did as he directed, the memory of the kiss still burning on my lips. An important boundary had been crossed in my heart and my mind and I knew there was no going back. I could no more prevent it than stopping the rain from falling from the sky. I was in free-fall, set loose on a path I did not know how to follow and I didn't know if I should feel thrilled or downright terrified. I, who endeavoured to control everything around me was now dependent upon another for my happiness. A state of affairs from which I would normally have run but my heart had other ideas. Beating its existence for only Jaya's good opinion and love. Oh, and how I wanted to bask under it, soaking up it's rays's like a person starved of food. I wanted it all, this moment, but now I felt awkward and clumsy. The years of abstinent affection had left their mark, making me feel uncertain and self-conscious. I'd been an island for too long and had forgotten how to live as a continent.

The river was not as deep as I'd supposed and I could feel the river bed catch as I found purchase against it's bottom. Gradually the raft edged out of the main current, and once we neared the riverbank it was easier to direct the raft into shore.

"Just a little further, we don't have to land just yet, but we need to keep out of the main current," Jaya cautioned.

I soon saw the reason why. The river had slowed down considerably and divided in two, several hundred meters ahead.

"They join up again eventually but where we want to go, we need to keep left," Jaya said giving the raft another strong push.

"How far is Sanuri from here?"

"Just over there, you can see a pass between those mountains. That's where we're headed."

I looked in the direction Jaya indicated with my heart sinking. The mountains were miles away.

We'd landed without incident and continued to carry Layla as we'd done before. Her skin felt clammy and cold and her face had taken on a dangerous tinge of blue. The fever had passed but I did not know if this was a good or a bad sign. Nonetheless, I took it as a dreadful omen.

Our progress was slow along the thin path. It was not well travelled, but then we were miles from anywhere. Who would possibly use it on a regular basis? My mind flittered onto another more pressing problem. How much time did we have before Chana reached Sanuri? Sanuri where the Stone Circle and it's secret lay. Chana would not leave the jungle without it but what lengths would he be prepared to go to obtain it?

In comparison to the small and narrow life I'd lived at home with all its problems, it now seemed minuscule in comparison to what we now faced. Layla slowly dying in our arms, the code to the Stone Circle in jeopardy, the Sanuri people's way of life at stake. We had to get to Sanuri before Chana, before Chana could stop us.

We rested for a time under the shade of a thickly leafed tree. The beads of sweat stood out proudly against Jaya's golden brown skin. His hair in disarray as was mine. The crazy ball of fluff hung limp and lifeless around my face. I swiped a cloud of frizz away self consciously. Although Jaya seemed not to notice. He sat with his back against the tree, his arms rested on his knees, head bent looking to the ground.

Jaya looked how I felt. Exhausted.

"How far now do you think?" I asked, then berating myself for sounding like a small child.

"A few hours if we hurry," Jaya replied in a monotone.

"Do the Sanuri people have anyway to protect themselves from Chana?"

"No," Jaya said simply, his answer hung between us, reverberating with it's darker meaning.

Fear gnawed in my stomach when I remembered the guns. The natives would have no chance against them.

*It was hopeless.*

Even if we did manage to get Layla to the Stone Circle, what then? Jaya would certainly never leave the Sanuri people in their time of need.

"How does the Stone Circle work? I mean, how can it heal people?"

"Stone circles are built over Earth energy points fed by ley lines. Ley lines traverse the entire Earth's surface and where they come close to the surface are the energy vortexes. Using ancient knowledge passed down through generations they use only specific stones which naturally emit high frequency energy and placing them over these vortexes the stones absorb the Earth's energy and then become like transmitters, like crystals."

"Like crystals?"

"Crystals are used in modern technology because of their ability to conduct frequencies, like quartz does in watches for instance. Many stones contain crystal formations within them. In fact, this is where they grow, inside rock. Stones are chosen for their unique energy frequency. To increase the energy within the Stone Circle, extra stones are placed outside the circle to absorb the energies from the moon, sun and stars. A feeder stone then conducts these frequencies into the circle. The energy in the circle is now complete. The combination of heaven and earth energy is very powerful, but at certain times of the year even more so. Too powerful for some people. This is when the Shamans perform special ceremonies and travel into other dimensions. The rest of the time the Stone Circle can be used for healing."

"What do you mean travel into other dimensions?"

"As humans, we live in linear time. Yesterday, today and tomorrow. When the Shamans journey, they can see in all directions at once. Know everything."

"And they can do this at will?"

"They have to enter a certain state of consciousness. The energy in the Stone Circles helps heighten this ability."

"What was the code Chana talked about?"

"In its most basic form it's a prayer. It's used to evoke the healing power of the Stone Circle."

"Did you know about its existence before you came here?"

"Yes and no. I'd heard a little about it through the grape vine, but that wasn't our reason for coming. We wanted to find out what had happened to my sister. Chana was my only link."

"And have you? Found out I mean."

"I think I know most of it. She got involved in something she knew nothing about, nor the dangers. Somehow stumbling upon or being privy to some sensitive information. I think she was planning to expose them. She knew how high this thing went within the CIA."

"How do you know that?"

"She told me."

"But....."

"I just told Chana what he wanted to hear. But I think he suspected I was holding back on something."

"And how high does this thing go?"

"Right to the top."

"You mean the President?" Jaya's silence told me all I needed to know.

"What's your sisters link to Chana?"

"He was her boyfriend." Jaya grimaced at my shocked expression. "Yeah, I couldn't believe it either."

"How...?" was all I could stutter.

"I think she had no idea who he was or how dangerous. Kara only saw the good in people."

"How did she find out?"

"I don't know all the details but I think she overheard some conversation or something and decided to confront Chana or whatever his real name is."

"So what happened then?"

"When there's an 'incident' there's a special 'clean up' division. Kara was cleaned up."

"He had her killed?" I said shocked.

"If she'd threatened to expose his actions it would be the only way to silence her."

"Are you sure?"

"No, but I wanted to find out one way or the other so my family and I can get closure on this."

"So your only link to all of this was the name Chana and when you started asking around at the Tribal Convention you discovered a tribe in the biggest opium growing area in the world, who had someone staying with them called Chana. Someone who had aroused the suspicion of the Elders. I'm surprised the Sanuri people told you anything at all, they seem so secretive about everything."

"Yeah, they are. They don't like what is happening all around them or how other villagers rely on the Americans' money to survive. The Sanuri people think they should live off the land like they do."

"Couldn't you take it anywhere higher to expose the CIA and what they are doing?"

"Expose them to who? They are the government."

"And that's it? You're going to leave it at that? How's that justice for your sister?"

"Assuming she is ........has been killed. Then we will get justice but by our own code our own way of doing things. We have been forced to take on the ways of the white man and live by his rules. But no longer. We've had enough."

"What do you mean?"

"Since all this happened I've imagined all the ways I would kill the bastard who took Kara or break a few limbs, rearrange his face but there are too many of them. So now I have a better plan." He looked up at me. "The plan is to find out where the opium enters the US, once it hits America's soil through military ports they won't be able to deny anything. I will expose them through the internet. Hit the government where it hurts most, their international reputation."

"You think you can do that?"

"Yes," he said simply.

And I knew I believed him.

We continued onwards as before. The heat of the day pressed in on us, sapping our already diminishing strength, making our progress laboured and slow. Slowly, I began to recognise some of the landmarks. We'd joined the path on which Jaya had originally carried me all those moons ago. When I had been innocent to the ways and wherefores of Jaya's underlying motives in being here, the drugs trade and the existence of a Stone Circle that could heal.

The steady walking had in someways helped Jaya's stiff and bruised body to loosen a little, but he still limped and strained to keep up even though our pace was far from hurried. I had lost all sensation in my arms and hands from the effort of keeping them clamped tightly around Layla's legs. If we did not reach Sanuri soon our strength would finally give out and we would be forced to camp under the stars.

I shuddered at the thought.

We would be vulnerable out in the open if Chana and his men did possess their heat detecting equipment and night vision.

"Keep moving," said Jaya through gritted teeth as if he had read my thoughts. "Only a little further."

Yes, we were nearly there. I recognised an outcrop of rock ahead, the precursor to the entrance to the cave network. I almost wilted in relief there and then to have made it this far. My step lightened and we pushed on until abruptly we reached the caves entrance just as the sun began to dip behind the trees. Even if we did not reach Sanuri before dark, at least the caves would give us some measure of concealment and a welcome rest I thought, hearing the ragged rasps behind me.

We entered the cool of the cave entrance groping our way inwards towards the central cavern and then between us, allowing Layla to slip gently to the ground. My heart contracted in anguish when I noticed only a faint rise and fall of her chest. Jaya noticed too, uttering an unintelligible sound before kneeling beside her.

"She's so cold. She needs to be warmer," he said hoarsely, before laying down beside her and wrapping his arms around her. Trying to press the vital warmth of his own body into hers. I watched in agony as a succession of wretched emotions passed over Jaya's face and suddenly I came to an uneasy decision.

"I'll run ahead and get help. I know the way from here." I said trying to sound decisive. Despite knowing the encroaching darkness would obscure the landmarks by which I would normally be guided. Jaya looked at me questioningly. His mouth drawn in a grim line. A hopeless misery sitting behind his eyes I wanted to kiss away.

"I'll be okay. You need to get some rest and look after Layla. I'll be as back as soon as I can."

He nodded distractedly before returning his attention back to Layla. I turned away, feeling my heart contracting. It was all down to me now. If I didn't get to Sanuri in time......... a feeling of impending doom settled over me. Nudging into my heart and mind like a draft of cold air. Perhaps I would never see Layla alive again, she'd looked so terrible. She wasn't going to last much longer. I shuddered, trying to still the panic and then the tears. The memory of my own grief was never very far away and now I felt the impending loss as keenly as a red hot poker stuck straight through my heart. I tried to push the painful memories aways but they hung like dark clouds gathering ominously in self loathing ferocity.

*Because I knew this was all my fault.*

If I had never stupidly slipped into that raging river, never collapsed in a pathetic heap at the village meeting, then Layla would never have been caught following Chana and would not be laying there dying. I suddenly felt the crushing weight of my shame cave in on me. Everything I touched never turned out any good. I was a walking disaster. I was pathetic, beyond useless and now I had brought my shameful world here too. Everything good collapsed around me, or was taken from me. It was only what I'd come to expect. Yet since my arrival here, I had begun to hope for something more. Something good that I could hold onto. Something wholesome and true that stilled my chaotic world inside. I thought I'd found it, but now I realised it had all been an illusion. A rotten apple always turns others bad.

How could it not? Like osmosis, nothing could stop it.

I'd run away from my home but I could not run away from the person still inside. I'd been tarnished, damaged and now I'd brought this evil upon the very people I'd come to love.

I hated myself. Hated who I was and what I'd become. Jaya said he loved me but he didn't know the real me, the one inside, but in time he would. I wouldn't be able to hide it forever.

I heard the sobs and felt the tears, but they never did any good, no matter how hard I cried.

Oh, for Christ sakes, stop the pity party right now, I chastised myself. This wasn't about me anymore, Layla's life was at stake.

Layla!

I plunged forwards, angrily wiping the tears away. Pushing the vile emotions back down to where they belonged in the pit of my stomach.

Stepping away from the largest cave I easily found the entrance to the tunnel I thought would lead me out of here. Yet, the constantly branching passages confused me, causing me to doubt my memory. I began to worry I was ever going to get out of here in time. This was taking far too long and Layla would die because of my own stupidity and foolishness.

I took pot luck and began down a tunnel I hoped would be the right direction when suddenly I was stopped in my tracks. A strange creeping sensation was spreading over my face and neck.

A sensation I remembered when I'd first been brought to the caves by Jaya. The strange feelings sent shivers up and down my spine in a shock of recognition. The spirit keeper of the cave was here. Making her presence known to me again in a way I could not ignore. The sensations pulsed inside, pulling tentacle like at my shriveled heart. Edging it open until the bliss swept through me unabridged. Sweeping the fears and phobias away. Filling me with her love.

But why? I thought, dragging myself back from being lost in the sea of glorious sensations. Why now? The last time I had walked through these caves, it had been to escape from what I had feared the most.

Being unloveable.

The spirit keeper had not made herself known to me then. When I'd needed her most. So why had she chosen to reveal herself now?

Up ahead, as if in answer I saw a faint golden glow glimmering in the darkness in a tunnel off to my left. I watched curiously as the light grew brighter and brighter until its golden resonance glowed lantern like against the tunnel wall.

As it drew nearer I felt no fear or need to run away, instead the loving sensations grew stronger until I felt bathed in love. The words 'follow me' formed insistently in my head and I knew then what I had to do. The compulsion to follow this strange light reached right down into my Soul. Pulling me towards this glowing oddity. Edging forwards the light pulled out of reach, never allowing me near enough or to gain any advantage. Drawing me deeper and deeper through a dizzying array of tunnels and into the cavernous bowls of the mountain. I hardly noticed, the light was all that mattered now, all I needed to follow.

A thought fleetingly probed my mind. What was I doing? I was on my way to Sanuri, I should leave right now. Yet the loving compulsion to trail the light distracted me and almost at once the thought floated away unconsidered.

Trance like, I continued in this ludicrous diversion, being led through the dungeon like tunnels for what seemed like forever. Until abruptly the diaphanous light suddenly drew to a stop and to hover just above the ground. Hesitantly I drew near, half expecting the light to dart away again, but this time the light allowed me to approach until I was standing right in front of it. As I gazed at it curiously I noticed something beneath over which it hovered. There, sat a largish oval shaped stone about the size of my palm. I bent down to retrieve it, noticing strange symbols carved into its smooth surface. Strangely they looked familiar, reminding me of something, jogging an impression, but then the memory was gone. Turning the stone over in my hand I wondered at its origin and where it had come from. Had someone placed it here or had it been lost? Even to my untrained eye the stone appeared significant or perhaps even valuable. For whoever had carved the beautiful symbols over its surface had owned considerable talent and patience going by the intricate design traversing its's surface.

Suddenly I remembered my original mission. I had no time for this, I had already wasted too many minutes in this ridiculous pursuit.

I had to leave immediately.

I looked about me in surprise as if suddenly becoming aware of my surroundings for the first time. I had no idea where I was or how I had got here. How stupid, for now I had no idea how to retrace my steps. The tunnel's network was like a giant rabbit warren. I would never find my way out of here.

A pulse of fear jolted through me when I tried to remember the way back. I hadn't taken any notice of how I'd got here. I'd only been watching the light. The tunnel was pitch black save for the golden glow beside me and now I felt foolish for being led here without even an ounce of resistance.

But now an idea began to formulate in my head. The golden glowing light had lead me here and now it could take me back. I had nothing to lose.

"Lead me back," I said. Not expecting anything would come from my fanciful request but almost immediately the light began to move, and back in the direction we had come.

Stuffing the stone into the pocket of my shorts I followed the light through the maze of tunnels. The spirit keeper had brought me here for a reason, of that much I was certain, but why would an innocuous stone be of any importance? It didn't make any sense.

But why had she brought me here? Why not Jaya or Layla or any of the Sanuri people? I wondered what possible significance this strange stone could have, but nothing came to mind. I pulled the stone out of my pocket to look at it again, searching for something, but I didn't know what. I would have to wait until I showed it to Jaya or Layla.

Layla. Oh God. This had been the most stupidest of diversions. How much time had passed following the light? I did not know.

I started jabbering incoherently in some semblance of a prayer.

Please, please God, oh God, please help Layla. Please, please help Layla.

How pitifully pleading I sounded, beseeching someone or something I had never believed in anyway. Regarding religions to be little more than an illogical fantasy, a fairytale that did not exist. Religion was supposed to teach us how to be better human beings, but the girls at school I'd known to be followers of a faith seemed to view God only to exist between the covers of a bible, or within the church walls they attended week by week.

Never on the outside, never in their everyday lives.

No, the whimsical claims of religion had turned me away from the idea of a God. Besides, there had never been a God in my life. Being buried under a ton of hurt and trauma had made me lose faith there could be anything else beyond.

The only belief I had was in myself because then, I only had myself to blame when I made mistakes. That was the way I liked it. I had to be free of all shackles and restrictions from outside. I had enough of those on the inside. When there is so much darkness within, when the process of life cannot be trusted, I'd had to live by my own rules.

Since spending time in Sanuri my perception of such things had begun to change. Perhaps the archetypal God wasn't sitting on his cloud shaking his fist at us whenever we sinned. That cruel and vengeful God inflicting floods and earthquakes and personal trauma upon us as punishment for our numerous misdemeanors. Perhaps God was not a He or even a person but as Jaya had tried to show me, was all around us and within us. Loving us no matter who or what we had become. That we were just extensions, little sparks of our Creator. This invisible energy field I'd learned I could feel all around me was in fact, the collective consciousness, the Source of all things.

A part of me. A part of God.

Jaya had said we were all connected through the matrix, the collective soup in which we existed and through this energy field we could influence others with our thoughts and feelings.

Suddenly I understood. That this was what prayer really was. Asking for Divine intervention combined with our loving intention. Energy follows thought Jaya had said, but love was the key. Love made the difference. Maybe all I had to do was to ask for Layla to be healed.

The spirit keeper had bestowed upon me this most precious of gifts, but how could I engender the feeling within myself? I cared about things yes, and I could arouse the feelings of compassion, but love?

I concentrated on my heart and willed the emotion to come, feeling it edge open by small degrees. Remembering how the spirit keeper had made me feel. That unconditional love, that infinite bliss.

I started again but this time saying it with my heart.

"Dear God, please, please, please help Layla"

No, that did not feel right.

And again.

"Dear God, if it is in Layla's highest good to live then send her all the healing she needs now please," I said repeating these words over and over in my head like a mantra. If this was the last thing I could do for Layla then so be it.

Then I had tried everything.

Suddenly I became aware of a strange heat emanating from my hand. I looked down at the stone forgotten in my hand. The heat was coming from the stone but it didn't look any different, only feeling warmer.

Over the years crystals had fascinated me with their beautiful array of colours and their fabled qualities to heal or calm you. Sometimes I could feel their subtle energies vibrating through my hand, but I had never considered a rock would have the same qualities. How could it? Rocks were just a collection of minerals. Crystals refracted light through their structures, imbuing their own unique frequency on whoever used them, but rocks were just..... dead weren't they? Jaya had told me the stones used in the Stone Circle had crystals within them, perhaps this rock had them too.

No time to ponder, the golden glow was disappearing fast round a corner, I could not let it disappear out of sight. I hurried after it, until eventually I emerged back in the main chamber I'd left some time ago and then the golden glow vanished from sight.

The last rays of the day still illuminated the cave faintly within. I still had sometime to find my way out of here but not for much longer. Scurrying forward to where I thought the exit tunnel must lay I suddenly heard approaching footsteps on the gravelly floor. Quickly I hid behind a large boulder. Maybe Chana had caught up with us in record time. Well, what could drive a man any faster than greed and revenge I thought? My stomach tightened in anticipation. Should I run ahead to warn the Sanuri people or remain hidden here? Either way Layla was out of options.

The footsteps came closer, then past me, receding into the far end of the chamber before I dared take a look. Seeing the outline of Jaya's diminishing figure disappearing from view.

Layla must have died and Jaya was following me to call me back from my pointless journey. A lump formed in my throat. I had wasted too much time following that stupid light and now it was too late.

"Jaya," I called out weakly.

Jaya heard me anyway, turning in my direction while a look of relief passed over his features when he saw me.

"Alice, thank God you're still here," He said. Yes, I'm still here because I've been chasing ridiculous moving lights when I should have been fetching help, I thought feeling terrible.

"I got lost," I muttered, but Jaya seemed not to hear me.

"Layla opened her eyes a few minutes ago and spoke to me. I think she's going to be okay," He grabbed both my hands joyfully and hugged me. "I can't believe it."

I stared at him shocked and hardly able to take it in. Layla had been hours from death when I'd left. I'd been sure of it and was now recovered?

"I had to come and find you before you went out into the jungle alone," Jaya said.

"Layla's okay?" I said disbelievingly.

"Yes, a few minutes ago she woke up, come I will show you."

Jaya lead me back to where Layla lay. Suddenly I was kneeling beside her. Only half an hour ago she'd been dying but now...... I pulled back.

"How......?"

"I don't know Alice," Jaya said from beside me. "One minute I thought she was going and the next she just........woke up."

Turning my attention back to Layla I gave her a more comprehensive once over. She appeared dazed, as if just woken from a deep sleep but how else are you supposed to look when you've just been dying? The hideous blue tint to her lips had gone, and a faint rosy glow had appeared on her prominent cheeks bones. Her breathing was deep and even and her skin felt warm. A miraculous change from the reptilian cold of before.

"Layla?"

Layla only nodded wearily, but did not speak. I looked up questioningly at Jaya, but he only shook his head.

"She's still very weak."

"I can't believe it."

"I know."

"How long has she been like this?"

"She woke up a little while after you left."

"Has she said anything?"

"Not really, only that she feels okay."

"But how? Why would......?" I couldn't even articulate what was puzzling me.

"She's going to be okay."

I looked back at her and knew Jaya was right, she'd only become stronger over the coming hours, I knew it deep in my.

"Yes," I laughed in relief. "She is." I stood to face Jaya. "I'm so glad. I couldn't bear the thought of losing her." I said hugging Jaya to me.

"Thank God you found us Alice," he said nuzzling my neck. "Even doing that and rescuing us was a miracle."

"Luck," I said.

"We make our own luck Alice."

"Yeah well, was it luck that healed Layla?" I asked glibbly.

"I don't know but I sure as hell would like to find out," said Jaya grasping my face in his hands and leaned down to kiss me, but not one that lingered.

"We still have to get back to Sanuri as soon as possible. I won't be happy until we have Layla safely in our hut."

"But shouldn't we........"

"No, but's, let's get moving."

It was pitch black by the time we reached the valley's floor. My eyes had adjusted to the gloom and could faintly pick out the path ahead. The fingernail slither of moon appeared above the trees, faintly illuminating the way ahead. Jaya would know his way better than I but we had reverted to our original method of carrying Layla. She was still too weak to do anything other than flop over my shoulders. At least she was alive I thought momentarily but I was too preoccupied by the need to remain vigilant to dwell on those thoughts for long. Every sight, sound and smell of the jungle could give us away. Our journey via the river and jungle had taken us only twelve hours to traverse. Chana had two days of walking to reach this place, but I wasn't fooled into a false sense of security. Men could travel much faster than a woman. Especially when a great deal of money was at stake.

Jaya called out just as we reached the first row of huts. Usually at this time of the evening the villagers would retire to their huts, but today there was a meeting being held in the centre of the village.

In the same place I had fallen apart.

The memory stung, but faces had already turned in our direction distracting me from the shame. Suddenly the villagers were running towards us and then stroking our arms and faces in greeting, murmuring words I could not understand. The Elders joined us soon after and Jaya then began to speak. The clicking noises coming in rapid bursts as he recounted all that had happened since we'd left. The villagers at first soothing in their movements towards us soon became nervous and agitated.

The conversation between Jaya and the Elders continued for sometime while some of the other villagers gently lifted Layla from our arms and carried her to our hut. She would be able to rest and recover for as long as she needed now. Maybe even be taken to the Stone Circle in the following days for further healing. That was if Chana did not get here first.

Eventually Jaya was done talking and then all eyes swiveled towards me.

"I've just told them everything, what you did."

I didn't know how to respond to that so I let it go.

"The Elders wish to thank you," I nodded nonchalantly as if this was an everyday occurrence. "For your courage, for rescuing

Layla and me." He paused. "The Elders and some of the villagers are heading for the caves. We'll stay here." Jaya said.

"Why?"

"To guard them. The caves are the only way in and out of this valley. Besides they don't need us to help them and we need to rest."

"What about Layla?"

"She will be taken care of. Tomorrow if Chana hasn't shown up we'll take her to the Stone Circle for more healing."

"And if he does?"

Jaya paused a moment too long. "Then the Elders have a plan."

"A plan?"

"Yeah."

"You don't sound too confident."

"I......have no experience in Shamanic practices."

"What's that supposed to mean?"

"Your guess is as good as mine." He smiled before taking my hand and leading me to our hut.

# Chapter 23

# Shamanic Practices

The Elders never made it as far as the caves. We heard shouting coming from outside the hut and then we saw them. The Elders walking back into the village preceeding Chana and his men. Despite the darkness I could still make out their stupid, triumphant grins as Chana's men walked behind. Smugly glancing about them as they made their way through the village while their guns glinted coldly in the faint moonlight. Other than the initial shouts from Chana and his men the procession walked in silence. Only the sound of their feet padding on the earthen path made any sound at all. The Elders wore bland expressions, yet with an air of calm as if they were just on their way to a routine village meeting.

The villagers stood somberly watching the procession but no one moved, no one rushed forward to help. The guns trained on the Elders saw to that.

From beside me I heard Jaya's sharp intake of breath when Chana's gaze found us within the thin crowd.

"Isn't there anything we can do?" I whispered hurriedly, but Chana had already drawn abreast of us and motioned for us to join the sombre parade.

"And where is the lovely Layla? Did she survive in the end?" His eyes flickered over me dismissively but I felt the weight of his interest. "Ah Alice, the heroic rescuer. Never thought you had it in you." He growled.

I felt rather than saw Jaya's anger bristle beside me but the cold butt of Chana's gun jabbing him in the ribs restrained him from making a move and Chana knew it.

"You fucking make a move and Alice will be mincemeat. Do you understand?" He smiled maliciously. "I've been feeling a little cheated Jaya. I was looking forward to that little sex show we talked about." Chana looked at me luridly. "But I think we've just found a replacement."

Chana leaned forward and whispered in my ear but still loud enough for Jaya to hear. "Those sweet lips of yours are sure to send a man to heaven and back. Warm them up for me babe." He leered.

I knew he was just playing with me to goad Jaya. Waiting for a reaction, wanting Jaya to make a foolish move but Jaya kept it together even as I waited for the explosion beside me, becoming deathly still, like a panther ready to spring. I knew he was contemplating it, working out the risks, only the gun was making him hesitate. I grasped his arm to caution him. Maybe there would be other opportunities, but not this one, not now. Instead I took Jaya's hand and pulled him amongst the Elders.

The procession headed west away from the village. An area Jaya had never taken me to before and now I understood why. This must be where the infamous Stone Circle lay and Westerners were not trusted or made privy to its whereabouts or even its existence.

Even if I had discovered this place on my own, I would never have given it a second thought. Such was the abundance of unremarkable Stone Circles back home. Silent statues begotten from another age. Few understood them or had unlocked their mysterious secrets, their reasons for existing. Many had contemplated their link to the planetary constellations, or the changing of the seasons, even as burial sites but no one really knew the real reasons for their existence.

Except the Sanuri people.

Now Chana wanted its secret, wanted to exploit these peace loving people's home and lifestyle, having no care for the aftermath and what this would cause. The flocks of desperate people looking to be healed from incurable diseases or maybe there was another reason. The pharmaceutical companies would not be pleased to discover the existence of a Stone Circle that healed or threatened their precious profit margins.

"Doesn't the Tribal Convention have any powers to prevent this sort of exploitation?" I asked Jaya.

Jaya smiled grimly. "Just take a look at the indigenous tribes of the world. Have they been able to keep their lands if there is profit to be made from them?"

I remained silent but saw the truth in what Jaya said. "Indigenous tribes are small fry and poor in comparison to the huge money behind large corporations. They cannot fight against them, only make do with the crumbs thrown to them afterwards."

"Do you think that's what will happen to the Sanuri people if their secret gets out?"

"I don't think so, I know," replied Jaya.

"Isn't there anybody who can help?"

"No," Jaya said with such finality I didn't ask anymore as a sense of helplessness washed over me. For we held no cards in our favour, no weapons by which to retaliate, nothing by which to bargain.

In Chana's words, we were fucked.

We'd filed into a large clearing filled with eight enormous stones standing magnificently silhouetted against the stars. Reaching over eight foot high, they towered over us, silently filling the space with their presence as completely as if they'd been alive. Vibrating a resonance I had never felt before.

In the early years of my childhood my family had visited another stone circle, Stonehenge. Just a short diversion from the road which took us to our holiday destination. Back then I didn't have any appreciation for this ancient wonderment or took the time to consider how the enormous stones had been transported over great distances by only rudimentary methods. Now the sheer force and majesty of this Stone Circle here in Sanuri pulled at something deep within, compelling me to wonder how anyone had discovered the power and energy which lay hidden within our landscape or even known how to tap into this hidden resource.

We came to a halt just short of the circle. Chana motioned with his gun for the Elders to come forward.

"I want the code. So which one of you speaks the words," he said questioningly, but no one answered.

"Aw come on. Don't go all shy on me now guys," he said glancing behind him at his men with a smirk before flinging an arm round one of the Elders almost half his height. "You know." He whispered into his ear. "If you do this for me I won't hurt anyone and I might even let you in on some of the spoils."

Chana's coaxing had no effect, no one moved or made any sound.

"Doesn't Chana speak any of the Sanuri language?" I said surprised.

"No, he supposedly came from another tribe, remember?" Came Jaya's reply.

Yes, but from where Jaya had never told me.

"Fuckers," Chana spat angrily. "Tell me." He said prodding his gun at one of the Elders. I cringed inwardly feeling the tension rising but the Elders appeared unmoved by the tirade. Although for me the reality was crystalizing. Like a cold draft of air under the duvet, waking me to our predicament. Chana was ready to explode going by the beetroot face and contorting tendons in his neck. I had seen those signs before.

"We have to do something," I said.

"Like we have any choices?"

"But he's going to ........." I had no time to finish before Chana spun round and grabbed hold of me.

"Ah Alice. What a shame I have to do this to such a lovely girl. What a waste, but beauty can't buy pretty houses, or fancy cars, eh" he growled into my ear. His gun pressing under my jaw. He turned me to face Jaya and the Elders.

"She's going to die if you don't cooperate," he said coldly.

The Elders appeared to hesitate and that was all it took. Chana took full advantage.

"Don't you fucking get it?" he snapped. "Alice will be the first to die and then I'll start on the villagers." He grabbed my hair yanking my head backwards. "And don't pretend you don't understand me, because I know you do."

Fear does funny things to your body. Paralyzing your entire being or driving you to accomplish miraculous deeds like lifting cars off loved ones or running miles with a severed arm. I did not fall into the latter. I felt the familiar freezing spreading though my veins. Crippling my mind and body and making everything, including my breathing, shallow and ineffectual.

Jaya looked on with a torn expression. One half wanted to jump the bastard and finish this here and now, but the other knew the odds were stacked against it. Our fate lay in the hands of the Elders.

"Well?" Chana said impatiently. "I'm getting really pissed here. Someone's got to start talking and soon."

The Elders turned to confer for a few moments before nodding at Chana. They'd agreed but in reality, there'd really been no choice at all.

A self satisfied grin spread over Chana's face. "Well, what are we waiting for?" He said waving the Elders forward. "Lets get moving."

Chana abruptly pushed me into the arms of one of his men.

"Shoot her if she moves," he told him before turning to Jaya. "Ah, young love, such tragic circumstances. Don't do anything stupidly heroic Jaya. It won't do you or your girl any good." Jaya didn't grace Chana's words with a reply but I could see the tension working in his jaw. "Just translate, that's all you need to do. I only want the code, there's no need for dramatics."

"How will you know if it's the right code?" said Jaya through gritted teeth.

That stalled him for a moment. "Ah, good question," Chana said considering Jaya's words.

"Then I will have the healing. I've seen what it can do," Chana mused. "Maybe it will help me to stop this fucking swearing," he said grinning at his men as he made his way into the centre of the circle.

"No funny business," he said sternly, pointing his finger at the Elders. "Begin."

The Elders assembled next to the a large stone and gazed in varying directions. I thought nothing of it at first as the Elders began their chant. Rhythmical and harmonic their voices blended pleasingly in melody, raising in speed and tempo their incantation took on a more insistent beat. I glanced back to the Stone Circle where Chana had taken a theatrical stance. Arms stretched out wide, tilting his face to the sky with a huge stupid grin spread over his face. Like Moses waiting to receive divine intervention, I thought. I almost laughed but the gun pressed into my cheek reminded me not too.

The Elders continued to chant, the voices blending, the rhythm quickening and it was then I noticed the change in Chana. His face had snapped forward, eyes bulging and staring intently at the Elders, but he did not move, or rather, he could not move. Appearing to be frozen to the spot, unable to move sinew or limb. A puzzled look formed over his face, his eyes flickered apprehensively from side to side, until eventually even they stopped moving. I looked around the clearing, Chana's men had frozen too. It was then I noticed the concentrated stares of the Elders each fixed on one of Chana's men. One Elder alone glared at Chana within the Stone Circle. Whatever the Elders had been chanting had paralyzed each man in some way. Then I realised the grip on my arms and neck had loosened too. I wriggled free and returned to Jaya's side.

"What's happening?"

"The Elders are doing something with the energy of the Stone Circle but I'm not sure what," he sounded puzzled. I looked back at Chana and his men standing like statues, inert, like marble.

"Why hasn't it happened to us?"

"I don't know."

We watched in fascination. The Elders still continuing to chant, fixing their eyes steadily on Chana and his men.

"They're not hurting them," said Jaya.

"Then what are they doing?"

But just as I had spoken, the Elders finished their chant and finally silence reigned over the clearing with an unearthly stillness. No one moved, no one spoke until eventually the oldest Elder called out to Jaya who nodded in accent followed by a lengthy dialogue.

"What are they saying?" I whispered before Jaya began to translate.

"They've hypnotized them."

"What?"

"Yeah, I know," said Jaya. I looked at the men anew, the simplicity of it made me smile. Of course, the Elders had known Chana wanted the code for the Stone Circle and that was what they had given him. Only this code had not been for healing, it had been a code to self hypnotize to enable them to pass into other dimensions.

"The Elders are asking us if there is any information we wish to learn regarding Kara and how she disappeared."

I stared at Jaya perplexed. "We can ask them anything we want?"

"In a hypnotized state people will speak the truth according to the Elders, don't ask me why or how. Chana will tell us exactly what we need to know. What happened to Kara and if she's still alive."

We walked over to the Elders standing beside Chana in the Stone Circle. He stood so still, inert as if he were in a deep sleep, only with his eyes open.

"Who are you and what is your real name?" asked Jaya.

"My name is Lee Corona, my parents are third generation Spanish immigrants."

"Who do you work for and what is your role?"

"I graduated from Princetown in 1995 and was recruited by the CIA soon after. I specialised in the transportation of narcotics and gather them at their point of origin. I'm also involved in which ports they are smuggled into."

"Tell me about the CIA and why they're involved in drug trafficking?"

"Many reasons, the CIA works with many underground groups involved in drugs. The CIA are involved in the criminal underworld who can provide us with useful intelligence information in exchange for allowing their criminal activities to continue. The CIA directly imports the drugs into the US and sells them to the Mafia and pharmaceutical companies, raising huge revenues to fund expensive wars and other government policies."

"Why? Why does the CIA do this?"

"Money. These drugs will never be legalised because that would eliminate the enormous profits being made. Being valuable commodities they are worth as much as precious metals with the advantage it can be farmed, in other words a renewable resource."

"Aren't you going to ask about Kara?" I said.

"I'll come to that," Jaya said. "What exactly is your role here?"

"I meet with the drug barons to do the deals and coordinate the collection and transfer of the opium back to military pick up points. This can be achieved by airstrips or ports. Sometimes I travel back to the US with the cargo," throughout Chana's discourse he had not sworn at all, I wondered if it was all just an act.

"How did Kara find out about your operation?" said Jaya gruffly. Even mentioning her name was hard for him.

"She was my girlfriend."

"How long did you date her?" asked Jaya with a hard edge to his voice.

Chana paused suddenly, hesitant to continue.

"How long did you date her?" Jaya asked again.

Even in his present hypnotized state he appeared uncomfortable. "Six months. I didn't see much of her during that time because I was here most of the time."

"And what ended it?"

"They took her."

"Who?"

"Those bastards from the agency."

"Why?"

"She'd overheard me talking on the phone to one of my colleagues. She put two and two together and then confronted me about it. She wanted the whole story so I told her. Then she got really angry, telling me how she was involved in helping native American drug addicts. That it was people like me who made the problem worse. Then she said she was going to blow the lid on it."

"What happened then?" said Jaya

"I tried to stop her, told her it would be too dangerous to expose them. The CIA don't want this operation and others like it reaching the press. Whatever she did, it was only going to get her killed. We had a huge argument and then she left and I never saw her again."

"So what did you do?"

"Nothing, I knew I couldn't help her if she'd spilled the beans. Then I got a call from one of my up line managers wanting to meet. I knew immediately what it was about. We met and he asked me a few questions about Kara. Her background, any fundamentalist groups she was affiliated with. Like they didn't know already. They knew the leak came from me, they would have got that much out of her at least before........ but at the time I was too valuable to let go. I knew too much and I had good relations with the drug barons here so they gave me a choice. To live in this stink hole for the rest of my life or to have my life prematurely shortened."

"What was your managers name?"

Chana hung his head not answering.

"His name," Jaya prompted.

"Mike Middleton."

"Do you think he was responsible for having her killed?"

"I don't know."

"But you think he might know something?"

"Yes."

"Do you know what happened to Kara?"

"Not really. If she's disappeared then she's probably dead. She knew too much and had already posted some of the information on the internet. Americans don't know the half of what their government agencies are up to and that's the way they want it to stay."

So far the story tied in with what Jaya had told me.

"What were your feelings for Kara?"

"I loved her. "

Jaya paused his questioning for a moment, clearly surprised. This Chana was different to the one we'd known since we'd been here. Was it possible there was a softer side?

"Then what?"

"Then I returned to Thailand to continue as before. There was nothing left for me back there."

"Who are these men with you?"

"Paid muscle. You can pick them up anywhere if you're happy to pay enough."

"Why was Layla shot?"

"One of my men patrolling our camp spotted her and fired. That's the only way to survive in this jungle. Attack first, ask questions later. And then you arrived on the scene. Very inconvenient, your timing sucked because then I had to make you look like the enemy as well. Two people following me about the jungle wanting to find out my business is very suspicious in my line of work. I can't trust anyone out here. The CIA would kill for anything less but because it was you and your sister.......... and Layla reminded me of Kara, I just couldn't do it. So I decided to find out how much you knew and what you were doing here."

"You would have let Layla die?" Jaya said accusingly.

"It wasn't in my plan no, but I had very little in the way of options."

"What about one of your military pick up points for the cargo, you could have had her flown to a hospital," Jaya said accusingly.

"And alert them to the fact I had people trailing me?"

I watched as Jaya's hands clenched and his jaw worked. "And this is how the CIA usually operate, terminating people when they become a problem?"

"And worse, they deal with criminals on a day to day basis. Set up smear campaigns against politicians who don't toe the line. What aren't they capable of?"

"The code for the Stone Circle? Why is it important to know this?"

"Because I thought it could be my ticket out of here. I've been dumped in this shit hole. I want to get out. I thought the CIA would be interested in the information. I could do a trade, have my slate wiped clean in exchange for the code."

"What about your phoney Shaman cover story. How did you get it?"

Chana laughed even in his hypnotised state. "The CIA, they have innumerable resources to tap into. It wasn't hard."

"Why did you want to stay in Sanuri when you could have lived with any of the other hill tribes in the region?"

Chana was silent for a moment as a look of confusion passed over his face.

"The Sanuri people like to think of themselves as separate from the outside world but all the tribes out here know about them. I was told there was still potential to persuade the Sanuri people to grow opium, that their valley was an untapped resource. No one had been able to do that before. It was thought that in the guise of a Shaman I could gain their trust and convince them of the benefits of growing opium for cash. How lucrative this business could be for them. Posing as a Shaman was just a way of gaining access into the community. I never knew about the Stone Circle. That was just a happy coincidence but when I found out I decided to stay for longer. I could still run my operations from Sanuri while I observed how the Stone Circle was used, but the Elders never divulged any information on 'the code'."

"Can you tell us anything else that could lead us to Kara's whereabouts?" asked Jaya.

Chana remained silent and shook his head.

Jaya turned to the Elders who'd waited patiently for our conversation with Chana to finish. I wondered how much they had understood of what had passed between Chana and Jaya. Then the realisation hit me that Jaya and Layla were done here. They had discovered everything they needed to know about Chana except what had happened to Kara. At least they had a name to follow up in the US. I suddenly felt immensely sad for them both. I knew how badly Jaya wanted closure on this, to know one way or the other what had happened to his sister. Then at least he and his family could put the ghosts to rest and get on with the rest of their lives.

"What's going to happen to Chana and his men?" I asked. The Sanuri people couldn't just simply return them to how they'd been before. The secret of the Stone Circle was still at stake.

"Chana and his men will be taken back to one of their old camps outside of Sanuri and then woken up from their hypnotised state. They will forget they have ever been here. They will forget its existence and everyone they have met."

"What if Chana has already reported he was being followed?"

"I don't think he did. He was concerned about his superiors knowing about any complications. So it is unlikely he mentioned anything about Layla and me. We'll still need to be careful though, just in case."

"Is it really that easy to erase a person's memories?" I asked.

"I don't know, but I trust the Sanuri Elders. They know what they are doing."

"But how do they do that? I mean, how can these natives know about hypnotizing people?"

"They're Shamans, Elders have always used the hypnotic techniques to enter into other states of consciousness to access information they require. In the West, hypnosis is a relatively new phenomena."

"What do they need to know? I mean why do it?"

Jaya turned to me with a solemn expression. "They do it to be merged with Oneness, the greatest state of grace known to man."

There was nothing I could say to that.

"So the Elders hypnotized Chana and his men by calling up the Stone Circle's energy not to heal but to allow them to enter other states of consciousness?"

"In a nutshell. Like I said the Stone Circle can be used for many purposes."

"Can anyone do that. Hypnotise people I mean."

"No, the Elders have trained for many years to be able to do what they do and they only work for the greatest good of all beings."

"That's a shame," I said thinking of the possibilities. "There'd be a few people I'd like to use that trick on."

*To make them forget the past.*

My mother being one for starters.

# Chapter 24

## Layla Recovered

Day break, the rose coloured light seeped through my open window pulling me awake. The sound of early risers already working on their chores filtered though the planks of the hut. Village life started early, before the heat of the day began, allowing the natives to relax when the heat was at its most lethal. I had managed to sleep only towards the later part of the night, tossing and turning, my mind never holding still long enough to slip under the blanket of sleep. There'd been too much happening over the last twenty-four hours and now I'd woken too early to feel refreshed.

I pulled the covers over my head to keep out the light, intent on snatching a few more minutes sleep, but then I felt the bed dip as the weight of Jaya fell in beside me, pulling my willing body towards him like a starving magnet. The sweet woody scent filled my lungs and then the feeling of those strong all encompassing arms as they circled around me, transporting me to heaven. Jaya had wanted to stay with Layla last night. She was still very weak and Jaya had thought she might need him still.

I felt the hot sweet breath against my ear as he nuzzled my hair. The hard lines of his body curving into mine and suddenly my whole world was here in this room, there was nothing else I needed.

"Sleepy head," he murmured as his lips brushed mine, pulling me fully awake as my lips responded to his. The kiss deepened, our lips danced across each other's. Then, feeling the fire of wanting him took me by surprise, hitting me deep in the pit of my stomach. I pushed myself against him, melting into the folds of his body, allowing myself the luxury of this closeness to Jaya. My fairytale imaginings had come true, even more wonderful in reality. Every fibre of my body burned for Jaya, my body only minutes ago woolly with sleep now became super sensitive to each sensation which cursed through my body.

Then I remembered, like being suddenly pushed into a cold bath. The knot of fear recoiling inwards, making me tense under the scorching touch of Jaya's hand. He felt me stiffen, his hand on my leg slid to a stop as he lifted his eyes to mine. Not judging or accusing, just holding my gaze with his soft golden brown eyes. Searching out my fear, the recoil and then the shame.

I looked away unable to look back at him. He cupped one hand under my chin to tilt my head so I could not escape his molten brown eyes. Could not doubt the gentleness or his ardor.

"Alice," he spoke softly." There is nothing to fear, it is only me. You know I would never hurt you." He spoke gently, his eyes gazed at me tenderly. I had to look away again, unable to bear it any longer, then pulling my chin out of his grasp to prevent him seeing the moisture threatening to spill.

"Alice, oh Alice," he spoke thickly pulling me tightly to him, pressing me into the strong safe planes of his chest, his hand in my hair, his breath on my cheek.

"If you could only know this thing between a man and a woman, it is nothing to fear, nothing to abhor, only an expression of love between two people," he murmured.

I'd promised myself I would not cry but suddenly the tears erupted unchecked, running silently down my cheeks.

"There is no hurry, no need to put yourself under any pressure. I want you to want me but only when you are ready and you'll know when that time is because you won't be able to resist me any longer," he chuckled to himself, trying to make light of the situation.

"Alice?" he bent his head towards me suddenly concerned I hadn't replied. Perhaps he detected the wetness on his chest or felt the reverberation of my stifled sobs.

Stupid, stupid, stupid.

How weak I must look, how stupid and pathetic.

Ever since I had known this man, all I seemed to be doing was crying whenever any shred of kindness was shown towards me. I seemed powerless to keep my emotions under control as they happily partied at my expense. Jaya's kindness had unlocked a deep vault of unresolved emotions, bubbling merrily at their new found freedom and embarrassing me at every turn. I felt guilty how I leaned on him for support, sharing the shame of the dark ghosts of my past which haunted me, each and everyday. The nightmares had never gone away and somehow, I had to learn to make peace with them otherwise my life would always be blighted like this.

But how could that be done?

Here I had everything I could possibly want, but I worried that Jaya's interest would wane if I could never give him this last part of me or experience everything a healthy relationship should offer.

What man would wait for someone like me?

I, who now knew how powerful this sexual desire could be for a man, strong enough to drive a man to take without asking. As vital to their constitution as the sun to a flower. Yet here and now, the aftermath of such an event would always extend way beyond that fateful night. It lay like the elephant in the room, unspoken and unresolved. Trauma does that to people. Working at an subconscious level. Like a computer, the trojan damaging the hard drive so that it cannot function as it was supposed to do. I had resigned myself to spinsterhood, never believing I could trust another man.

Until I'd met Jaya.

For a long time we lay entwined. The tension of the moment had long since passed. I was content just to nestle against the warm golden brown skin so smoothly silky, and luxuriate under the lazy movement of Jaya's hand caressing my back until a movement beside the door made my look up.

"Layla!" I jumped out of bed to hug Layla too me.

The beautiful young woman who stood before me today held no resemblance to the one who'd lain dying only yesterday. She looked so healthy, her hair glossy, the skin golden and fresh. While her cheeks and lips had returned to their former rouged glory.

She tutted when she examined my hair. All semblance of control had long since passed, the curls had morphed into the crazy frizz of before.

"What have you been doing to this," Layla said in mock disgust. "Haven't you learned anything about how to look after your hair?"

"I'm sorry, I've been busy," I said smiling back at her.

"And what of you brother?" she said. "Sneaking into this girl's bed without asking? What would the villagers say to that?"

"You already know the answer to that. We'd have to marry!" Jaya grinned.

"Yes, you would."

" Hang on a minute, marriage?!" I said aghast.

They both turned to grin at me. "It's the Sanuri way. When you lie with the one you love the next morning you're married!" Said Layla laughing.

"Well, that's a relief. Jaya's only been here a few minutes!"

Jaya rose from the bed, his height and size seemed to fill the entire room and grabbed Layla around the waist in a backwards hug.

"Stop teasing Alice," he murmured into her ear.

"So you haven't dated any of the native girls here?"

"No, for that very reason."

"And what about you Layla. What were you doing spending all that time with Chana?"

"Ladies," Jaya interrupted as he exited the door. "You have your chat. I'll go make some breakfast." He said leaving Layla and I alone together.

"Chana. Well, he wanted me to help him you see. We were studying the Stone Circle and the unusual energies in this area. I thought it too good an opportunity to miss to spend time with him. Jaya wasn't keen on the idea but what choice did he have? It was a chance to find out what Chana was up to and any information about himself."

"And did you?"

"Yes and no. He was very clever, never really revealed very much about his past or tribe that he supposedly came from. Of course, we checked his story out, we wanted to know how he orchestrated such good cover. Someone within America's tribal community undoubtably covered for him. We still want to find out who that was."

"That reminds me," said Jaya coming to stand in the doorway to my bedroom with something in his hand which looked alarmingly familiar.

"What's that?" I asked, although I already knew. I just couldn't believe it.

"A satellite phone," he said looking at me apologetically.

"You had a phone here all the time?" I said.

"Yes."

"But you decided not to tell me," I said flatly, belying the indignity I felt inside.

"Yes, no.....I" he didn't get the chance to finish.

"You didn't tell me you had a phone. All the time I thought I was trapped here, unable to get home........."

He interrupted. "We only use this cell in emergencies, the line is unsafe. We have to be careful in case other people are listening into our conversations."

"But...."

Jaya held up a hand to silence my protests already speaking into the receiver to someone on the other end of the line.

It seemed strange to see him with a piece of twenty-first century kit. The most technical piece of equipment I'd seen him use until now had been a home made spear and his little gas stove.

"We have to be careful. Satellite phone lines are never secure so we only use them when absolutely necessary," Layla interjected.

"You're worried people might be looking for you too?"

"It's still likely Chana reported back to his contacts in the US. He may have told them he'd been followed and had captured them."

I looked off into the distance for a moment.

"What does that mean?"

"We're not sure. Our father is trying to find out. The CIA may have been alerted to our presence here in Sanuri. They may want to talk to us."

"Will you be able to return home?"

Layla smiled sadly. "We don't think so, not yet at least."

Jaya finished his phone call. "My father's onto it, he's going to ring back later. He suggests we stay put for now and not do anything until he has more information."

We sat in silence digesting this information.

Layla turned to me. "I'm going to make some coffee, would you like some?"

I nodded.

We wandered into the communal area to make coffee and suddenly something caught my eye. One of the tapestries hanging on the wall held a shape that seemed oddly familiar. I walked closer. Yes, there was something within the swirling shapes I recognised. Suddenly I remembered something, the strange stone I'd discovered in the caves. I pulled it from my shorts and held it up to the light. There, the patterns on the stone were the same as drawn on the tapestries. I walked to the other wall hangings and found they also held the familiar shape. What did it mean?

"Layla, come here a sec," I said continuing to look between the stone and the tapestries. Layla came to stand beside me and followed my gaze.

"That can't be possible," she said. "Can I have a look?"

I passed her the stone, watching as she turned it over in her hand.

"Where did you find it?"

"Back in the caves. It was odd because I would never have found it had it not been......" I stalled suddenly feeling foolish. It seemed so ridiculous now.

"Because of what?"

I looked at her warily. "I followed a light, it led me down one of the tunnels and where it stopped I found this stone."

"You followed a light?" Layla asked in an incredulous voice, her eyebrows arching in surprise.

"Yeah, I know, I should be locked up, right?"

"No, that's not what I meant. What type of light was it."

"Ah, golden and it had a strange energy. I'd felt it before, when Jaya first took me through the cave network. He said it was the spirit keeper." I looked at her closely to see any signs of guffawing, but there was none.

Layla looked down at the stone and then back at me with a wondrous expression. "You've found it. There are legends about this stone and it's symbol, I never believed it was real."

I stared at the stone perplexed. "What do you mean?"

"Let me see if I can remember the story correctly," she became very still, concentrating on the stone in her hand. "The stone was lost many centuries ago during a war between two tribes. It has amazing powers, the stories have been handed down in folk law for just as long. Someone hid the stone to keep it safe but this person was killed soon after. No one knew where he'd taken it. It is believed to contain special energies like the Stone Circle, and now you've found it." She looked at me quizzically. "I didn't believe it. The Elders were right, you really were sent to us for a reason."

I suddenly remembered something. Lifting my hair I showed it to Layla. "Does this mark look anything like those on the stone?"

Layla laid a finger on my skin, tracing the outline of whatever she could see. "Yes." She said quietly. "It's almost exactly the same." She drew back to look at me with a strange expression.

"Didn't Jaya tell you about this?"

"Yes, it was talked about at the Elders meeting, but of course you wouldn't have known what was said. There was much debate about what it meant to have found a symbol on a strange foreign girl. No one could work it out so it was decided to see how events panned out. The Elders believed that your purpose in coming here would be revealed to us and now it has."

I nearly said 'and you believe all that stuff', but by the expression on Layla's face she clearly did.

Layla continued. "This is not just a stone, it's the symbol drawn upon it which is the key." She paused to think. "The legend tells us this stone and others like it are linked to the Stone Circle somehow, that it contains the same magical powers."

"But Jaya told me it was the combination of earth and planetary energies which created the healing energies. How can a symbol have the same powers?"

"Yes, that's true but this stone is a key to unlocking something and I'm not......I can't quite remember what was said about it."

"So the tapestries, the stone and the mark on my neck have the same symbol drawn upon them. If the stone has the same magical powers as the Stone Circle, does it not mean that anything which has the symbol drawn upon it also has these powers?"

Layla looked at the symbols on the stone thoughtfully.

"The Stone Circle requires a code to evoke the healing energies, perhaps this is all that is needed. Maybe it is linked in ways we cannot even imagine and yet still it can still heal."

I looked at her as a new thought came to me, then everything fell into place.

"Then that's how you were healed back in the caves. I thought you were dying so I prayed for you to be healed soon after I found the stone," I exclaimed.

Layla nodded. "That could explain it."

"Could it really be that simple?"

"It must be, I'm proof!" she said laughing. "There's no other explanation."

"Do you think it could work anywhere, I mean somewhere far from this place," I said as a nugget of an idea began to formulate in my head.

"I don't see why not," said Layla happily. "But the Elders will not want this rock to leave the valley. I will need to return it. "She said holding out her hand to retrieve the stone. Reluctantly I handed it over, before another nugget of an idea, larger than the last, began to roll insistently around inside my head.

Then I knew exactly what I had to do.

# Chapter 25

# The Elders

It was early morning. A golden sun rose hazily just above the line of trees. Morning mist hung heavily over the jungle like etherial gauze, shrouding the shapes of the trees and vegetation in great swathes.

I glanced back towards the sleeping figure of Jaya strewn untidily across the bed. Marvelling at the perfect features, the strong set of the jaw, the fine but strong nose. His beautiful golden skin contrasting against the paleness of the bed covers. How had I got this lucky I wondered? How had I managed to find such a place and such a man? I shook my head hardly able to believe my good fortune.

These last few years I had striven to be content with just myself. To never need or depend upon anyone else ever again. It was just too painful, but this resolution had been thrown to the wolves. Now my new found contentment depended upon Jaya. A happiness as fragile and delicate as newly formed butterfly wings. I hardly knew how to act in this uncharctered territory, this vast tundra of new discovery and I worried I could easily ruin it with my clumsy fears and phobias.

I padded back to the bed and lay down beside Jaya, nestling into the curves of his body. I could feel the gentle rise and fall of his chest and the steady beat of his heart and suddenly I was transported back to my childhood. A time when I would sneak into my parents bed on a weekend morning. Contented just to listen to them sleeping. My whole world there in that room.

We'd grown up on a brand new estate in Harpenden's poorer suburb Southdown, our house backing onto the St Pancras line. Not the best of locations by any stretch of the imagination, but it meant we could afford the four bedroomed house my father had always aspired to provide for his young family. My mother became entrenched within the estate's community. Organizing baby sitting circles, being the helpful neighbour and encouraging the estates children to come and play at our house when others shoed us away.

Kids loved coming to our house to play. Envious of our fun loving mother, baking cakes and taking us and our friends to the local swimming pool or adventure parks.

Frankly, I enjoyed my friend's admiration of my mother, a big kid herself and who frequently joined in all the fun. I was too young too appreciate that other mothers were not like mine or even half as good.

Although our father was a far more distant figure, it didn't mean he loved us any less. He just found it hard to tell us, that was all, but that did not mean we felt deprived. Our father was a stoic steadying influence, but now the memory of him was beginning to fade. I struggled to remember the timbre of his voice or the sound of his laugh. Even his features were difficult to recall and frequently I needed a photograph to remind me how he looked. Somehow this frightened me, that I was beginning to lose the memory of my father. One of the biggest influences of my life and now I hardly remembered who he was. Was that what happened over time when we lost someone we loved? That slowly they faded from your heart and mind until eventually they became just a fragment of before? Or maybe it depended upon how much space they'd taken in your heart. Perhaps ten years had not been long enough to indelibly imprint my father to memory forever.

I let the thoughts slide away. The ache in my heart would never go away if I continued to think of the past. Best not to think of it at all. Living in the moment was best and keeping busy, busy, busy. That had been my motto back home when every corner of life had been a reminder of what we had lost.

But not here in Sanuri. Here I had been able to largely forget the past. I'd found a good friend in Layla, and a man who had given me somewhere soft to land. What more did I need to be happy? Yet, these good times made me tense and apprehensive. I knew how fragile happiness could be how easily it could be taken away.

Nothing ever lasted.

I rolled away from Jaya and padded into the communal area of the hut to make some tea. A nagging uneasiness settled over me, and I knew what it was. I did not want to think of my mother all alone with only her bitter sadness to keep her company. I did not want to think of her pain or how similar her coping mechanisms were to mine.

Because I needed someone to blame.

In my mind it had had to be my mother. For not living up to the mark and getting over my father like other people did. For escaping into her drunken world and leaving Harry and me to pick up the pieces of our life on our own. For taking my savings to fuel her addictions. Cashing in the bonds my father had invested for me to mature when I reached the age of eighteen. Wasted and burned on useless cigarettes and booze.

I shook my head sadly, although I understood the reasons why she drank and why she'd become the way she was, but that didn't make it easier to love the person she'd now become they way she was, but that didn't make it any easier to love this person who had taken her place.


Later, I sat on the balcony over looking the village waiting for Jaya's return. Jaya had left more than an hour ago to attend to some chores. Layla had still not risen.

Eat, sleep, find food.

I was getting used to doing very little.

It was not until the sun had risen high in the sky that I noticed Jaya making his way towards me through the village and I wondered idly what had kept him so long.

"Alice, I have some fantastic news," he said enthusiastically flopping onto a chair next to me.

"You've won the lottery?"

He smiled that jaw dropping smile. "No. I've just met with the Elders. Well, to cut a long story short they want to offer you the healing of the Stone Circle."

I stared at him perplexed. "Me?" I said stupidly.

"Yes you!"

"I don't understand."

"It's a thank you for everything you've done. Without you, Layla and I would most likely be dead."

"No, you would never have got into this mess in the first place if it hadn't been for me," I countered.

"You found the stone, discovered it's healing powers and you rescued us, do I need to go on?"

I stared down at my hands suddenly anxious, picking at an old scab that had almost healed. "They want to offer this to me?" I repeated.

"Yes, silly!"

I looked away into the distance finding this news strangely disturbing. "And you think this could work for someone like me?"

Jaya was silenced for a moment. "Is that what you think? That it couldn't work for you too?"

I nodded mutely.

"Alice, the Stone Circle doesn't pick and choose who it works for it heal everyone on all aspects of ourselves not just the physical. It will help you as well. I know it will."

"How, how do you know?" I said annoyed. "You have no idea what I'm like inside."

"You're saying that to the wrong person Alice. I do know what's inside and it's not all bad. It's just mixed up."

I stayed silent for a moment.

"What if I'm not me anymore, afterwards?" I said.

"You will still be who you are, just without any baggage."

"But if this can't help me.....?"

"It can and it will," Jaya said picking me up to pull me onto his lap.

"You think life has been a big disappointment. Am I right?" I nodded.

"And you're worried this will be too," said Jaya matter of factly. "I understand that, but why would you give up a chance like this just because you're afraid of what might not happen? You've seen the result of Layla being healed with just the stone with the symbols. You know it works. Don't even think this can't help you because I won't let you." Jaya leaned back to look at me. "Understand?"

"Yes."

"No one's forcing you to do this but you might never have a chance like this again. To get shot of the past and worst case scenario, even if it didn't work at least you tried, at least you gave it a go. Believe it or not that's the biggest step, making that decision to have help. We can't do it all on our own. Okay?"

Before I could answer, the creaking of the hut's wooden steps and the sound of numerous feet upon them told me the elders had come to hear my decision.

The Elders had come to hear my decision.

I quickly recovered my composure, pulling my hand down over my face to wipe my bewildered expression away.

We stood to greet them as they stepped onto the balcony. I faced them with a smile that belied the turmoil that twisted inside.

Jaya began to translate when one of the Elders began to speak.

"They have come to thank you in person for everything you have done for the sons and daughters of Sanuri. A most valuable artifact has been returned to them and they are eternally grateful."

The Elder paused and turned to retrieve an object being held by one of the others. A palm leaf folded many times over was being handed to me. I looked at Jaya who nodded I should accept the gift.

"This is a gift which signifies your place amongst the Sanuri people. They welcome you as an adopted daughter."

Slowly I opened the emerald green wrapping and inside nestled a handcrafted beaded necklace similar to Layla's. It was beautiful. Immediately I put it on much to the delight of the Elders.

"Thank you. I don't know what to say," I said.

"They offer you the Stone Circle's healing."

I gave Jaya a sideways glance. I knew he was watching me closely in how I was going to reply. Was this really what I wanted? Yes, I wanted to be rid of my defects but.....

"Yes, I would like that. Thank you," I blurted out before I could change my mind.

The Elder who had spoken took my hand and squeezed it tightly smiling up at me.

"You are now officially a Sanuri daughter," Jaya said smiling.

I looked down at my feet not knowing how to act. I was overwhelmed by their generosity and their kindness. The healing in the Stone I hoped would enable me to find a new perspective a new set of protocols by which to live. Yet if it didn't, if I stayed the same as before, then I decided that would be okay too.

I would take whatever was being given and hope it was good enough to keep Jaya by my side.

# Chapter 26

# The Stone Circle

The journey to the Stone Circle seemed arduous and long. Each step dragged as if I was walking through snow. The monsters of my past had reared their ugly heads, taking it in turns to terrorise my thoughts and feelings. Filling my cup of fear to full and then overflowing. Yet, despite the agony they brought with them, they'd become familiar, woven intricately into the very fibre of my being. I knew my limitations, my boundaries and now the thought of these being taken from me brought a stab of disquiet. How would I know how to act when they'd gone? A shiver ran down my spine as I wondered how such characteristics could be extracted at the same time without also removing my inner most being.

Now I felt like the proverbial lamb being taken to the slaughter.

The sweat ran down my back and collected under my arms, indelibly becoming impregnated with fear.

I could almost smell it.

Every fibre hummed with tension, my gut churned and coiled.

What on earth was I doing? I asked myself for the umpteenth time.

I knew with certainty, I couldn't go back to my self inflicted prison anymore. That dark cavernous place I'd created inside devoid of all light. I had to break free from those chains once and for all and perhaps this would to be my only chance.

Still, it scared the hell out of me.

I clung to the fact Layla had been miraculously healed when she'd been dying. There'd been nothing different about her afterwards, in fact, she'd positively glowed. Perhaps if I was as lucky ...........no don't get too hopeful, I chastised myself.

I still had to protect myself from disappointment.

*Just in case.*

Being with Jaya had thrown up all my defects I'd been trying to bury these last few years. Weaknesses I now knew would never go away if I did not face them and face this. At least I was not doing this on my own, I had Jaya and Layla with me flanking on each side.

I reached out and grasped Jaya's hand, holding it between both of mine. Whatever happened in the next hour or so I had to trust it would be okay. Yet trust had never featured much in my life when my experiences had shown me it was safer not to. Now I hoped this was going to change all that. To become that person I never thought I could be.

*To be who I really was.*

Was it really possible to change habits of a lifetime or even change your personality? I hurriedly pushed the thoughts away. Too much speculation never did any good. I would take one step at a time and get through this as best I could and I'd promised myself I wasn't going to break down into a gibbering idiot in front of everyone again.

Once was more than enough.

The path lead steeply upwards and panned out on to a level plateau. I recognised some of the rocks and unusual plant life from when we'd been brought here by Chana.

Taking the last turn, suddenly we emerged from the jungle into a large clearing. There, the magnificent stones stood just as I remembered but less mysterious in the light of day. I glanced round the clearing which was much bigger than I'd imagined the darkness having concealed it's true size. We pulled to a stop and everyone turned to look speculatively at me.

This was it. I gulped.

The Elders began speaking and appeared to be relaying instructions as they prepared to begin the ceremony. I felt my stomach summersault in response. I wanted to run away and as fast as I could but then Jaya lowered his back pack and pulled me into his arms.

He understood, he knew how scared I was.

Normally I would enjoy being pressed into the hard lines of his body, to feel the strength and shift of his muscles beneath the golden skin. Now I hardly noticed.

"Hey," he said looking down at me, stroking my hair. "It'll be okay."

"Yeah, whatever," I said trying to sound cool. He cupped my chin to raise my head to look at him.

"I'll be right there with you," he said with his hand on his heart. "Every step of the way."

I nodded unable to speak, a large lump was forming. I should be getting used to having feelings again, but these were the ones I'd never wanted back. I willed them away with great effort. I'd promised myself no more emotional outbursts, it was just too pathetic.

Jaya was directed to lead me into the centre of the Stone Circle and wait for further instructions. The waiting seemed to stretch for eternity.

Finally the Elders signalled they were ready.

"It's best if you lie down," he said gently looking down at me. The golden flecks in his eyes glinting in the sunlight. His glossy hair worn loose today, framing those fine features and never looking so handsome. Taking one last look into Jaya's eyes and then all around me I sank down to the ground. Jaya knelt down beside me.

"Don't fight it Alice, but you're good at that aren't you?" he said smiling, trying to lighten the situation.

I averted my eyes, the panic was beginning to set in and I didn't want him to see the sheer terror in my eyes.

"That's your best advice, don't fight it? Anything else I need to know?" I said shakily.

"Yes, just this," he said, leaning down to kiss me gently before moving away to join the others.

Suddenly I was all alone. The Elders, Jaya and Layla all stood at least twenty meters away well outside the Stone Circle, their faces bright with anticipation.

I took a deep breath and closed my eyes. Trying not to notice my heart careering away in panic, my palms hot and sweaty and the dreadful hysteria beginning to take over my body. The Elders began their incantation with a rhythmic chant evoking the power of the Stone Circle. Calling on the heavens and the earth to unify their energies for the divine purpose of healing.

Their voices clicking and blending in melodic harmony that went on and on.

The atmosphere within the clearing suddenly became deathly still and charged with energy, like the calm before the storm.

Then I felt it.

The sensations began as a buzzing. Gradually gaining in strength and then moving over my body. Pins and needles prickled through me and then intense heat swirled into my hands and feet.

I kept my eyes squeezed tightly shut. The sensations inside me were more than enough to scare me, I didn't want to see what was happening outside of me as well. The sensations pulled and pushed, strobing up and down, warm then cold and then a strange buzzing sound filled the air. Like standing under an electricity pylon, causing the hairs on my arms to stand tall and the skin on my scalp prickled. My heart raced at an unbelievable gallop, the pressure inside and out was building and building until I could bear it no more. I raised my head to look for Jaya in hope the sight of him would still my frazzled nerves but nothing was there, only the blurred outline of the stones shimmered as if a heat haze were all around me, beyond that there was nothing.

What was happening?

Stupid question.

Then I realised. The energies of the Stone Circle were distorting the visuals. The frequencies and vibrations danced and shook in tune to the Elders chant.

Heaven combining with earth.

Had it been the same for Layla too?

I could not wonder for long because a new feeling had entered my body.

Now it was love which moved through me.

Like that of the Spirit Keeper when she had visited me in the caves, my father cuddling me in his arms or my mother comforting me on her knee. They had all shown me their love and now I was being healed with it.

As the love continued to surge through me, I knew with a sudden certainty, it was this which had been absent from my life, this I had been searching for all this time. Not only to be bestowed upon by others but for me to love the person within. All these years I had hated who I was, loathed the faults and failures, detested my weaknesses and defects, the shame I'd felt after the rape. I had thought I'd been irrevocably changed and become different from everyone else. An emotionally handicapped, vandalized and frigid person so disfigured inside I didn't deserve to be loved.

Now I knew I'd been mistaken.

The gulf by which I'd kept myself separate had always been an illusion. I was no more separate than the sun from the sky. We are all connected. By love, this love, this beautiful force which moved within all things. Mostly buried or ignored within us yet still our divine inheritance. I understood now. I understood it all. This light was in us all, good, bad or ugly. Only most of us had forgotten it was even there and now I had found it. This eternal flame within and the true shining light of my Soul was being allowed to emerge.

Illness is a self inflicted state of being, manifesting when there is an absence of light.

My emotional and physical were being healed with this loving energy, this light.

I could feel it.

I'd been broken inside all these years, until eventually it had felt normal. The darkness, the shame had all but extinguished the person hiding within.

The Stone Circle filled me with its unconditional love, entering every cell, every molecule of my being, filling me, enriching me and allowing me to become whole.

The tears began to fall, then faster, but not from sadness or hurt.

They fell for joy.

Joy for feeling alive, joy for remembering who I was, joy for being loved, joy in the process of life.

The landscape of my life was being irrevocably changed, transmuted. The fears were being melted away, replaced with much nobler emotions lain dormant for so many years. The true light of my Soul was being allowed to emerge, as if from a self inflicted cocoon. I felt myself stepping forward and slowly unfolding my wings. This was my God self, the divine spark entrusted to me by God and I had all but smothered it in darkness.

Until now.

I felt the warmth of the divine presence around and within me. This was the Oneness Jaya talked about, this was what it felt like to be connected to all things. I was being reborn. I would never walk in darkness again, not now I had felt this.

How could I?

Now I knew this love existed I could never return to the person I had been before. It would be like living in the freezing lands of Antarctica when I'd glimpsed the tropics, eating stale bread when I'd tasted caviar.

There was no going back. I was changing, morphing into someone new. Someone I wanted to be.

*Someone I could finally like.*

# Chapter 27

# Making a Decision

"Does everyone have the same experience in the Stone Circle?" I asked over breakfast one morning

Layla replied "Everyone is different, with all our own unique set of problems. Of course the Sanuri people have used it for a long time and they have very little in the way of health problems nowadays."

"So what do they use it for?"

"Snake bites, broken arms, that sort of thing."

"Do you think any other stone circles can heal like the one here?" I asked.

"Probably."

I contemplated that for a moment. Thinking of the possibilities, but how would anyone know which ones could heal? I got up and walked over to the tapestries, examining the whorls and colours as if hoping to see something else.

Even if I found a stone circle back home that healed like the one in Sanuri, it would be useless without the code. I knew that, but there had to be a way to get this amazing healing power home.

A skeleton of an idea had began to formulate in my head. Something that had been niggling away ever since I'd found the stone with it's special symbols. The healing powers could be evoked elsewhere away from this place, but I didn't know exactly how. Yes, I'd said a few words in prayer in the tunnels in the cave network and more by luck than anything else Layla had been healed. I'd been told it had been more to do with pure intention than anything else. An exact code was needed to unlock the healing power for people who did not believe in divine intervention or were able to project loving intent.

Over the last few weeks I had revisited the Stone Circle several more times. The results had even been amazing to myself. The angry blaze of eczema on my elbows and behind my knees had disappeared completely. The anxiety, fears and phobias had melted away like butter, leaving me feeling at peace and happy for the first time in years.

Jaya had noticed the difference too. A look of speculation had been evident in his eyes. I knew what he was thinking and I'd been imagining it too.

I smiled inwardly. That was something I would soon be finding out. Jaya was right, I was finding him increasingly hard to resist. The feel of his hands on my body, the slow play of caresses evoked something deep in my belly. A fire which Jaya was gently stoking. But I knew the fire had to be truly blazing. Only then would I be ready to take that last final step.

I dragged my thoughts away and back to the idea still rolling around in my head. What if I could take this amazing healing back home? What if my mother could be healed like I'd been?

There, the notion had surfaced. I could not unthink it.

The thought of my mother alone with her depression had begun to play on my heart and mind. A mother who had only shut herself away within her alcoholic world to escape the hurts and pain. A mother who had turned inward to stop feeling the pain.

*Like I had done.*

How had I not seen the similarities? How had I not understood?

I knew why.

Because I had been too wrapped up in myself and my own problems to see beyond. Like driving a car at nighttime, I had only been able to see the pool of light illuminating my own road, my own world of troubles. I had cocooned myself in my own cave so that I could no longer see or absorb other people's pain.

The guilt hit me deep within. I had run away. I had endeavored to forget my troubles at home and with them my mother. She could not run. She'd had to stay. To work, to pay the bills just to survive. There'd been no escape for her.

The liquid in my eyes spilled over. I should have helped her more. I should never have left. What had I done?

The sobs came in pitiful bursts as the full weight of my selfishness hit me. I thought I had left to save myself but now

I realised this had been the easy option. I had left so I did not have to face my mother's pain mirroring my own.

In my way I had blamed her for the miserable life we led back home. For not living up to the mark, for not coping with the loss of our father. Yet who was I to judge her? I had not come to terms with my traumas either.

Yet, that had been before I'd been healed by the Stone Circle and I knew it could do the same for my mother and Harry. Harry who had left the house as soon as he was able, had his own ghosts to exorcise. We'd all been in need of healing, trapped in the private rooms of our own traumas. Now I wanted to help them too.

Silently I made a vow to myself. I would find a way to take this healing power back to my mother and Harry. I would help them just as I had been helped.

I felt an arm circle around me. I had forgotten about Jaya and Layla. Annoyed with myself I angrily wiped the tears from my face.

"What is it Alice?" said Layla softly.

I hesitated, I'd never spoken much of my past, mostly to avoid the pitying looks in peoples eyes.

"Home. I was thinking about home," I said eventually.

I felt the weight of their stares and then it all came out. I'd only given snippets about my family before and now I filled in all the gaps.

"I have to help her, I have to help them both. Maybe I could find a Stone Circle like this back in the England."

It was Layla who spoke. "Even if you did find a Stone Circle that healed, you'd never get it to work. You still need the code."

"I know," I said hopelessly.

Silence sat between us. There was nothing to say.

Eventually I turned to Layla. "Is there anyway I can learn the code and take it back home."

Their sombre faces gave me the answer. "That would be for the Elders to decide." Jaya said eventually. "And to be honest, it's pretty unlikely."

Still, I didn't want to give up, there must be a way although right now, it seemed impossible.

Morning again, time was flying by. It had been more than a week since my last visit to the Stone Circle. My body felt strong, my emotions true and free. Life was good. Apart from the guilt when I thought of my mother, but there was nothing I could do to help her. So I'd pushed these negative thoughts away. I did not want it to spoil the time I still had left or how happy I'd become.

In the beginning, the feelings had felt almost alien having been absent for so long. My face ached from smiling so much, the muscles unused to such use. And I was in love. With this gorgeous, amazing man who slept next to me every night. Just holding me in his arms, never forcing the issue. Letting me come round to it in my own way and my own time.

I felt Jaya stir beside me. I turned to watch him. I'd never stopped marvelling at the lovely golden skin, the strong handsome features and toned body. I drank in his appearance, taking in every small detail, wanting to keep this image like a photograph in my head. Knowing I would need it when my time came for me to leave because in my heart I knew I could never stay here. This was not my life or what I wanted. I had a University course to get back to, a new life to lead. But I didn't want to think of that yet, didn't want to face the future.

Jaya and Layla would be leaving soon too. Since Chana had been returned to the jungle with his men, they'd been waiting for news from their father if the CIA had any interest in them still.

But before I left, there was still one last thing that Jaya could do for me.

I leaned over to kiss him awake.

"Sleepy head!" I said, repeating the words he'd whispered to me all those weeks ago. My comment drew a small curve of a smile. His hand came over to pull me close, wrapping me into his chest where I could feel the soft thud of his heart. I listened to the comforting beat beneath my head and then I spoke. Having weighed and measured the words carefully, almost feeling too shy to say them now the moment was here.

"Jaya, I'm ready," I said quietly. For a moment I wondered if he had heard me at all for he made no sound or change of movement. Until I noticed his breath had stilled and then the sound of his racing heart beating beneath my ear. He lifted me level so he could look me full in the face. His expression serious.

"You're ready?" he repeated questioningly.

I nodded.

"Are you sure?" He said searching my face.

"As sure as I'll ever be," I said smiling back at him. "But not here, I want us to be alone. Just you and me. I want it to be special." I said.

He looked at me gently. "You will have your wish Alice and it will be special. Special for me too for I know what this means to you."

I snuggled back down onto his chest, running my hand over the hard muscles beneath. I smiled inwardly on hearing his racing heart. How cool he played it with me but underneath I knew how much this meant to him too. To show me this physical love and to know every part of me.

"Have you ever been in love before?" I asked dreamily, my hand now tracing the light hairs on his forearm.

"No, not even close. You?"

"No, I've never even had a boyfriend."

"Not even a crush on a pop star or something like that?"

"Are you having a joke?" I said, hearing the laugh rumble through his chest. "That's fantasy stuff. Like I'd have the hots for someone I didn't even know!" I said chuckling to myself when I remembered how I'd felt from almost the first moment I'd laid eyes on him.

"Hey, what's so funny."

"It's nothing," I said smothering my smile into his chest.

"You know, for an English person, you have a weird sense of humour."

"For an English person? What's that supposed to mean?"

"It means I can't work you out."

"I like keeping you guessing, it adds to the mystery."

"Yeah well, eventually I'll know everything about you."

"It may take a while."

"Time is definitely not against us Alice, I have all the time in the world!" he said pulling me to my feet, then leaning down to kiss me deeply.

"You don't have to do that anymore Jaya!" I said weakly.

"Just warming you up!"

"You've been doing that all week!"

"It's worked then!"

"More than you can ever know."

"Tell me how, for future reference!" the smile twitched at the corners of his mouth.

"Never!"

"Go on."

"No."

"Fine."

"Whatever."

"I won't let you into my secret then."

"What secret?"

"Ah, can't tell you now!"

"Oh, you're impossible."

"You'll like it."

"What?"

"The secret."

"It isn't a secret if you tell me."

"Well, you'll never know then," he said turning away, but he had me now. I hated secrets. So I told him everything. How much I loved him, how he made me feel.

"So what's this secret then?" I asked eventually.

"It's Layla. She went to see the Elders," he said slowly.

"What about?" I said in anticipation, wondering at the serious expression, the slightly uncomfortable look behind his eyes.

"It's about the code," he said simply.

Then somewhere deep inside, I knew exactly what he was about to tell me.

# Chapter 28

# Physical Love

Jaya resumed what he'd been saying. "Yesterday Layla went to see the Elders. To make a request." He paused. "Perhaps I should let Layla tell you the rest. It's her story after all."

"Please carry on," I said eager to hear his news. I couldn't wait for Layla.

He looked at the ground for a few moments before replying. "The Elders agreed."

"Agreed to what?"

"You can have your wish."

I looked at him questioningly. "You mean I can take the code back to my mother?" I said excitedly.

"Not just the code, the symbol as well."

I stared at him dumbfounded, not knowing quite what to say.

"Yeah, I know, it's awesome," he said flatly, watching the multitude of expressions passing over my face.

"Well, this was what you wanted. I guess it means you're going to leave now. That this is it."

I was brought back abruptly to earth suddenly realising the significance of what Jaya was saying.

"I'm not leaving yet."

"But you will."

"I don't want to leave you, but I have to."

"It doesn't make it any easier."

"You always knew there was a good chance I would leave, there were never any guarantees."

"Yes, but not so soon. I thought I'd have you here a while longer."

"I'm not going to leave tomorrow, or even the next day. I've still got some time left here!"

"It's never going to be long enough Alice," he stopped, clearly upset and I felt something turning over in my heart. This part I'd managed to prevent myself thinking about by fooling myself I'd be with Jaya forever. That things would work out.

"I know what I have to do now, I know this is the right thing."

He nodded. "It's just sad that's all." He spoke in a low murmur and I felt something tugging inside me. Was I making a mistake?

"I'll come straight back. After I've taken this back to my mum."

"I know you want to help her, but I'd come to hope that you could stay with me despite the dangers."

"What are you saying?" I whispered hardly able to speak.

"I'm saying I want you here with me Alice, for always," he pulled me into the circle of his arms and whispered. "Isn't that what you want too?"

"Yes."

"Then don't leave," he said simply, studying me with his golden brown eyes, their intensity burning at my resolve, weakening my decision. Here, in this man I had found everything I could ever hope for.

Why would I ever want to leave?

My mind whirred as my heart contracted. The life Jaya was offering me was so tempting. I could almost imagine the happy and blissful times we would spend together, the ease in being with the person who I had come to love above all else. The perfection of it all but then an image of my mother sitting at home with only her unhappy memories for company filled me with regret. I knew only too well the pain and suffering she was feeling. The nirvana in my head would always be blighted by the knowledge I should have helped her. I should have been there in her time of need just as Jaya had been there for me too. Yet, the realisation of what this could cost me sent a blast of cold panic through me.

How could I leave?

How could I not?

It was an impossible choice but through it all I knew there had never been one, never any life with Jaya. Our relationship had been doomed to fail from the start. Two people from opposite sides of the world, two different cultures. When had there ever been any common ground? How could I have imagined an even playing field?

"I have to go Jaya, I'm sorry. I would never forgive myself. My mother, she's....... "

"Alice when you leave here I can't be certain how much longer Layla and I will be able to stay. My father called last night. We can't return to the US yet until this mess has been sorted out."

"What mess?"

"There's still a strong chance the CIA are looking for us. Chana reported back to his superiors about suspecting he was being followed."

"How do you know this?"

"We have our own contacts."

"Within the CIA."

"Wherever we need them. It works both ways."

"Do you think it will ever be resolved?"

"Yes, but we need to move from Sanuri as soon as we can and then lay low. I have no idea where we will go after this."

"We do live in the twenty first century you know, there is technology."

"We cannot use phones in areas where they'd be monitoring all cell phone calls or the internet in case we're traced, we cannot be obvious in our movements, we have to stay hidden."

"Maybe someone in Sanuri could get a message to me?"

"And put them in danger too? Besides, once we leave this valley we won't burden the Sanuri people with the knowledge of our new location. It is better for them that way."

"Isn't there some way you could call me?"

"It was never going to be easy."

"You knew this would happen?"

"No, the Elders did."

"The Elders did," I repeated.

"Yeah, when they raised the energies of the Stone Circle to heal you, they saw your future."

"And my future doesn't involve you? I said, the words catching in my throat.

"I'll just have to hold on to the hope that one day we will see each other again."

"Don't talk like that, I can't leave here believing I might never see you again."

"Alice you have to go, I know that. I just hoped you would stay. I was being selfish."

"I can't lose you now, not after everything. Come with me, come home with me," I said as a tremor came into my voice even though I knew he couldn't, but I asked anyway.

"I can't leave Layla, you know that."

"There must be a way."

"No, the Elders have seen this, seen us parting. I just hoped they were wrong."

"We will see each other again," I said, more to hear the reassuring words out loud. "I know I will see you again........"

"I hope so Alice. I really hope so," he said tightening his arms around me and bending his face to rest against my cheek. Then I felt the cold brush of fear seep through me at what I was about to lose. The tendrils curling a new darkness, a new chill inside and I wondered what I was going to do if I lost Jaya forever. Yet, I should not be surprised in how fate had played it's old hand as a thought came back to me. Something I'd known for a long time ever since my father had died.

Nothing ever lasted.

*And forever was always a lie.*

Later we ate our breakfast in silence, there was nothing to say. Jaya was preoccupied with the thought of me leaving. The time and day had not been discussed yet but its inevitability hung over us like a dark ominous raincloud. My heart was torn in two. Half wanted to help my mother, the other to stay here cocooned within the blissful embrace of Jaya's love and follow him wherever he needed to go.

I knew I had to at least try to help my mother one last time. God only knew the number of times I'd already done so. Finding phone numbers of drug abuse Charities for her to attend their group meetings. Trying to get her to talk, to face up to herself, but in the end I had given up, we all had.

She did not want help.

Relatives had tried, my Aunty Sarah, my mother's sister, had attempted to help on numerous occasions. But an alcoholic doesn't want help, they become sick in their minds, furtive in their behaviour, secretive in their habits. Hiding their dependency and tricking us all to think otherwise.

There'd been no quick fix treatment to cure her. Only a long and painful road lined with psychiatrists hashing over the traumas again and again. Going over the details with fine tooth combs and scrutinising the rubbish components of her life under a magnifying glass. No wonder she refused help in the end. For to live the trauma once was bad enough, but to relive it time and again had been more than she could bear.

I was certain the Stone Circle could help her and that finally there was hope, but was this act of mercy going to cost me my relationship with Jaya? The one shred of happiness I had found in all this time? I could not know, could not begin to think of the aftermath when I left. Both options were cutting me in half, both breaking my heart.

Layla appeared on the balcony, looking refreshed and beautiful, holding some bottles of potions I recognised in her hands. She made some adjustments to my curls, then stood back looking pleased with herself.

"I never thought we would completely tame you hair, but the result here is great," she said in her happy sing song voice, sitting down opposite me and Jaya. I fingered an obedient curl absentmindedly.

"Wow, we do look glum this morning, anything I should know about?" she said taking a bite from a banana. I watched the lump in her cheeks, swapping from side to side as she chewed, looking almost comical in such an exquisite face.

"Alice, will be leaving soon," said Jaya distractedly.

"When?" Layla asked in surprise. Looking between Jaya and me. Perhaps she was thinking we'd argued.

"Jaya told me you went to see the Elders and made a request."

"Yes, I did."

"What did you say to them?"

"I wanted to do something for you after everything you'd done for us. So I went to ask the Elders to allow you to take the code and symbol back to your mom. That's it."

"And they said yes?" I stared at her with a shocked expression. "Just like that?"

"Well, it did take a little persuasion."

"Like how?" I said, thinking how the Sanuri people had fiercely protected this secret.

"It was just a matter of reasoning with them. Letting this code be taken from here didn't mean it endangered their way of life in Sanuri, but more than likely protected them. Once this symbol and code is taken out into the world, no one will be interested in Sanuri or the Stone Circle because they will already have the all the healing they need within the code and symbol. Besides, who better to launch this into the West than you Alice?"

"I still can't believe it."

"Well believe it, they only wish you do not talk about Sanuri. They still want to live anonymously."

"I think I can do that," I said with heart felt gratitude.

"Good, then that's settled then."

We finished breakfast and without even a glance Jaya took my hand and pulled me in the direction of the river. I noticed how the light seemed hazier today, its glare hurting my eyes, not the usual perfect deep turquoise sky. The jungle buzzed and hummed from the early activity of insects but I hardly noticed, my focus was on Jaya looking pensive and distant. A far cry from the ardor of this morning and I was beginning to worry.

"Penny for your thoughts," I said lightly, but he didn't speak or give any indication he had heard me, only looking distractedly away into the distance. We'd walked a long way from the village to a place I'd never been to before when Jaya finally turned to me.

"What you said this morning, that you where ready for........" He said quietly before his voice trailed away.

"Yes?"

"Perhaps it would be best not to take this any further Alice. Not now you'll be leaving." He looked deep into my eyes and I caught a hardness I'd not seen before.

"What do you mean?"

"You're leaving Alice, what would be the point?" he said, a bitterness in his tone.

"But I want you Jaya, that *is* the point," I said.

"I think it would be better to save yourself for someone else Alice. Someone who'll be able to take care of you," he set of his jaw told me this was what he'd been chewing over all morning and he'd made up is mind.

"No!"

"How can it mean anything if you leave now? It's for the best if we ended it here and now. No more dreaming, just reality."

I felt my heart contracting, the air sucking out of my lungs, hardly able to believe what he was saying.

"Jaya it's you, only you I want, nobody else," I felt the lump forming in my throat. "Don't do this Jaya, not now, not after everything." He looked down at me, but I couldn't tell what he was thinking.

"It's for the best Alice," he said in a monotone voice before looking away.

"No Jaya, no!" I stepped forward to wrap my hands around him, feeling his arms hesitate then reluctantly circle around me. I was suddenly aware of the gaping fissure. Feeling his distance, not believing he was doing this now. I tilted my head and cupped my hands around his face to pull him down to my lips. Desperate to feel the passion that I thought might still be there, to feel his desire, to know he wanted me still. His lips met mine, still and unmoving, like marble, stiff and unyielding. I held him there, willing him to kiss me back and to feel the warmth of his caress, wanting him now, aching for him. My emotions ran riot, the fear of losing him, the fear of not being wanted, the rejection I thought would never come from Jaya was here and I could hardly believe it. I whispered 'I love you' as I kissed him again and again beginning to give up all hope. Unable to comprehend it was ending, that he had chosen not to want me, when I'd all but given everything. Suddenly I felt his lips moving over mine, his hands pulling me to him, pressing me into the hard plains of his body. The need for him had set me on fire as I lent into him, my breath coming in gasps as he lowered his head to kiss my face then lower under my throat. I could feel his hands roaming freely now but I was not afraid, I wanted this now, I wanted him to touch every part of me. Suddenly he picked me up in his arms, the feeling so familiar but yet strange. For it had been so long since he'd held me like this.

"And this is really what you want?" he said. The dark molten look in his eyes burned me with their intensity and I felt weak under his gaze. I knew what he was thinking. I was picturing it too.

"Yes," he whispered, suddenly shy now under the study of his golden brown eyes.

Satisfied, he carried me away from the path, towards the cool of the trees. Lowering me gently to the ground before joining me at my side. He pulled me into the fold of his body, kissing me deeply. Gone was the restraint or the need to conceal his desire. Now his ardor ran unchecked as did his lips, covering my body in hot, butterfly kisses. Slowly he removed my clothing, leisurely and with all the time in the world, until finally I lay before him naked as Jaya gazed down on my body. Taking it all in with a long slow sweep of his eyes.

"You're beautiful Alice, so beautiful," he said his voice coming thickly as he leant over to kiss me again. Taking his time with me, unhurried in what he did. Wanting me, but waiting for the fire to burn in me too, playing my body to some beautiful tune which only we could hear. Evoking responses I never knew I had.

I wanted him now, so much. My ardor was burning in every part of my body. The suspense, the waiting and wanting blazed scorchingly inside me.

Jaya looked into my eyes, the gentleness still there but his desire like an inferno melting me into him and then we were moving together. The feeling of being complete, so natural, so right.

"I love you so much Alice," he said.

The passion with which we moved as one, the beauty and pleasure of the moment consumed all other senses. I had never imagined physical love to be like this, never would have known had it not been with Jaya. Jaya who'd gentled me like a wild animal, taught me to trust again, shown me the wonders of the world we lived in, was now uncovering a new person within. A woman, not a girl. Her body revealing the beauty of physical love shared with the one she loved. The unbroken melody of movement and sensation swayed rhythmically through me. Jaya rocked me to his song, carrying me on his lullaby to an unimaginable odyssey. My body responded, opening to the bliss, then the rapture, the intense pulsating ecstasy which tore though me and I knew then I would never be the same again, because now in every sense of the word, Jaya had made me a woman. His woman.

Much later as we lay entwined in each others arms, Jaya had fallen asleep but I stayed awake, thinking back to our love making. Jaya had been right, this thing between a man and a woman was as beautiful as he'd said and more. I loved him even more now, the physical closeness evoking a deeper need, a more complex love. Wholesome in its entirety, like the halves of two coins fitting exactly to the other. My heart swelled with emotion as I remembered each moment. Jaya had made this experience as complete as it could ever have been, showing me its beauty, the ecstasy, and through it all, his love for me. This moment was perfect, too perfect. For everything that came after would only bring sadness and heartache.

But not yet. I still had now.

I turned to trace my hand over the perfect body, marvelling at the taut muscles, the smoothness of his skin. The lovely jet black hair falling back from his face creating a dark glossy halo beneath his head. I felt him stir under my touch, but his eyes remained closed even as a smile began to play over his lips.

"Have you not had enough!" he said huskily.

"Enough of what?" I said coyly, then giggled when Jaya suddenly rolled over to pull me to him and then there was only the fire burning in his kiss. Melting me all over again, melding me to his body until we were together once more and this time Jaya showed me, there were so many ways to be loved.

More than I could ever have imagined.

# Chapter 29

# Leaving

Everything had been leading up to this point. From the moment Jaya had found me on the river's shingle beach, battered and barely alive. To the sweet and perfect way in which he'd led me through to my own self discovery. Helping me find new places within to explore, finally rediscovering the real me. Life had an uncanny way of surprising you and now this new experience brought new feelings, a new outlook on life, one I'd least been expecting.

This moment had erased the traumas that had lain before, replacing them with a different perspective by which to live. Enabling me to leave behind those hideous memories as if a blindfold had finally been removed.

I had thought this life could only contain pain and suffering but now the slate had been wiped clean. I was starting a new life, a new cycle of growth. Jaya who had understood my deep seated fears, had looked beyond the false facade and seen something I'd never dared hope for.

A person worth loving.

A person whose light had been obscured by the darkness of emotion and trauma, who'd lived under the dark cloud of believing she was worth nothing, less than nothing. Somehow Jaya had reached into that void and pulled me free. He could never know what making love like this had really meant to me, how he had dissolved the shackles of my fears.

Transforming the ugly duckling into a swan.

And now I was leaving.

Jaya lay beside me on the bed, the physical love had deepened the feelings in my heart and just now had been no exception. The sweetness in each moment, the depths to which we showed each other our love had never ceased to amaze me.

I lay with my head nestled in the hollow of his shoulder, still in the after glow of our love making, the languid warm pleasure now turning to winter as my thoughts returned to today. This was the last time I would lie with Jaya, the last time I would feel the closeness of his body next to mine. For I would be leaving Sanuri today, forever, to trek back to the road leading to Chang Mai, take a bus and from there a train to the airport in Bangkok.

Now the bitter sweetness of this moment filled my eyes with tears. I was losing him and when he'd only just been found and maybe forever.

The tears rolled down my cheeks onto his chest, the warm drops pooling under my cheek. I felt him pull me in tighter, feeling the wetness and the soft sobs which shook my body against his. I wanted to say I would not go, that I would stay, but the words would not come.

Because I knew I had to leave.

*For my mum.*

The weight of leaving had hung heavily over us these last few days. Spoiling every remaining moment I still had with Jaya. I saw his sadness in the way he would look at me for too long or held me in his arms.

"Where will you and Layla go, when you leave here?" I asked Jaya.

"It has not been decided yet. We will have to leave soon. Probably we'll stay with another tribe somewhere, another country, another place. It will be the easiest way to hide."

"Do you think you'll eventually be able to return to America?"

"I hope so. We'll need to lay low for a while until this thing gets cleared up."

"Do you think it ever will be?"

"My father's working on it. Besides, I want to visit you in England."

"Really?"

"Yeah, really."

The thought filled my heart with hope. Jaya seemed to read my thoughts "I'll find you Alice, you can't escape from me that easily."

"You know what? I wouldn't want to escape from you."

"Even though there'll be all those college boys to date at Uni?"

"No, not even then," I said truthfully.

Jaya began to remove the beautiful beaded bracelet I had noticed on his wrist the first time I had laid eyes on him.

"I want to you to have this," he said tying it on my wrist. "It was made by my sister Kara. I want you to have it.'

I looked down at it in surprise. "I can't take this from you."

"I want you to have it Alice. So you'll remember me every time you look at it," Jaya said simply.

"But..."

"No buts, it's yours now."

I looked down at the bracelet already tied to my wrist and then back at Jaya. "But I have nothing to give you," I said.

"You've already given me more than enough," he said pulling me into his arms again.

"You've given me your love, your trust and you've given my sister and me our lives. What more could you give me?"

Silence fell between us.

"What's going to happen to us Jaya?" I said.

"We'll get through."

"How? We"ll be so far apart, I won't even be able to talk to you on the phone."

The satellite phone Jaya had used was now null and void. It couldn't be used just in case the CIA would be listening. Jaya had said if they were looking for them they'd be monitoring all phone calls in and out of the area.

"I wish we could have been together Alice, that we could have met under different circumstances, believe me," he said tightening his arms around my body. "But we both know you have to do this. For you and your Mom."

"I'd give it all up tomorrow if I could."

Jaya pulled back to look directly at me. "I know." He murmured softly. "We will be together again." He said seriously. "I promise."

His words broke the dam I'd been holding back for so long.

"Hey." Murmured Jaya into my hair, holding me close, letting me cry myself out but nothing could comfort me. Not even the feel of Jaya's strong compassionate arms pulled tightly around me and

I knew this yawning hole inside me would never be filled without Jaya being right by my side.

We walked to the centre of the village where the Elders and villagers had gathered to say their farewell. My heart swelled with emotion when I saw them all assembled. They'd come to mean so much to me over the last few months and now I couldn't believe I was finally going.

The Elders walked forward and embraced me in turn. Each saying in their own language their own special goodbye. Lastly one Elder handed over the stone I had found back in the caves.

"Thank you, "I said finally. "For everything, especially for this." I said turning the stone over in my hand. They merely nodded smiling. Carefully I put it into my rucksack.

There was nothing else to say. I went to turn away but Jaya stopped me.

"There is one last thing."

I looked at him puzzled and then I saw the oldest Elder offering me a small green folded palm leaf with twine holding it together. One for me and one for Jaya.

Jaya took his with a look of surprise.

I removed the small package from the Elder's hand and began to open it but the Elder only waggled a finger at me and said something to Jaya.

"Don't open it yet. Wait until you get home," I looked at Jaya questioningly but he only shrugged his shoulders.

It was nearly time to go, I only had one last person to say goodbye too. Layla stood by our hut waiting for me.

"Goodbye Layla," I smiled weakly. "And thank your for everything, including what you've done for my hair!"

She embraced me before pressing a small pot of her hair potion into my hands. "There, now there's no excuse!" She said smiling before bending to retrieve something from the hut's steps. "You'll be needing this," she said holding a folded piece of paper. "It's the code translated, keep it somewhere safe."

"Oh Layla," I laughed through my tears. "What am I going to do without you?"

"You'll be fine," she said.

"Time to go Alice," Jaya said from behind me.

"Yes," I said slinging my small rucksack over my shoulder and looking round me one last time. This was going to be harder than I thought.

Much, much harder.

It took only a few days to reach the road which would take me to Chang Mai. We had taken a more direct route than the one back to the waterfall, thereby reducing the likelihood of meeting any drug lords or Chana along the way.

This protracted goodbye weighed heavily over me. I was finding it hard to say anything at all without the familiar lump forming in my throat or the tears threatening to spill.

How was I ever going to get through this I wondered? It felt like grief without the death. And the thing that stung most of all was knowing Jaya was going to be somewhere living in the world and without me.

It was killing me.

Finally we were there. Reaching an assortment of ramshackled buildings along the roadside. A service station, if it could even be called that, where buses stopped between towns for refreshments.

It looked as I felt, desolate and empty.

We were the only ones there other than a pair of workers manning a couple of food stalls and some bus staff. We settled ourselves on a bench in the shade and waited.

"It's okay," Jaya said breaking the silence and taking my hand. "This is the way it was supposed to be."

I nodded unable to speak.

"Tell me about your home so I can imagine you there when you've gone." Jaya said squeezing my hand.

It took me a moment before I could begin and then I told him about our house, it's hideous decor and the nondescript garden. I told him about Harpenden, about the shops and the park. I told him about the commons and the people I'd known, until finally a bus bound for Changi Mai swung into the bus station.

This was it.

Jaya pulled me into his arms for one last time. The feeling so familiar, so bitter, so sweet.

Then it was time to go. I mounted the steps and turned to wave before taking my seat beside the window.

Jaya mouthed 'I love you' but I only saw it through a blur. I wanted to run right back into his arms but already the door was closing and we were pulling away. I turned to catch one last image of Jaya disappearing from view. One hand held up in farewell, his hair blowing round his face before being obscured by the plume of dirt kicked up by the bus.

Jaya was out of my life, but never out my heart.

# Chapter 30

# Home

In the two months I had lived in Sanuri the jungle sights and sounds had become so ordinary. Even the night time spine chilling animal calls had no longer caused me any concern. The jungle had been more than just an experience, it had become a way of life. In the short time I had been there, Jaya had shown me how to watch and listen for danger, how to notice any interruptions in the flow of life, any change in the energy and atmosphere. He had taught me not to just look with my eyes but to feel the jungle. The subtle nuances of vibration, the flow of life circulating through the plants and animals. At first I had been sceptical, these new ideas so alien to my Western upbringing. Yet, gradually as my senses had developed with practice I'd begun to feel the faint pulsing of energy beneath my fingertips and sense the electrical charge permeating the air. Perhaps my hypersensitivity had been born to do this. The empathy by which I absorbed other peoples emotions and feelings had always been one of my greatest weaknesses. Overloading my highly receptive being, pouring still more darkness within. Now I realised this sensitivity when allowed to emerge was also my greatest gift. When I cultivated thoughtless awareness I could tune into the things around me and feel the subtle changes within my surroundings. This palpable infinite energy field I could now feel not only bathing all living things within it, but also encompassing our living, breathing planet. The macrocosm mirrored within the microcosm. The Earth's ley lines no more dissimilar to the meridian network of energy lines transcending the human body, carrying our life force to distant parts of our bodies. A system discovered thousands of years ago by the Chinese which and now formed the basis to their unique form of medicine. Jaya had said we absorbed this universal energy into our bodies, as essential to our health as the food we ate and the air we breathed, needing it to drive our life force within. Just like our bodies, the Earth ley lines connected far reaching parts of the Earth, transferring energy from place to place, bathing the Earth's organic body with its life force to keep it strong. Where these ley lines converged with underground rivers running over their path, huge energy vortexes were created. Like the one I'd encountered with Jaya back at the cave.

Only we'd lost the significance and meaning to why our ancestors had expended tremendous effort in constructing stone circles and places of worship upon these sites. We'd forgotten the importance of these energy lines and through them our connection to our Earth. Our mother and provider. Today these magical stone circles of energy lay dormant and forgotten amongst the fields and hedgerows.

An untapped resource.

A forgotten legacy.

Now I held the secret to unlocking their amazing healing powers in my rucksack and I was taking it back to my mother and Harry.

In Chang Mai I'd luckily managed to retrieve my large rucksack from 'Changs,' the backpackers hostel in Chang Mai, still intact with all my belongings.

Sitting on the Thai Airways plane, set to arrive at Heathrow in less than two hours I allowed myself to think of Jaya for the first time since leaving him at the bus station. With it brought a fresh stab of pain in my heart. Leaving him had been one of the hardest things I had ever had to do. I had never felt so empty.

My thoughts returned to what lay before me. My reunion with my mother. I'd not contacted her in months. I had decided not to call from Bangkok airport to tell her I was on my way home. I'd be back in the country within a matter of hours anyway, what difference would it make when I had been absent for months? Besides, I wanted to see her reaction when I walked through the door. Then I would know for sure how she really felt about me. My life had been devoid of any semblance of her love for so long I had come to accept she no longer loved me. Now I suspected another truth. That like me, she had buried her emotions to simply survive. That underneath that harsh and bitter exterior there was still the mother I had once known. A mother who loved me like I had always loved her.

Suddenly I remembered the little green package the Elder had given to me before I'd left. He'd told me to wait until I was home before opening it, but I was impatient to know what it contained. Rooting around in the hand luggage I'd carried onto the plane, I found the small gift still perfectly wrapped at the bottom of my rucksack. The package was rectangular in shape, the edges not sharp, but I could feel its hard angles underneath. The twine fell away and as I pulled back the folds, there in my hand was the last thing I would come to expect as a gift from a tribe such as Sanuri. Something so out of place in their world it made me smile. For nestling in the green wrapping was an up to the minute twenty first century satellite phone. Its phone, the number neatly written on a piece of paper and beside it Jaya's name and another phone number.

Of course! The Elder had given Jaya an identical green package to mine! A wave of joy tore though me and suddenly I knew somewhere deep within I would see Jaya again.

The taxi from the train station wound its way through the familiar Harpenden roads. The summer was full blown and the trees on the little greens in front of the smart shops were lush with their lime green leaves while beneath them, the grass was neatly mown. Within a few minutes I would be back at the small house that had been my home for the last ten years. The house where all I had ever known was sadness.

*Now I was going to change all that.*

I wondered if my mother would be there. Smoking her usual brand of cigarette and drinking her whisky, sitting beside the lounge window over looking the garden. That was how I always remembered her while I'd been gone, and in truth, a place from where she hardly ever moved.

As the taxi passed through the high street I looked out the window in search of faces I thought I might know but the town and its people had become as strangers to me in the nine months I'd been away. The memories of before now felt distant, of another time, a different story to the one I was living now.

I had changed beyond recognition. Living in Sanuri had seen to that. It was as if I could see with new eyes, my soul reborn, free of the past. As if the fragmented parts of my soul and been returned, the missing jigsaw puzzle replaced and the picture was now completed.

The taxi pulled up outside the nondescript terraced house identical in every way to the other houses within the small cul-de-sac. Everything looked just as I had left it. The white, false clapper boards I'd painted a couple of summers ago, the single garage jutting out in front to meet the narrow drive, the same small patch of grass that made up the tiny unremarkable front garden adorned with only a concrete molded bird bath. Everything looked exactly as I had left it. Even the cars in the street sat in the same positions. Nothing had changed, even though I had.

*Beyond description.*

The taxi driver had already placed my dusty rucksack beside the front door before I'd even emerged from the car. I was hesitant, oddly nervous, unsure of the reception I would receive. The months of non communication and the way in which I had contacted her, by email, was sure to have angered her.

And I couldn't blame her.

I'd probably be upset too.

I took a moment before entering my old home trying to steel the nerves inside, the fluttering in my stomach. What would my mother say when she saw me? A year ago I would hardly have cared, or that was what I had thought. It had taken my time in the jungle to brush away the hurts and horrors. To realise I loved her still, like perhaps she still loved me.

Now I was going to help her too.

I opened the front door into the narrow hallway, the same dirty mustard coloured carpet welcomed me as did the smell of a fresh cigarette burning somewhere inside.

*She was home.*

Seven strides and I was already in the lounge and there sat my mother in her usual old armchair beside the window over looking the small garden. Just as I remembered. The short permed hairstyle with hardly a greying hair, the hand knitted cardigan and the faux sheepskin slippers on her feet. Now the large blue eyes were becoming shiny behind her glasses and suddenly I felt the wetness on my cheeks too. A huge grin spreading helplessly over my face and I knew then that everything was going to be all right.

Dipping my head to touch her cheek with my lips and wrapping my arms around her, I hungrily pulled in the familiar scent of her soap, felt the sweet softness of her skin. I murmured the words I had been longing to say ever since I started this journey back.

"Hello Mum, I'm home," I said, my voice ringing in the stunned silence of the room.

Then there was only the sound of her sobs that followed and the feeling of rivelets rolling down my own cheeks and the years of the love lost between us were rolling into the past.

Suddenly through the tears and swell of emotion, a huge revelation came to me.

Forever wasn't a lie or even a promise.

It was how we lived between hello and goodbye that counted.

The End.

# MY STORY

The stone circle is a fictional story based on my own experiences. The discovery of the code and symbol described in the story represents my own journey of self discovery and healing. I have placed everything I have learnt through studying complementary medicine within the code 33 and symbol command code to help others heal themselves just as I have healed. Sadly, my mother died ten years before discovering how to help clear emotional trauma and you can still find her memorial bench on Harpenden Common.

Many of you who have read this story will be wondering at the significance or purpose of the code 33 and symbol healing code. I will try to explain how it came about, who I was all those years ago, why I was in search for answers to my problems and the process by which I discovered ways to heal myself.

Many of you like myself, will know what it is to have suffered emotional pain through loss, abandonment, sexual abuse and many other issues. They leave scars that no one can see and their effects extend far into a persons life, changing the way they live their lives forever.

Many years ago trauma devastated my own life and to contend with the trials of everyday living, I buried the pain deep inside, numbing any emotional responses to prevent my already overloaded being from being hurt any further. Nonetheless, the pain unconsciously ate away at me until I loathed the way I looked and hated the person I was inside. I believed I did not deserve to be loved like other people. How could I expect anything after what had happened to me, who would want someone like me?

Eventually I learned to exist on two levels, the one that people saw everyday and the other who loathed and hated everything I had become. I had little expectation of anything that life could offer or had any trust in anything or other people. I thought my life as it stood was as good as it could get and I just had to get on with it.

At the time, I had no idea how traumatised I'd been or low I'd become after the rape, my father dying or my mother becoming an alcoholic, but looking back I realise I was probably suffering from post traumatic stress disorder, common in those who have suffered traumatic events.

So how do you pull yourself out of such a quagmire of self loathing? How can you rise above the duff hand that has been dealt to you? How can you ever get over anything?

After a lengthy search, the answers to these problems came in the form of complementary therapy. Until this point, I had never been interested in massage treatments or had even known what an Osteopath did for a living, but one day on impulse I booked a Shiatsu treatment. The session consisted of finger pressure on acupuncture points combined with massaging the body. The after effect created profound sense of wellbeing I had not felt in years. Immediately I knew I had to find out more about this form of treatment and how to experience the immense sense of peace I'd experienced afterwards.

How did it work? Why did it work?

Later, I went on to study Shiatsu and found that I had a natural aptitude for working on people, that my hands and sometimes my entire body would become incredibly hot when working on people's deep energetic problems. Shiatsu is based on the same theory as acupuncture, a form of medicine that had been developed over five thousand years by the Chinese. It is an incredible system by which seemingly unrelated problems like insomnia and palpitations are in fact very much related because they share the same meridian. When the meridians become weak or out of balance they create problems within the physical body and when the physical becomes weakend by perhaps a toxin, it can in turn affect the energetic bodies.

Now I had a new road to explore, a journey into complementary medicine where I would find the answers I'd been searching for. I would discover how to treat my over active thyroid genetically inherited from my mother's side, clear emotional traumas, toxins, colds and other infections. This new road became a journey into self discovery and a return to health physically, mentally and emotionally.

The thirst for knowledge drove me to learn increasingly more. I undertook courses in Touch for Health(kinesiology), Muscle Energy Technique, Dowsing for Health, Muscle Energy Technique and Divine Healing Master Key. I learnt there were eight main categories which contributed towards disease states including emotional trauma, mental stress, physical injury, spiritual issues, genetic, radiation, toxins and viruses/bacteria/parasites, etc.

Perhaps the most useful tool I leaned to use to diagnose where illness lies is dowsing. With the use of a pendulum, a conical shaped weight at the end of a thin chain, I can locate where problems lay within the body and measure the percentage of function and what have been affected including glands, organ, systems and energetic bodies, the original cause of illness, when the problem started and after the treatment which percentages in the body have changed. The pendulum spins one direction for yes and another for no and by asking specific questions I can access all the information I need.

In the past I used homeopathic remedies to treat clients, but after studying the Divine Healing Master Key developed by Mary de Tute, I discovered healing could be achieved just by asking in a very specific way. Of course, I was sceptical at first with this new method of healing, just as I am sure you are too, but after extensively testing this method on myself, family, my animals and clients, the results unquestionably convinced me. Using the knowledge from all the years of study and combining it with asking for healing, the code 33 and symbol command code was born.

You well be may asking why did I write the book, why not continue to treat clients and my family just like before?

Well, while walking our family dog one day I was thinking about a distressing documentary I'd watched the previous evening showing African children who had contracted a face eating bacteria. Having children of my own it at upset me terribly. I knew the methods by which I used in my practice could help these children, but how could I get this method to them or any other people who suffered with trauma or disease? It was at this point the book idea germinated. If I could use my experiences to write a story, it would act as a vehicle in getting this code out into the public domain, perhaps then it could also reach places like Africa and poor disadvantaged people who could not afford health care or others who had suffered terrible emotional trauma and illnesses. I only knew that this method of healing had the power to help heal people in ways that had never been seen before and it deserved to be available to everyone.

It has not been an easy decision to make public events which I have kept very private, but I knew it was the only way to launch this healing method out into the world so people could find it and in doing so, be of benefit to people like you my dear reader and I do very much hope you will give it a go.

If you are planning to use the code 33 and symbol command code you do not need to know where or what the problems are that have created illnesses or when it started. I only check the progress in my clients by dowsing the percentages of the meridians, organs etc and have included them here for your interest. Below are some case studies which I hope you find of interest.

You do not need to know anything about your condition or even believe in divine healing, healing is not reserved just for believers!

## INSTRUCTIONS FOR USING THE HEALING CODE AND SYMBOL

To be able to monitor the improvement of your symptoms I suggest that before you start, use a note book to record the severity of your problems from a score of 0 to 10. 10 being the most severe and 0 having no symptoms at all.

Make a note of where you are emotionally. Are you feeling anxious, fearful, angry, worrying, depressed etc

Physically how severe are your symptoms? Give them all a score.

Every month make a new note of how you are emotionally and physically.

## Pregnancy

If you are pregnant you will also need to ask permission for healing for your baby as well. If this is the case replace the beginning with;

Healing Team, Archangels and Angels of Healing if it is in my highest will and my baby's highest will and good and as our souls direct.

Continue as normal using 'we' instead of 'I'

If you are planning to become pregnant it is advisable to use the code for several months before conception to cleanse your body of toxins and other interference.

## Who is healing us when we use the code 33 and symbol command code?

We all have beings 'on the other side' who help and guide us throughout our lifetime, they can only work in your highest will and good and can do nothing to harm you. These beings may be loved ones who have passed over, spirit guides and Angels who are just waiting for you to ask them for their help. 'Ask and you are given' is the phrase in the Bible and using the code 33 you are asking to be healed in a very specific way.

As human beings we have created many blockages between us and the Divine or God which prevent us from receiving healing. Blockages we have created include negative beliefs, vows, thought forms, cultural beliefs, emotions etc. By clearing these blockages we can open ourselves to receive healing from our guides and Angels.

## Why do we have to repeat the code so many times?

Each time we ask for healing the request becomes more powerful. Some issues are harder to clear than others and is the reason why the number of times you need to repeat different sections are different.

## Do I have to read all the sections of the code 33?

Yes, it is very important to do all the sections within the code 33 and symbol command code as each part has a different function.

The first two sections clear all blockages between us and the Divine and the two further sections clear the distortions within our bodies which are creating illness and also encode vibrations and frequencies that will bring us back into balance. You can say the code out loud or inside your head, it does not matter.

## How long will it take to see any results?

The majority of people will not be see results immediately unless you are clearing a cold, virus or bacteria and even this will take several hours for you to feel better. Our bodies cannot assimilate or restore itself all in one go. A system, gland or organ usually has to be strengthened before more healing can be assimilated and there needs to be complete cellular change to take place before the condition is completely healed. Over the years we accumulate a variety of different problems that have contributed toward creating illnesses and rather like peeling back the layers of an onion these issues have to be gradually removed. I suggest you use the code is twice a week if you suffer with fungal infections like Candida, otherwise once per week should be sufficient for approximately 3-4 months.

If you have a cold or virus etc, it may be necessary to also ask for healing for all the family members of your house hold at the same time yourself to prevent reinfection.

## Should I continue to take my medication?

Yes, the code 33 is not a replacement for medication prescribed by your doctor, but will complement any treatment you are already receiving.

In addition, it is advisable not to drink coffee during the weeks you are using the code as this can interfere with the treatment, but tea is absolutely fine.

## CASE STUDIES

All names have been changed.

Percentage changes occur in the meridians first before affecting the physical and I have included them below. When I talk about the functions of certain organs I am referring to the meridians as described in Traditional Chinese Medicine (TCM).

## Case study 1

Sam is an adolescent male who had had trouble getting to sleep. He eats a well balanced diet, played sport and had no stressful situations or emotional problems. He spends a significant amount of time playing on the computer. His sleeping problems had developed over the last six months and sometimes Sam could not get to sleep at all. There are many other causes of insomnia but in this case electromagnetic radiation the from computer had disturbed the oscillations in his energetic body. Our energetic body is made up of three parts - subtle bodies(aura) chakras (energy centres) and meridians/nadis(energy lines). Each play a different role in maintaining our physical body. If any are disturbed they will create distortions within the other parts of our energy system as well affecting in the physical body. Disease states always start in the energetic bodies first. I dowsed to locate where the problems were in Sam's meridians, each meridian corresponds to an organ, gland or bodily system as follows;

## Before treatment 1

Heart Protector (heart)- 33% cause - electro magnetic radiation
Triple Heater (heart) 32% cause - electromagnetic radiation
Large Intestine 41% - cause - mental/electromagnetic radiation/ pathogen
Bladder 33% - cause - electromagnetic radiation

The code was encoded and I asked Sam to return to see me the following day because electro magnetic radiation can take longer to clear than other issues and I wanted to check the progress of the treatment.

The Heart Protector meridian protects the heart, Triple heater meridian has many functions but mainly governs the circulation of nutrients, blood and the immune system. The heart houses our soul, when the heart is disturbed it affects our mental processes including sleep or manifesting as neurotic behaviours and mental problems.

The following day Sam's meridians were as follows;

## After treatment 1

Heart Protector 83%
Triple Heater 51% Lung 75%
Bladder 73%
Kidney 53% - deficient Essence, cellular memory of a virus in the past was depressing the kidney's function

Sam needed another treatment in 25 days time.

In Traditional Chinese Medicine, Essence is essentially our constitutional strength or life force. If we inherit from our parents and ancestors Essence that has been damaged by poor diet, bad life style, genetic impairment, toxins or smoking when pregnant, the baby will be born sickly and in poor health. Health can be helped to be restored through eating nutritiously, taking supplements or herbs, living a healthy life style and using the Code 33. Infection caused by bacteria or viruses can also affect the function of our cells. Cells can remember anything that damages or impairs their function including shock and trauma, negative emotions or even the memory of a disease. In Sam's case the memory of a virus infection needed to be cleared to help restore health in his Kidneys.

## After treatment 2

Heart Protector 87%
Triple Heater - 67%
Lung - 85%
Bladder - 77%
Kidney - 75%

Sam reported that he was able to sleep soundly every night and was feeling generally much better.

## Case study 2

Lucy is a lively five year old girl who suffers with eczema covering nearly 70% of her body. The eczema was very itchy and Lucy would scratch the skin until it bled. As far as her mother could remember, Lucy had always had eczema and used steroids to control it when the sores became infected. Lucy could almost be called hyperactive, could never sit still and at times could be described as uncontrollable.

On dowsing I located where the priority problems to treat lay.

## Before treatment 1

Stomach 32% - cause - genetic, toxins, pathogens (Candida)
Triple Heater 42% - cause - physical, pathogen ( Candida)
Spleen 31% - cause - genetic, pathogen (Candida)
Large Intestine 21% - cause - toxin, pathogen (Candida)
Lung 32% - cause - genetic

I discovered that the genetic problems came from the mother's side who herself had suffered with allergic reactions to certain foods and suffered with skin problems. When looking at the Lucy's meridian percentages most of the problems lay in the digestive system. According to Traditional Chinese medicine, problems in the large intestine affects the skin and due to the huge amount of toxins we ingest in this day and age skin problems are becoming increasingly common. In Lucy's case, she had inherited faulty genetics from her mother, ingested toxins and had a Candida (fungus) infection which had further depressed the digestive system.

On dowsing after the treatment the percentages were as follows

## After treatment 1

Stomach 44%
Triple Heater 62%
Spleen 62%
Large Intestine 62%
Lung 75%

Lucy had made good progress but due to the Candida infection she needed to use the code 33 twice a week.

## Two weeks later

Gall Bladder - 71% - candida
Stomach - 72% - candida
Spleen - 73% - candida
Large Intestine - 74% - candida
Lung - 85% - candida
Bladder - 82% - candida

Candida is a fungus that lives naturally in the digestive system but if allowed to get out of control and grow almost anywhere in the body. Candida can be difficult to clear in one treatment as it becomes endemic. Frequent use of the code 33 can help to remove it. In Lucy's case, the Candida had been cleared after treatment 2 but had grown back, although her skin had been clear of eczema, some small spots had reappeared due to the use of a well known pain killer with a purple dye (colourings and food additives can be toxic to our bodies). On dowsing, Lucy needed the code 33 to encoded once a week for 3 weeks. Her mother also had Candida when she gave birth to Lucy passing on the infection to her daughter. She was advised to use the code 33 three times a week for three weeks.

## Eight weeks later

Stomach 91%
Triple Heater 92%
Spleen 95%
Large Intestine 96%
Lung 96%

Lucy has become much calmer and now can sit for extended periods of time and has been clear of eczema ever since.

## Case Study 3

Jane is a lovely 83 year old lady who has suffered with back pain for most of her life. Doctors had given up on being able to alleviate her pain. At the age of one she had been badly injured after falling down some stairs and had had to remain in a full body cast for a whole year and did not walk for three years. She also suffered from thrombosis, varicose veins and asthma. She had recently recovered from a heart operation to replace a valve in her heart but still complained of being very breathless and had not experienced any improvement in this area of her health since the operation. She was also falling asleep up to ten times during the day and used an inhaler for most waking hours. Her passion was singing and she was finding it extremely difficult to do so because of her breathlessness and this was depressing her very much.

## Before treatment 1

Liver 24% - emotional, spiritual, toxin, pathogen(candida)
Lung 23% - genetic, toxin, pathogen(candida)
Bladder 22% - physical, toxin, pathogen(candida)
Kidney 13% - physical, genetic, toxin, pathogen(candida)
Spleen 23% - spiritual, toxin, pathogen(candida)
Stomach 23% - physical, toxin, pathogen(candida)

After discovering Jane's Kidneys were functioning at only 13% I was not surprise she felt so breathless, poor kidney function in TCM is involved in anchoring the oxygen we breath in before it is circulated round the body. Poor kidney function can affect the amount of oxygen that is made available to the body resulting in feeling breathless. I didn't find anything wrong with her heart.

Jane also had a problem in her spiritual bodies(made up of the aura, chakras and meridians) in this case, a layer of her subtle bodies was weak and therefore was not supporting her physical body.

The physical issue in her bladder meridian related to the shock and trauma her body suffered as a result of her accident and the reason behind having chronic back problem. The bladder meridians runs either side of the spine and if weak will not be able to support the vertebrae.

Toxins had also lodged in all her organs.

In all organs I dowsed, Candida was also contributing in depressing their function.

I also found a genetic issue in her lungs and kidneys. Genetic problems aren't as difficult to treat as is believed. They arise from our ancestors having experienced emotional, mental, physical, spiritual, genetic, radiation, toxin and pathogen issues which subsequently suppress the DNA function. Miasms are one example of this. The inherited ancestral memory of a disease can still affect us even after many generations further down the genetic line, for example syphilis and gonorrhea. Our healing teams can clear the memory of these issues from the genetic code just as they can clear the above contributors to disease that are affecting us in our present lives.

## After treatment 1

Liver  23%
Lung 42%
Bladder 42%
Kidney 31%
Stomach 23%

It was decided that because of the candida Sarah required to do the code 3x per week.

## 5 weeks later

Lung 85%
Liver 86%
Bladder 89%
Kidney 73%
Stomach 93%
Spleen/Pancreas 91%

Jane's breathlessness has gone and she has started singing again having had to give up due to her breathing problems, in addition, she now only uses her inhaler twice instead of at least ten times a day. Before the treatment she would fall asleep constantly throught the day and now only takes a couple of naps. She now actively takes part in yoga once a week and has reported in feeling so much better.

## Treatments

I offer a monitering service to follow your progress over the weeks and months and to discover the original causes of illness and when the problems started. This involves send me some of your hair (root included) so that I may dowse to find where the problems lay. I can then advise how frequently you need to use the code 33 and monitor your progress over weeks and months. If you are interested in this service please contact me at kecracknell@hotmail.com

# HOW TO USE THE CODE AND SYMBOL

Look at the symbol once for 20 seconds or count slowly to 20.

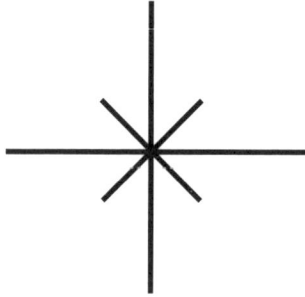

Healing Team, Archangels and Angels of healing, I/we give thanks and open my/our heart, mind and being to receiving your divine love, presence, grace and healing. For my/......... highest will and good, I /we relinquish the need to control or sabotage this healing. I/we request an alignment and synthesis with the Body Consciousness and a clear and perfect channel to be kept 100% activated, protected and clear between myself/...........and my/...........Healing Team and all those who work co-creatively with me/..... in only the highest will and good. Please protect me/........ and my/our work space and give me/us access to all causes of dysfunction, distortions and all other factors creating dis-ease. Please encode each of the following sections at the most beneficial and appropriate time. Thank you

## Repeat twice

Healing Team, Archangels and Angels of healing, I/we command a pendulum spin rotation is activated in the speed, direction, rate, strength, rotation size and the most beneficial number of rotations through all my/............. bodies, subtle bodies and personal fields to 100% clear, extract, remove and release all conscious and unconscious blockages, obstructions, interference, imprints, messages, programming, harmful, negative, detrimental and hostile issues, limitations, intrusions, all non-beneficial protection seals, vows, pacts, agreements, low frequency and discordant energies, life forms without any cell walls, resistance, inhibitors, shadow energies, negetive feelings, emotions, thought forms, dark energies, illness/disability programming, illness, perceptions, misconceptions, judgements, internal interference programmes, external influences, interference at soul level, negative cords, beliefs, attachments, radiation, habits, low frequency energies all associated and residual energy and anything else which you know needs to be cleared and released but which I/........ do/does not know about or have forgotten including the core issue, the source of its power, the original cause and time of cause, effect, memory and record so that healing work can begin. Thank you

Please reverse the spin and seal my/.......... energetic fields at the most appropriate time. Thank you

## Repeat 7 times

Healing Team, Archangels and Angels of healing, Higher Self and all other specialists required, I/we command E remedy and all other organic synergists, homeopathic remedies, vibrations and frequencies and anything else that you know I........ need/s, are radionically applied and encoded into my/.............. Holographic Matrix in the most beneficial vibration, frequency, potency for maximum benefit and for as long as required to action a 100% cleansing, clearing and protection from all inappropriate energies, interference, attachments and residual energy from all my/....... subtle bodies, bodies, energy systems and work space through all levels, dimensions and timeframes. Thank you

## Repeat 3 times

Healing Team, Archangels and Angels of Healing if it is in my/.............. highest will and good and as my/......... Soul directs I/we command the code 33 is encoded into my/............. Holographic Matrix and work space at the most appropriate and perfect time and for as long as you know I/.............. need/s in the most beneficial vibration, frequency and potency to clear, extract and remove all harmful causes of distortions, suppressions, dysfunction through all levels, dimensions and time frames for maximum benefit. Thank you

## Repeat 3 times

Healing Team, Archangels and Angels of healing I/we command the perfect and most beneficial regenerative, restorative, nutritional, repairing, healing, protecting, maintaining vibrations, frequencies and homeopathic remedies that you know are required to create 100% health, vitality, strength, wellness and optimal functioning of the whole organism through all levels and layers of my/........... holographic matrix, multidimensionally and time frames for maximum benefit. Please protect all encoded vibrations and frequencies from interference.

Thank you, thank you, thank you.

That is it!

Just remember to say thank you afterwards.

Some people can feel the changes taking place, others may not. Please be aware that sometimes the reactions can be very powerful. Please do not drive or use heavy machinery until several hours after using the code if you have a strong reaction. I find it is best to use the code in the evening when you aren't rushing around. Please try to stay still for at least fifteen minutes after using the code so your healing team can work on you.

If you feel you have picked up a pathogen then don't wait for morning or evening, use the code straight away.

If you do have a strong reaction or feel a little odd do not be alarmed, it is only the healing taking place and it will take the body a little while to rebalance itself.

If you are taking any medication please continue to take it unless directed by your doctor.

Your healing team are waiting to be asked to help you and heal you with their love, know they will only work on you in your highest will and good.

Check your progress by looking at your original score for your illness.

You do not need to believe in Healing Teams, Angels or God for this to work , but hopefully you will believe in them afterwards!

Lastly the code does not work by a placebo effect, it works because it works!

Love and Best Wishes

God bless you.

KC

# Acknowledgments

I would like to thank my husband Jeremy and our kids Josh, Ben and Kieran for putting up with me over the last year while I wrote this book. Thank you for all your support and love and the life we have together. It has meant so much to me over the years and I love you all.

For my late mother Eileen, who taught me so much about myself. I will always remember how you loved me and I still miss you.

Mary de Tute a huge thank you for teaching me we only need to ask to be healed and without her amazing teaching this book could never have been written.

It is Mary who discovered and developed the method by which to ask for healing and I am incredibly indepted to her for allowing me to use some of her work. Mary has not only been a true pioneer in this field, but a wonderful friend, teacher and healer, thank you.

I would especially like to thank my sisters in life Debbie de Vito, Shirley Lowry and Sue Ayling for all you're wonderful support even when I had my wobbly moments.

Thank you Ian, even though I know you probably don't think you have done very much, I know you will always be there if I need you and I love you for that.

I would also like to thank my Aunt Rose and Uncle Pete who have been a tower of strength, love and support all these years.

For Kaz Field who has been an invaluable friend and helper with this book.

Ali Kaplan and Janine Lillie my two oldest and best friends, thank you for just being in my life, it's all the better because of it.

Thank you to Anne Field, Anne Dickins and Clare Neville who are the kindest and funniest group of people I know, you light up my life.

Nessa Harrison and Ali Westcott who have been a great inspiration to me, but above all in showing me new ways to have fun!

My yoga girls, Sukie Burne, Jeannette Eccles, Chrissie, Judy Macdonald a great big thank you for helping me through those difficult child rearing years and helping me stick to my guns.

Chris de Tute who gave me some great ideas for the book.

Carron Coakes a great friend and fantastic hairdresser, thank you for all you have done for my hair!

A big thank you also goes to Paul Stiffle and Bill Ayling who both showed me there is a whole new world out there waiting to be discovered.

Thank you to my first boyfriend Jacko who helped me in so many ways you could never have known.

For Karen and Alan, founders of the Association of Osteomyologists, a fantastic organisation for complementary practitioners, thank you for all your wonderful support and keep doing what you are doing, the courses are fantastic!

A big thank you to Bernard Cracknell for proof reading the manuscript. Thank you all those people who allowed themselves to be guinea pigs when testing this healing code, especially Sarah Haywood, Nicola Gill, Clare Neville, Ian Martin and Madeline Westcott and many others.

For the very special animals which have been in my life in the past and present, Cindy, Tikka, Major, Fern, Shay and Paddy.

For all those people who have shaped my life with the good and the bad, thank you for making me who I am today. You have been my best teachers and healers.

If there is anyone I have led out, well, you know who you are and thank you!

Lastly and not least I thank with all my heart my spirit guides, Healing Team and Angels who have lead me on the most amazing journey through this life which has culminated in this book.

I could never have done it without you!

# Biography

Karen was born and grew up in Harpenden where she lived for eighteen years before leaving to attend De Montford University in Leicester. After completing her course in Contour Fashion she worked briefly in the fashion industry before leaving to take a sales job for an industrial chemical firm.

After having her first child with long term partner Jeremy, Karen changed career, having always had a strong interest in alternative medicine she qualified as a Shiatsu practitioner. From here, she continued to take courses in Kinesiology, Quantum Shen (similar to reiki), Dowsing for Health, Muscle Energy Technique, Divine Healing Master Key and now belongs to a professional body of alternative health practitioners, the Association of Osteomyologists.

Karen now lives in Surrey with her husband Jeremy and three children, two horses, one dog and one cat.

You can follow me on twitter@kecracknell or my blog - kecracknell.blogspot.com.